Raventower &
Merriweather

2: War

By

Lazette Gifford

Raventower & Merriweather 2: War
A Conspiracy of Authors Publication
www.aconspiracyofauthors.com
Copyright © 2020, Lazette Gifford
ISBN: 978-1-936507-91-7
Cover Art: Copyright © 2020, Lazette Gifford

First Print Edition, February 2020

Dedicated to Russ who is the best friend a person could ever have and who has never stopped believing I can do this writing and publishing thing.

Thank you.

TABLE OF CONTENTS

CHAPTER ONE

L ord Micalus Raventower clamped his fingers around the chain, his feet balanced on the large hook as it swept outward over the ocean. He could feel the cold metal even through his gloves, and the wind off the water numbed his face where the scarf did not cover his skin. He blinked half-frozen tears from his eyes and tried to focus on the work at hand. However, his mind clearly focused on only one point.

Merriweather is going to kill me when she realizes what I'm doing.

Mica knew he had to be the one who took on this delicate part of the job, though. He could judge the weight and movement of *Flash* as the newly built cranes, made to his design, pulled the scout ship out of the water. The airship had crashed during the battle, but Admiral Rose had directed the crew so that the ship went down on her side and kept the huge hole as much out of the sea water as possible. He'd not had a good look at the ship yet, but he thought they had a chance of repairing her and getting *Flash* back in the air. They needed as many craft as they could salvage because the war was far from over.

Mica looked out at sea where the enemy still lurked. Billowing clouds rose over the turbulent gray ocean. They'd had nothing but storms of late: storms and cold, and more cold. Snow, gone dirty gray through most of the city, would not melt for some time and treacherous ice clung to everything. Mica felt as though both nature and the Atrians had turned against them, and the people of Kamere suffered through the winter with glares and growls as everyone waited for the next disaster.

The crane creaked ominously in the wind, ice cracking where it had formed along the edges of wood and metal. Mica held his breath, but nothing gave way, so he gave the signal to lower him closer to the pounding waves while the second hook began to drop into place.

He blinked, ready to shout instructions to the person who held on there, and then realized it was not necessary. Merriweather, who had sat in on all the discussions, had hold of the second chain.

Maybe she didn't want him to have all the fun.

As the chains lowered, the sea cliff cut off the view of the land, for which he was oddly relieved. While an assassin with a knife could not attack him out here on the chain, a marksman might get a lucky shot. He couldn't say he trusted everyone who had come out to watch the operation. Too many people went bundled in warm layers of clothing during the winter, inadvertently disguising themselves, and making Merriweather, his guard, more than a little nervous. Even voices muffled behind thick woolen scarves could-could hide a hint of an accent.

Mica did not like being paranoid. He refused to give into the fears and hide away in his tower -- as though Raventower was actually safe.

Mica glanced once more across the stormy sea as the chain lowered, link by link, through the winch secured to the land above them. He could barely see the outline of a ship holding off outside the bay. An Atrian ship, without a doubt;

Mica knew their blocky shapes. This one had sails down and no plume of steam from the small engine, so they were sitting at anchor out there, watching him as he watched them.

The Atrians had the bay sealed off which might prove difficult as the winter wore on. Many of the city dwellers had already left for the backcountry and smaller villages. Those places, though, might have more trouble than the people in Kamere if the war went on too long. Many of those smaller communities had swollen to four times their usual size and already experienced problems with housing and food --

The hook clanged against the edge of *Flash* and Mica cautiously stepped down, keeping tight hold of the chain. The airship bobbed up and down in the water making footing on the curved edge difficult. Water and ice conspired in an attempt to land him in the ocean, but Mica was not going to drown. Merriweather would be mad at him.

Mica smiled as she landed beside him and held as tight to her own chain. He almost reached out to steady her, but she caught her balance quickly enough. Better not to waste time here.

They'd built a ramp of wood and sand starting at the foot of the cliff and up to the airfield. A wooden cradle waited there to take the craft if they could get her that high. The angle was steep and the structural integrity of the airship doubtful. It might come apart with the strain.

Mica looked up and saw someone peering over the cliff at them -- that would be Admiral Honeysuckle Rose. Mica suspected it was lucky they couldn't hear her.

"Find the places to hook in, Lord Raventower!" Merriweather shouted above the wind and the crash of waves. "We're already soaked -- let's just get this done!"

He gave a quick nod of agreement and worked carefully around the hole in the hull of the craft. Water had gotten in, of course, but it hadn't reached all the way to the top and dragged the ship to the bottom. The damage didn't seem to have reached the engine, either -- another good sign, though there was doubtless going to be damage from water. Still --

They needed the airship back in the air where she belonged. The Atrians had an advantage there right now, and they were making it difficult for the city to get any coal in by rail, let alone by ship. A shortage of food was bad enough, but one of coal for heat would be devastating in this weather. Many of the buildings had switched from wood to coal over the last few decades, but they could use wood if need be. However, the only wood on hand came from destroyed buildings, and that supply might not last through the winter.

They needed this airship to fight off the enemy. Mica intended to see her out of the water and repaired. That was something he could do to help.

"Well?" Merriweather asked, her voice a croak behind the scarf she wore.

"There, on your side," Mica shouted with a wave to the corner of the hole. "Do you see the metal beam there? Hook in. We'll test it out."

She knelt and pulled the hook downward as he gave the signal to those watching to lower it another foot. Then he did the same for his side, hooking onto another beam, so they didn't put too much stress on any single one.

"Ready?" he called out when she stood again.

"Yes!"

He gave the signal, and those working the devices began to turn both winches to pull upward. The angle would be difficult -- they didn't dare just drag the ship straight up out of the water, and that's why they had the ramp with soft sand to cushion the hull. Even so, the ship bounced and creaked with sounds he didn't like to hear. He signaled a stop and adjusted his hook. Then they started upward again.

Something dragged, and he feared he heard wood

breaking. Mica looked over the edge and snarled as he signaled another stop. "We need to cut the last of the sails away, Merriweather! Take my hand! I'll get you over the edge and join you --"

"You stay here and keep hold of the chain!" she replied and caught his hand. "Otherwise, we'll have to cut handholds into the hull so you can get up here to keep watch when the ship starts upward again!"

She was right. Besides, Captain Merriweather had her knives, and she knew how to use them effectively. He lowered her over the side where she caught hold of the metal bracing and worked downward until and she dropped onto the sand. Merriweather took hold of one of the broken masts and made quick work of cutting away the cloth and shoving it free of any entanglements. One sail and then another dropped away. She looked up at him, but he could only see her eyes and glitter of frost on her eyebrows and on the scarf.

"Take her up! I'll follow!" she yelled.

"No! Not follow!" he shouted, appalled by the thought. "Go up along the far edge and stay clear of her path. She might still break loose!"

"Oh. Yes." She gave him a bow of her head. "Take it on up, your lordship. I'll be there as soon as I can."

"Move carefully, Merriweather."

"And you, too! Don't, for the love of the gods, let someone shoot you before I'm there to kill them!"

He gave a little laugh, but she did have a point. "I'll do my best," he promised. Mica did not say what he intended, which was to come back down and get her if he needed to.

Mica signaled. The others started the work of pulling the craft upward again. He kept a close watch on the area where they'd hooked in, but with the sails gone, they moved far easier. He realized that the water inside the hull had dropped by a couple feet, too, which mean they had an opening somewhere on the other side, but one that must have been offset by water pressure. It might only have been a door or porthole open.

Mica peered into the hole again, already trying to map out the damage. A few warped metal beams would have to be replaced along this side of the craft and at least half the hull as well. Except for the control deck and engine room, most of the interior work could be put off, if need be. They only needed to get the airship stable enough to take to the sky again.

Mica could no longer see Merriweather without leaning precariously out from the hull, and each time he did so, she shouted in dismay or anger. To keep from annoying her more, Mica knelt and listened to the sounds of *Flash* as they inched slowly upward. He hadn't realized how cold he felt until just now, though. He held convulsively to the chain and planned, if he lost his hold, to throw himself inside the ship. Wet in there, but out of the wind and less chance of being crushed as the ship went upward.

Slowly, slowly upward. Mica almost signaled the others to work faster, but that wouldn't be wise. He thought about Merriweather trudging up the sand, wet and cold with the wind blowing on her. He should have been the one --

Stupid thoughts. He turned his attention to the ocean and frowned. A second ship had slipped into view, a bit of steam showing over the top. Atrian again, and this one larger and more powerful.

"Damn!" He gave the signal he didn't like, but they'd been ready for it. The cranes began to move a faster, pulling upward along the sand. They only needed to get to the top, then swing over to the cradle wagon that would take the ship away from the edge of the sea where it made too easy of a target.

Squinting, Mica spotted at least one airship tethered to the hull of the Atrian ship. If the enemy cut that craft loose to come after them, they might not get *Flash* to safety. Or him and Merriweather, either. Granted, the Atrian Airship wouldn't survive considering the weapons the Sedina forces had lined up on the cliff, but that would be a small solace.

Chances were that they wouldn't think it worth the trouble. Salvaging ships from the sea wasn't something they worried about so much as seeing the craft in the air. Besides, the Atrians didn't have any airships to waste, either.

Sedina could hold out longer than the ships, as long as they could disrupt the Atrian supply lines often enough. It would be an odd war fought that way, but he would rather have the trouble stay in the ocean and the bay rather than an invasion of the Kamere streets of the city again.

That was a forlorn hope, of course. The Atrians still hovered along the Kamere coastline for a reason.

The edge of *Flash* came up over the top of the cliff and then bounced a bit onto the solid land. The others winched the craft up a little higher and began to maneuver *Flash* onto the tandem wagons which were drawn by oxen. By such contrivances, they would move the ship across the field and onto another cradle where it would be repaired.

Mica slid down off the hull, landing badly and twisting his leg, but he was back up in a moment and heading for the incline. Admiral Rose joined him. He needn't have worried. Merriweather came up over the edge and grabbed her weapons, having left them on the relatively drier high ground. She checked one of the two flintlocks; she'd started keeping one loaded and ready, despite the risk of the powder getting wet. She gave a quick nod and shoved it into the holster beneath her cloak.

"Got it!" she said with some satisfaction and waved to the departing craft.

Mica grinned behind his scarf and turned back to see the chains released from the cranes and crashing down to the ground. People gathered them up and shoved them on the edge of the wagons. The hooks were still in place on *Flash* so the chains would have dragged along and probably caught in the wheels. They would use the hooks and chains to lift her into the cradle.

The oxen began to move. The ponderous creatures were more often used to pull farm equipment; they walked with steady steps toward the distant goal. The road was already cleared of snow, if not ice, and they had only a couple miles to go. He could hear a couple of them bellowing a complaint, though. He suspected they didn't much care for the weather either.

Mica's clothing had frozen in places. His hands, still inside the gloves, felt stiff and painful. Merriweather would be no better -- but they'd done the work and gotten the ship up. If it could be repaired, they'd have another much-needed airship back in service.

Admiral Rose watched the departure for a moment, but then she turned and waved toward the building that housed the headquarters for the Air Patrol. Mica thought he heard her say 'warm' and followed her just on that promise. His mind, however, had already started working on a schedule of repairs.

Merriweather stayed beside him and kept watch on all sides. Admiral Rose didn't have a guard of her own, and Mica felt suddenly self-conscious at having his own protection. Not that Merriweather wouldn't leap into help Admiral Rose, of course. Maybe the woman realized she didn't need protection with Merriweather around. His guard -- and future wife -- did have a reputation for taking care of any trouble.

He looked back at the Atiran ships, neither of which had moved closer. The airship still remained attached to the anchored ship. Good.

Mica wished for help from other lands and armies. They had allies in the south, but those people were not likely to come this far north until the spring. He could hardly blame them, either. The southern sailing ships were flimsy things, and their only airships were show craft and used for travel, not fighting. The Argine did, however, possess some of the best land-based soldiers and cavalry to be found, most of them mercenaries. They might need that help by spring if they couldn't hold the Atrians off. For now, though, they would be on their own.

Just as they reached the door to the building, Mica heard the sound of gunfire and spun to look for the enemy. Merriweather shoved him and the Admiral inside the door. Wise, he supposed, though he muttered a curse and then an apology to the Admiral whom he had nearly tripped.

"What is going on out there?" Rose demanded as she tore off her scarf. She tried to see past Merriweather who held the door mostly closed, peering through a small slit.

"Gunshots in the southwest corner of the airfield," Merriweather said with a snarl. "I counted at least four shots, and they came quick enough that there must be more than one or two people. "I can see movement, and I fear --"

Whatever she feared, she didn't say aloud. Something exploded. By now the people working in the building started to crowd into the little area by the door though the Admiral ordered them away.

Merriweather unexpectedly threw the door open. Mica saw her draw the already loaded flintlock, and she fired as a figure rushed closer, something burning in his hands. He fell back. Merriweather yanked the door closed and shoved people back --

The bomb exploded. If it had gotten to the door, or worse inside, none of them would have survived. As it was, the door flew off and hit someone. Parts of the building shattered. Blood splattered everywhere, and there was no longer a clear sign of the enemy's body --

But the lights appeared: frantic life lights trying to reach him. Mica hoped the others didn't see beyond the smoke and after the shock of the explosion. He did not dare let too many others know this secret. He had to get clear --

Merriweather caught Mica by the arm and pulled me out past the bomb and towards the cradles where ships were being repaired. One was already on fire, and there would be no way to salvage it. Another bomb went off by a second ship being repaired. He couldn't see how badly that one might be damaged.

They had other problems. People swarmed through the area, and he couldn't easily tell an enemy from a friend, at least until someone attacked him. Merriweather had taken on someone coming from the side, her sword in hand now. Another man came straight at Mica. This one was not as encumbered in heavy clothing, and the growled words were definitely not Sedinan.

Mica brought up his own sword and proved far better with the weapon than his opponent. He focused on the fight which was not easy with so much else going on around them. *Focus just on the movement of the enemy's arm and sword and deal with it as quickly as possible.* Mica easily saw the pattern of the man's moves and circumvented them. The kill was quick. The man seemed surprised.

Merriweather grabbed him away from the second set of life lights. There were dead all around the area, and the bright little vestiges of their lives would be hard to avoid. Mica's head already pounded from the few lights he had fought aside, and he hoped that the smoke and battle kept others from noticing this odd problem.

Merriweather had gathered Admiral Rose to them again. They headed along a path between sheds that gave them a little cover. "We need to get to the guard house at the gate," Merriweather warned. "That's the best place to find some help we know we can trust. Some of these people are not Atrians."

"I noticed," Mica added. "Damn them."

"Fools," Rose growled and looked back at the burning ship. "They're getting the fire in hand. A loss, but they won't take more of them. Must have moved in while we were all so busy watching *Flash*."

"Before that," Mica said. "We were all on guard too much for something that simple to take place."

"Agreed," Merriweather said, somewhat breathless. She'd thrown back her scarf, and he could see the strands of her hair glittered with ice. "This was no sudden attack, Admiral. They did wait for everyone to be busy, though."

"And people already in the Air Patrol probably helped them," the older woman added. Her voice had gone as hard and angry as Mica had ever heard her. "I will find out who it was that got the bastards close enough to do this damage."

Mica didn't doubt her.

The fighting had already lessened, and the three had only one more encounter on the way to the guard house. Merriweather took care of that trouble without help from either of them. Mica could see the anger in her eyes and decided to do as she said and hope they all survived.

When they had left behind the sheds, he could see that only one ship still burnt, so they had held off more damage to the others, including to the ones that could still fly. Three of them had taken to the air and were no longer easy targets.

A close battle still raged around one of the docks, but Mica could see that the Air Patrol wouldn't have much trouble getting the problem in hand. Nonetheless, he was glad to see an army patrol heading up the road at a full run. They must have spotted the smoke from the fires in town --

No. Too soon.

"Don't let them in!" Mica shouted as they hurried toward the gate.

"Oh hell," Merriweather yelled, realizing the problem as well.

It was possible these men were a patrol that had already been on the path and heading their way, but Mica had the feeling they were not, and they dared not take the chance.

Admiral Rose shouted as well, and it was her familiar voice that at least prepared the Air Patrol guards for trouble. They could not get the gate closed in time, but the band of twenty didn't make it through unscathed. Rose, Merriweather, and Mica raced to join the battle, the Admiral directing her people while he and Merriweather took on anyone who came way.

Chaos at the gate: Mica saw Admiral Rose's second in command, Greenwood, rush into the melee and fight at her side. The younger man took a wound and nearly went down, but kept fighting. The focus of this battle had changed to killing Admiral Rose, but she fought like a wildcat. Mica moved to her left and Merriweather beside him and together they fought the last of the attackers back out of the Air Patrol field. Whatever they'd come to do, they'd failed, because almost immediately they grabbed horses from the pen and prepared to escape again.

Neither Mica nor Merriweather wanted to let them go. Mica moved with her as they chased off the mounts and tried to engage the enemy one more time. Rose shouted something about being crazy, but it was better for Mica to be out here away from where the others had died. Merriweather knew it, too. Besides, all but two of the Atrians had gotten away, and he didn't think they could have much trouble --

Well, they wouldn't have had trouble capturing them if the damned men hadn't headed straight for a cliff to throw themselves into the sea. Merriweather tried to grab one -- but the Atrian caught hold of her instead.

With a cry of dismay, Mica raced the few yards where she

struggled with the larger man. The other had already thrown himself off the edge, and that was all that saved her. If there had been two, Mica never would have reached her in time. She held on long enough for Mica to give a vicious swipe of his sword, nearly severing the enemy's arm. The fingers released her, but with her balance off, she nearly tumbled over as well. Mica shoved her back, and they both tripped, but landed safely on the ground and did not go over the cliff.

"Damn!" Merriweather shouted. "I wanted one! Why do they keep doing that?"

"It does seem rather melodramatic," Mica agreed.

"You can get up off of me now, your lordship," Merriweather suggested.

"Are you certain? The cliff is still very close. There might be more Atrians nearby."

"I think we're safe. And here comes Admiral Rose to lecture us. Let us be as dignified as possible."

He gave a sigh of agreement and stood, offering his hand which she took with a nod of thanks. Then, unexpectedly, she put a hand on his arm.

"Thank you, Lord Raventower."

"My honor, Captain Merriweather."

Admiral Rose arrived, breathless for a moment, but then she did start a litany of complaints about what they'd done, only to cut it off just as suddenly.

"If anything happened to you, Mica, I don't know what I'd tell your brother," she finally admitted. "Don't put me in that position."

"Admiral Rose," he began. Then he stopped. "We'll all do whatever is needed."

She agreed with a reluctant nod and turned back to the gate with four of her own people taking up guard positions. Mica looked them over. They'd thrown back their scarves making it easy to see faces and he recognized three of them.

He had to assume the other three knew the fourth member or else they would not have let her so close to the Admiral.

The guard's shack was the only place of any cover. They found warmth there, and both he and Merriweather leaned against the wall, exhausted and dripping sea water still. The small brazier that warmed the little area did an excellent job, though. While Admiral Rose gave orders and listened to reports, they took off their cloaks, and both leaned closer to the warmth, letting it dry out the woolens they wore, ice melting away to puddles at their feet.

Admiral Rose and Greenwood finally stepped back into the little cover. Her face was red, his pale -- but that came from the wound in his left arm which he cradled close to his chest.

"Damned mess," Admiral Rose said. "But it could have been a damned sight worse. You saved my life, Merriweather -- along with those of Lord Raventower and others. We're lucky the bomber didn't get inside."

She gave a little shrug.

"If I may make a suggestion?" Merriweather said. She was Army, not Air Patrol and had always been worried about overstepping her position.

"I would appreciate any help," Admiral Rose replied. She'd signaled Greenwood to take the only chair and had drawn out a first aid kit to deal with the cut in his arm.

"Let no one close to you or the ships who is not recognized by two other people," Merriweather suggested, looking out the small window at the crowd that had begun to gather near the shack. She didn't trust them any better than he did. "Work out in circles as people are cleared. You won't be able to catch any Sedina traitors, but you should be able to limit their access to Atrian allies."

"Yes," the woman agreed and went to the door. Mica heard her giving the orders.

He saw two people backing away in haste already, but he wasn't the only one who noticed. The fight was brief, and lucky for him it was far enough away that the life lights did not notice him.

Admiral Rose gave other orders, which included clearing out a set of sheds to be used as cover and to take care of the wounded. When she left, he and Merriweather trailed behind, though he avoided any area where there might be more people dying.

"How are you doing, Lord Raventower?" Merriweather asked. She had stopped and stared at him, clearly noting how quiet he had become.

"A headache," he admitted. "And -- too much going on. Too many things around me. I don't do well."

"We should --"

"I want to see *Flash* and make certain she's taken no more damage," Mica said, nodding in the direction he had been headed. "And help get her in the cradle for repair."

"We are both covered in ice," Merriweather reminded him. "But you're right. We went through a lot to get the ship this far. We might as well help make certain she's as safe as possible."

The oxen had been spooked by the battle and the fire, but their handlers had stayed with them, and they were already moving again. Good men. They'd come from the local farms with the animals, and they knew how to handle the creatures. Mica and Merriweather walked along the side of the wagon while Mica took note of all the scratches and scrapes on the hull.

"You told me once that you had sponsored airships," Merriweather said as they began to fit the ship with thick rope netting that slipped underneath and cradled the craft as they lifted her. "I assume that *Flash* is one of them?"

"Sponsored and designed a great deal of her," Mica

admitted. He hated to see the damage done, but he had faith they could make repairs. Krogor, the engineer, was ready to crawl in and look at the guts of the machine as soon as it was in place. He gave Mica a nod and a grunt, which was as friendly as the man ever got.

They had no trouble setting the craft in the repair cradle. It was, in fact, the only calm thing that had happened since they'd pulled the airship out of the water. More sea water washed out of the hull as the work crew turned her. Mica climbed up to look inside again, and Krogor joined him. Merriweather kept as close as she could, and only made way for Admiral Rose when she arrived.

Mica and Krogor went over the engines, mostly tapping, grunting and nodding in a way that only two engineers would have understood. He supposed it might even sound funny to others and he suspected Merriweather of grinning now and then, though he did not catch her at it.

"Not as bad as it could be," Mica finally said when Admiral Rose asked. "We'll have considerable work to do, but she's going to need half the hull refitted anyway, so it's not as though she'll be flying soon anyway. I'll start in on some plans --"

"After your meeting with General Gregorian," Merriweather reminded him. "And we had better go soon, or we'll be late."

He'd forgotten the meeting. He wanted to protest, but there was no point in it. Besides, after what had happened here, Gregorian would need a first-hand report.

Mica climbed down and back into the wind. The repair crew began stringing a tarp up over the area. They'd probably start work this afternoon still. He wanted to stay --

"I have some warm cloaks for you," Admiral Rose said, leading them back toward the gate. "And Greenwood is writing up a report I would like you to take back to General

Raventower and the King."

"Certainly," Mica agreed.

"Guards will --"

"Not go with us," Mica said. "Keep them here for now. If we left with a group of people to protect us, we'd only draw more attention."

Merriweather nodded agreement, which apparently did more to convince the admiral than his own words. He couldn't imagine why people didn't listen to him most of the time. He also wasn't certain why they thought Captain Merriweather more reliable. Or sane.

The two had the cloaks, horses, and the report before they left the walls of the Air Patrol field. Mica looked back after they'd gone no more than half a mile. Except for some smoke in the air, he could see no sign of the battle. That didn't seem right. People had died -- but the cold seemed to have blotted away the anger. He couldn't even draw it up in himself again.

The weather had turned cold and brisk, but no new snow had fallen since the battle in the city a few days before. That was why they'd taken today to get *Flash* up out of the sea before the next storm blew in. The weather would soon change. He didn't even have to look at a barometer to know the next storm would soon swoop down on them.

The city had already suffered a difficult winter, and it had barely started. Damned mess. Mica huddled in the cloak and wished for spring again.

They didn't linger on the open trail, but at least they would see if anyone came along the way. Merriweather even moved off the road itself when it came too close to the cliffs. They had slower going there, but it did seem wise.

They passed two squads of guards riding in from the city to help in what they knew must be trouble. Both seemed legit, but Mica couldn't say he felt any better as they went past.

They reached Kamere by the North Gate. The guards recognized them and let the two through with only a quick bow of the heads and a salute to Captain Merriweather.

"Any trouble here?" she asked, looking back the way they had ridden.

"No, Captain," the man in charge said. "Seems quiet today. More so than usual."

The man didn't appear to trust the quiet. Well, neither did he and Merriweather. They rode past the guards and into an area with inns and taverns, all of them closed except for local people staying there. Faces watched from windows, seeing not their own Lord but a stranger and his companion. Mica threw off the hood of his cloak since that might stop some people from confronting them. Merriweather did the same. The day was cold and their hair still damp, but they did not have far to go.

The castle stood on a promontory, the hill leading upward past a few dozen estates belonging to high-ranking and affluent locals. The Merriweather estate was located on the western flanks of the hill, probably the most protected area in the city since it had no view of the sea and was hard to reach. The path they took curved upward, splitting from the road to the sea. The estates here had guards at their gates. Most of those retainers were older men and women, or else ones too young to go into the army.

Moving past them did not make Mica feel any safer. Merriweather had gotten twitchy again as well, but he could hardly blame her.

They reached the heights with a view back across the city. He turned to see Raventower itself rising on the far side of sprawling Kamere. They were a long way from home, but at least he could see the place.

They rode on to the castle gates and yet more guards, and nowhere safe.

CHAPTER TWO

S hacks built of salvaged wood and tents made of blankets clustered everywhere in the castle grounds, the makeshift housing crowded with people who typically would not have spent more than an afternoon near Kamere Castle and then only on festival days. The King and Queen had encouraged many of the poorer people to come here for refuge since their areas of town, being close to the sea and filled with factories, had been among the hardest hit.

Many others still held to the ruins where they'd always lived. Mostly women and children had gathered here for safety, and even many of those from the fishing village at the edge of his own tower had taken refuge in this mass of people. They were safer here, and Mica was glad to see some of the familiar and smiling faces as he and Merriweather rode by. He thought those people probably felt the most out of place though, so far from the sea and the lives they'd always known.

The scent of food came from some of the communal cook fires. Nothing fancy, but the smell could have drawn him to the company of people he got along with so well. What kept him riding past was not the idea of Gregorian waiting for them so much as the realization that these people had little to share.

They rode on to the Kamere Castle that stood towering over the grounds. Like most royal and noble abodes, the building had been constructed in various ages, with wings and towers sprouting whenever the royal family decided they needed something new and spectacular to impress the people. The newest section was already almost one hundred years old. He thought they could use something new. After the war. It could mark their win.

He would suggest it. Later.

Raventower was probably the only noble house that had not changed, at least outwardly, since the original building. He wondered if he should add something on, but that felt like defacing the ancient -- older than the castle -- home of his ancestors.

Many of the commoners knew Lord Raventower well. He heard his name shouted and waved in that general direction. These were worried people, but they were grateful for a relatively safe place with food and warmth.

Only relatively safe, though. If the Atrians ever got a foothold in the city, they'd be heading straight for the castle to attack the King and claim the rule and wealth of the land.

Well, Atrians might be surprised by how much opposition they found in these poor people. Mica didn't think that was why the King brought them here, but he might learn to appreciate them as more than the workers who kept the city running.

Off to the right, Mica saw a group that had taken themselves apart from their poorer neighbors, just as they had in the city. He scowled that way, but at least that group had stopped purposely creating trouble. The King had come down and talked to the two groups, but it was clear that the not-so-poor did not like that they had to share this place with the abject poor. They acted as though everyone here was not caught up in the same war.

Mica really didn't understand people.

Another set of guards held the steps leading to the castle entrance. One of the stable boys took their horses.

"At least we don't have to climb up to the army camp," Mica said as he stood before the steps and tried to ease the ache in his legs. He couldn't tell if he trembled from cold, exertion, or just nerves. This had not been a pleasant day so far, and he couldn't see it getting better.

"True," Merriweather agreed and gave him a little nudge. "It will be warm inside, you know."

"Ah. Warmth. I know this word, Merriweather, but it's been a while since we've experienced it."

They'd left Raventower before dawn. From the moment they stepped outside the tower until now, they had not had more than passing warmth like the few minutes in the guard shack.

The steps were somewhat icy. It couldn't be helped, Mica knew. Snow had covered them and people coming and going packed the bits of snow into ice. Mica slipped once going down on one knee, cursed under his breath, and stood to go on.

A guard at the door gave a coded knock, and the door opened to one of the King's stewards who ushered them in with some haste.

"Prince Gregorian said to keep watch for you," the man said, barely giving them time to strip off the cloaks. He seemed to sniff disdainfully at the clothing underneath and the pervading odor of sea water, but he wisely said nothing.

They moved swiftly through the building despite the equally crowded halls here. Most of these people were members of the various temples. The Temple Square had been severely damaged by bombardments from the Atrian ships which had seemed a waste of weaponry at first. Now Mica wasn't as convinced. The people had always gone to the temples in times of trouble.

The priests and priestesses did spend time with those who had taken refuge in the grounds by the castle, and sometimes a few even went down into the city itself, which helped somewhat. Temples that had been holding private grudges against one another had put aside all their differences for now.

So, the Atrians might not have gotten what they wanted after all.

The rush of people everywhere unsettled Mica again. His headache grew, and he felt as though he had started to fall into a morass of colors and sounds with no way out. He wanted to close his eyes, to hide in a corner --

Merriweather moved up closer to his side and guided him, an unobtrusive barrier between Mica and the rest of these loud, moving people. Mica gave a little nod of thanks and leaned slightly closer to her.

Would they never get clear of these people? Chants, shouts, incense, more noise: Mica could not bear the cacophony much longer. His head would explode. The army camp might have been better. Fewer sounds, less chaos. He couldn't say the warmth was payment enough for --

They stepped past another guard and into a quiet, calmer hall.

"Too many of them," the steward mumbled. "Gods help us, the only peace we have is when they sleep. Lately, though, I swear they are taking rounds at staying awake so that we always have something going on. Ah, forgive me." The man stopped and ran a hand through his graying hair. "I should not say such things."

"I am glad to hear the words," Mica confessed. "I thought it a bit too much as well. Let us hope the war ends soon, for all our sakes and for our sanity."

The man gave a quick nod of agreement and left them at the hall to Gregorian's office. Two guards stood there, both neat -- but both wounded and no doubt taken off active duty to handle this task. Anyone who reached this door had already gone through a dozen or more guards.

One with a cane in hand made a soft knock and won a gruff order to enter. Mica found himself straightening slightly, an automatic reaction when he faced his older brother. Half-brother, as he had lately learned, though that made no difference in their relationship.

Merriweather opened the door and stepped aside, the perfect guard again. Mica went in --

Gregorian was not alone. The King sat in a chair beside Gregorian, looking over the notes and maps strewn across the desk. The oil lamp had been pushed aside, precariously close to the edge.

"Your Highness," Mica said somewhat belatedly as he bowed. Merriweather had moved up beside him and bowed as well. "I had not expected you here."

"Sit down, sit down both of you," King Abertus ordered with a wave of his hand to the two chairs. "What is going on out there, Lord Raventower?"

"We've brought a report from Admiral Rose," Merriweather offered and pulled out the message that had been wrapped in water-resistant cloth. She sat the envelope at the corner of the desk where it dripped as much as she and Mica, and at the same time she surreptitiously pushed the lamp to a better position. "There was, as you no doubt know by now, an attack at the Air Patrol Field."

Gregorian asked a few questions about what had happened and got concise replies from the Captain. Both King and General appeared to be content with hearing what Merriweather had to say, and Mica had nothing to add until they got down to the repairs that would be needed to do on *Flash*.

By then Mica had sorted out much of his own thoughts.

He gave a litany of the damage to their prize airship, but he reassured them both that everything he'd seen had been repairable. They'd also been lucky to lose only one other ship in the recent attack, and that one had already been damaged.

"I'll know more when I can actually look at the engine," Mica admitted. His headache had eased in the relative quiet while Merriweather did her report. "What I saw was not beyond repair, though. I will be going back out to take a look and help once they get things cleaned up."

"I don't think --" Gregorian began with a shake of his head. Mica's brother looked, reasonably enough, harassed and troubled. He also looked as though he needed some sleep, which made Mica feel all the more tired and more than a little guilty. He at least had a chance to sleep sometimes.

"This is the work I do, you know," Mica said before his brother could speak again. He even lifted his hand to forestall more of the argument, a movement that seemed to surprise both Gregorian and the King, who wisely stayed clear of this part of the discussion. Arguments between the three Raventower siblings were legendary. "And they will need me. I designed that engine. I can rebuild what needs to be done."

"Yes, yes," Gregorian gave way with a sigh. The King had opened the report from Admiral Rose. "I won't do anything stupid like try to order you to stay away. You'll be needed. And we will have better patrols along the road, though from what you said, it wouldn't have helped. *Traitors in the Air Patrol.* I'm not surprised since I know we have a few in the army, too. Still, this is not why we called you here. We need to talk about the statue."

"The statue," Mica repeated, surprised by the sudden change in direction. "What about the statue?"

"How can we get it up?" King Abertus asked.

"I had not considered -- well not much," Mica admitted. There had been other things to keep his attention. He sat back in the chair and stared at the wall, but in his mind, he saw the moment when he and Merriweather had taken the submersible too close to that strange statue and had almost become the victims of the strange thing that sat the sea floor. It had glowed, being made of sea metal, a rare substance that sometimes washed up on the shores near Kamere and which he had not realized came from something so malevolent and dangerous.

"Mica?" Gregorian said and sounded only a little frustrated with his silence. Gregorian and the King had both known him long enough to be used to those moments.

"My apologies" Mica sat forward and pulled his wandering thoughts back to the present problem. There was simply too much he needed to deal with right now, and the statue had not been anywhere near the top of the list. Mica recalled all he could from their brief encounter with the device, though he would rather not have remembered that moment when the eyes opened and seemed to see them in the little craft. He managed not to shiver at the memory as he focused on Gregorian. "The statue is huge and heavy, being made of metal. I do not think it is solid metal, so that gives us some hope, but in my opinion, we would be wise to leave it there for now. Get the rest of this matter settled."

He had left out all the troubling magical problems that went along with the statue. They simply did not have time to try and deal with those things right now.

"Ignoring the statue may not be possible," Gregorian said. He quickly sorted through some papers on the desk and drew out a note on a piece of scrap paper. "We intercepted this last night."

He handed the note to Merriweather who was closer. She glanced over the words and grimaced before giving it to Mica.

Cheap paper, torn from something else, but not anything obvious to give a clue to the original use. The words were scratched hastily with a poorly tipped quill or perhaps pen.

Must take Raventower before we can get the statue.

Well, that probably made sense; Raventower sat close to where the statue sat in the ocean. However, he didn't like the idea much at all.

"Why do they want you, Mica?" the King asked softly.

"Not me," he replied before he handed the scrap back. He doubted more study would reveal anything important. "They want Raventower itself. They've made it clear that they are not interested in keeping me alive, you know. They want Raventower because the statue lies off the cliff where my tower stands."

"It has been there for at least five hundred years," Merriweather said. She sounded angry. "Why are they coming for it now?"

"We had no idea anything was there until about seventy years ago when --" Mica stopped and then shrugged. "When it came awake, for want of a better word. Something triggered the device which I think might be some sort of clockwork construction. I don't know. The sea metal has magic, and it has been wearing away. Even the priests and priestesses of the Temple of the Unknown Path could not tell me how the magic works in the little pieces I have brought to them. Because we don't understand, we don't want to be too quick to bring this thing up to the surface and have to deal with it."

"It's been pulling ships down, you say," the King said. He nodded. "Yes, we have lost ships there, and it cannot be a coincidence, especially given what you saw."

"Why do the Atrians want it?" Merriweather asked. "And how do they even know it is there? We forgot it existed, so how did they remember?"

"Many of them are descendants of people who were exiled when we abandoned the God of War," Mica reminded her. "And that's what we're dealing with down there, you know. That is the statue that was thrown into the sea at the time they were exiled. They may have kept the legend alive."

"Or else someone came across it of late," King Abertus offered. "We know they have an archive of sorts, written in an old style of our own language. That might have started them on this war."

They all nodded agreement.

"No matter what set them off, they're here," Gregorian said with a growl. He drew out his pocket watch and scowled at it as well. Clearly a busy man. "We can't let the Atrians get the statue."

"No, we don't dare," Mica agreed. "It might be nothing more than the mass of sea metal they want, but even that would be dangerous in their hands. If the statue is something more, I would not want it in the control of the enemy, either."

"And it now makes sense why the Atrian assassins were trying to kill Lord Raventower," Merriweather offered as though everything had become suddenly clear. "If they want the tower, they might have expected the place to be abandoned if the eccentric young lord was no longer around."

"I resent that description," Mica said with a glance her way. "I am not that young."

A moment of silence had passed before the King laughed. Gregorian had looked appalled at the joke, but now he grinned as well. Mica thought the humor helped them all.

"It does make sense of something so odd," Gregorian finally admitted. "Not that it helps."

"They haven't killed me yet," Mica pointed out. "And knowing they want the statue makes me all the more curious about why and what we might do to get it up and out of their hands --"

"Or would bringing it out of the water only make the work easier for them?" Merriweather dared to ask.

"Good point, that," Gregorian admitted. "Right now, we

can keep their ships away from the area, and they have to try and control at least Kamere if they want access to it. They might think they can get it if they hold Raventower. Should we destroy the tower?"

"I would really rather you didn't," Mica replied. "At least not unless the Atrians do take it, and then I suspect they'll knock it down to make a camp where they can raise the statue. We are warned, though. I think we can keep them out."

"Let us hope so," King Abertus said. He glanced at his own watch. "I do not like the idea of destroying our own property, but if we must do so, the tower will be rebuilt. You know that, Mica."

"Yes, thank you," he said, and neither of them spoke about what would happen if Mica and his people -- including Merriweather -- didn't survive. A nice memorial built there, he supposed.

This was not the time to get morbid.

"I think that covers everything for the moment," King Abertus said with a glance at Gregorian. The general nodded.

"I will begin work on plans to bring up the statue," Mica promised. "I'll have a day or two before we can start work on *Flash*, so I might as well put them to good use. If I come up with anything useful, I'll get the notes to you, though not by the usual pouches. I don't think we want to risk such a thing falling into the Atrians' hands and giving them help in their own plans."

"Yes, good idea," Gregorian said. "How then?"

"I'll send them with Shipley and Bear," he said. "Have your guards aware that the boy may come to see you tomorrow or the next day."

"Shipley? Bear?" the King asked.

"A young man and his rather large dog," Merriweather offered. "Completely trustworthy and not easy for anyone else to mimic."

"True," Gregorian agreed. "Good."

"I will leave such things in your hands," the King said with a nod toward Gregorian.

"I am putting more guards on the tower," Gregorian added and looked at Mica as though he expected some argument. Mica said nothing. "Huh. We dare not let it fall to them, so we had better make certain there is a sufficient force to keep them out. I'll trust Merriweather to keep watch over you. She's managed it well so far, and not complained, either. I thought you'd drive her insane by now."

"Maybe I have," Mica replied. "After all, we are going to wed. Eventually."

"Ah, yes," the King said with a bit of a smile. "Congratulation on your betrothal."

"Thank you," Mica said with a forced smile of his own. Not that he didn't want to marry Merriweather, but he noticed how uneasy the King seemed to be when he gave his congratulations. Mica couldn't imagine why.

However, as Merriweather gave her own thank you, Mica thought he understood the problem, and it was one that had not occurred to him or to Merriweather. Given that the King had to order the assassination of Mica's father because of problems dealing with gathering souls, and since Mica had inherited the same power, he suspected King Abertus might be worried about the ability passing to a new generation.

It was not something he had even considered. In fact, the thought of children at all had not occurred to him until now.

He would have to talk to Merriweather about the matter. Later, when they had time to stop and think clearly about such mundane things. She might, after all, have second thoughts of her own when she realized some of the implications.

He tried not to let the dismay at that thought come to his face, though he saw Gregorian glance his way with a frown. Mica sat up straighter and did not look at Merriweather. They had other matters of concern, and there would be time enough to discuss marriage and children later, after the war.

They talked for a little while longer. Gregorian laid out some of the wider plans for the placement of the army and drew Mica into a discussion about the cannon on the tower and how best to use it if they ran into more trouble. The conversation drew him away from the darker thoughts, and he wondered if Gregorian hadn't done that on purpose, though he doubted his brother had understood the reason for his sudden silence.

Another glance at his watch and the King stood. They all did as well, though Mica felt a strain in his legs. More rest would have been nice. At least they were a bit drier.

"Take care, Lord Raventower," the King said. "And Captain Merriweather."

"Thank you, Your Highness," he replied with a bow of his head.

"The two of you are in the thick of things," King Abertus said, "and you have handled everything well so far. Thank you."

He turned and headed out the door. Mica frowned, but he supposed a guard would be there to escort him. They would not be careless here in the castle.

"I need to get to the camp," Gregorian said as he began to shove papers and maps into his case. "King Abertus needed to know about the statue and what we should plan to do. It's easy for the rest of us to keep rushing off and handling matters, but he's the one who has to appear as though he knows all and can deal with the rest of the Lords and the people who come to him."

"True," Merriweather agreed. She appeared to be happy to be going again. Mica did not look forward to going back out into the weather, though it gave him a hope of reaching the tower yet today. Home -- whether safe or not.

"Damned mess here in the castle," Gregorian admitted as they headed out the door. "The servants are going insane along with everyone else. It does not help. The rest of the royal family, including my wife and children, are going to remain out of the city until this is settled."

"Wise," Mica said. "It is becoming increasingly more dangerous out in the city. I would like to think that people in the castle are safe beneath the shelter of all the temples, though."

"Well, as long as we can keep them from going at each other," Gregorian replied. They headed toward the louder areas again, and Mica at least tried to get some control this time, knowing what they were going to face. "We've had a couple minor incidents, but nothing too serious. I think it helps that the Temple of the Unknown has moved off as far as they can from everyone else. That would be where I would expect the most trouble, though not because they'd start it."

Many of the other temples did not trust people who worked blatant magic, though all of them had their own special abilities. That was why Mica had to be careful of displaying his own odd skills.

People cleared the way for General Gregorian which proved the wisdom of walking beside his brother. For once Gregorian wasn't lecturing him, either. Merriweather walked a little behind and to Mica's left, while another guard had moved up to cover the General. Mica tried to feel safe.

"I have been trying to talk King Abertus into leaving," Gregorian admitted softly. He shook his head. "It is not going to happen, but I keep at it. He's right that he should stay, and I know it. I'm starting to think we do have the protection of the gods. The castle and the grounds have not taken any direct hits. Granted, we are some distance from the bay, and it would be a difficult shot, but I would have expected something to head our way. We have also had good luck at catching a few people trying to infiltrate the castle itself."

"Then this chaos may be worth it," Mica said, though he looked around with a frown.

"I am going to believe so," Gregorian replied. He slowed again, which was fine. Mica had started to limp. He'd had a long, rough day already. "Here is a bit of news, though."

News he wanted to be spread elsewhere since he said it out here amongst all these people, despite his lowered voice. Mica saw how some of them already attempted to move along with them, though the people stayed clear of the guards.

"Something is going on?" Mica asked.

"Not yet, but it will be. We are starting to work up the plans for an invasion of Atria in the spring. King Abertus agrees that it is time to put an end to this constant trouble."

Oh yes, that might worry Atrian spies and if word got out to the fleet, would they retreat and prepare for a different war? No, not likely -- at least not before they lost another battle or two. It was a seed of trouble that Gregorian planted at that moment, and Mica appreciated the move.

"What do we do for now?" he dared ask.

He thought Gregorian came close to shrugging, but that would be a bad reaction for the General in charge of keeping the city safe. His brother caught himself barely in time.

"The Atrian fleet is still holding off, what's left of it. We can't get a clear idea of how many more ships might be on their way since it is too dangerous to send airships out over the ocean this time of year. However, the fact that they are not retreating means that they are not done."

A point they had all realized, of course. "Any hope of getting help?" Mica asked.

"We're trying to draw people in from the south," he said. "But it is far to the border, and we have rumors of trouble down that way, too. Damned mess, Mica. All of it."

The sight of white robes moving down a side hall brought

another question to Mica, and one he was almost worried to ask. "Have you seen Honoria?"

"She's here. We've passed in the hall and said hello, but she hasn't come to visit. I suspect we are both too busy with our own ends of the war to take the time to gossip about you."

"I didn't mean --" Mica began but realized that his brother was joking with him. Mica tried to hide is frustration. "Ah. Sorry. I'm a bit jumpy today, I guess. This has been a hellishly long day already, and I don't know what I might find back to the tower."

"You could stay here," Gregorian offered. "I have room in my own quarters with all the rest of the family gone."

"I can't," Mica replied. He felt sorry that Gregorian was alone -- but then he realized that his brother probably wasn't around much either. "I need to be back to the tower."

"True," Gregorian agreed and didn't even pretend to argue. "We both know where we need to be."

"I don't like that Sedina stands alone in this," Mica admitted as they neared the outer door. He stopped and looked back while the servant got their cloaks. People watched, of course. He tried to study their faces, to find guilt in some so that he knew whom not to trust. Oh, it was never that easy, but he wanted it to be.

"We are not cut off," Gregorian replied and took his own cloak in hand. He looked no more in a hurry to go out than Mica. "The big question is why we had no real warning of the ships coming our way. Oh, we had rumors, but there should have been something far more substantial before they showed up on the coast."

"Nothing from the Middle Islands?" Merriweather asked with a frown.

"We suspect they sailed wide of the islands, which means they had stashes of supplies in place somewhere else. Likely on a few of the rocky outcrops where no one would see what they were doing."

"Still --" Merriweather started. Then she stopped and shook her head. "The Atrians are not known for using magic."

"And that's the question," Gregorian said as he pulled his cloak tight around him. "Did they use magic to get here? Have they used magic, as we have, to focus the weather the way we want it?"

"If so, that might be all they could do," Mica replied. "They haven't used anything blatant that I've heard about since they arrived."

"I've heard of a couple minor incidents, both of them outside the city during the fighting to the north," Gregorian said. They were heading outside, the door held open to the frigid wind. "I am trying to get them confirmed, but it may not matter since I don't think any of the Atrians in those incidents had survived."

"Is that why they want the statue?" Merriweather asked. "The magic metal?"

"Maybe," Mica agreed. He had wondered too with the way this conversation was going. Now they stood out in the cold wind and Mica snarled at the weather. Though he didn't like the wind and ice, it did seem to be normal for this time of year, though. "If they are using magic, it does change things somewhat."

"More than somewhat," Gregorian mumbled as he started down the steps.

People brought out the horses for Mica and Merriweather while a band of soldiers gathered to go with their commander up the long stair-step path to the army camp. That was not a climb Mica envied. At least he wouldn't be walking through the dangerous city, and there would be no climbing on icy stairs.

"I've talked to people from the Temple of the Unknown Path," Gregorian said as Mica took hold of his horse. "They have not been entirely forthcoming and helpful."

"And that surprises you?" Mica asked. "Remember that it is their High Priestess who was so very helpful with that warning about putting time in its place that got the damned spiders released."

"True. Still, you have to hope." He put a hand on Mica's arm. "Take care, Mica. The enemy hasn't used magic much before, but that doesn't mean they don't know how to do spells. Raventower may not be safe."

CHAPTER THREE

Gregorian's warning stayed with Mica as he mounted the horse, and as he and Merriweather rode away. Mica hadn't considered Atrian magic in the equation. No one had used it to try and kill him, even though they apparently thought it worth their while to send assassins.

Mica felt slightly better at that thought as they rode past the refugees and into the streets again. The lowering sun already cast long shadows, and Mica looked forward to being home beside a warm fire in the kitchen, and perhaps with a cup of soup. A little quiet to end the day did not seem like too much to ask.

Merriweather wasn't talkative, which he had expected. She got nervous when they rode through town. Mica wondered if he shouldn't hire some guards to help her out. Maybe not, though. He suspected she would go crazy trying to watch them and everyone else as well.

They passed by piles of debris as they neared the center of the city. He didn't like to think about the effort it would take to rebuild everything. The city would suffer for years after this war. And why? The Atrians couldn't believe they could hold the land, could they?

"Maybe we should give them the statue and see if they go

away," Mica suggested suddenly.

Merriweather looked his way and gave a sharp shake of her head. "No. If they want it this much, we really don't want to find out why later."

"I suppose not," he agreed and shrugged his cloak up higher on his shoulders. "Just looking for an easy answer."

"There are none in a situation like this. The best answer would be for the Atrians to back off and go home. I don't see that happening."

"Which brings us back again to wondering why they are here at all."

They had a brief view of the bay as they reached the Temple Square. The fog and wind hid much though he could see men at work repairing damage to the temples as they rode through that area. Mica thought that might be premature since the Atrians still sat just outside the bay, and there was no guarantee they weren't going to come and attack again.

Maybe it was important to repair the temples. Mica had never found himself drawn to organized religion, and though he offered prayers to the Gods in turn as their seasons began, he took no untoward interest in any except maybe Tulac, the God of Iron. He'd taken a liking to him through Nyle, Mica's smithy. Mica worked in metal most often, even if it was only small pieces of the material.

A few guards in uniform were on duty in the temple district, but he noted that they were using prisoners to do the manual labor. That didn't sit well with Mica -- but then he thought that if there had not been a war, they would have been shipped off to work in the coal fields to the north or the copper and silver mines to the west. This work might be somewhat better, he supposed. He watched as they carted stone from one place to another, worked on walls, and shivered in the cold. Not humane, he thought -- but what else could they do with prisoners? He trusted the Temple of Justice to have assessed these people for their crimes. Now that Honoria no longer sat on the throne of judgment, he believed they were doing their work properly.

But still, but still --

So much to think about and he should focus on the war instead. One problem at a time.

They had reached the edge of the square and skirted around the temple of Rozen, the god of winter. Mica had formed a silent prayer to that the God that grew in his mind, vaguely asking for kindness to those suffering in the cold. As they passed beside the mostly intact walls, he heard something on the roof and looked up -- and pulled aside just in time as a large tile clattered down close enough to brush against his arm and crash into the pile of snow beside him.

"Damn!" Merriweather shouted. She leaned sideways and grabbed at his bridle since the horse was startled and uncooperative as they moved quickly away from the edge of the building. Merriweather stood up in her stirrups and tried to see up on the roof. He stared too, but though he thought something might have moved there, a mere shadow, he couldn't say it was more than a cat or a rat.

"We should go check --" Merriweather began. Then she stopped and shook her head. "No, we shouldn't. That would only put us in a dangerous position again."

"True," Mica agreed. He patted his horse and hoped the animal calmed and didn't bolt. "I thought I saw a shadow, but it might only have been an animal."

"Maybe," she agreed and let go of his horse, though she looked ready to grab hold of the bridle again.

The animal remained skittish, but Mica kept control. A glance at his cloak showed a line of dust where the roofing had brushed against him. If it had not landed in the snow, the brittle tile might have shattered and injured the horse. He'd gotten lucky.

"It was probably just chance," he said, staring upward where she did.

"It's not like there isn't damage to the buildings and some of the walls are still unsteady. I'd like to believe that was the cause," Merriweather agreed. She finally turned her horse aside.

"As would I," Mica agreed. They started away, though Merriweather kept glancing back as though she expected someone to follow -- which did not help Mica's worries about enemies. He wanted to be back in the tower walls where he felt marginally safer than here.

"There are too many Atrians in the city still," Merriweather finally said. She didn't glance back quite so much, but that was because they had reached more dangerous territory with factory and warehouse buildings on both sides, and areas where people could easily hide. If someone did wait for him to head home, they would likely be along here. "How long are we going to worry about where an enemy is hiding and what they will do next?"

"A miserable thought," Mica agreed. "I fear it might be long after the rest of the city recovers before the two of us feel safe again."

"The rest of our lives," she agreed.

"Merriweather, there might be reasons why you don't --"

"I am not going to break our betrothal," she said without stopping to look at him.

He wanted to let the discussion go, but there were matters they simply had not discussed. Maybe he should wait until they got back to the tower, but he'd started the discussion and now seemed a better time than letting the conversation slip comfortably away again. He might not get this brave again.

"There is something we need to discuss, though. Something neither of us knew about at the time of the betrothal."

"I know," she replied.

He wasn't certain she did, so he went on anyway. "The King reminded me that there is a matter we hadn't taken into account. Children, Merriweather. Specifically, my children who might inherit my problems."

"Yes," she agreed with a quick glance at him and then back to watch for trouble. They were not safe. However, she glanced his way once more, and he held his breath. "It is something we'll deal with when the time comes."

She turned to look for enemies again. He smiled, and though Merriweather didn't see, he suspected that she knew.

They left the factories behind and entered into the poorer part of town, an area that some would consider by far the most dangerous. The poor, though, had never frightened Lord Raventower.

Damage here was noticeable, but only because the area had already been in such disrepair. Mica funded some attempts at improvement through the better months of the year, so the buildings were at least livable.

There had not been as many bombs lobbed in this direction. Mica still could not be certain why they had not fired on Raventower itself, except that they wanted it. The statue must be the reason --

Movement to the right.

He and Merriweather turned, reaching for weapons --

The glowing woman, the High Priestess of the Unknown Path, had appeared again. Mica sighed. Merriweather mumbled under her breath, and the words didn't sound polite.

The woman glided towards them, not fully in this reality. They'd seen her more in the flesh once, and this was like a ghost of someone. The woman blinked and focused on them with her mouth drawn into a frown.

"Things are not what they seem," the woman said, her words echoing when there should not have been an echo at all.

Merriweather urged her horse a little forward and looked down at the woman. "You do realize that's not a lot of help, right?" she demanded.

"Merriweather --" Mica began, worried about what the woman would do.

"And you know that your last cryptic advice set the damned spiders loose, right?"

"Yes." The woman stared up at Merriweather. A brief, odd look came across her face, but then she turned and walked away, disappearing long before she reached the shadows of the buildings nearby.

"Well, damn," Merriweather growled.

Mica sighed and watched the shadows where the goddess had gone hoping for ... something. He didn't know what, exactly.

"I had hoped we were done with that part," he admitted when he looked back at Merriweather. "I fear things are going to get worse."

"Of course, they'll get worse," she said with a bit of a snarl. Then she turned her horse and forced Mica's to move along as well. "Let's get to the tower."

"So, we can make some other find and let loose something worse than spiders?" Mica asked.

"Ha. Well, at least we're warned, right?"

"Things are not what they seem," he repeated. "Oh yes, that's a helpful warning."

Merriweather made a more amused sound this time, but he could tell she felt no better about the warning. He couldn't imagine what they should make of it, either. Best not to consider the supposed problem since there were far more real troubles to handle.

The road began to twist and turn a bit, the buildings becoming more dilapidated and the scents overcoming even the cold of winter in places. He usually didn't mind so much, but this evening it seemed as though every shadow moved, and he began to fear that evil gathered here along with misery and poverty. He hated that this place sat just beneath his tower -- though granted, the tower didn't look much better, and he at least did not put on an ostentatious display of wealth. He even tried to help where he could, much to the surprise, and sometimes derision, of some of his fellow lords.

This area of the city often seemed to grow darker earlier than anywhere else, and there were places where he knew that daylight never reached.

Like Shadow Walk. That dark tunnel between buildings was an area where most people would not go, even if invited. Mica felt relatively safe in parts of it since he had made friends with people that some of his fellow Lords would throw in prison simply for crossing their paths. Mica glanced into Shadow Walk, hoping to see someone there and feel as though they had allies close by. Nothing moved in that darkness.

They were a long time until spring, he thought. Spring would be helpful. The cold sapped at everything and made them weak. A few people had already died of the chill this winter, though mostly drunks who hadn't the intelligence to leave off the drink (wherever they were finding it these days), or to make certain they were already in some warm hole before they passed out and froze to death. Those deaths were not only found in places liked Shadow Walk. Soldiers drank their pay and even those of higher class had been found passed out, and one dead.

The road took them past another path. This one led down to the fishing village. Mica saw no movement there, which bothered him, although he knew the women and children were mostly up at the castle. He didn't like to see the emptiness -- and the faint shape of a foreign ship far in the distance. He wanted the Atrians to go away and once again considered the idea of giving them the statue.

Not wise, he knew, but he wanted this over with so he could return to his quiet life.

The gate to his courtyard stood partly open, but only because there were so many guards in place and they often needed to come and go, sometimes with wagons or carriages. The two nodded to the guards, and Mica felt his shoulders relax for the first time all day, even though this looked nothing like the quiet little courtyard he was used to. Wagons crowded in around the walls, most of them with supplies for the soldiers. Mica tried not to scowl, but he really did want his old, peaceful world back. The soldiers moved everywhere, and their fires sent smoke up through the windows of the tower. He could hear them even with the shutters closed in his workroom.

The soldiers would remain until the war ended. Since they had no idea how long that might take, Mica supposed he ought to get used to them.

At least they were mostly polite. Mica couldn't tell if it was his title, his brother's rank, or Merriweather's scowl that sent them scurrying out of the way as they came through the gate, but he appreciated that no one stopped them.

Nyle came to take the horses, but he looked harassed. A couple soldiers followed the smithy and were discussing something about sheds and metal. Mica came close to ordering them away, but Nyle just gave a signal, and the two soldiers fell quiet. He must have it in hand, despite looking bothered.

"Thank you, Nyle," Mica said as he slid off the horse and forced his legs not to give way. Mica thought he could still hear the soft tinkle of ice breaking away from cloth. "It has been a damned long day."

"How many people tried to kill you?" Nyle asked. That won raised eyebrows from the soldiers.

"I don't think anyone specifically targeted him this time," Merriweather replied as she gave her horse over to one of the soldiers. "But there was both gunfire and bombs."

"Ah, all pretty normal then," Nyle said and took the horse away. The soldiers followed Nyle, silent this time.

Merriweather grinned and headed for the tower door, herding Mica along with her. "Well, that certainly brightened my day. Good to be home -- good to be back, Lord Raventower."

Merriweather's words brightened his day. So, she did consider this odd place her home, too? Wonderful! Though, if it came to it, he would find them somewhere better to live once this madness ended. While he didn't mind living in such a rundown building, she might like something a bit less drafty, and perhaps less ancient. Something built in the last two hundred years might suit her better.

Merriweather had gotten a quick report from one of the men as they crossed to the building. Nothing out of place today. No bombs here. Mica gave a nod of relief and pushed the heavy door open.

Once inside the hall with the door firmly shut, Mica found peace again. He could smell something sweet from the lower level kitchen, though not a scent he was used to. Gram, who had taken over the kitchen with Ada gone, had a different style of cooking. Mica enjoyed the food, but he still missed Ada, Fern, and Roe and wanted them back, too. He wanted a return to the world he understood.

That didn't mean he didn't appreciate Gram any less. She had stepped in when they might have been reduced to eating army fare with the men out in the courtyard. Mica relished that they ate so well. He had to be careful not to overindulge, though he suspected climbing up and down the Tower would probably take care of any extra weight.

"I am going up to the workshop," he said and started for the stairs. "I need to relax a little, Merriweather. I'm sure it's fine -- you need not come with me --"

"Go, go," she said and urged him to the stairs and followed.

He wanted to argue, but he started up the stairs. Gram had come up out of the kitchen, though and they both paused.

"Captain, your ma, she arrived unexpected like a few hours ago -- oh the bread!" she rushed back to the kitchen again.

"Well damn," Merriweather grumbled. "I'll send her a note of apology, though she might have warned me she intended to visit. Go, Lord Raventower. What she was doing out at a time like this is really beyond me."

Gram might have more to say, but they'd hear it all later at dinner. The older woman didn't come to the stairwell and yell anything else up after them. Quiet here. Silence and peace. Maybe he would just stop at the floor with his rooms and head to bed and sleep, though then he would miss dinner. That wouldn't do. Gram worked hard on the cooking, and he did not want to disappoint her.

Besides, he'd had nothing but some bread and cheese when they left this morning. The same for Merriweather. Food would do them both some good.

So, he barely paused at the floor and took the last flight of stairs, hearing Tippet give a little bark just before he stepped out into --

A room filled with horror.

Silks, lace, and other clothes of all types were draped over every spot he could see. Ruffles hung from the necks of clockwork animals, finished and unfinished, on the shelves. Dark velvet covered his desk, the top thankfully closed to protect the delicate work within.

Even Tippet, his oldest clockwork creation, had a bow on his head. The creature danced around, apparently pleased with the addition.

"What in the name of the Gods --" Mica began.

Merriweather had moved up beside him and stopped, her face flushing and her mouth moving, though she could not actually find words to say at first. She finally shook her head, looked at Mica in dismay, and then turned back to the room.

"Mother!" she said at last.

An older woman appeared from behind the columns that rose halfway across the huge room. She held a bundle of cloth in her hand. A small, stout woman, but Mica could see traces of Merriweather in the older woman's face and her bright smile.

"There you are!" she said as though they had just arrived at her sitting parlor. "I feared you would not get back before dark, and I do so hate to travel at night these days!"

"What --" Merriweather began. Her voice squeaked slightly. She cleared her throat as the woman came closer. "What in the name of all that is holy are you doing here, mother?" she finally demanded.

"Oh, do watch what you say, my dear. We wouldn't want Lord Raventower to think you are coarse, do we?" Baroness Merriweather said. She smiled, and Mica had the feeling of a little joke. "We have not been truly introduced, Lord Raventower --"

"Mica," he corrected automatically. "Please call me Mica."

"That's very kind of you. Call me Magina," she said with a nod of her head. Pleasant woman, he thought. "Jewel --"

"What are you doing here?" Merriweather demanded again.

"We must look over some of the cloth that I thought might make a nice bridal gown," Magina said with a wave of one arm, draped in lace, towards the other items in the room.

"Are you crazy?" Merriweather finally demanded. She even sounded sincere.

"Jewel --"

Captain Merriweather had begun moving through the

room, hastily grabbing cloth from every spot she could until her arms were full, and she clearly had no idea what to do with it now. Her mother had simply followed behind and took cloth back out of her arms and began draping it here and there. Mica watched with morbid fascination and wondered if this kind of behavior was typical for families.

"Oh, do calm down, Jewel," Magina finally ordered, and Merriweather did stop. He supposed she was used to that tone. "Going over the cloth and lace will not take that long."

"Mother, you do know that we do not intend to marry for some time, right?" Merriweather asked. A piece of lace had somehow drifted up over her head and now brushed over her nose. She didn't have a hand free to knock it aside. "We don't plan for the wedding to be any sooner than five years or so --"

"Good!" Magina said and clapped her hands in delight. "That is *wonderful* news. I'll have so much longer to prepare! Now, I know that the colors will need much black and gold --"

"Years, mother! *Five years!*" Merriweather shouted, waving her arms in exasperation this time.

"Yes, I heard you. Five years just means I'll have all the more time to enjoy planning the affair --"

Merriweather looked at Mica, shaking her head in dismay. He moved to his desk and cleared the chair, trying very, very hard not to laugh. This was not a battle Mica wanted to take part in because he did not understand the rules. Merriweather was appalled, but he also saw a hint of amusement beneath her words. He would leave this to her. She'd faced far worse trouble than her own mother armed with some lace.

"We are in the middle of a war, mother," Merriweather said, trying to sound, he thought, a little more reasonable. "Coming here, of all places --"

"The tower has not been hit, even when the rest of the town was bombarded," the woman replied and sounded serious enough herself. "I daresay this might be safer than home."

She did have a point, thought Mica didn't say so aloud. Merriweather sighed.

"Who knows what might happen to any of us these days," Magina added and removed the lace from Merriweather's nose. "You and Mica both go into danger all the time, my dear. I know what you do, and I fear for you, so I am fighting in my own way. Besides, I'm old. I might not survive another five years, even without the war."

"Oh, don't be so melodramatic," Merriweather said with a sound that came close to a laugh. "This just simply is not acceptable, mother. This is where Lord Raventower works, and not just on the cute clockwork creatures. You cannot come up here and throw cloth everywhere and expect me to stand around praising it all."

"I do rather like this velvet," Mica said, brushing across the cloth on his desk. "Do you think I could get a vest or two of it?"

"You are both impossible!" Merriweather shouted, throwing her arms in the air and tossing cloth everywhere.

Mica grinned at his future mother-in-law. He thought they might get along very well.

"Oh yes, quite beautiful cloth. A vest would look exquisite, perhaps with some gold detailing?"

"Yes --"

"I am living in a nightmare," Merriweather mumbled with a shake of her head. "Where are the assassins when I need them?"

She began picking up cloth again and stood, precariously balanced.

"Oh, do put that back in the case," her mother said with a wave toward a trunk at the side of the room. "But we must discuss things..."

Mica settled into work, carefully putting aside the velvet

and a bit of ruffle before he opened the top of the desk. He went to work on the small insects that he'd found were excellent distractions against someone attacking him. The fire Nyle must have set blazed in the middle of the room dispelling most of the cold. He wasn't used to other people talking while he worked, but he was able to ignore most of what the two women said, which did help.

Despite battles and all they'd done, the army had only pushed the enemy out of the city -- mostly -- for a few days. The ships still held off the coast and more might be on the way. They would be in the thick of war again soon.

Mica needed to consider how to raise the statue out of the water; his mind worked at that problem while his fingers worked with gears and bolts, and whirligigs. They had no idea how much the statue weighed so he would have to design something that could handle probably more than would be needed. Something far more complex than what they used to bring *Flash* up to land, though that design would be a good place to start.

What would they do once they had the statue out of the water? Especially a statue that probably had some sort of unnatural abilities.

Somewhere behind him, Magina and Merriweather discussed cloth, his guard making appreciative noises as her mother apparently pointed out one sample after another while they packed them away.

This was another side of family life he had never imagined. Although Merriweather had many disagreements with her family, her arrangement to marry *Lord* Raventower had settled the major trouble with her parents. Her father had not wanted Merriweather to go into the army, but rather to be a dutiful daughter and marry someone of wealth and title to bring the family up the social ladder.

Why the man wanted to hobnob with the current run of

lords and ladies was beyond Mica. For the most part, they were unrelentingly tedious. No one could be that dull without working at it, he had decided. They made it into an art form.

Magina had left the bow on Tippet. Mica looked down and found the clockwork dog sitting at his feet, tail wagging. Apparently, Tippet liked bows. He did not order it removed.

"That's it, then," he heard Magina say. The trunk closed with a thump. "We have time to make decisions, and I was thinking of importing some of that exquisite Argine silk that your father says is too expensive."

"Mother --"

"Oh, he won't mind, you know. Since we did it for your brother's weddings, he certainly will not complain about the cost of yours. Did you know that Helsta and Burnis are expecting another child?"

"Another? Doesn't she have anything better to do? The woman needs a hobby that does not include changing diapers."

Mica buried his head in his work and tried not to laugh. He'd had the same feelings towards some of the young women at court, the wives of courtiers and lesser nobility. There had been a time when he was certain they were having a contest to see who could have the most children in the least amount of time.

"The next question will be about jewelry," Magina said. "You never did collect anything much --"

"Well, that's changed," Merriweather said with a sudden laugh. "Lord Raventower?"

He turned back, and she gave him a nod, her smile hardly hidden. Mica stood and went to the cupboard and came back to the desk with the two jewelry boxes, which were in themselves quite ornate.

"These are Merriweather's now," he said and waved a hand to the boxes, letting Merriweather led her curious mother over. "They belonged to my mother and my grandmother."

"Ah," she said with a bit of a frown. Livinia Raventower, his mother, had left behind a reputation that went unmentioned by most people.

Merriweather opened the cases.

"Oh, Gods and Goddesses," Magina whispered. Her hand hovered over one case and then the other, not quite touching the jeweled pendants, earrings, necklaces, and rings. "Oh."

Mica pushed his chair over so she could sit. He had not expected quite that reaction from the woman, who stared, mesmerized for a moment, before she shook her head.

"As you can see, the problem will not be finding jewelry, but rather deciding which ones to wear."

"They're real?" she said, still stunned.

"Oh yes, all of them," Mica replied and smiled. "The King had them in his keeping until I took Raventower. He had them appraised --"

"I don't want to know," Merriweather said with a shake of her head. "It's hard enough to even look at these pretties, let alone consider the amount of money they represent."

Her mother nodded agreement, but Mica had the feeling that Magina knew good jewels when she saw them and had a fair idea of what she looked at now.

Mica reached into the older of the two cases and pulled out a pair of earrings, the jewels perfectly shaped teardrops and glittering enough to send sparkles around the room. He'd always been fascinated by diamonds and their rainbow effects.

He looked at Merriweather and gave a subtle nod to her mother. Merriweather smiled with delight. He had thought she might have wanted to give something to Magina, but still could not quite get used to the idea that these were her jewels, not his.

He supposed that made her wealthy. Mica suspected she hadn't put that fact together yet.

"Those were my grandmother's," Mica said and held the two clusters of jewels out to her. "I think they'd look lovely on you. Consider them a gift for our betrothal."

"Oh. I couldn't --" Magina blushed with surprise as Mica put the two clusters of jewels in her hand. She stared down at them, too stunned, he thought, to say anything.

"You should put them on, mother. They'll look lovely."

"I cannot accept! The money --"

"The money means nothing," Mica replied with a wave of his hand. "Please accept the gift."

She stopped talking and studied her future son-in-law for a moment before she nodded. Her fingers fumbled, and Merriweather helped. Then the two went downstairs, Merriweather dragging the trunk behind her with a steady thump from one step to the next as they went down one stairwell and the next until Mica could no longer hear the two.

Mica put the jewelry cases back away, locking them back into the safety of the cabinet. He thought they had surprised Magina, and he also suspected the woman better understood the situation. Lord Raventower was not poor. He might not dress in the latest fashion (though the velvet vest did appeal to him), and he might not live in a fancy townhouse, but he was not poor.

More than that, though, he suspected she had come to see if Merriweather was happy, and he liked her all the more for the concern.

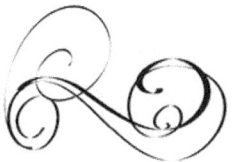

CHAPTER FOUR

The silence in the workshop seemed odd after Merriweather and her mother had left. Empty. The tick of the clock became too loud, something he had never noticed before. The wind rattled the shutters and whispered icy promises.

With a force of will, Mica went back to work on the insects, setting one after another on the edge of the desk as he finished the little bodies. They were easy enough to create, and he'd been gathering the pieces whenever he had the time. They kept his hands busy and allowed his mind to focus on --

Well, not on things he should think about like the statue, *Flash*, and whatever else needed his attention for this war.

Mica glanced at the stairs, thinking Merriweather took too long to return. Granted, the sun had not yet set and with all the soldiers around the building he doubted anyone could get in.

Mica thought he could even hear the guards up on the roof and the soft whisper of their words. *Safe*. He thought heard the word, and heard it again, as though the wind had taken up the duty to reassure him. He had thought it might be his clockwork ravens, nestled into the nook he made for them to stay during the winter. They tended to gather ice on gears and snow, so he didn't use them much during the winter. Besides, Gregorian sent reports with the changing of the guards.

It had not sounded like a raven. Just the winter wind.

Mica heard Merriweather hurrying up the steps. He knew the sound of her boots against the stone and how she did not pause at the landings. Tippet let out a little bark but settled back in the corner again, apparently content, bow and all.

Mica smiled and looked up from the desk when she entered the room. Merriweather glanced around the area as though she expected her mother to appear again and she shook her head with a cross between amazement and shock.

"I can't believe my mother --" Merriweather began. She stopped and shook her head. "Actually, I'm not so surprised she showed up here. I should have anticipated it. My apologies, your lordship --"

"I like her."

Merriweather stopped and stared for a moment. Then she smiled. "Good. But even so, this is going to be a problem. Five years or more of problems if I don't get her in hand. I fear we do not have enough jewels to distract her, Lord Raventower."

He laughed agreement. Merriweather sat in the chair by the steps, but he could tell she was still too antsy to settle into their usual silence. She gave a sigh and looked at him again.

"I had never considered how thrilled she would be with the idea of me marrying," she admitted. "When I was a child, she always talked about my wedding day, but I grew out of those daydreams when I hit my teens. Mother, though, continued the dream she had started when I was born. Nothing -- not even a war -- is going to interfere."

"So, we can expect more visits and lace?" Mica asked.

"I fear so. And don't even think about going to my father to get her to stop. You don't want to know the kind of conversations they've had when he's tried something that stupid. My brothers are even worse. And stupid. They'd just annoy her into coming more often."

He'd only really dealt with Burnis, and that in a sword fight, but he could see she was right about him at least. Mica suspected that having already annoyed Burnis, it would be best not to antagonize his future brother-in-law more, though he doubted Merriweather cared. She did not deal well with idiots.

"We will simply have to find a way to work with her," Mica offered, and she gave a reluctant nod of agreement. He did not point out that she still had a bit of lace in her hair. "This is not a problem, Merriweather. We simply have to make certain she's safe if she decides to rush here with more cloth to show you."

"Yes," she agreed and took a deeper breath. "I shouldn't react this way. What do we need to do, Lord Raventower? About the statue, I mean."

"I need more time to consider that one, but there is something else we need to do that might help with it later." He pushed aside the bits and pieces of insects and turned so he could watch her instead of getting lost in his work again. "I want to get the submersible up, Merriweather. If it is at all repairable, I think it might be useful in the coming battles, besides possibly taking another look at the statue before we decide anything."

"Not too close of a look this time," she replied with an almost frantic shake of her head.

"Not too close," he agreed. "First, we need to find the craft and bring it to land, most likely in the fishing village. There was far too much going on when we had to abandon it. I have a general idea of where to find the craft, but this is not the time to go poking about out into the bay with the Atrians watching us."

"Yes, an excellent point," she agreed. "We have ships cleaning debris in the bay, though, and so far, the Atrians aren't attempting to stop them."

"Of course not. The Atrians want the area cleared so they can invade easier. They don't seem to get the idea that cleaning the bay will help our ships as well."

"I heard a rumor that our ships are putting bombs in the water so that if a ship tries to come in, they can blow it up."

"That would be handy," he said. "And something more we need to consider if we are going to try to get the submersible."

He stopped and ran a hand through his hair.

"The problem is locating it," Merriweather said. "The water was not too deep, but I doubt we'd be able to spot it from above without some help. And we won't have much time to look."

"Because if we do spend time, someone is going to wonder what we're doing," he agreed.

"What about a hollow pole with glass seal on the end and a light to illuminate the area? Something that can be attached to the side of the ship and can be used to spy what is down below --"

"Oh, now that is a brilliant idea!" He grabbed some paper and began to make a quick sketch. "Something like this, maybe --"

She brought the chair over to the desk, and they went over the design, which included mirrors and an oversized globe of sea metal at the end to illuminate the area.

"I am leery of working with the metal now that I know where it comes from," Mica admitted and waved toward a few small gears that still sat in the corner of his desk."

"I don't blame you," she said and seemed to eye the pieces with the same distress.

"I knew the metal had some magic," he admitted. "Though no one could trace why, and so far, only I've had any luck working with it. I certainly never associated it with a God, and especially not with Torger."

"But you have used the metal often," she said. "And not seen any evil in it, have you?"

"No? I trap souls with it, Merriweather."

She looked at him, her head tilted. "You said they were not trapped, and you give them a choice, and some do not stay. Isn't this true?"

Mica took a deeper breath. Panic had almost gotten the better of him. He'd been holding those fears at bay ever since they saw the statue. Merriweather, though -- she helped him through this part. He hadn't needed anyone before. It was a difficult adjustment.

"The spiders --" he began.

"Even they didn't turn out to be as bad as we assumed," she reminded him. "I think they only wanted to get to the north and put the submersible together. I almost regret destroying a few of them."

"Those were my father's work," he said and looked at the clock. Seconds ticked away. "I have other reasons for not trusting them."

She didn't argue that point. "Can you come up with something else for the light? Can you design an enclosed oil lamp?"

He picked up his pen, looked at it, and put it back down again. "Yes, I probably could," Mica admitted. "But that would take even more time and need testing. We don't have time to waste, and I don't want to go out more than once, if possible. We must figure out how to collect the ship and bring it to land, especially if it is in more than one piece. If we find it is not mostly intact, I see no reason to gather it up just now."

Merriweather nodded. "We have to believe the ship is salvageable and that it will be of use. Since it also uses the sea metal, you'll need to decide if you can deal with working in the craft."

"Yes, true," Mica agreed. "I'll put aside my worry over the metal itself for now and focus on making things work. I like your pole idea. I think Nyle can put the frame together without much trouble. There should be pipe enough that can be welded into one long pole --"

"Or like the air poles on the submersible so that it can expand outward, each piece nestled together. Wouldn't that make the device more adaptable? Besides, we don't want it to draw attention when it's taken to the ship."

"Yes," he agreed again and began to redesign the idea.

He enjoyed sitting with Merriweather and sketching what they would need. How odd -- he never would have thought he could work with someone else.

Shipley came up to let them know dinner was ready and then darted back down again before either of them could say anything. Merriweather gave a quick laugh, though.

"Obviously hungry," she said and stood, stretching. Mica reached over and retrieved the little piece of lace from her head and handed it to her. "You could have said something before now."

"I thought it was cute."

"Cute?" she replied, as though she didn't even know what the word meant. "Goddess help me. Don't go all sappy on me, Lord Raventower."

"I will do my best," he agreed and gave a little shudder that was not entirely faked. "I remember those people at court. No, it is not something you need worry about with me."

"Good." She turned and headed for the stairs with Mica close behind her. Food would be nice --

But he thought he heard a whisper of words just as he reached the steps and turned back, startled. Was that still the people on the roof? It had seemed --

"Lord Raventower?" Merriweather asked, a hand on his arm as she prepared to face whatever might be there.

"Sorry," he replied and shook his head. "I am too easily spooked right now. I must have heard the wind blowing past the shutters. Let's go and find out what delicious foods Gram has for us today."

"I am grateful for the stairs," she admitted, giving the room one more quick look before she turned away. "The steps are the only hope I have for keeping off weight. I had gotten used to army food, even when I worked in the castle. I can't say that I miss it."

Mica gave a little laugh and followed her, though he still found himself looking back at the room at the last moment. Would he ever really trust the tower to be safe again?

The thought bothered him as he followed Merriweather down the stairs, past the floor with their suites and then on to the floors with rooms and windows still sealed shut.

Payton Honorgate said there were still secrets in the tower, and the man had believed it enough to convince the Atrians. They wanted the tower.

What could be here? He had done more searches again after the clockwork spiders had emerged from hiding. He'd never suspected they had existed so he couldn't say he trusted there were no other secrets to be found.

Every odd sound worried him. Every whisper of a breeze through the drafty old place made him fear something had gotten loose. Maybe it wasn't Merriweather who would want a new home, and he should consider the change for himself. Someplace new and calm, where he could work again.

After the war? Perhaps he would find peace here again when the rest of the troubles ended.

They reached the bottom of the old, worn stairs. The scents of dinner drifted his way and drew Mica's mind instantly from anything troubling. Merriweather was not, after all, the only one who appreciated the food here.

Nyle was just coming in the door as well, Shipley and Bear

at his heels. The boy must have run out to get him as well. The wind came through the area, cold as ice, and dancing with a little snow though it appeared to have been gathered from the steps and was not actually falling from the sky again.

Mica hadn't even considered opening the shutters on the workroom once he and Merriweather began discussing the design. Usually, he liked to know what was going on outside.

They went down the last stairs and into the kitchen for a companionable meal, all of them at the huge table set by the cook stoves. He missed Ada, Fern, and Roe, but that did not make this company any less pleasant.

They were, like everyone else in the city, conserving food as best they could, but they didn't eat poorly. Gram, in fact, might have been better at this sort of meal making than Ada. Gram had spent most of her life poor and making ends meet as best she could. That she had once cooked for high-ranking members of the city showed in her deft control of spices, though. Not many others would be eating this well.

"Shipley has been helping me sort through the remains of the smithy," Nyle said when asked what he'd been doing besides fielding questions by soldiers. "We've found most of what can be saved, and it looks better than I had hoped. The anvil appears to have come through without even a chip. Good piece of equipment that is. I would have hated to lose it."

"I think I'll have a project for you in the next couple days," Mica said, holding fresh, warm bread in one hand as he spoke. "Nothing too fancy, and I'll show you the plans later so you can get an idea of what you might need."

"Good enough," Nyle said. He looked pleased. Maybe having a project for Lord Raventower would get him out of reach of the soldiers for a bit.

"How about you, Shipley?" Merriweather asked. "How are you taking to living here?"

"Oh, I like it well enough Captain," he admitted but with a worried glance at Gram. "Not that I don't like our place in Shadow Walk, but --"

"But there be safety here," Gram said. "And food and warmth, and we can do good for others."

"Yes," Shipley agreed, and Mica thought he had relaxed a little at those words. "But if there be anything you want me to do in town, your lordship, just send me off --"

"Not yet," Mica replied. "I might need information before too long, but I'd rather everything settled a bit more."

"I could go to the beach and gather metal, though."

"No," he said. "For the moment, I don't want any more of the metal."

"Ah," Shipley said and looked bothered.

He would have to tell the boy about what they'd found and the trouble around the statue, but not here at the table. Nyle took up the conversation again, which helped. Mica hadn't thought about all the work that needed to be done with the soldiers in residence. Merriweather made it plain that she expected the soldiers to start doing their fair share of what Nyle had been doing for them.

Oh, Mica didn't want to be out there in the courtyard when she called the soldiers to order and explained how things were going to work from then on. He was glad, though, that she thought enough of Nyle to realize she needed to right matters.

"It's not so bad," Nyle said as he pushed away his empty plate. "But it might get worse, you see. I know I'll need to do work for Lord Raventower, but I suspect they don't realize that I'm only willing to help them until then."

"I will handle it," Merriweather replied. Mica thought he heard a bit of pleasure in the words. No doubt it would make a nice change after her inability to handle her mother.

He did not say so aloud.

"Can you ask them not to try to tease Bear and make him angry?" Shipley asked, looking a bit nervous at the request. "I don't think it is wise, you know. But they seem to think his anger is a thing they want to see."

"No, not wise, at all," Mica agreed, and Merriweather gave a decisive nod.

"I will see to that one, too," she agreed.

The group lingered at the table, Merriweather helping to clear away the plates and waving Shipley to sit down. Bear continued to gnaw on a bone as he sat in the doorway which was not quite as warm as the lower room. The huge dog had long fur which was probably great when he went out into the snow, but not so fine here where the humans huddled close to the warmth.

The building moved.

Mica stood, and Merriweather took a step toward the doorway and stopped. The room moved a little again, but not so strongly this time.

"Quake," Mica said, his voice a bit unsteady. "Not a bomb, I think."

"That's what it felt like," Nyle agreed. "I'll go out and check."

Mica had started for the door as well, but Merriweather caught his arm. "If it is other than a quake, you don't want to go out there, your lordship. Should we check the tower?"

"Yes," he agreed. "But it seems to have held up nicely again. This isn't the first quake we've had here."

"Better 'an the walls of Shadow Walk," Gram said and patted the stone beside her. "Come on boy and help me wash the dishes now."

She didn't want Shipley slipping out either, so the boy gave a sigh and went to help her.

Another short jolt. The area didn't usually get clusters of quakes, and Mica hated to think how this might be affecting those in the city, with ruins already tottering.

He and Merriweather made a quick check of the floors, and especially of the gas line that never seemed quite safe to him anyway. Everything appeared to have come through fine, though a few clockwork animals had fallen from the shelves in the workroom. Mica sent a raven off to his brother saying they'd come through fine and by the time they got back downstairs, Nyle had come back in as well.

"Found a crack on a seaward wall to the southeast of the tower, but not so bad it looks ready to fall," he said. "Had some rock falls to the south but weren't nothing there to get hit. I couldn't tell if there is much damage in the city. I went down to the edge of the fishing village. A couple buildings collapsed there, and a man told me the sea moved funny." He stopped and shook his head, so Mica knew there was something more and probably worse. "There was a light in the water, Lord Raventower. A bright blue glow in the sea, off the side of the tower."

The statue. Mica almost said so aloud but shook his head instead. "Well, good that it is no worse. We'll see what help we can be."

"As I expected, sir," Nyle said with a brighter smile. "I can't say many of the soldiers think they'll be doing some good, though."

"They will be," Merriweather promised.

"Don't be too hard on them," Mica replied as they headed for the door. They both grabbed their cloaks, preparing for the colder weather.

"They're no good if they're lazy," she said and frowned at him.

"And worse if they resent having to be here," he replied, though he hated to say anything that might anger her.

She started to say something and then stopped. "Damn. You are right. I'll have to coerce them into helping rather than ordering them. And here I thought being a captain would make this part easier."

"Nothing is ever as easy as it should be," he replied. "I thought becoming a Lord rather than a younger brother was going to make my life easier, too. Look at this mess."

She laughed agreement at that one. Mica liked the sound of her laughter. The soldiers she was about to deal with were going to be happier for the change of mood, too.

The door opened to a brisk, cold sunset. They'd had one situation after another today, and far too much of standing out in the cold and wind. Mica would be happy to see everything calm down for a few days, but he suspected that would not happen soon.

The soldiers milled about, clearly uneasy. Mica supposed having a quake and being encamped at the base of a massive and ancient stone tower had not helped their nerves much.

They spent some time with the soldiers, and by the time the sun had gone down and the night turned cold, he was more than willing to go back in and head for bed. He deserved it. They'd had a very long day.

Mica didn't rest that well, though. He awoke twice to find the building trembling and at least once more when he thought someone called to him.

No, he did not rest well at all.

Not much changed over the next few days and they fell into a sort of sullen calm. Mica found himself going up to the roof one or two times a day to stare out at the Atrian ships holding off the coast. On the third day, the weather was far too clear and the ships too easy to see. He had rather liked it better when they were partly hidden in snow and fog, as though they didn't truly exist in this world.

Merriweather always went up to the roof with him, of course. He ought to have felt guilty about making her stand out in the cold with him, but when he glanced her way, Mica could tell that she was just as interested in the scene spread out before them. The four guards who watched the various directions always left the two alone. He would have been annoyed if they tried to order him around at his own home.

"The Atrians can't sit out there forever," Merriweather said on the third day. She leaned forward, studying the ships with more intensity today. "They have limited supplies, which will be worse for them in this cold winter weather. I don't care where they come from, they can't survive by eating ice."

"True," Mica agreed. Her words gave him a little hint of hope. "Gregorian says airships are trying to bring in some supplies and they might have convoy ships farther out, but the Sedina fleet is hunting those down."

"I still don't understand why they are here." Merriweather stared as though she could find an answer. The blustery weather promised worse to come, but she leaned into the wind with her eyes narrowed against the cold. "They don't have enough people on those ships to invade."

Mica did not mention the statue. Neither did she, though they both likely thought about it, sitting down there at the foot of the tower.

While he appreciated the quiet days, part of him would rather have had things moving forward. Anything. Waiting had never bothered him so much as it did today. Sometimes he found that even working at his desk did not help.

Something was going to happen, and he'd rather it just started. Trying to guess what the Atrians would do next would drive them all crazy. Maybe that was the plan.

When they climbed back down the ladder, Mica was glad to find a letter from Gregorian on his desk. Shipley must have brought it while they were up freezing on the roof. Mica held his hands to the fire, Merriweather beside him, before he went to look at the note. They both took their chairs by the desk. Merriweather often sat there rather than going to sit by the stairs.

"I'm not sure why Gregorian keeps me informed," Mica admitted as he opened the missive. "Until recently, he treated me like a bothersome little brother."

"He's had reason to see a different side of you lately," she reminded him. She also accepted an envelope addressed to her and from Gregorian as well. The General was scrupulous about making sure Captain Merriweather had the same info as his brother, and sometimes adding matters that dealt with the army to hers.

"Panic spreading through the city," Mica said with a finger tapping the note. Merriweather looked up from her copy and nodded, grim-faced. "That would explain some of the fires we've seen lately."

"I'm sure there are still Atrian spies stirring up trouble," she added. "In fact, that could be most of the problem."

"I suspect you are right. All a spy would have to do is get things going and then sit back and nudge the people one way or another." He read a little more and nodded. "Gregorian suspects it as well. Worse, though -- he says there is a lot more unrest in the countryside already."

"Well, that was bound to happen with everyone from the coast heading inland." Merriweather lowered her letter and gave another rueful shake of her head. "You and I had our hand in that, you know."

"The two of us?" he said, startled.

"Our rather spectacular trip to Windmere is almost the stuff of legend at this point, not helped by the fact that some of the worst parts of the tale are true, like the Atrian airship in the mountains."

"Ah. But nothing much really came of that trip, at least not directly."

"That doesn't matter. We went rushing off to the mountains. We rushed back again. Or maybe I should say that *you* did these things since it is Lord Raventower who drew the attention. Add to that the problem with clockwork spiders and a ship that travels underwater, and you, Lord Raventower, are becoming quite famous."

"But -- but --" He couldn't think what to say. "How do you know these things?"

"Notes from my mother, of course," she replied with a bright smile. "You knew she'd written to me a couple times in the last few days."

"I thought she wrote you about bridal things," he admitted.

"Oh that, too."

"How can you find this amusing?" he asked, probably as appalled as he had felt in a long time.

She put her own letter in her lap and looked at him, her head tilted. "I am amused because nothing that has been said about you -- and about me, since I am mentioned now and then -- none of it isn't true. The exaggerations are small, Lord Raventower. I regret that some people are using those tales to create fear and worry, but I think anyone who looks logically at them will realize that what we've done proves things are not out of hand. We've stopped the trouble so far. Give the people some time to think about our adventures. Oh, and let my mother handle that sort of thing, too. Once she gets going, you are going to be the hero of Sedina."

"That does not exactly appeal to me, you know."

"You and I are not likely to have any say in it."

Mica thought about Magina and the forcefulness she applied to what she wanted. He gave a nod of agreement. They'd simply have to ride out whatever happened. Once the war ended, things would go make too normal again.

Another note arrived that night at dinner, this one in a cheap envelope and with handwriting that he didn't recognize. Mica put aside his cup and opened it, curious and worried --

Reason to be anxious, too, it seemed. He must have made a sound, or maybe they all watched his face. When he looked up, he had the attention of everyone at the table.

"The note is from Roe," he said. Nyle looked disturbed. "They're fine, but he says they need to come back to the tower. It is not safe out there for them."

"Ah," Merriweather said with a quick nod, likely seeing the problem's they would have faced quite clearly. "It will be good to have them back."

"He seems to think they'll be safer in the tower," Mica said and felt a welling of doubt at that idea. "But given how much trouble is directed at me --"

"We all been safe here so far," Shipley pointed out. He gave a sudden nod of his head, brown hair bouncing in his enthusiasm. "Safer here than anywhere, I think."

Gram gave a nod too, though she frowned. "Ada should come back to her place."

"I'll want you to stay on as well," Mica said. He still didn't like the idea to bring them back, but Roe and everyone else seemed to think they needed to be here. "Things are going to start getting hectic here, Gram. We're going to be feeding a lot of people who are destitute this winter."

"Ah," she said with a grateful glance from him to the back of Shipley's head. He hadn't considered how she might want the boy to stay, and how he would have followed her, no matter where Gram went. "Yes, I can help with that cooking. Your lordship is a good man to think on such things."

"We are all doing what we can to help," he reminded her. "And I appreciate that you have been here, Gram. You and Shipley both -- and Bear. This is going to be hard winter for people. We'll do what we can to help them. There might even be people staying in the tower before the winter is out -- though I suspect Captain Merriweather would never sleep again if that happened."

"Strangers all through the tower?" she asked, so appalled that it won a laugh from all the rest of them.

Mica smiled as well, but that didn't ease the worry he felt.

CHAPTER FIVE

Mica did not sleep well that night or the next. Exhaustion should have driven him into oblivion, but nightmares riddled the night, and he couldn't say he was better for spending any time in bed. Mica woke often, and on the third night spent much of the time simply sitting on the edge of the bed hoping that the sleep would catch up with him and he could rest for a few hours without waking, startled by something that had seemed too real.

He finally slipped under the blankets when the banked fire began to die down and the room cooled. Mica knew the dawn couldn't be far away.

The wait did not help.

Mica awoke not much later with the odd hint of a voice still whispering nearby. He sat up, grabbing at the candle by the bed and lighting it while his fingers shook.

He was alone, of course. Not even a mouse squeaked in dismay and ran for darker corners. A little steam hissed out of the pipe by the window, lending some warmth to the room but winning a curse from Mica who had nearly thrown the candle at the sound.

No, this was not good. Mica had never had so much trouble sleeping before and knew that if it kept up, he'd be in no fit shape to help anyone soon.

Was he going crazy?

That was a question he'd tried to avoid, but it sprang into his mind before he could stop the thought this time. Was this another sign that he was, after all, his father's son? Greyland Raventower had gone mad because of the power that had rested in his hands.

Mica sat down at the desk and looked at his own hands. He could deal with souls just like his father. If he wasn't there, the life lights simply did not manifest, and the person went to whatever reward his God of choice had promised. However, Mica's presence created a change in the natural order. Some souls wanted to take his body. He fought those off and sometimes forced them into a different shell, like his clockwork ravens. Those souls either stayed there or left for the afterlife of their own accord.

Mica did not, like his father, go hunting for souls. The idea made him ill. He had thought that act was what had made his father crazy, but now he wasn't so certain.

He saw the faintest hint of gray at the edge of his shutters and heard the wail of the wind outside, which he had not noticed until now. Another storm? He couldn't decide if that was good or bad, either.

Up and get dressed. Merriweather seemed to have a sense of when he would be ready to leave his rooms, and she never took more than a moment or two after he knocked on her door. Today she stood waiting in the hall, and he gave her only a quick nod and mumbled hello before he headed toward the steps and went up to the workroom rather than down to the kitchen. Merriweather didn't ask why. In fact, he thought she looked a bit worried.

"We need to talk," he said as he settled at the desk. "We need to talk about me."

"You," she echoed. The idea seemed to take her by

surprise. "Is something wrong?"

"I fear there might be," he admitted and ran his fingers through his hair. He hated this. "I think, maybe, there might be a good reason for you not to marry me after all, Merriweather. I fear I am going mad, like my father. I am hearing voices at night --"

"You aren't the only one."

He stopped and stared at her, thinking he had misunderstood what she said. Then he frowned for another reason. "You heard voices, too?"

"I have for a couple of nights," she said. She sat back and her shoulders relaxed. Mica wondered how much she had feared for her own sanity. "More clearly last night, though I couldn't make out the words and they stopped as soon as I awoke.

"You said nothing."

"I thought it was only my overactive imagination," she admitted. She even offered a wry smile. "Tell me that you didn't think the same thing."

He thought he ought to be annoyed, but she was right. He nodded instead, toyed with a clockwork insect for a moment, and then turned back to her. She waited patiently, sitting there in the too-cold room with the wind howling at the shutters.

"I am not sure if the idea that we are both hearing the voice is better or not."

"You think we're both going crazy in the same way?" she asked, her right eyebrow raising slightly.

"No. I believe that this might mean there is something dangerous in the tower still."

"Yes, I was starting to fear the same thing. Perhaps we ought to go check our rooms and that floor. Gram won't have breakfast ready for a little while yet."

"True," he agreed, glad to be doing something.

They started with the hall, looking for recesses, for bricks that might move, for places on the floor that might be weak under the carpets. Then they meticulously went through his room and by the time Shipley arrived, he was standing on her bed and checking the ceiling.

Shipley appeared at the door, took in the scene, and gave a slight shake of his head. "Breakfast," he offered and then backed away and hurried down the steps.

Merriweather laughed, finally, when the boy was well out of hearing range.

"We'll have to explain over breakfast," he said and accepted her help to step back down to the floor.

"Oh, it might be more fun to let the boy think what he will."

"Maybe so, but I want to know if they've heard anything."

"Ah. Good point. But we have found nothing but a few unlucky spiders. Maybe we both have let our imaginations fabricate more trouble than we need."

"Maybe," he agreed, but Mica could tell that neither of them believed those words. At least the exercise had woken them, and he didn't feel as though he had missed much sleep after all.

They went down to breakfast, which was a sweet oatmeal, warm and soothing after such a night. Merriweather was the one who explained what they'd been doing, and he saw the boy's look of relief.

"Bear wakes up too often," Shipley admitted. "I took it to be living in a strange place, but it might be something more."

"I sleep like a child," Gram said. "Hearin' ain't what it was, you know. Shipley has to shake me awake some days, so it's no use asking if I hears anything. More oatmeal?"

Mica accepted a little more and a sprinkling of dried apple on top this time and realized it was like eating cookies for breakfast. He hoped they didn't have anything too strenuous for the day. Nyle had reported some snowfall and a bad wind, so he thought maybe even the Atrians would stay huddled into their ships. Some weather was not fun for anyone, no matter how used to the cold, wind, and ice they might be.

He slept better that night and the next. No voices at all and Merriweather reported the same.

On the afternoon of the third day, Shipley rushed into the workroom, so breathless he couldn't speak right away, bringing both Merriweather and Mica to their feet.

"Sorry, sorry," he said with a wave of his hand another gulp of air. "Wagon coming through the gate. Roe, Ada and Fern are back."

"They made that journey quickly!" Mica waved the boy on back down the stairs. "Don't run down them! And watch out for the gas pipes."

"Yes, me lord."

He and Merriweather followed, and not very slowly either. He'd be glad, really to have his friends back home. If they truly were not safe out in the country, then better here after all.

The wagon jerked to a stop as they came out the door, having navigated through the crowd of soldiers. Another band of army men followed on horses and had ridden with them, he suspected from farther than the city gate.

Roe was the first off of the wagon, and though bundled in warm clothing, he still looked happy as he pounded Nyle on the shoulder, patted Shipley's shoulder, and gave a quick bow to Lord Raventower.

"Good to be back, me Lord. Nice change to be out in the country, it were -- or would ha' been in better weather, but it's nice to be home again."

"I'm glad to see you three," Mica admitted and noted that the soldiers were starting to ride away. "You had guards?"

"Almost all the way from the farm, Lord Raventower," Ada said as Mica helped her down. "Seems you must have mentioned to your brother that we were coming back? And good thing they were with us, too, or we might not have gotten through some of the spots."

"I will have to thank him," Mica said, more than a little surprised that Gregorian took those steps to help his people.

"They was in the area," Roe said. "And heading for the city anyway. Would ha' made it faster without us, but we're right grateful to have had the company."

Mica helped Fern down from the wagon as well. She looked pale, but her eyes had turned to Raventower, and he could not have mistaken the relief he saw there. He gave her an impulsive hug, and she smiled back at him, even though he thought she might be a little shocked.

"We brought what supplies that we could from the farm," Ada said with a wave of her arm to the wagon. "Not much, but it were plain things would be bad here in the city."

"I'll see it unloaded and the supplies brought in," Merriweather said and eyed soldiers who were suddenly starting to back away. "Hold it right there!"

The men laughed as did many others. It really didn't take much to get the wagon unloaded, and the items dropped into the kitchen.

Ada shed her cloak and went to the table and sat down, the others following her example. The three travelers looked exhausted, and they didn't appear to have done any better for having been sent away.

Merriweather sat by Mica. Gram got tea and some cookies, and Mica thought this seemed like a nice little gathering, despite the circumstances.

"The others on the farm thought we was crazy to come back to the city," Roe said with a shake of his head. "Especially after they heard about the clockwork spiders and that trouble."

"They're gone now," Mica said and hoped it was true. He was surprised to see Fern give an emphatic nod and not look at all frightened by the thought of the creatures.

"We're glad to be here, me lord," Ada said, drawing his attention back again. "It was good at first, out there -- but the weather turned cold, and we was all trapped in a house that weren't big enough for half of us. And some of them weren't so nice. One of her cousins broke a wing on one Fern's butterfly --"

"Oh, let's get that fixed!"

"Can you?" Fern asked. Tears appeared at the edge of her eyes. "I love the pretty so, and I'll love her anyway."

"Let me see," he offered.

She pulled the butterfly from beneath her apron and held it out. The wing had been twisted and some of the metal broken, but Mica could see it wasn't severely damaged. He sat the butterfly on the table; the wings moved slightly, and he had a sense that the creature was troubled. Well, better to have them all back here, butterfly and all.

Merriweather went up and got the box of tools and parts that he kept on the desk, and he worked on the little thing while they talked at the table.

They told about the farm, about the people, and about the problems of dealing with so many people in one place.

"I don't much lose my temper," Roe said, and Mica knew that was true. "But I can't abide by fools, and that's what they seem to ha' raised out there on that farm. I hope it isn't the same at the rest of the country. I'd have to think the only wise people are in the city -- and I don't count many of them as all that wise, either."

"Too true," Mica agreed. He tested out the work he'd done and then lifted the butterfly into the air and tossed the clockwork creature towards Fern. The wings fluttered for a moment and then flew to her, sweeping around her head.

Fern laughed with delight.

"That's better," Ada said and patted the girl on the shoulder. "But you look ready to fall asleep in your chair, child.

Go on to your room now."

"My room!" she said, still smiling. "Just my room!"

Mica didn't think he'd ever seen anyone so happy to go to bed. Fern walked away, pausing at the hall to look back, making sure the butterfly remained with her. She laughed again and hurried to her room.

Once her door had opened and closed, Ada gave a sound that could only be a sigh of relief. She gave a nod to the others. "It were hard on Fern. I hadn't thought how bad it might be, the way they'd treat her."

"I'm glad to have you all back, but --"

"We had to return, me lord," Roe said. Ada gave an emphatic nod which made Mica realized there must be more going on. "We heard things, and there was trouble coming our way."

"Trouble?" Merriweather asked.

"First, the thing we heard," Roe said. "It were easier for me to hear these things, being out working with the men. Seems there was a lot of talk about Torger and how we done wrong to turn or back on the God of War. Some said that if we brought him back all proper, we wouldn't have this trouble with Atria."

"Did they?" Merriweather said, and her face had a hard look.

"Yes, Captain," Roe said with a snarl of his own. "But it turned worse there towards the end. I heard a lot of bad talk about the temples and the royal family. Things I ain't never heard from any good villager before. And since we worked for you, Lord Raventower -- and your brother is Prince Gregorian -- it just were not safe anymore."

"Well damn," Mica said. He had his hands around the tea and frowned. "I'm sorry --"

"Weren't nothing you did wrong, me Lord," Ada insisted. "Don't even think you have a reason to apologize. They are all fools like Roe said. And I say they'll pay for it, too, by the end."

"Unless they get smart," Roe said. "There's a chance, I think because a few didn't take kindly to those words about the other Gods. I did some scouting around the farm. It were easy since I volunteered to go out and check the fences and the fields. I also spent time in Grover, the village a mile or two from the farm. The little estate close by that belongs to Lord Honorgate -- we was told it was shut down, but there be a lot of people going in and out of the gates, and some through the woods, in the middle of the night. I got close enough to hear some of what they said, but all I could make out was Torger, Atrians, and war."

From the look Ada gave her husband, this was the first she'd heard of what he'd done, too. Mica didn't berate the man for taking such chances. He had the feeling that she was going to do enough of that herself.

"This sounds serious," Merriweather said. "We'll need to go over a map tomorrow, Roe. I'll want to know where this took place and get an idea of how many people might be involved. Not tonight, though. I want you to rest and think about it. Right now, you and Ada both look as though you are apt to fall over in your chairs."

"It were hard going getting to the city," Ada admitted. "We didn't dare stop last night. Even the soldiers said so, with so many people on the road and our wagon so tempting. Then we reached the city, and I have to say it broke my heart, it looking so bad. But we're here. We're home. That's all that matters now."

"You know this is not a safe place," Mica said. He lifted a hand when she started to speak. "Just listen a moment. You have to promise me that if things get bad, you'll get clear and find shelter elsewhere --"

"We can help them, Gram and me," Shipley said. Gram

gave an emphatic nod. "We can get them safe, me lord. Don't think none on that. We'll all do what we have to."

That relieved Mica of a few worries, though when he looked at Roe, he saw that the man's face had unaccountably grown dark with rage. Was it the idea that the boy had offered to find them safety and Roe didn't want to follow behind him --

No. Mica should have known better.

"I don't like how people are willing to take any help from Lord Raventower, but they still talk about the nobility as if they're all involved with the Atrians and are enemies," Roe said with a snarl. "It weren't right, me lord --"

"Nothing about this war is right," Mica offered and hoped to calm the man. "And remember that for most of the country folk, the lords and ladies are as much outsiders as the Atrians."

Roe snarled but nodded. His big, rough fingers played with the small cup as he spoke, the words not quite as heated. "Truth is, the talk started with the Honorgates since it's been no secret where the Lord's heir had gone to ground all those years ago."

"I hadn't thought of that connection," Mica said. "To me, it seems like a local scandal." And he tried not to think about Honoria and Gregorian, who now knew they were the children of a traitor. Was that worse than being the children of a madman?

"It weren't long before such talk started to include all of the nobility and the royalty as well," Roe said. "At first, I tried to talk sense to some of the people, but they'd have none of it. Those of us who still held to our loyalty just learned to be silent. It got worse, though, it did. I didn't see no reason to stay some place where we had to guard ourselves, night and day."

"Yes," Mica agreed. "Better that you came home. I'm sorry it turned out this way. I thought you would be safer away from the city."

"So did we," Ada said and patted her husband's hand. "So did we or we wouldn't ha' gone at all, even for Fern's sake. That poor child suffered the most. Children can be cruel to anyone who is different from them. I mostly kept her close to me, and we did some of the work --"

"Truth be told, you did almost all the work, the two of you," Roe said with another growl. "And they weren't much grateful for the help, either. I'm sure they're regretting it now that they have ta' make their own meals and clean their own floors."

Ada smiled. "And a dirty lot they were, too. Well, it is in their hands now. There was other talk, me lord. Many of the people were nervous about the tales of clockwork spiders. They was real, weren't they? Your work?"

"My father's creations," he said.

"Oh now, that's troubling, ain't it?" she said, looking out to the hall with a nervous glance.

"We've looked everywhere, and I don't think there are more in the building. Do be careful, though."

"Some people talked about them spiders coming down from the north and hiding in the hills far west of Grover. Now I knowed it was probably just talk, but it were persistent like. And I listened and heard it twice from people just passing through, so it weren't just a local tale."

"That might need checking," Merriweather said and looked troubled.

"There might be some truth to it," Mica admitted. "It wouldn't take the spiders much work to go from the area of Headaway along the hills and end up where they've been seen. But why would they do it?"

"There's a troubling question," Merriweather agreed. "Seems to me that they would need a purpose to wake up and move again. Could someone else have ordered them to some work?"

"I wouldn't think so," Mica admitted. "My father didn't appear to be working with anyone else, and it seemed as though I only had nominal control because they recognized me as his son."

"This sounds dire like," Roe said with a look of worry.

"They aren't here," Merriweather repeated emphatically. "And if they are in the hills, well that is still better than many places they could be."

Mica nodded, but he had to worry about what the creatures might be doing. Though maybe it was all just tall tales told by people who heard things and hadn't anything better to talk about, being cut off from the war. The fighting age men and women would have gone to the shore to join the work there. The rest could only talk about the trouble, and sometimes create stories to make everything more exciting.

"I am glad to have all three of you back," Mica told them as he stood. "And I can see that you are too tired to sit here and gossip with Merriweather and me. I'll leave you to get settled back in and rest. I've asked Gram and Shipley to stay on since we're going to be helping to feed some of the poor --"

"I am so glad!" Ada said, taking hold of the older woman's arm as she stood. "She and the boy are like family already. I can't imagine the place without them and the dog around, and I would worry every minute if they were out there living beyond the tower."

Much the way Mica felt, so he was glad to hear the words. They had plenty of room down here since he'd never hired more people to help at Raventower. They didn't need a bevy of servants rushing here and there. He'd seen too much of that at the castle and didn't want to get involved in those kinds of servant wars and politics. This group got along, and they were all happy to be here in this odd place.

"Oh, I suppose I should tell you before you hear it from other sources," Mica said with a quick smile towards

Merriweather. That glance had not gone unnoticed by Ada. "The Captain and I are betrothed. We do not intend to marry for a few years, though --"

"Betrothed!" Ada all but shouted, startling Mica. "By the Gods and Goddesses, you wouldn't joke about such a thing, would you? No, no. Betrothed! Oh, we must discuss galas and parties --"

"Years, Ada," Mica repeated more loudly. "We will not be wed for years."

"Yes, yes," the woman said. Gram smiled and nodded as well. "But we have to prepare. So many things to consider --"

She and Gram began talking about galas and baking. Their excitement and joy grew with each word so that even Roe and Nyle got drawn into the discussion. Mica backed away, and Merriweather came with him.

At the edge of the kitchen, she stopped and shook her head. "They're as bad as my mother. We're doomed."

CHAPTER SIX

M ica and Merriweather both wrote notes for Gregorian and sent them off with the changing of the guard. The word that had arrived with the new guards did not look very promising.

"Fighting in town," Merriweather said as she looked over the reports the guards had given her.

The guards on the roof changed while she still scowled at her notes. The men who went off duty gave salutes to Captain Merriweather and bows of their heads to Mica. He still couldn't say that he liked having people constantly on the roof, standing over them, but he knew this was a strategic point to get a view of the city and the bay. He didn't complain, but he wanted the quiet life back again.

Mica watched one group of four guards leave, and the others climb up the ladder to the roof. Once that opening had closed, he gave a sigh of relief, glad to have everyone out of his workroom. Except for Merriweather, of course; she still looked over her notes with a sudden shake of her head and growing frown.

"Is it that bad?" he asked at last.

"Bad enough," she admitted. "The fighting is sporadic but growing. They've caught a few more Atrians starting trouble, so it's plain where most of the initial problems are beginning."

"Making trouble so that it will be easier for their army to move in?" he asked.

"Most likely," Merriweather agreed. "Or just making trouble because they're annoyed that they can't simply step in and take over. There are too many fools who are willing to help them out, even if they don't realize that they're aiding the enemy. Buildings have been burnt down, but we saw that from here. There's worse, though."

She sorted through the notes and handed one paper over to him. He didn't recognize the writing, so it wasn't from his brother.

The news was grim. Four families, supposedly safe in their homes, had been murdered, including the children and a couple servants.

"Why?" Mica asked, handing the paper back. "Why target them? They were merchants and clerks --"

"Ordinary people," she nodded agreement. "No ties to anything dangerous as far as the preliminary reports go. We'll see if anything else turns up, but I suspect the people were just chosen at random. Just spreading terror. There are also notes about patrols being drawn into traps. They'll all be more careful now, but it is still going to get worse, you know."

Mica wanted the war to end, but peace wasn't going to happen soon.

Over the next few days the incidents in Kamere grew worse, and soon tales of serious trouble in the villages outside the city reached them as well. One village had been almost entirely destroyed by fires and looting, and rumor said that the group that had perpetrated the crime were gathering more members and heading for other villages.

"I don't understand," Mica admitted. "I just don't know why people would do this because it clearly cannot be just Atrians at work here."

"Think about all the people who are perpetually angry at their situation, whether they made the trouble for themselves or not," Merriweather said, though she sounded no happier than he felt. "People who make trouble just to make trouble -- and now they find companions who will stand with them so that what they'd ordinarily avoid for fear of being punished, they can do in a group and expect never to be caught."

"Fools," he said. Tippet barked. He listened for a moment. "Gregorian."

Gregorian came up the stairs at a fast pace, too, which meant trouble. Mica and Merriweather were both on their feet by the time he arrived. He nodded and waved to the ladder.

"Need to check things out," he said, crossing to it. "I was in town when I heard."

He started up the ladder. Mica grabbed the cloaks he and Merriweather had begun keeping in the room and threw one to her. She followed Gregorian up the ladder and Mica came last. He was too curious to stay behind.

"There was an invasion just to the north of the Air Patrol field," Gregorian said and waved a gloved hand in that direction. His red face might have come from rushing up the stairs, too much time out in the cold, or rage. Mica suspected all three. "They apparently think that is a weak spot, but I doubt they will make that mistake again."

"It didn't work then?" Merriweather asked as they crossed to the edge of the tower and stared in that direction.

"The initial report sounded bad, but the second one, hardly a few minutes later, was much better. The Atrians retreated in haste when they found that there were far more soldiers to face than they had expected. It also helped that Admiral Rose was in *Flash*."

"They didn't get it flying yet, did they?" Mica asked, appalled. He'd seen some of the damage reports yesterday.

"She didn't have to take the craft up to use the cannons."

"Ah." He smiled brightly at the thought.

"Scared the hell out of the army men, but apparently her people were not at all surprised. At any rate, she saved the ships and has kept the Atrians from invading from that direction. I had rather hoped to see the ships retreating, but they are holding in place so far." He patted one of the four guards who had been on duty there. "Let me know if anything changes out there."

"Yes, sir," the man said. An unnecessary order, Mica knew. They reported if the ships so much as bounced more than usual on the waves.

They went back down into the workroom and found that someone had brought up tea and cakes while they were out on the roof. Gregorian looked at them as though he wasn't sure what tea might be. Mica pushed his brother into a chair while Merriweather got another one from across the room.

"Rest for a minute, Gregorian," Mica ordered. "A cup of tea will help. I suspect a little food won't hurt you either."

Gregorian looked at him, eyes narrowed. There were dark circles beneath his eyes and his brother, the usually immaculate General, might not have shaved for a couple days.

No one in the army could have so much as suggested General Gregorian sit down and relax. That was probably the problem. The King might get him to rest, but Mica suspected the King had troubles of his own.

"Yes, tea," Gregorian agreed and pulled off his gloves. "Sit down, both of you. I can stay for a little bit. We've had a busy couple days out there. A lot of activity, and I had the feeling the individual actions were leading up to something more serious. We've held them off this time."

He sipped at the tea and picked up a cake, looking it over as though it might be a map of some sort.

"Gregorian?" Mica asked. He and Merriweather had both taken chairs at the little desk.

Gregorian sat up straighter and shook his head. "Too many things to consider, but I do believe I'm going to be able to get more than a couple hours sleep tonight. It's not that I distrust the others in charge, you know -- but when there was so much going on, it just seemed impossible to get away long enough to rest. There is something more we can talk about, as long as I'm here. The reports from your people about the trouble they saw have already helped. We wouldn't have thought to study some of the rumors. I've had some studies done on the general feeling of people out in the villages. One thing that my people have already noted is that the leaning towards Torger is rather new, just as we suspected."

"Someone reviving the old God so that they can align more people with the Atrians?" Merriweather asked.

"That would be my guess," he replied. Gregorian ate the cake in several quick bites. Mica wondered when his brother had last had a meal. Someone should have been watching over him. "The odd thing is that the revival doesn't seem to have started in any central location."

"Agents trying to light fires in many different places?" Merriweather asked.

"I think so. We might still learn more. It might also help if we could discover anything specific about the practices the people held. Is there a holy day? A gathering? That could be something important to know, but I can't even begin to figure out how we could learn about a God who disappeared -- mostly -- from Sedina centuries ago."

"Leave that work to me," Mica said.

"How could you find out anything?" Gregorian asked and seemed honestly curious.

"Priests, mostly." Mica ate part of a cake and sipped some tea while he thought it out. "The first place to go would be the Temple of Knowledge."

"In the Temple Square, which has sustained a lot of

damage," Merriweather reminded him.

"The priests of Eligeius keep their information far underground to protect the manuscripts," Mica replied. He doubted either of them realized the extent of the archives. "I can't say how far back the knowledge goes, but if anyone has information from five centuries ago, I would expect it to be that group."

"I saw a few priests at the building the last time we passed through," Merriweather admitted. "I did wonder why there were not at the castle with everyone else. It never occurred to me that the priests of knowledge would have anything to guard."

"I'll write you out a note and put my seal to it, just in case they think to argue with you," Gregorian added. He pulled up his shoulder pouch and drew out the paper, though Mica provided ink, pen, and even some wax so that General Prince Gregorian could put his official seal on the note.

Mica picked it up afterward and read the brief note.

"You did not address this to the priests of Elegius," he pointed out.

"No, I didn't. Keep the note with you and use it whenever you think it might work."

This note was a sign of confidence that went far beyond simply asking Mica to do a bit of research. Gregorian proved that he trusted his younger brother to do whatever was needed in these matters.

"I'm heading back to the castle --"

"We'll ride as far as the Temple Square with you," Mica said. Merriweather stood with a nod of agreement. "The sooner I start in on this, the better. I can't believe the priests will have what I want conveniently at hand, you know. Since many of them are at the castle, the work of finding the material may take longer than usual. Best to get them started now."

"Ah. Yes." Gregorian stood, but he poured himself a little more tea and sipped with a show of pleasure. "Good idea. Besides, you will ride with a few guards to that location. I don't trust anything out there right now."

Mica wondered if they ever would again, but he didn't say so. They went down the stairs at a nice sedate pace, which felt odd. Lately, it had seemed as though they rushed everywhere all the time. Maybe that had affected some of how they looked at the trouble, too. Everything happening too quickly?

Trying to stay ahead of all the trouble, Mica supposed. He didn't think they dared slow down, except for a few steps down the tower and out into the perpetually cold day. If they hurried, would it make spring come sooner?

Someone handed Gregorian a note as soon as they came out of the building. So much for the little bit of peace and calm.

"Ah. The ships up north are moving somewhat," Gregorian said. "But they do not actually appear to be heading towards us. They might be trying to draw the last of our ships out of the bay and into an attack. It is not going to happen."

"What about the rest of our fleet?" Mica asked.

"They're spread out and hoping to intercept more of the Atrian supply line. The Atrians are moving, but the weather makes it difficult to spot the ships once they are away from the shore."

Mica nodded and looked back as Shipley and Bear came out of the door behind them. The boy seemed surprised to find the three standing there in the weather.

"I'm headin' for Shadow Walk," Shipley explained. "Bear needs a good run anyway, and it's been a few days since I talked to any of my boys there."

Mica had not forbidden the boy to go out, even though he didn't like it much. He had the sudden feeling that Gregorian felt the same way towards their young friend.

Shipley trotted through the gate with the huge dog running ahead and back, rolling in the snow, and generally having a good time. Mica, Merriweather, Gregorian, and ten guards followed, though the boy had disappeared into the Shadow Walk before they got that far. Gregorian didn't appear to be in a rush.

Mica hadn't been out of the tower for two days or maybe more. It was hard to keep track of what they'd done lately. He could taste smoke on the air and heard shouts not far away. Gregorian detailed two of his guards to check for trouble. They were not gone long.

"A bit of a scuffle, but they scattered when we showed up, sir."

"Good," Gregorian said. "That's most of what we've seen the last half day, Mica. Otherwise, I would have suggested you hold off on this study. I don't know that it will help --"

"Anything we can learn about the followers of Torger is something more they can't surprise us with," Mica replied. "And I think I was starting to feel like Bear and needed to get out and run a bit."

"Do not go rolling in the snow," Merriweather ordered.

Gregorian laughed. "Mica always did like winter."

"Not so much these days," Mica admitted. "It seems too bleak rather than pretty this year."

Gregorian looked his way with a shake of his head. "That's because others are suffering in the weather and you cannot bear that thought. But the winter will pass, Mica. The war will end. We'll recover and do better."

Gregorian believed those words. Good. Gregorian gave him hope on this dull, gray, cold day.

The slums gave way to the rows of tall square factories, at least the ones still standing, and the view looking no better for it. Some showed signs of damage. Mica tried to consider how much work it would take to get their city back to working order once the war ended. He might start plans based on the factories they would need most to begin other work.

The others left Mica to his thoughts. He began to make mental lists and pushed the thoughts aside as they reached the edge of the Temple Square.

The temple of Eligeius stood not far off to the right. Gregorian stopped and looked that way with a nod. "I'll go on to the castle," he said. "I need to make several late reports to the King. He's been patient about the occasional delays, but I know it bothers him to be out of the picture. I'm leaving two guards with you Mica, to keep watch here and on the way back to Raventower."

"Gregorian --"

"You cannot argue with me anymore now than you could when you were ten. Just give up now, and neither of us need be embarrassed."

Mica laughed at this truth and gave way with a bow of his head. He wondered how Merriweather felt about the guards. She might be relieved to have someone stand guard over the horses while she went with him and counted that as another reason not to argue. He supposed she got nervous every time they left the tower.

"You be careful too, Gregorian," Mica said before his brother rode off. "A great deal is depending on you."

Those words made Gregorian uneasy, but he nodded agreement and rode on with his people. Two soldiers remained, both of them looking as alert as they had when they guarded the General. Mica supposed they worried what Gregorian would do if something happened to Lord Raventower.

"We're only going to the Temple of Knowledge," Mica explained to them. "I'll ask a quick question or two and probably look at the archives, but I won't be long. Captain Merriweather will make certain that I don't linger. Then we'll head back to the tower. I will not make this any harder for you than necessary."

"That would be appreciated, Lord Raventower," the one on the right said, and the other nodded. "It looks calm enough here, sir and Captain, but there has been trouble around the Temple Square of late, and I think it would be wise if we didn't remain too long."

"We haven't had any trouble with assassins lately," Merriweather added. That might be a reminder of the problem for the two men. "Let's not invite it to spring up again."

"They have to run out of the damned assassins at some point," Mica replied as they rode toward the temple. "I can't believe they brought an entire ship full of them."

"I don't discount anything with the Atrians," Merriweather mumbled.

The building had taken damage with part of the portico down but that debris cleared away into a huge pile of rock that stood almost as high was the building and a few yards across. The group rode along the side of the Temple of Justice, and he was not surprised to see Honoria on the steps where priestesses and priests were handing out food. She looked up when they rode by, and for a moment he saw the distrust in her eyes. At least this was something he still understood in the world. Even with the war raging around them, Honoria remained Honoria.

He smiled at Merriweather, which she clearly did not understand since she was all but glaring at Mica's sister. He dared not say anything so close to the Temple of Justice, though. At least Honoria was not yelling about Dark Magic whenever she saw him. He rather hoped she was not saying those things to others, but he couldn't count on it.

He had never understood Honoria, and though he had better knowledge of her childhood and how that had affected her later life, he still couldn't say that he knew why she acted the way she did.

No matter. They avoided each other as much as possible.

Besides, he spotted something far more interesting just to the right as they cleared the side of the temple.

Lord Honorgate stood on the path near a work area. He'd been talking to someone overseeing the prisoners who worked clearing the area, but as Mica and his group came around the corner, the man immediately moved away from the others and headed straight for him.

This was going to be worse than any confrontation with Honoria.

Merriweather started to get out of her saddle, but Mica stopped her. "No. We'll ride around him if we can. Remember that he is a Lord, Merriweather, and he has his followers."

Lord Honorgate had been close enough to hear those words, and he must have had some trouble deciding which of them he wanted to chastise more from the way his head snapped left and right a couple times.

He finally focused on Mica.

"How dare you," the man snarled. Was he drunk? Mica couldn't tell, but he had the feeling that for once the man was completely sober. No wiser for it, though. Honorgate reached for Mica's horse and nearly got a hoof on his foot before Mica pulled the horse back. "How dare you spy on me!"

"Spy?" Mica asked. "You are not important enough to spy on."

No, not the most diplomatic thing he had ever said to Honorgate or to anyone else. Gregorian would have handled this far better -- even if the man was his grandfather. Mica found that troubling when he considered the ties to his family.

"You think you can win this --"

"I have no reason to deal with you at all, Lord Honorgate. I suggest that we both go on about our business and pretend that the other doesn't exist. That seems the best answer to me.

There are far more troubling matters these days than whatever vendetta you think you have against me."

"I know things about you and your family --"

"So does most everyone else." Mica leaned closer to the man's face despite Merriweather's hiss of warning. He lowered his voice. "I know, others know -- Gregorian and Honoria know."

The statement stopped Lord Honorgate for a moment. He glanced to where Honoria still worked. Mica did as well. She was watching, of course. Everyone watched this little show. He couldn't begin to guess what his sister thought, or what Lord Honorgate meant to do here.

Merriweather had brought her horse around so that she could cut between Mica and Lord Honorgate if the man made any kind of suspicious move. Mica thought she might want to see him try. He wondered what the older man intended.

"I am going to ride on," Mica said, his voice still neutral. The guards were making unhappy sounds now, too. "Good day, Lord Honorgate."

"You can't ignore me, you little bastard. I know about your father and --"

He had moved to grab Mica by the leg. Mica kicked him, and he staggered back. Merriweather pushed forward and ordered the other two guards to stay and deal with the man while they went on.

The guards were not happy with that job. Honorgate might make life hell for them later, but Mica knew a few words to Gregorian -- and from his brother to the King -- would put an end such trouble. Besides, he suspected that once he rode past and was out of sight, Lord Honorgate would calm down again. He wondered if he could stay in the Temple of Knowledge long enough that the man went away again. Merriweather might not complain about remaining there if it meant less trouble.

He glanced her way and shook his head. "I have no idea why he made such a show," he admitted. He could hear the man still arguing with the soldiers, though he did seem a bit politer with them. "What can he hope to gain?"

"Nothing," Merriweather replied. "You are just a focus for all his anger in the world, Lord Raventower. That makes him unreasonable, and irrational people are dangerous. Even so, this seemed odd -- and he was not drunk, either."

"That's what I thought," Mica agreed and glanced back --

A group of the prisoners stood not far from Lord Honorgate. Most had pails filled with rocks or stood with picks in their hands. One did not: Mica thought he might be some sort of foreman directing the others --

But then he saw the man's face.

"Payton Honorgate!" he said and pointed to the man on the pile of broken stone.

"Damn!" Merriweather shouted. "Soldiers! Go after him!"

Payton scrambled down the far side of the rock pile. He'd had chains on his ankles and wrists like the others, but he pulled them off and tossed them aside, proving they were only there for show.

Mica saw another half dozen other men do the same.

Mica pulled back in haste, and so did Merriweather. The soldiers slowed but kept going, their own weapons in hand.

"This way," Merriweather said and started off to the left so they could skirt around the debris. At least she wasn't trying to keep him away from Payton, and from the look on her face, he could tell that she had every intention of catching the man.

They didn't have any such luck. By the time Mica and Merriweather came around the side of the stones, and the guards had gone over the top, there was no sign of Payton or his companions.

CHAPTER SEVEN

Mica remained with Merriweather as she checked the area, though they did so on foot so they wouldn't be easy targets sitting up above everyone else. Mica kept his hand in his pocket and a half dozen of his mechanical insects ready. The guards worked with the Captain, but nothing came of the search.

Mica stopped long enough to scratch out a note from supplies he begged from one of the Priests of Eligeius.

When the guards finished their searches for Merriweather, he gave it to one of them. "Take this to Gregorian. He'll want to know what happened."

"But --" the man began, worried about not obeying the General who had set he and his companion to watch over Mica.

"No, he's right," Merriweather said. "This could be a serious problem -- spies pretending to be prisoners. We're using them everywhere, you know. And Lord Honorgate is also gone, of course. He knew his son was here and tried to keep our attention from him."

Mica looked around and sighed. "Well, at least I won't have to deal with him. Damn."

"He knew his son was here, I'm sure of it," Merriweather

added as she nervously kept watch. People began to gather in small groups, most of them priests and priestesses of the various temples, their different colored robes making them look like wildflowers popping up among the ruins.

"Honorgate was a fool, but I'm not surprised," Mica admitted. He had started to feel uneasy under all those stares, and his hand in his pocket played with the insects, fingers moving nervously over the little bodies. "If the man had kept quiet, we never would have seen Payton."

"Fool," Merriweather agreed. "I'm going to talk to the guard that Lord Honorgate was speaking to before he saw us."

"I'll just stay here with this soldier and look noble."

"Yes, that would be a good act to try."

The guard looked as though he might be having trouble breathing. Merriweather stalked to the guard, but she maneuvered him, so she had an eye on Lord Raventower. Mica didn't think she would get any information, whether the man had been aware of what was going on or not.

The implications of what they'd stumbled across bothered Mica more and more, however. Prisoners who were really Atrians, or locals who were Atrian sympathizers, would be a problem for the entire city. What damage had they done already? Or was this simply a fertile ground for Payton to find local followers among the real prisoners? Even that would be trouble.

The other prisoners had been gathered up by the guards, and it was clear they were heading back to confinement somewhere. There would be questions, but Mica could leave that work to others.

They'd been close to grabbing Payton again. Mica hated that the man had gotten away once more. He felt the war would be all the harder to win, though he supposed that was silly. Payton was not all that important.

Merriweather came back and mounted the horse again,

looking around with the same sort of frown as Mica had on his face.

"Nothing helpful," she said, which didn't seem to surprise her any more than it did him. "I didn't expect anything. I think the guard was not working with them, though. He seemed quite put out that Lord Honorgate had been questioning his ability to do his job properly."

"Interesting. Keeping the man's attention while Payton did something? Slipped into the group? Slipped out of it? What about the other guards?"

"None of them would be in a position to clearly see Payton's actions, which is all the more reason to think Lord Honorgate knew exactly what he is doing. The guards will check the entire area. The prisoners have been here in the Temple Square the last few days and done little else in the city."

"Good. Let's go on to our work. No, I am not going to turn around now and go back to the tower."

"I suppose that would be silly since we'd only have to come back out again another day." Merriweather started onward with the last guard close at their backs. "But I think we should get back as quickly as we can."

"I will not argue. I fear the weather is going to change."

"And not for the better, right?"

"You really have to ask that given how things have been going?"

"I think you should be quiet and just look noble again."

"Ah. Then I *can* look noble. Excellent. I'll practice more."

Neither of them looked back, but Mica was certain he could hear the guard trying very hard not to laugh.

Two priests of Eligeius stood on the steps of the Temple of Knowledge, both looking bothered. Mica supposed that this entire war had been a strain on people who were used to quiet and contemplation. He had certainly felt that way about his own life.

Merriweather stationed their guard at the bottom of the stairs, and the two of them walked up the ten steps to where the priests waited.

"Lord Raventower, isn't it?" one of them asks, squinting rather myopically at him.

"Yes," Mica said with a bow of his head. Then he thought of something to asked. "Were the prisoners scheduled to work here soon?"

"Later today," the other priest said and seemed to understand the implications right away. "We hadn't expected it since we had so little damage, but we were told that they were going to examine the walls. That sounded legitimate, actually."

"Yes, it does," Mica agreed. He still frowned. "We'll look into it, but it may have been that they were after some information. Perhaps even the information I hope to find."

"In the archives? I'm not certain I have the authority to allow you there, sir."

"I have orders from my brother," he said and tried to make the words sound at least a bit like a joke as he waved the paper. He did not want to annoy the priests who could then be less helpful.

"I suggest that you are, in general, careful of whom you let in," Merriweather added. "However, in this case, it is important that we see if there is ... certain information available."

Mica glanced around and could see why Merriweather became so circumspect. People had begun to gather in little groups, and none of them looked happy. He couldn't take that as a sign of their guilt; no one in the city was happy right now. Still, he thought there was something sinister in the way they glared at him, as though they had all caught that attitude from Lord Honorgate.

"Oh, that's not good," Merriweather said, looking around

as he did. "Lord Raventower, if you would just step back closer to the covering of the temple? I won't ask you to go hide, but I do ask that you take cover if things go badly."

"I will."

"Good. Then I'm going to try and break up these groups before trouble gets started. Stay out of trouble."

He nodded, and she darted down the stairs. He heard some disagreements, but no one actually argued with Captain Merriweather, and soon the square looked more like it had when they first arrived, with a few of the people gathering back where Honoria and her people gave out food. He did not stare that way and try to figure out what she might think of this mess. He really didn't care.

Merriweather came back with a shake of her head. "Well, that was annoying but illuminating," she said. "Many of them thought the trouble was your fault, Lord Raventower."

"Mine?"

"Yes. Some people saw that some prisoners escaped as soon as you arrived and began arguing with Lord Honorgate. They know that you often help the poor, so --"

"And they wouldn't recognize Payton," he said with a sigh.

"Exactly. This is probably going to be more trouble, you know -- but that's for later." She looked at the two priests who still hadn't moved and hadn't decided what to do next. "Can we go in?"

"Inside, yes," the first priest agreed. "But I think we need to ask the High Priest for permission to access the archives."

"This will be ancient information. I understand the formalities have to be handled, so if we can send a message to High Priest Irwa, then we might get things moving --"

"Oh, he's here already," the other priest said. "He's been examining the temple and preparing for classes again. We don't have much damage, you see --"

"Let us see if we can go talk to him, shall we?" Mica asked, somewhat amused.

At least something seemed to be working in their favor. The group went into the temple, which was one large room surrounded by halls, stairs downward, and areas with desks. The place seemed empty and without the welcoming echoes of others working. This had been one of the places Mica had always enjoyed visiting when he was younger. He had always felt closer to the God of the Knowledge than to any of the other major gods.

He wondered if Merriweather had ever been in here. She looked around with a sort of curious stare. Sounds echoed oddly today. Mica could hear voices but couldn't tell where the speakers might be standing. Lights dotted the walls, all of them magical.

"Please stay here," one of the priests said. He waved his companion to the right as he turned to the left. "One of us will find the High Priest."

Mica nodded and watched the two hurry along their chosen paths. He moved to one of the desks and looked at the dusty book sitting there. It must have been abandoned during the attack, and no one had come back to clean up yet.

"Ah. Studying Argine history," Mica said, tapping the page before him. "Not the best book on the subject, though."

"Maybe you should leave the person a note for when he comes back."

He smiled at the idea. Paper, ink and a quill sat by the book, and the ink was not quite dry, so he was able to scribble out some suggestions of better books.

By the time he had finished High Priest Irwa had arrived. The man looked down at the paper and gave a gruff laugh. "Yes, Mica my boy, you are so right. I wish you would write us a bibliography on the subject."

"I will keep that in mind," Mica promised. He thought it

might be something nice to work on when he needed to step away from the rest of this madness. Or maybe a project for the end of the war? He could look forward to that time. "You aren't going to ask me to join the priesthood again, are you?"

"Not today," the man said and still smiled. "My people say that you want access to the archives. You are one of the few people I would let down there without question. Can I ask what it is you seek, though?"

"Any information you have on the followers of Torger and about the downfall of the God. So yes, we are talking about material that may well be centuries old."

"Ah. Yes, that may be a problem."

"More of a problem," Mica said. "I cannot do the search myself, sir. I'm sorry -- but there is so much else going on --"

"No, no. I can put my people to it. But there is something I think you should see first. This way. Yes, yes, you as well, Merriweather."

Of course, he knew Merriweather. Everyone did.

The High Priest turned and hurried down one of the halls, passing by dozens of doors and coming to one that was at the end of the passage, and only a few feet from the steps that lead downward. He pushed the door to the cell open.

"This is the room that belonged to Fasin, the priest who was killed at the castle. That is his desk. He was copying, translating and annotating an ancient history from the archives. One that happened to cover the very time of your own interest."

"Well," Mica said and inched closer to the desk where both the ancient and the new work sat side-by-side. "I do not really believe in coincidence, you know. Not right now."

"Coincidence that he was working on this, that you now need it, or that he was killed?"

"All three," Merriweather replied.

Mica nodded grim agreement. He looked at the work but

didn't touch it yet. "This is a surprise. I would like to take this with me."

The man looked uncertain this time, but after a moment he gave a quick nod. "Yes. I don't like what I heard about the prisoners and knowing that someone might have been trying to get in here already. His case is there by the bed. Pack it all up and take it with you. I trust you will be careful of both the older material and the new."

"I will be as careful as I can," he replied as he did the work. "But you know that things have not been altogether calm at the tower."

"Not calm anywhere," High Priest Irwa admitted.

"There was calm here, though," Mica said. He looked around the room and felt sad for the priest who had been killed and forgotten in the midst of the rest of the war. His part in it had been more complicated than they had imagined -- cousin to Payton, but perhaps something more dangerous if he was working on material dealing with Torger. "This is a nice room."

"It is," the other man agreed. "A place where you could work in peace. Or so it seemed, but we all know better now, don't we? This is no safer than anywhere else in the city. We need to see this war done. Come with me. I have one more thing to show you."

Merriweather didn't seem to mind. She took the case from Mica and held it carefully while the older priest led them down the stairs and into an area lit with a soft blue glow -- bright enough to read the titles of the books on the shelves, but still somehow calm and relaxing.

"Usually there would be a hundred priests and priestesses down here, busy at their work. I want that back, and I daresay Talis, the archivist at the castle, would be glad to have them out of his hair. This way. This way."

They passed by hundreds of shelves. Mica always had a

problem when he came to this place because he wanted to stop every few steps, pull out books, read things -- learn new things, discover secrets. The lure of this priesthood was stronger than the others probably realized, though he would not have made a good priest.

He didn't have the dedication to choose some subject and stick with it for very long. Oh, he learned a great deal. He read everything that came into his hands, but he didn't have the discipline for one subject and to dedicate himself to learning and expanding that knowledge.

They went down another set of stairs and into carved bedrock now. The smaller room seemed overrun with more shelves. Mica wondered how many books --

Irwa led them to another set of stairs, set well back in a dark corner. Mica hadn't even known there had been another level below this one.

This time they came into a room about twice the size of the one above, the shelves crammed with manuscripts, scrolls, and a few books bound in crumbling leather. The walls glowed with magic, both for light and warmth to protect the treasures buried here so deep in the earth.

"These are our oldest archives, Lord Raventower," the High Priest said and with some pride. "They are protected by magic that keeps them from simply disintegrating. We rarely ever take anything out of the room, but that is mostly because it is so difficult to find what we want. It will take my people a day or two to find what you need, but I will put them on it yet tonight. I just wanted you to see this so that you knew the problem we faced."

"I appreciate the work," he said and reached out to brush his fingers over a scroll case. "I wish I could stay to help."

"Later, after the war, we'll lock you down here for a few weeks," the High Priest said.

"Promise?"

The man laughed and patted Mica on the shoulder. "Just know that you are always welcome here. You are one of the few true scholars in the country, you know."

"Ha. Windmere has --"

"Windmere is a beautiful place, but unfortunately filled with far too many lazy young people who are wasting the resources of excellent professors," the man replied and herded them back to the stairs. "But that is the way it works. The professors are good teachers, and some of them quite wise -- but they are not scholars in the way you are, Mica. You are willing to learn anything."

Mica only nodded, thinking about what he'd considered earlier. Maybe he'd looked at it all wrong. Maybe it wasn't that he couldn't limit himself, but rather that others couldn't see any wider.

What an odd thought.

They went back past rows of books and Mica tried to imagine being here for as long as he liked. He had imagined that when he was younger, too -- but this time the dream included Merriweather, though he wasn't certain she would have enjoyed the time spent buried underground with the knowledge of the ages.

They reached the upper floor and went out again to the vestibule, leaving that haven or paper and parchment behind. They went again to the trouble that lurked outside the building. Mica didn't want to go back to the war.

"I will have whatever we find sent to you at Raventower," the High Priest promised. "And I hope that it will help."

"There should be soldiers in the square at all times," Merriweather said as she looked at the door. "I'll arrange for one of them to take the material to us whenever it is ready. We must be careful. If the Atrians were trying to get into the archives, let's not make this easy by bringing the material out and handing it over to them."

"Excellent point," Mica agreed. He thought he might be getting some of his senses back. "I'm sure Gregorian will agree --"

"I'll agree to what?"

Mica spun, finding his brother just coming in the door. Gregorian looked bothered.

"Guards to take the material from here to Raventower, sir," Merriweather said and gave a quick salute.

"Yes. Excellent idea. There is no sign of Payton or our good Lord Honorgate," Gregorian said and sounded annoyed. "I can't leave you two alone for five minutes without there being some sort of trouble, can I?"

"We do our best to keep things interesting," Mica replied. He nodded to the case that Merriweather still carried. "We do have something to work on. The priest who was killed at the castle just happened to be translating something from the archives about the fall of Torger that we probably want to read."

"Oh yes, that's a coincidence, I'm sure," Gregorian said. He looked more bothered now. "I don't like any of this."

"None of us do," Mica agreed. They bade farewell to the High Priest and stepped back out into the light of day. Things seemed calm, but he really didn't trust it much.

Someone in uniform rode up, passed through two sets of guards, and finally reached General Gregorian. Mica watched how the people around his brother acted and knew that they were taking this the Honorgate problem very seriously. Gregorian took the note from the man, broke the seal (royal, Mica noted) and quickly read the note.

"Good. King Abertus has sent a request to the Honorgate townhouse that he come to the castle," Gregorian explained. He waved the paper in the air as though they could read it like that. "I sent word to him at once as soon as I got your note -- I wasn't even to the castle yet, you know."

"I hoped so. I wanted you to know right away."

"Yes. It would have been delayed if I'd been inside. I don't suppose they'll find Lord Honorgate at home."

"Probably not," Merriweather agreed. "However, the worst part is that I couldn't find anyone who saw the two together. He'll be able to say it was only coincidence."

"And he ran because?" Gregorian asked.

"Because Mica is so unreasonable," she replied. "You can both laugh but that is how this is going to play out. You might as well be ready for it."

"She's right," Gregorian agreed, though he still looked amused. "But even so, Lord Honorgate knows he's been caught with his hand in the pot this time. If he is in contact with his treacherous son, then it's going to be all the harder for the two of them to work together now. If Honorgate isn't at his townhouse, then we'll go for him at the estate."

"Payton will have more trouble hiding in the city now as well," Merriweather pointed out. "All of the Honorgates and their friends will be under watch. My mother knows Lady Honorgate, by the way. They live close to each other. If you have my family watched, do try not to annoy my father. I don't want to have him come ranting to me about it."

Gregorian laughed again. Merriweather had a good way with him. "I wish we had caught them both," he said with a shake of his head. "But at least we cut them off from more allies among the prisoners."

"I wonder how many he already has there," Mica said. None of the prisoners were around now.

"They'll be more circumspect in where the prisoners are used," Gregorian promised. "I hope we can get a look inside the Honorgate Estates, to be honest. Along with the material, you reported about the smaller property and the rumors we've had from the larger one -- well, I can't say we trust it at all. Come on. I'll ride back with you to the tower."

"You don't need to escort us --" Mica began.

"I'll feel better if I can see the two of you -- and that case you carry -- safely behind the tower walls," Gregorian admitted. Then he shook his head. "Well, as safe as it can be. I've sent others to check into the prisoners, and until we have word on Honorgate, there is nothing I can do there. The Atrians appear to be sleeping or something, and the search for Payton is too wide flung for me to do any good. I'm not going to go to the castle and sit and wait. I might as well go with you two rather than wandering around and driving everyone insane."

"So, you'll just drive me crazy instead," Mica said. They'd reached the horses. "Well, come along then. I think dinner should be about ready by the time we get there."

"I can't stay for --"

"If you go with us, you are staying for food," Mica replied. "Besides, you really don't want to miss the magic Ada and Gram can do with the few supplies we have. It will be the best meal you've had in a while. I can pretty much guarantee that much."

"Ah." He frowned as they all mounted, and the guards fell in around them. They turned towards the tower, which Mica could barely spot above the tall buildings that stood between them and home. "Yes, a good meal might be nice. Thank you."

"It's going to be a long war," Mica said, admitting the truth to himself at last. "I don't want it to be, but it will drag on. We need to be prepared for it, Gregorian. You need to take better care of yourself."

"Don't lecture me," Gregorian warned.

"Someone has to since Princess Jenlyn isn't in the city. Don't worry. I won't embarrass you in front of your men. Well, not often at least. I think you owe me a few such times, though, considering how often you embarrassed me in the past."

Gregorian didn't argue. He looked around at the temples and shook his head again. "None of this makes sense. Do you think it will by the end of the war?"

"War is chaos," Merriweather said. "You don't make sense of it; you only survive to the other side."

Gregorian nodded, and they rode away.

CHAPTER EIGHT

A da quickly set another place at the table, being a bit more polite than usual and fretting that they didn't have the good china out. Merriweather helped put the woman more at ease. Gregorian had taken dinner with them before, but not often. Mica supposed it was the war that made her so nervous.

The others sat down. Shipley was not there, which worried Mica, but he and the dog arrived only moments later.

"Ha. Knew the boy wouldn't miss a meal, now didn't I?" Gram said but looked relieved as well. "Go wash up and come back quick before we eat it all. And give Bear his bone. It's there on the plate by the stove."

Shipley did so, giving Gregorian a quick nod of greeting. The boy wasn't nearly as nervous around Mica's brother as he had been when they first met. That was good, too, because Shipley was often a fount of information that neither Mica nor Gregorian could get from anywhere else.

They were already eating the baked pork and vegetables by the time Shipley came back. Gram had taught him manners. He would have done justice to the King's own table, where a few of the lords and ladies could have stood to learn a few manners of their own.

"I ha' some news," Shipley said before he began eating, though his finger's twitched toward the bread. "Some people were tryin' to hide in Shadow Walk today, but they was either killed or run out. The guards got the bodies already. They looked like they wanted to find someone who was not one of the dead."

"Ran there after he left Temple Square," Mica guessed. "That would have been Payton Honorgate, Shipley. Do you think anyone in Shadow Walk saw Payton?"

"They wouldn't know if they did, would they? But I think he wasn't one of the dead the way the soldiers acted."

"Could Lord Honorgate have run there, too?" Gregorian asked.

"Ah now, him they would ha' known," Shipley replied. "And I heard no word of it. I don't see how he could ha' tried to hide there anyway. He is no friend of the poor."

There was no question about that part. Honorgate took great joy in proposing anything that would hamper the poor and help the rich. No, Honorgate would not expect to find help in a place like Shadow Walk. They'd find him hiding in a more genteel location.

Gregorian let the boy eat some of the food before he began to ask questions. Shipley didn't hold back on the answers, including pointing out that some of his own soldiers were making more trouble than they ought to.

"I want to know which ones," Gregorian said. "The best descriptions you can get me, if you would Shipley. I suspect some of them are fools, but we know a few side with Honorgate in other matters. He has allies in the Army, the Air Patrol, and the Navy. If we can weed some of them out before they make too much trouble, all the better."

"I'll do what I can," Shipley agreed. He looked pensive, but Mica didn't think it was because he mistrusted Gregorian or even the army. The war was weighing on the boy as much as it did the rest of them.

The meal had gone well, though. Everyone relaxed, and Gregorian thanked them all, including the cooks, before he left.

"Come back again for dinner," Mica told him as he escorted his brother to the door. "If you are in this part of the city and you have some time, just come to eat. You can use a little time to relax. I think you see things clearer for it."

"I think you might be right," Gregorian agreed as he took up his cloak from the hook by the door. "And I will if I can. Don't count on me. Things are bound to get more intense now that we've brought the Honorgate's part fully to light. I don't mind the work, though. It is progress."

Mica watched his brother mount his horse, his guards quickly finishing their own meal and joining him. Mica suspected the guards wouldn't mind coming back here again. Gram had been teaching them campfire cooking since she'd been appalled at how poorly they ate. He suspected they were going to adopt Gram, Shipley, and Bear before the war was over.

And that was good. Mica wanted his people to have more allies and friends outside the tower, which was not a very safe place.

Once Gregorian rode away he went back inside. Merriweather was ready to get back to work.

"We still didn't mention the ghostly woman with a warning," Mica pointed out.

"And what would we say? Things are not what they seem? I'd rather not have that discussion just now."

The next two days remained relatively calm, with only a few outbreaks of trouble and those, Gregorian wrote, seemed more the common sort of people who were suffering the stress of still being in the city. Mica wondered why they didn't leave. Some, like the Merriweathers, seemed to have a stubborn streak that they'd passed on to their daughter. He was not at all surprised to find that the parents had not left, and the sons wouldn't dare look like cowards. Torlin, the youngest of the boys, was even in the guard now, though they posted him close to home.

"Sir?" Ada said, pulling him aside before he went back upstairs. Merriweather stopped nearby but tried not to intrude. "It's a small matter, me lord. About Fern." She stopped and then seemed to gather her thoughts. "I thought she was fine coming back, you see. We told her about the spiders, how they was like her butterfly, and that they'd gone on to other places. She seemed okay with it. But now she's spooked, sir. She says she hears a voice sometimes when she's working on the top two floors. I am going to keep her working more down here with Gram, and I'm going to take over that work and do the dusting and such if that's all right?"

He put both his hands on her shoulders. She was the opposite of Gram who was stout and short. Ada had always seemed more bone than flesh, but the worry since the war began had worn her thin.

"Ada, I don't care if the dust grows to a foot thick and we have to fight our way through curtains of cobwebs. I'm just glad to have Fern -- and the rest of you -- back with me."

Ada smiled with a radiant look that he'd never seen before. Tears touched the corner of her eyes. She pulled away and gave a quick bow. "Thank you, sir. We are glad to be back, even Fern. She were afraid to come to me at first, in fact. She feared we'd have to go away again."

"You never have to leave again, even if you don't do another day's work. Oh, but do remember that Shipley can help, too. He did the work on the upper floors while you were away."

"Yes, I'll keep that in mind," she said and seemed more herself again. Thank you, sir."

Mica turned to the stairs, and as they went up the steps, he began to rethink what she'd said.

"Voices," he said to Merriweather as they reached the upper floor. He looked around with a frown. "She might have actually heard something, and that makes me wonder if I ought to send them all away after all --"

"No," Merriweather said, and she stopped by her chair placed there by the steps. "So far, even if the voice is real, that's all it's been, Lord Raventower. Where would you send them? Not back to the country --"

"My estate should be safe," he said. Then he shook his head. "But it might not be since it has a direct connection to me. The castle is the only other place, and I know Gregorian would take them into his care. We'll save that possibility, though. They're happy here, and I don't think I need to warn them to be careful."

"You already have," she said and sat down.

Mica felt that trouble ease from his mind as he went back to work. He'd been trying to design equipment that would get the submersible out of the water as a sort of trial to getting the statue out as well. The day passed with relative calm. No voices whispered to them, and only a couple notes arrived from his brother along with a quick report from Shipley. Even the boy said things were uncommonly quiet.

That didn't last. Just as the sun went down, a storm blew in. An odd storm for the midst of winter: lightning rent the air and thunder shook the tower. Gregorian sent word to get his men off the roof where they were likely to attract the lightning -- and there was another note attached.

"The word from the temple is that there is far too much magic in the storm, but it doesn't seem to be directed at anyone," Mica said as he started to follow Merriweather up the ladder.

"Stay down there," she ordered. "I'm just going to yell for

them to come down. There's no reason for another to go up."

He had wanted to go look at the storm, but he supposed she would not be happy if he did. When she opened the trap door, he was glad enough not to be there. The wind sounded fierce, and hail had started to drop in pieces large enough to crash to the floor beneath the ladder and explode into shards of ice.

Merriweather shouted something and then scurried back down. The four soldiers followed her, their faces pale with the cold and more hail caught on their clothing.

"Came in fast, Captain," one of the men said as the other stopped at the stairs. They would not rush to go back outside. "Don't seem natural, ma'am. "

"I'm sure it's not," Merriweather agreed. The storm winds blew hard off the sea and pounded against the east side of the building. Hail pinged against the window, and Mica threw the shutters closed in haste in case the glass broke. The soldiers hurried away with worried looks at the ceiling. It did seem as though the lightning and thunder came far too close.

"You do remember we have some bombs still up there, right?" Mica asked as he looked at the ceiling.

"Oh, excellent point. You know, I think Gram was baking cookies. Superb cookies."

"That sounds wonderful to me."

They had a pleasant evening in the kitchen, and Mica had relaxed so much that he thought he might sleep all through the night this time.

Something woke him.

A voice again? It might have been, and it left a sense of urgency. He started to roll out of bed and stopped in mid-move, aware of a sound out in the hall. Not Merriweather; he knew that without a doubt. Not anyone, or anything, that should be there.

He slipped from the bed and didn't hunt for his slippers

even though the floor felt icy. He grabbed a robe out of habit, though and pulled it on while he put his ear to the door.

Movement out there. And oddly, a bit of a breeze leaked in around the door frame. Was the window at the end of the hall open?

Damn.

Having expected trouble at all times, he'd kept his sword by the door. He carefully pulled it out of the sheath and then listened again --

And heard Merriweather's door open. He wasn't even surprised that she was moving before he did.

He was also not surprised, when he opened the door and found four men in the narrow hall. The assassins were surprised to find them attacking, though. They had not expected to be heard, and the hall was not the best place for them with their small daggers facing the long swords both Mica and Merriweather had in hand.

She also had her flintlock loaded and ready to fire. The explosion of sound was deafening in the small hall, but one of the men fell before he got close enough to engage.

They were still outnumbered, and there was not enough room for Merriweather and him to work side-by-side. She could not hold all three off though she tried for a moment and then wisely let one through for Mica to handle while she took on the other two.

The man threw his dagger, but Mica had expected that move, and the blade went harmlessly past as he stepped aside. His enemy had drawn another though and lunged in so quickly that it almost caught him off guard. He slashed with his sword against the arm with the weapon and deflected the blow. He had cut deep. The man gave a gasp -- the only sound any of them had made -- and stepped back, blood flowing.

Mica dared a look beyond his enemy to Merriweather. She was having trouble holding the two back --

His attacker lunged forward again. The blade cut Mica's arm, though hardly a scratch. Mica had let him close. It was easier to use the sword then, and it went straight through the man's heart. The assassin looked annoyed rather than startled as he fell.

Mica was about to step forward to help Merriweather when Bear barreled past him and leapt straight at the man closest to Merriweather. Mica gave a cry of dismay, but he needn't have worried. The dog took the man down, and Merriweather killed him with one quick stab and started for the last one, Bear at her side.

Shipley arrived a moment later, took in the bloody sight, and gave a nod of grim approval.

The last assassin backed towards the open window. Mica supposed the storm, with all its own magic, had weakened the seal they had on the windows. He'd have a priest or priestess in as soon as they could rouse one and have the magic replaced and reinforced.

Merriweather brought her sword up and moved for the attack. It would not be a killing blow, Mica knew. They wanted one of these men --

But they would not have this one. He gave a feral, silent grin before he spun and threw himself out the window and down on the rocky shore.

"Damn! Not again!" Merriweather shouted and rushed to the window.

Mica went with her, not looking at the three dead bodies in the hall. Merriweather had stuck her head out into the icy rain, and Mica did the same. The storm had died down, though Mica thought the rain was more snow than water now.

They could not clearly see anything on the stones below. The waves washed high, though, and if a body were there, it would be taken out with the tide.

Merriweather pulled back and looked at the hall, then at

the window. "I don't think we'll have any more trouble tonight. Shipley, can you go down and tell the guard what happened and that we'll need people up here to take the bodies and clean up. And try not to worry Fern if she happens to be about."

"Yes, Captain," he agreed. He looked at Bear. "Stay here and stand guard, Bear."

The dog went to the window and sat there, a better deterrent to trouble than either of them would be.

"The magic in the storm weakened the window's spell," Mica said. His arm hurt a little, but not so much that he was ready to have it cared for yet. "I'll write to Gregorian and see if he can send someone to reset the spells."

She nodded. "We'll go upstairs, I'll make certain things are safe there, and you can write and the note off as soon as the soldiers get here. I am going to guess that this is the only window they could get open, though. It would have taken quite a bit of magic to do it, even with the help of he storm. We'll check, though. Ah. Here they are."

The soldiers arrived in a rush and were quick to both move the bodies and clean up the blood on the floor. Merriweather watched over them for a moment while Shipley and Bear stood watch by the window, both of them looking ready to attack even a gull who might have been blown that way.

Mica and Merriweather went upstairs to the workshop. She checked the trap door and the clockwork lock there, but no one had come in. The shutters were still closed in the room, and when they turned up the lights, they could see no one was hiding.

They bandaged wounds.

"We got lucky --"

"Something woke me again. I think it was a voice," she said.

He nodded and said nothing more. Mica wrote a quick note to Gregorian explaining what had happened and asking for help with the magic. Then the two of them made a round of the entire building, checking all the windows, all of which still appeared to be sealed.

The storm had died down by the time they were back to the floor with their rooms. Bear and Shipley had not left the window.

"We'll stay here until this is fixed," Shipley said. They'd pulled the glass closed, but it still seemed cold in the hall. "We'll be okay here."

Merriweather got him a blanket anyway, and the boy sat down by Bear. Mica knew he would be a good guard, but he was not ready to go back to bed. Instead, they went back to the workroom. The clock clicked out the minutes; almost five in the morning so the dawn would not be too far away. He thought he might feel better once the sun rose again.

He played with clockwork insects.

He heard Merriweather shift in her chair, something she rarely did. He wondered if her injuries bothered her and if they shouldn't be here --

"Lord Raventower, do you believe in ghosts?"

Mica turned his chair to face her. "Yes, I do. I think they might be the residue of the life lights that remain active for one reason or another and linger even without a body. Or perhaps they are strong enough that they invest themselves in something without the help of someone like me."

"Like a building?" she asked.

He looked around the room. "Yes, like a building. There could be ghosts here. Raventower has had a long, strange history, even before my parents."

"Yes, I suppose so," she said and finally sat back, looking relieved. "And if the place is haunted, then they've certainly done us no harm, have they?"

"None that I have seen yet," he agreed. "But whatever we have been hearing, Merriweather, it is not natural. We can't be confident that it won't be a problem."

"Yes," she agreed. She glanced at the clock, and Mica thought she might be considering the clockwork spiders that had spilled out from around the device -- but Mica was more interested in the clock itself these days, though he hadn't the time to do any real examination. The war drew too much of his attention.

He pulled out the plans for lifting the submersible and even drew Merriweather into looking them over and making suggestions. She learned quickly about angles, weights, and levers.

By first light, the storm had disappeared, leaving behind a sullen sort of cold wind, like the remnant of a winter storm that never had a chance to grow. Hail stones sat in piles outside the building where the soldier had swept them up. Some of the tents had taken damage, but the men were already at work on them.

Roe and Nyle had come out with the two and Mica stopped to talk with them before he and Merriweather headed out.

"We had four assassins in the building last night," Mica said.

"Gods all!" Nyle exclaimed. "I thought I heard the dog take off, but I didn't consider -- damn, I'm sorry, Lord Raventower --"

"We managed," he said and did not rub at the bandage beneath his long sleeves. "Bear came to our aid, and he and Shipley are guarding the window where they got in. It was weakened with the help of the magic in the storm. I imagine Gregorian is going to send help to get those seals reset before the day is out, but I thought you better hear the news from me -- and not with Fern about."

"The storm not only weakened the magic, but it also let the men slip in without being spotted," Merriweather added. She frowned at the soldiers, but they were already looking worried since they knew what had happened.

"It's not their fault, Merriweather," Mica told him. "They've done as much as any of us. This was not an attack that anyone could have predicted. I just hope that they are running out of the damned assassins."

"Where are you going?" Nyle asked.

"Just down to the fishing village and the bay," Mica replied. "And no, you need not come with us, either of you. There are soldiers everywhere along the way, you know. Get to your own work here. And be certain someone takes a warm breakfast up to the boy and Bear."

"Yes sir, we will," Roe said and tapped Nyle on the arm.

They were going to go off to discuss things they didn't want Lord Raventower to hear, he supposed. He gave a little bit of a smile to Merriweather and went with her to the gate.

He was right about the soldiers being everywhere. They did not, however, make him feel any safer. Merriweather cast worried glances left and right as they went down the road and around the corner.

"We should have ridden horses, I suppose," he said. "It would have been faster."

"But no safer," she replied and fixed her attention on him as they reached the first of the buildings. He remembered running from the clockwork spiders along here. One problem after another. "The ground is icy, and the horses wouldn't have been as sure-footed as I would have liked. And it would only make you an easier target."

"I suppose so," he agreed. His foot slipped on the ice, and he almost went down. "I'd take the chance with Kandlis."

The massive clockwork horse rarely had trouble on ice, and he thought even Merriweather might think about taking him next time, despite that he was rather showy.

The village remained almost empty with only a handful of the older fishermen and a few stubborn women still holding out. A couple walls had cracked in the earthquake, but for the most part, the place seemed relatively untouched. That seemed odd after everything they'd seen in the city and all the destruction there. H wondered if he ought to feel hope here, but he couldn't quite capture the emotion.

The fishing pier was gone, of course. That had been destroyed by the spiders. Worse had happened out in the bay where many ships had been destroyed and sank. The bay had been choked with bodies and broken pieces of wood, along with anything else that had been on the ships when they went down. People had reported a couple cats and a dog swimming to shore, but not many of the sailors made it that far.

Local craft had gone out using nets to clean up most of the mess. The tide had gone out and left smaller slivers of wood, glass, and metal along the shoreline where he and Merriweather stood. Mica stared out at the dark water and shook his head.

"I don't think we can do it," he admitted and ran a hand through his hair. "The Atrians might be on us before we could even find the craft, and they'd certainly try to stop us if we brought it to the surface -- providing, of course, that it isn't in a hundred pieces down there."

Merriweather looked where he did, as much at the distant ships as at the water where he thought the submersible had gone down. She seemed to be contemplating the scene before them with more hope than he felt.

"The water isn't going to be clear enough to see much," Mica said. "And I can't tell quite where we went down. If a ship took us out and we started making circles and crossing back and forth, we'd only give the Atrians an idea where to find it."

"True. We have to work carefully," Merriweather said.

"I've used the diving suit, and I could go down into the water," Mica said but shook his head. "However, it has a very limited range, besides being damned awkward to wear. I might have to use it when we find the ship, though."

"We need to find the ship without doing something obvious," she added.

"And I can't see how we can, even with the pipe to see down below. The water is too dark even in bright daylight." Then he stopped and shook his head. "We won't get anything if we don't at least try. Let's start finalizing the plans."

They started back toward the tower. Mica thought about the ships, the pole, and the submersible. So many things to consider --

His foot hit a patch of ice, and he slipped, landing on his back and staring up at Merriweather's bemused face.

"Yes, yes. Pay more attention to where I am," Mica said with a sigh. A soldier passing by snickered and then moved faster when Merriweather turned to the man. He almost fell as well.

Merriweather helped Mica back to his feet. They weren't far from the tower, and he could grab breakfast and then head straight up to work. Having a project helped.

They were detained, though, by a couple of the local fishermen. Mica didn't mind and greeted them brightly.

"What keeps you here?" he asked. "The King would be glad to have all the rest of you up at the castle. It's safer there --"

"Safer, yes," Pegrin agreed. "And we be grateful that the families are there. But we stay here. We keep watch for General Gregorian. We knows these waters better than any sailors what go far out to sea."

"Yes," Mica agreed with a nod. How interesting that they named Gregorian specifically. They didn't much trust the army, he knew. They honored King Abertus and were grateful for the help he gave them in this mess, but the person they trusted with their reports was Gregorian. Not even him.

Interesting.

They bade farewell to the men and the soldiers they passed and hurried on up the hill to the tower. The road was icy, but the edges were less treacherous. Mica was glad enough to go back through the gate. Soldiers stopped to report to Merriweather, and he had been tempted to go on without her, but that would have been unwise. He had no reason to hurry.

Mica waited. They went in and had breakfast, and then the two of them went up to the workshop. Shipley and Bear were still at the window, but they had food, so Mica only waved, and he and Merriweather went on.

Mica reached the table at last. He pulled out paper and began making sketches, once again including Merriweather in the work. If they could get in the right area, they might have a chance of finding the submersible. What they did afterward, he wasn't certain.

CHAPTER NINE

N yle worked for two days on the pole. The device was too damned heavy to carry around, so they had to move it to the ship in pieces and as quietly as possible. They took all of another night to attach the pole to the side of the *Gull's Flight*, a ship that had been doing most of the cleanup in the bay. The craft went out again the next morning, the new addition disguised as part of the rake used to clean up debris.

Mica never enjoyed sailing on the big ships. He enjoyed the freedom of the airships where he could stand on a deck and see the world spread out below them. Standing on a seabound ship made him feel unsteady, and he could barely see beyond the flashing waves to the shore. The Atrian ships stood on the other side of the ship, and Mica had agreed to stay out of their line of sight.

Sailors rushed back and forth on the deck, mostly ignoring Mica and Merriweather where they stood by the railing, anonymous in their oiled cloaks, and looking like two more of the crew.

The crew threw out nets as well as working the rakes. They dragged up debris and a few fish. He hoped that the schools of fish returned soon since that could be a primary source of food needed for the rest of the winter. And fish oil, too. If this war dragged on --

Mica didn't want to think of a war that lasted for years. He took his turn at the pole and stared down at the ocean, watching to within twenty feet of the sea bottom. A few fish moved there, and some crabs and a lobster or two. That gave him hope of food if nothing else.

The ship moved on. Merriweather took over. The swept a bit to the south and stopped. The day had gone like this for hours already. Wasted time, he feared. He should signal them to head for port, and he could get back to the tower and do something. Anything. Standing here unable to even work with a few gears had started to drive him insane.

"I see something," Merriweather reported. She quickly stood back from the pole. "I'm not sure -- there is so much stuff down there -- but point it a bit to the east. Tell me if you think that's our ship."

He didn't hold much hope until he saw what she had. He stared for a long moment as fish swept by, and the scene cleared again.

"Yes, that is it. A big piece of it, at least. I can't tell if it is the entire craft or not." He pulled back from the pole and stood up straighter. "I'm going down. We had better move fast."

The diving suit, a huge, cumbersome affair of metal and bolts, had been lying on the deck beneath a tarp. Merriweather gave the news to one of the crew who hurried off to the captain. They would need to anchor here, and the captain had to make it look natural. A net was about to get 'caught' on something, and they'd have a hard time working it free. That, Mica hoped, would keep the Atrian's watching the other side of the ship.

He climbed into the suit, grimacing at the weight and the smell. The air pump turned on, a grinding noise that was far too loud, but there was no hope of working on it now. Maybe he should have been doing that while he waited.

Merriweather sat on the rail, helping to balance the massive bubble headpiece that would connect to the rest of the suit.

Merriweather started to get the helmet into place and then stopped. She leaned close to him. "You know what is going to happen if you get killed down there, right?" she asked.

"I would think I would be dead, but from the sound of it, that wouldn't be the worst of my troubles."

"Right."

She helped secure the helmet. The air tube worked well though the oxygen tasted a bit of fish oil. They really needed to have the generator repaired --

Out over the water and down. Mica had done this before a few times, but he still hated when they swung him out from the ship. Once he was under the surface, though, he forgot all his dislikes.

The weight of the metal dragged him downward, but the chains attached to the arms and shoulders kept him from dropping too fast. He signaled to descend and paused part way when he thought the air was not flowing well. He reached up and twisted the tube; the system seemed to burp a bit and sent a flood of air again.

Mica did not plan to be down here for long. He did still find it fascinating, though. He couldn't see far until he got to the edge of the pole they'd used to study the ocean floor, and the sea metal there let out a helpful glow. He removed the glowing metal and held it in his hand, an excellent light as he moved out from the ship.

Such an odd feeling to hear only his own breathing. He wished Merriweather could have come down here as well, though not because he feared for his life. He just thought she might like to see this unique world as well.

Fish swept past him. He spotted more down here than he had expected. Good. Debris had fallen all over, much of it the heavier metal. The entire hull of one ship stood off in the deeper water to his right. They were lucky the net really hadn't caught on it, though it lay on the side. One of their own, he thought, though he couldn't be certain.

Such a damned waste.

Had he lost his directions? He couldn't see anything that looked like the submersible, and it had to be close. Ah, but the ship had moved slightly before they'd put down anchor, so maybe off to the side --

Yes. He could see the metal now, a shiny bit of surface sticking up out of the rock, sand, and seaweed. Not much of a piece, though, and that made him worry again. The ship had probably blown up after all.

Moving was difficult. He had to give the signal for more chain and air tube, but he knew there wouldn't be more than a few feet of it left now. He might have to go up, get them to move the ship a few yards, and back down again. That, though, was bound to draw attention.

Damn. Mica wanted --

The ground sloped slightly away on the other side of the metal fin, and there on the far side sat most of the submersible and almost entirely intact. The fin had blown off, and there was a hole in the side, but as he got closer, he could tell that it was not otherwise damaged.

Oh, there was water inside, of course. That could be a problem. Mica would only find out how much of a problem once they had the craft back on dry land.

Now he crawled up on the surface, unhooked one of the chains from his arm, and latched it securely to the side of the craft. There were places where the ship had been secured by chains in the cave where it had been built. It wasn't difficult to find a couple of those places. They'd have to pull it up by those since he didn't have enough tube to move down the other side.

Mica pushed a few rocks and such out of the way. A long eel came out from under one such spot with a look of indignation and a flash of his huge teeth. Mica was glad for the metal casing after all.

He would have been less worried about being down here except that he was too aware of the statue. He could even see a slight glow in that direction, out and down into the abyss. He found himself quite happy to have the craft between him and that location.

The statue had not reached out to pull the submersible in so he had to believe it would not find him here, in this little suit. He only had to get this done and get back to the ship -- and make certain the ship did not go too close to the statue. He went back to the fin and began to dig it out. He might be able to reattach it on the ship rather than making an entirely new one.

Something odd dropped past him and into the sand.

He stared at the spot -- and another swept down past him.

Cannonballs? He was lucky they were not the kind with bombs in them! He grabbed the fin out of the sand as he felt the tug of the chain that still attached him to *Gull's Flight* showing that they were about to bring him up. He did not even consider arguing the point. He got clear of the chains attached to the small ship and then returned the signal.

They started him up. He could not turn his head to look upward and see if the ship had taken any hits. He could not look down to see if the craft they'd come to rescue had taken new damage. He could only move slowly upward, inch by inch, as they cranked him back up from the ocean floor. Not too fast -- he did not want to be ill once he returned to the real world.

He saw another cannon ball sweep past. He felt the chains

give a sudden rattle that probably indicated that the ship had been hit. Damn! They needed to get to safety. They'd have to drop the chains that attached the submersible to the larger ship and hope that they could come back some other time. He knew the spot now, and it would be easier --

Something bright flashed off in the direction of the abyss, a sudden blue glow spreading upward like a fountain of light in the dark. He thought his heart would stop with fear. Was the statue moving? Was it coming his way after all?

He could barely breathe, not helped by the limited air supply. Calm, he reminded himself. Calm. Nothing more than light. Fish swarmed out of the area apparently frantic. He held his breath, but nothing except the fish had moved and the light died back down again.

He really hated the idea of that thing sitting at the foot of Raventower. Was knowledge of the statue what made his father first interested in clockwork creatures? Was there a connection Mica had not realized until now?

Mica still held tight to the fin and felt a wave of relief as the water began to lighten. He hadn't seen any more cannon balls go past, but he had the impression of the battle still being fought. Some wood spun past him, a sure sign that the ship had taken a hit.

And they stopped pulling him upward. Mica growled with frustration and waited, though impatiently, for them to bring him the rest of the way. He could see the glitter of the surface, so he was not very far down.

The water around him churned and then settled to a deceptive calm. A moment later they pulled him upward once more until he dragged metal along the side of the ship itself. He tried to push away for fear of doing damage as he slid upward and around the curve -- and into the air. He had his back to the ship and flailed, trying to turn and hold on to something. Impossible, of course, even if something had been in reach. The weight of the suit, now out of the water, made it impossible for him to move much.

They yanked him up on the deck with such force that he knew he'd have bruises all along his back. His head had hit the helmet as well, and he feared that combined with the sudden lack of air --

The helmet came off, and Merriweather knelt beside him.

"Sorry," she said and helped the others with the rest of the suit. We had to get you up fast."

"They figured out what we were doing?" he asked, still gasping for the fresh, clean ocean air.

"Don't think so," one of the sailors said. They nearly had him out of the suit, tossing pieces of it under the tarp. "I think they just thought we'd be good target practice, just sitting there like."

"Oh damn. You took hits --"

"Nothing serious. And they got a hit from us, too," the man said with a grin. "Captain!"

The sailor got to his feet and saluted. Mica, unencumbered now, stood and gave a bow. "My apologies for the trouble, but I did find the ship, mostly intact down there. The chains are attached to it, but I don't think we dare try to bring it up now. I hope I can find her again later --"

"Not pull the craft all the way up," Captain Murkin said, staring out at the water. A full beard hid most of his face, leaving his bright gray eyes as the most expressive feature. He rubbed at the beard and considered the situation, as though no enemy ship still tried to destroy them. "We can pull it part way up, so she doesn't drag and get her closer to the shore. There's no reason, is there, to have people come all this way and risk themselves again? Closer in would be better. Not to the dock, though. We can't get in close there."

"Closer to the fishing village?" Merriweather suggested.

"Yes, that would be best."

"I won't argue, but I expect you to drop the submersible anywhere along the way if this turns out to be too dangerous."

"Thank you, sir. It's good for you to think that way. We'll do what we can, though. Fire the steam!"

The sudden shout sent men rushing everywhere. Mica and Merriweather stored away with the diving suit before it slid across the deck. The fin went in with it, too, which he had held to, even with everything else going on.

"Are you alright, Lord Raventower?" Merriweather asked. "You look pale."

"Did you see the light over by the statue?"

"No, but I suspect a couple of the sailors did. I heard some shouts, but I was more interested in getting you up since we had the Atrians firing at us. What happened?"

"Just light. Fish panicked. At first, I thought the damned thing might be moving, but I didn't see anything more. We found the submersible, Merriweather. I don't know if that's at all important."

"The craft has been helpful in the past," she reminded him. "Getting it closer means no other ship has to come out this far and into danger."

"I had hoped to get it up to the Air Patrol field and use their facilities to do repairs," he admitted. "But I can make do with whatever I can put together. There was water inside. It might be that I can't get her seaworthy again at all. Oh, and I think I know a name for her."

"What?" Merriweather asked and already looked suspicious.

"Jewel," he replied.

"You wouldn't," she snarled at the sound of her hated personal name.

He grinned brightly. "I might."

Her face went red, and her hand went to her weapon. Mica still smiled. He wouldn't dare annoy her much more, but it was fun to see her reaction.

"We could always name it after your mother," she suggested. "Livinia --"

"Ugh. No. Okay, we'll look for other names."

She agreed with a quick nod.

The *Gull's Flight* turned in a slow sweep away from the dangerous area. No other attacks came as they left the outer bay, making a wide, slow circle. The Atrians might think the ship took damage and couldn't maneuver well.

Mica and Merriweather kept watch on the ocean beneath them and the distance to the shore. Mica chose the spot to drop the submersible and hoped that it wouldn't be spotted since the area was quite shallow here.

Gull's Flight hardly slowed as they went on to the docks. Mica thanked the Captain for his help and offered to pay for damages to the ship.

"It was an honorable wound to the old *Gull*," he said with a bright smile. "We been doing our best for the war, and if that little ship of yours can help out, then we'll call it good, Lord Raventower. But you take care. Good day to both of you."

They hurried off the ship with the rest of the crew. Mica had to leave the fin behind, but it would be brought to him later, slipped in with supplies to the tower's guard. Meanwhile, he would have to think about everything he had seen at the site and perhaps have a start on how to repair the ship later.

Merriweather said very little on the way back to Raventower. They'd left their horses near the dock early that morning, and it was not an unpleasant ride back, even with the smoke in the air and the brisk winter wind. They both stopped, though, when they reached the road that curved down to the fishing village. The sea looked choppy, and Mica was glad they'd gotten back before nightfall and wouldn't have to go out again tomorrow.

"I hope the submersible goes unnoticed," he said. "I hope

that it's heavy enough that the tide doesn't move it too much. I don't know what we can do with it later, but I suppose we need to consider every possible weapon."

"We will win this war," Merriweather said.

Odd, but he didn't doubt her.

CHAPTER TEN

Mica woke early the next morning knowing he had important work to do but uncertain if he wanted to get out of the warm bed. Food would be nice, though, and the draw of Gram and Ada's cooking finally took him from the bed to the privy. He cleaned up in haste. The bruise on the side of his face, where he'd hit it against the diving suit's helmet, looked rather spectacular this morning. He shaved anyway, found Merriweather in the hall, and went downstairs, to apple bread, fresh butter they'd brought from the farm, omelets, and tea. Yes, this had been worth getting up to face the day.

Reports from Gregorian arrived with the changing of the guard, so he and Merriweather went over them as they sipped the last of the tea. Looking at the papers, he suddenly realized what a wonder it was to have Gregorian trust him that much.

"More tea, your lordship?" Ada asked.

"Yes, thank you." He started to smile and changed his mind when a slight pain moved through his bruised cheek.

"General Gregorian says there was a confirmed sighting for Payton Honorgate last night." Merriweather handed over the paper.

"Damn. I hoped Payton would leave the city," Mica

mumbled and scanned the note. "High-class area of town. Someone was hiding him, and it wasn't his own family, either."

"True," Merriweather replied with a scowl all her own. "The general says he'll be putting more spies in the area. Soon they're going to number more than the people who live there."

"Maybe they should go to their country estates. I wonder if the King could, if not order them, strongly suggest they leave."

"Would that help? At least here there is a chance of seeing them do something wrong. Do we want more people like the Honorgates out there, stirring up trouble at our backs?"

He hated the thought that they couldn't trust the nobles to behave, but the problems in the hinterlands kept growing, and he did not like to think about the city of Kamere with enemies everywhere.

Another report said the Temples were all cooperating in the attempt to keep the city safe. A quiet priest from the Temple of the Unknown had, along with Nyle gone through and sealed the Raventower windows the day after the attack, which made him feel safer. Mica hadn't seen any material from the Temple of Knowledge yet.

The book and translation Mica had gathered from Fasin's room proved fascinating but turned out to be an esoteric look at the gods, not something historical. Mica continued to translate, though, since he had nothing else to keep him occupied. He'd known the basic tales that were told to all children, about one god creating, another tearing down and creating new, and so on until they came to an agreement and each took on some aspect of the world. Mica had always thought it a tale to teach young ones to cooperate with one another, but he found a more serious version here.

The vision of the murky world of the gods, filled with mists, unused power, and little else, made him think about how the gods could imagine his world from nothing. The idea intrigued him.

Mica thought about Honoria suddenly and wondered what she did now. She had seemed changed when they spoke before the King, but then she'd glared as much as usual when he saw her at the temple square. He wasn't surprised because he hadn't trusted her sudden epiphany.

Besides, there was still the fact that he was involved in matters that were not normal. Honoria knew that he'd inherited the gift from their father and that he did have some connection with the souls of the recently dead. If she had thought their father's work had been evil, she certainly could not now accept the same *gifts* in him, could she?

Did he care?

Mica sipped his tea and wondered why he had let that thought suddenly invade his mind. The entire problem with Honoria was nothing compared to the rest of the trouble. Still, what might she say to others? He had to believe she had some fear of what the King would do if she annoyed him. He also thought that High Priestess Surrey might not be entirely pleased if she did something to make trouble for her younger brother.

"Lord Raventower?" Merriweather said and handed him another note.

More material about trouble from the night before, and nothing serious. A report from the guards who had been on duty at Raventower proved to be something more troubling, though.

"Someone on the sea wall?" he said, waving that paper.

"It appears so. The person didn't get into the grounds, so they didn't bother us in the middle of the night. I think we should take a look now that it's fully light. The guard is off duty but camped here. I'll have him brought to the tower if he isn't already waiting for us."

Mica nodded agreement.

In fact, the man waited on the steps, bundled in his cloak and anxious to move before he froze. They headed to the outer wall, and he pointed out the spot. It was close enough to the sea's edge that someone climbing there might have avoided the village entirely. Mica didn't like that the intruder gotten so far before he'd been frightened off.

"Not an assassin," Merriweather decided after she'd climbed up on the retaining wall. Mica had wanted to follow but changed his mind. "Might have just been someone curious, but it's good to keep watch them off."

"Let's go check with the fishing village. They may have noticed someone in the area," Mica suggested though he didn't want to go wandering off in this weather. The wind felt bitterly cold, and bits of ice touched his skin. They were going to have snow before the day was out and he only hoped it would not be too much.

He and Merriweather went down to the village. One of the men reported hearing a sound in the general area, and when he'd gone to look, he saw a boy run off. He hadn't known the boy had gotten all the way up on the wall.

"Fool child," the old man said with a grumbled of anger. "Fool to even try such a thing. But some of them, they be wandering back in from the castle grounds, you see. They be saying it's all stupid, locking them up there. Says it's a plot, but don't know what the plot might be."

"Thank you, Depar," Mica said. "Warn them away. I would hate to see a boy killed just for curiosity."

"Yes, me lord. I'll warn the young fools. Can't say it will take, though."

He was right, of course.

"That was an interesting bit of news," Merriweather said as they headed back to the tower. Guards passed them and saluted her and bowed to him. "Someone is starting trouble up at the castle."

"Yes, I caught that too," Mica agreed. "We'll have to send word off to Gregorian right away. He's going to be so pleased to hear this one."

She grunted agreement. Once back at Raventower she called a man aside to take the message, and they wrote out the note at the kitchen table and sent it off within minutes. They looked grim, and that probably made the soldier all the more careful to get there as quickly as possible.

"It can't be Payton or his father," Mica said as he stood. "Not there in the castle grounds. There would be far too much of a chance of being spotted."

"I don't know," she said. They headed for the stairs to the workroom. "With so many people, someone in a cloak could go unrecognized, especially if the person never came close enough to the castle itself or took any of the paths where someone of high rank might spot him. Stay back in a corner, whisper about mistrust and plots and how they can't trust anyone ... soon people who haven't anything else to do will start listening. The tales will grow."

"I always hope for better from people. I am also seriously considering moving my workroom down to the main floor. These stairs are getting longer."

"Maybe so, but how else are we going to work off all this delicious food? I don't want to have to buy new uniforms every few weeks."

He laughed a little. The truth was, though, that he ached from the bruises he'd taken in that dive into the water. And what good had it been? He still had no idea how --

An odd sound. They were on the last steps heading to the workroom, and they both stopped, Merriweather just ahead of him. She quietly drew her sword but paused to hand him the weapon before she pulled two blades from her corset. They moved on, one silent step after another. He could not tell what he heard, but it did not sound human, that swish of noise coming again and again. He hadn't been paying attention. Had Tippet barked? What was --

They cleared the landing.

Ada swept the room, the broom brushing up bits of dust and dirt by the window. She eyed the weapons with a raised eyebrow and perhaps a touch of amusement.

"Ah," Merriweather said as she put her blades away and took back her sword.

"The room needed a quick cleaning," the woman said and continued to sweep while she talked. "I hadn't expected you back so soon, truth be told. But I am good as done here. I'll get your rooms next, by your leave."

"Thank you, Ada."

"No trouble," she said with a smile that showed she didn't mind cleaning the rooms. "We be getting a lot done, me, Gram, and Fern. The boy's a help too. I'd only known boys that age who were more likely to make messes than clean them up. Shipley is right good at the work, though."

"Good. Ada, would you like Gram and Shipley to stay on?" he asked. He'd wanted to put the question to her, but he hadn't been certain how to approach the subject until now.

Ada stopped and leaned against the broom. "I wouldn't mind none at all, as though it were any of my business who you hired."

"You run this place. I won't do something that would make things difficult for you."

"Thank you, me Lord. But the truth is, Gram and me get along right well, and if she wanted to stay on, I'd be happy to have her here. I know she wants to go back to her own place, though. Maybe she could come and help some days? And the boy, too. He's right handy for getting into places that Fern don't like. Polite too. And that dog of his is a real deterrent to people what think they should rush into the tower to see you."

Mica smiled, thinking about how that might have been a

problem, especially if Roe and Nyle were not around. He'd noticed how at first the guards had tended to think that since they camped here, they should have full run of the place. He had not talked to Merriweather about it, though. She had enough on her mind.

"I'll leave it all in your hands, Ada. Full or part time, whatever you and Gram can decide."

"I'll think on it, then," Ada said. She swept up the dust into a pail and headed down the stairs to do the work on the next floor. Ada never stayed to gossip or take advantage of Mica's good nature. Nor would she rest when there was work to do.

Mica sat down at his desk, looked over the piles of notes and drawings, and just shook his head, unsure where to begin. Merriweather took her spot by the stairs, but she had a stack of papers of her own to go over. When he glanced her way, Merriwcather nodded as though they'd been in the middle of a discussion.

"I suspect, despite how she feels about her home in Shadow Walk, that Gram is going to want to stay on here," Merriweather said, surprising him.

"Why?"

"She's always looking out for the boy. She was the one that helped him get his place in Shadow Walk, and that might have been the best she imagined for a boy like him. Now that they're here, she can see what an opportunity this is for Shipley. If she goes back to Shadow Walk, the boy will go with her, no doubt, and she won't have any say in it either. I don't think she'll do that to him."

"You are probably right," Mica agreed. "Good. I'd like to have the boy here, too. We don't have to worry about any of this until after the war, though. And right now, I can't say it will ever end."

"Like this winter," Merriweather said and looked toward

the shuttered window. "But it will. We're holding them off, you know, which they apparently had not expected. I think they meant to take us just as winter hit, a time when they'd have the advantage. They failed. We're going to survive."

By late afternoon there were more notes from Gregorian. They ate a quick meal in the kitchen, little more than an afternoon snack, at the table there in the nice warm room that smelled of spices. The others worked around them, and it made a nice change from the upstairs. Mica realized that he couldn't hear the wind down here. There were no windows for the snow to brush against, either. The only time winter touched the room was when someone went in or out of the main door, and the draft blew down the steps and into this little refuge from the storm.

Going over the notes proved easier because he had no little bits of clockwork material to distract him. There were days, like today, when even the pattern of the wood on the table seemed more interesting than another report about trouble in the backcountry.

The preliminary report from Gregorian about the potential for trouble at the castle was brief. Merriweather read it aloud.

"Gods curse them all. Thank you for this wondrous new message and the trouble it implies. I'll be looking into the shadows of the castle grounds. If I find anyone, I'll consider handing them over to Merriweather. That should be entertaining and probably far more productive for getting answers than anything we've done so far."

"You seem to have a reputation," Mica observed as he sat aside his notes.

"One for getting things done. Anything in those?"

"The usual. More trouble in the villages again. I am glad the others came back to Raventower. If I'd seen these reports and they were still on the farm, I think I might have had to go and get them myself, the weather and the war be damned."

"The trouble is spreading even outside of Sedina, too," Merriweather said and picked up a note, waving it a bit. "A lot of trouble down south along the Argine border. It doesn't appear to be Atrian, though."

"Atrian allies?" Mica asked. They'd seen no sign of any such people here, at least.

"Or some group taking advantage of our troubles to make some gains down that way. I know Prince Kistrin is down there to hire mercenaries, but I suspect this is going to make it difficult. The Argines are not going to want to give up soldiers if they are fighting their own war."

"Should we hope that their war is quick then?" Mica asked.

"Their war, our war -- let's hope for a quick end to all this trouble." She sat back in her chair and gave him a weary nod. "Prince Kistrin is good at negotiating, though. He might get us a few companies of mercenaries and maybe even some ships. They'll be expensive, but if they can help end the war, I'll be happy to contribute my own pay to hire them."

"I've never liked the idea of mercenaries -- of people who fight only for money and not for what is right."

"In principle, I agree. On the other hand, I worked with a company of Argine mercenaries on the Middle Islands during the last war. I have a lot of respect for what they can do. See, this is the important part, Lord Raventower: we have an army, and we keep it well trained, but the men come and go with each year. No one is dedicated to the military except those of higher rank. The Argine mercenaries, though -- they join young, and they rarely leave. They have better discipline and training -- and they just have this better sense of working together. I've seen a squad attack the enemy and work with precision without ever uttering an order. They just know what to do and what the others will do."

"Fascinating," he admitted. "I had never considered such a thing."

"Most people don't. Even individuals in the army don't think much about it. But I was in a position to work with them. I wasn't good at it. I learned very early on just to stay back and do any mop up after they'd gone through."

They headed up to the workshop but took another detour by going to the roof to look at the city and the ships. The guards, wrapped in their cloaks and looking miserable in the cold, mumbled greetings and saluted Merriweather. Snow fell, though only a light sort of mist that did not hide the world. A spyglass brought the ships into clearer focus, but the men on the decks looked just as bundled and miserable as the Sedina guards on the roof. It was harder to see the castle, but Mica could make out the movement of people and see the line of smoke from the cook fires. He suspected this would be a day when everyone took to what cover they could find.

Mica feared, though, that there would be trouble at the castle before too long. Should the King send everyone away?

Send them where? Back to the rubble-filled city? Damage appeared everywhere he turned, from the edge of the bay to the hills circling the castle. He thought he ought to be getting used to the sight.

Merriweather gave the spyglass back to the soldier beside her, a sign that it was time to go back into the tower without her ordering him. They went to the trap door and the ladder, a little clumsy in the cloaks. The room felt warm, the fire bright. They'd gathered a lot of wood before winter, but he felt guilty, thinking of the soldiers on the roof and the people at the castle grounds -- and all the others who huddled in the cold and waited for the next disaster to strike.

Mica created more insects. He had started building a third new raven; he feared he would need them and carried at least one empty raven in his pouch whenever they went out. He had given insects to Merriweather and even Gregorian, showing them both how to toss them up and out so that they moved straight at the enemy. They worked best with the wind at their backs or no wind at all. In a gale coming in their direction, they'd simply not have the power to move forward.

Both of them thought the little things ingenious, though. Mica found them only practical.

He worked at making more of them, preparing for a war that might last through the entire winter and into the spring. Why end then? If the people in the back country were not with them, how long could Kamere hold out surrounded by enemies?

He feared this was going to be a very long war.

CHAPTER ELEVEN

When Admiral Rose sent a note asking if he could help with some of the work on the airships, Mica almost considered it a miracle. He'd started pacing through the workshop the last few days, looking from one unshuttered window to the other, watching for trouble. The feel of something about to go wrong had made sleep difficult -- that along with the echoes of whispered words.

Mica wondered if Gregorian had suggested keeping him busy to the Admiral and almost snarled at the idea -- and then decided he didn't care how Admiral Rose came to write the request. There would be gauges, engines, and other devices he could work with, and what he did would be helpful for everyone.

Merriweather didn't argue though she did make certain the note actually came from Admiral Rose. With that confirmed, she only insisted that they not go by the main road through town.

He didn't mind, except the work stretched on for the next ten mornings, and he wondered how Merriweather found so many unique paths to get through Kamere. She even managed a couple that took them away from the cliffs in the open area between town and the Air Field.

Mica's expertise with steam and mechanical works did prove helpful at the Air Field. He'd only seen Admiral Rose in passing, but he sent reports to her just as he had sent reports to the General. The notes sometimes delivered bad news. On the tenth day, he pointed out that someone must be sabotaging controls in some of the airships. The damage simply was not in line with what they would have gotten in battle.

Rose asked that he have lunch and talk to her that afternoon. He and Merriweather trudged across the snow-covered grounds and up into *Flash*. The hull had been rebuilt, and they were just now refitting the engine that had been cleaned up. Some of the parts had been stripped away and cleaned. Engineer Krogor was hard at work but grunted a greeting to Mica when he peeked in. Mica, for his part, wanted to leap in and help, but Greenwood arrived and led Merriweather and him up to the control deck.

"Prompt as always, Lord Raventower," Admiral Rose said. She sat in a chair by the table that had a glass covered map on it. There were several other chairs ranged around the table and the wall -- unheard of before this and he looked at them with some consternation.

"Oh, sit down, boy," she ordered and smiled. "They're chairs. The rest of the rooms are still being refitted from water damage, so we take our meals, such as they are, here. I don't suppose you've had anything to eat?"

"We had a quick breakfast at the tower before we headed here," he said and gingerly sat down.

Merriweather nodded agreement. Mica made a note to have Gram and Ada cook up some cookies and other treats to bring out.

"Join us, Greenwood. You need to hear this too," Rose said and waved to the chair beside her.

"Thank you," he mumbled and settled in with the sort of

movement of someone who maybe hadn't sat much in the last few days.

Cook and his helper brought in some plates and food, settling everything on the glass-topped map table before they scurried away again. They had cups of bean soup and fresh bread and butter. The food helped calm Mica.

"I appreciate that the two of you have come out here to help us," Rose said and sounded surprisingly sincere. "I am sure you have other --"

"Should I be sitting in my workshop making butterflies?" Mica asked. He waved away whatever she was going to say. "This is the work I do well, and as long as I am here, under your watchful eyes, Gregorian is less likely to worry."

"You are not a child."

"You might mention that to my brother."

Rose gave a sudden bright laugh as Mica had hoped. She probably got notes from Gregorian now and then asking about his brother, though how he found the time to even think about Mica was the real question.

The conversation turned better afterward. Mica didn't like to deal with people who were not at ease around him. He had trouble interpreting their emotions and worry often looked too much like anger to him.

He glanced at Merriweather. The fact that she rarely let emotions take hold of her was the reason he had so little trouble dealing with her.

"You've been here so often, Mica, that a couple of my captains sent me a note suggesting you build a summer home on the grounds and enjoy the area in better weather." Rose smiled brightly at his laugh. "We all do appreciate the work you are doing. Now tell me why you think some of the problems have been sabotage."

"Damn," Greenwood mumbled then lifted a hand in apology.

Mica went through a detailed list of the suspect damage he had found and why it could not have happened during battle. The two members of the Air Patrol listened with growing frowns, but neither of them questioned the finds.

"I'll have to put guards on everything," Rose said with a sigh. She sipped at her tea and frowned. "More trouble than we can afford, but I don't suppose I should be at all surprised."

"I could go over the enrollment," Greenwood said. "Though I wouldn't know what to look for in them."

"Any apparent ties to Honorgate," Merriweather said. Knowledge of the role of the Honorgates in other trouble had spread, even outside of official lines. "But that would be too easy to find. I suggest you look specifically at people who joined just before or early on during the first battles."

"Good idea," Admiral Rose said. She smiled again and waved a hand to Mica. "Run along and help Krogor. I won't keep you any longer from the work."

They spent the rest of the day on *Flash*. Mica got to crawl around the engine and make connections, test power, and adjust things. He and Krogor mostly communicated with grunts and mumbled curses. Merriweather handed over tools; she had gotten quite good at knowing what they wanted.

The work could not go on forever, but on one morning as they sat at breakfast in Raventower, the notes brought something Mica had not expected.

"Gregorian says there have been too many reports of spiders in the foothills to the west," he said. "He wants us to go out with a group of guards and have a look."

"Yes, that would probably be wise," Merriweather agreed. "We know more about them than anyone else. Do we leave today?"

"Apparently so. The guards will meet us on the way to the Air Patrol Field, and we'll ride out from there. We best take packs then. Gram --"

"Ada and me will get some travel food together," the older woman said and went straight to the work

Mica nodded his thanks and headed up to his room. The idea of riding out in winter did not appeal to him, and for a moment he considered taking Kandris and the carriage -- but that would only draw attention.

They rode out a little later, and weighed down with the food the two women had found for them. Roe, Nyle, and Shipley saw them off, though from inside the tower door. There was no reason to advertise to even the guards that this was anything more than the usual trip to the airships.

"I doubt this will take more than a few days," Merriweather told the others. They already fretted. "And since we have spent a night or two working on the airships, it shouldn't draw too much attention when we don't come back tonight."

"Take care, though," Nyle said. "If it is more spiders --"

"We've dealt with them before," Mica said. He did not mention the lack of a convenient ocean to drag the spiders into, but since they'd simply swam away from that trap it probably didn't matter so much. "All of you take care here. Anything could happen. If you must leave the tower, just do so."

They all nodded.

Then he and Merriweather went outside, climbed onto the horses as usual, and rode away. Mica glanced back at the gate. Everything looked normal enough -- at least as normal as it had been since the war began.

He hoped the journey did not take long.

The soldiers joined them just outside the city gate, a silent group of ten, nearly anonymous in their own cloaks. Mica saw Merriweather look at the man who must be in command -- his jacket beneath the cloak showed the red of a lieutenant -- and frowned. Since she said nothing, he didn't ask, but he suspected some trouble there.

Gregorian waited at the gate to the Air Patrol Field. The two brothers and Merriweather gathered in the gate house, leaving the others outside. He thought the lieutenant snarled some nearly silent curse.

"I hate to send you off in this weather," Gregorian said with a shake of his head. "It is just that if there are truly some more of the spiders out there, you are the only ones who can do anything with them."

"I agree," Mica replied and held his hands toward the small fireplace, too aware of how long it would be until he found such warmth again. "We'll be back as soon as possible."

"Good. Anything else I should know?"

"I think we have the airships in hand," Mica said with a wave of his hand toward the field. "Rose and her people can handle the last of it. Is there any reason why the Atrians are still holding off?"

"Not a good one. We think the Atrians are expecting reinforcements. Our fleet is covering the ocean as best they can. There is nothing within at least a week of us, though."

"Good."

"Anything more to add, Merriweather?" Gregorian said a glanced her way.

She had been looking out the window at the soldiers. With a sigh, she looked back at her General. "You don't miss much, sir."

"It's part of my job."

She laughed a little. "I served under Lt. Karto, General. We didn't get along."

"Ah. I could remove him --"

"No," she said. "I don't mind if he's surly. Removing him now would only slow us down, and also make the men uneasy."

"Karto is from that area," Gregorian said. "That's why I thought he'd be a good choice."

"Good," Merriweather replied. "I'm sure we'll do fine with him."

"You are not under his command," Gregorian reminded her. "I hope that you'll cooperate as much as possible, but I also expect that you will order him if need be. This is a situation where you have more expertise as well as rank. And that's all I'll say about it," Gregorian said. He patted Mica on the shoulder. "If you can, do stop by the Raventower estate and see how things are going there. You should be quite near to it."

"I will if it is possible," Mica said. How odd that his brother should worry about the estate -- but then he and his family did spend more time there than Mica had in the last few years.

They stepped back out into the cold, Mica pulling his cloak tighter and still wished for Kandris and the carriage. Nyle had done repairs on both, and the single mechanical horse could easily pull the vehicle. He'd seen the soldiers amazed by the huge metal horse, and Kandris had seemed to like the attention.

"Good luck on your journey," Gregorian said. He had placed himself closer to Karto's horse. "This might not amount to anything important, but it has to be done. Captain Merriweather is in charge of the overall expedition, though Lt. Karto will direct the soldiers unless she has other orders. I expect there to be no trouble."

He said the last words with an obvious glance at Karto. The man gave a steely eyed glare and salute in return. Mica couldn't say that his brother had helped with those words, but at least Karto knew Merriweather had rank over him and that he had to obey.

This was not, however, the most pleasant way to start out

the journey.

They were soon on the way, though. Farmland filled most of the area to the west of the Air Field, all of it covered in the stubble of plants and snow. They made their way to the edge of a broad stream, frozen over, where they had some cover beneath the barren trees.

"I'll scout ahead," Karto said, finally. They were more than an hour out, and no one had said much of anything.

Merriweather gave a nod. Karto signaled four of his people and rode off. He did not salute.

"Well, this is going better than I hoped," Merriweather said after the others had gone more than a mile ahead of them.

At least half of the remaining six laughed, which surprised Mica and put him in a better mood. They even joked with Merriweather about her cushy new job. Some of the others were likely spies for Karto, but Merriweather didn't discuss him or the assignment. The jokes ended when they caught up with Karto again. He had nothing to report and rode on once more.

They spent the rest of the day in that manner and finally, just after sunset, took refuge in a barn with a few chickens, goats, cats, and owls. Karto looked Mica's way too often, expecting him to complain about the accommodations. Merriweather ignored the man, who took his soldiers apart from the two of them and set up the guard.

The truth was that Mica was just as glad to have the little area to themselves. Merriweather even agreed that she could trust the others to keep watch, though she slept close by. Mica didn't sleep well, though. There were too many odd sounds and whispered words. He wanted the quiet -- mostly quiet -- of his tower back.

By the next day, they had started to collect what information they could from the locals. Karto proved to be less than helpful in this work, which didn't surprise Mica much but began to annoy Merriweather as the day went on. The man stepped into every conversation they had with people, whether on the trail they now followed or in the small villages they passed through. Karto *demanded* information and snarled when Mica pointed out that there were better ways to deal with these people.

"Why don't you just throw coins at them, then," Karto replied with a growl. "Maybe you can buy them like you bought --" His eyes went to Merriweather, but he said nothing and pulled his horse aside.

Mica was ready to pull his own sword.

"Calm, Lord Raventower," she said and moved her horse closer to his. Karto and his usual group were riding on. The soldiers who stayed behind looked shocked by the lieutenant's words. "I'm not in the least bit surprised to find that's Karto's take on why I am doing better than him. Don't let his bad manners worry you."

"Ah. True." He took his hand from the sword but frowned for a new reason. "It is odd, though. He clearly has no worry about the nobility. Not only is he rude to me, but he hasn't even considered that you will be Lady Raventower at some point."

"I hadn't thought of that," she said. She looked to where the man had ridden away. "That is something to consider."

They were still four days from the foothills, and Mica feared that the journey was not going to get better. They had snow on the second night and into the day so that they were all glad to take refuge early at an inn. The place was mostly deserted, and the owner only shrugged when Karto said they would be staying there and expected to be fed.

Mica, however, paid the man.

"These people are having a hard time," he said looking at Karto. It was, he thought, the first words he had directed at the man.

Karto's lips moved into a sneer of contempt. "A waste of coin. They'll do what they're ordered."

The owner of the establishment took that moment to duck into the kitchen.

"You will be polite in my presence, Lt. Karto. I won't ask more of you -- but do remember that requirement."

Karto started to say something. Changed his mind and stalked away.

"Well, that will probably keep him away from you," Merriweather said at his shoulder. He wondered if it hadn't been her reaction that had chased the man away. "Which is fine by me, Lord Raventower."

They had a good dinner, though the rabbit stew was a bit undercooked and bread hard. Mica missed the food at the tower, and he would appreciate it all the more when they got back.

He did manage to get the innkeeper to talk to him about the rumor of spiders.

"Yes, sirrah," the man said with a nod of his nearly bald head. He frowned back at the other soldiers but then continued. "Can't say where they are exactly, though some ha' said in the abandoned silver mines."

There was the first helpful bit of information he'd heard if he turned out to be true.

"Mines. Like caves," Merriweather said when the man had gone off to serve the few locals who had come in, mostly out of curiosity Mica guessed. "That makes me think this might be something after all."

"I thought the same thing," he agreed. The cider, at least, was excellent. "We must be a few days out from there, though."

"Yes," she agreed with a sigh.

The next two days were much the same, though some of Karto's usual companions had started trying to trick

Merriweather into chasing out after rabbits or deer, saying they were about to be attacked. They seemed to think it a good joke, even if Mica's guard was not taken in by any of it.

The others relaxed more, though. Even Karto only frowned and refrained from saying anything to Mica, which was as close as the man apparently came to being polite. Merriweather didn't trust him, though. She stayed awake until Karto slept and watched his favorite companions as well. She also made certain that Mica slept with one of her knives close at hand.

Then on a late morning that was more fog than snow, Mica found some interesting prints on the edge of the river they were following. Merriweather must have spotted them as well. They were both off the horses and checking them out before the rest of their companions had come to a stop. Karto and his men turned back as well.

"It could be," Mica said, though he wasn't certain. "It is possible that the spiders were strong enough to swim up the current."

"Or they could have come down from the higher lands," Merriweather said as she stood. "They either came from or headed into those marshes."

Mica had not seen the water expanse not far from the river. A human-made bridge of rock had been built by the river where it must sometimes wash over into the lower land. Birds were there, even in the winter. He thought it might be a beautiful place at better times.

"There has been too much wind and ice," he finally admitted and stood. "I can't be certain. They might be closer than we thought, though."

He had not expected Karto to be spooked by the idea that they might find something out here. Had that been part of the problem? If the man thought this was a waste of time, when everything else was going on along the coast, Mica could almost understand. Karto probably wanted to prove himself in battle, like many fools thought to do.

A village sat not far from the marshland. They dined on duck that night and won a few more cautious tales from the locals. There might have been something in the marsh five days or so ago, but it was gone now and heading to the foothills.

They would be going on after all. Mica had rather hoped this was the end of the journey, though he supposed they would have had to check out the hills anyway.

He wanted to go home. The journey had been more annoying than difficult, and that was the fault of Karto. If it had just been he and Merriweather, they would have made better time and perhaps found something by now.

Another day out in the increasingly cold and snowy weather did not improve anyone's mood. They camped that night with a line of trees to break the wind, but no one was comfortable.

"There is nothing out here," Karto finally brought himself to say as they sat around a fire that night. "We're chasing children's tales. We should go back to the city."

He did not, however, order it. Instead, he looked at Merriweather and waited for her to make a decision. She, wisely, did not turn to Mica.

"I am considering it," she replied with a civil enough tone. "Even if we went on to the foothills, we'd have a hellish time trying to find the abandoned mines, let alone one that might or might not have spiders in it."

Karto grunted and still stared.

"I'll let you know in the morning."

Karto nodded and, as usual, moved off with his men. Good. Mica wanted to discuss the situation with Merriweather, but he didn't want to make this position difficult for her. He had kept out of the trouble as much as he could.

"I suggest you send them back," he said when they were mostly alone on their side of the camp. Someone might hear them, and he didn't want his words to sound like an order. "We can go on to the Raventower Estate -- it isn't more than twenty miles away."

She looked in that direction. Mica hadn't been aware that she knew where his lands were, but she gave a slight nod. He slept better for it because he still didn't trust Karto. With any luck, they might get some information from people living at his estate. Those were people whom he trusted and whom Karto could not intimidate even if for some reason he came with them.

The morning meal of hard bread, weak tea, and a little cheese did not go well.

"Well?" Karto demanded, looking at her over his metal cup. His eyes gleamed. He wanted trouble.

"You and your men will return to the city," Merriweather told him. The man's eyes narrowed knowing there was more to be said. "Lord Raventower and I will go on to the Raventower estate. General Gregorian had asked us to look in on it."

That was true. Mica had even forgotten.

"You can't possibly believe --"

"You have your orders."

"And what do I tell General Gregorian then?" Karto demanded. He stood. Merriweather did not. "He sent us out here to protect his precious brother --"

"He did no such thing," Merriweather replied. Her voice remained steady, and she did no more than blink when she looked at the man. Mica needed to learn how she managed to show such calm in these circumstances. "Your orders were to help find and deal with clockwork spiders. We have not found any. You are *ordered* back to the city."

Karto still wanted to argue, but some other thought must have crossed his mind because the anger disappeared almost in an eye blink. Perhaps he was happy to be going back, but Mica suspected something more sinister in the near smile he gave.

"Of course, we'll obey your orders, Captain Merriweather."

He turned away and went to the horses, one of his men with him. Merriweather looked at Mica and frowned. She had seen the change and didn't trust Karto for it, either.

Merriweather wrote a quick report to send back with the soldiers and to be given to General Gregorian. She put a seal on it, but Mica suspected that was not going to hold and he wondered if the report would reach his brother at all. Karto was cooperating far too well. Mica didn't trust the man.

Both groups headed off in the same direction. After a couple hours on the trail, they found a path leading southward which was the general direction of the Raventower lands.

Merriweather gave a nod to the soldiers and they rode off, Karto not giving a single word at the parting. A few of the friendlier soldiers glanced their way and seemed to look worried.

Mica would have to remind Merriweather that there was another of those absurd little Honorgate holdings somewhere along the way, but for the moment he was simply glad to be away from the soldiers. Merriweather said nothing, and the silence with the others gone was a welcome change.

The ubiquitous morning snowstorm had started, but even the weather could not dampen the relief Mica felt when the others rode one direction and he and Merriweather another.

"Damn," she mumbled after a while. "I don't know if this is wise, Lord Raventower, but staying with Karto was looking increasingly dangerous."

"Dangerous?" he said, startled by the word.

"Some of us thought that he and his chosen few might be meeting with others when they'd ride off ahead of us."

"Ah. I wondered, but since you made no show of it --"

"I feared that would only get us killed." She looked back over her shoulder, but the snow fell harder now. He glanced back and realized he could no longer even see the path they'd been on.

He didn't feel any safer for having parted with them.

CHAPTER TWELVE

They had already gone more than two miles without any trouble, but Merriweather didn't look any better for it. The harder fall of snow didn't help either since they were at least half a day's ride from the estate. Although they'd faced no hostile people on this journey, that didn't mean he thought it was safe to wander around.

Mica soon realized he should reconsider those thoughts. They had faced at least *one* hostile person.

The ambush came less than three hours after they'd left the soldiers behind. The gunfire came from the left of the trail, the attackers hidden by a thick line of brush and tall snow drifts. Mica thought there might have been four or five guns fired. He couldn't be certain because one of the first shots caught him in the left shoulder and tumbled him from the horse.

Merriweather threw herself from the other horse and let both animals run. Was that wise? Mica tried to say something, but she grabbed gun by one arm and dragged him across the trail and into a few bushes of their own. The land sloped slightly downward there, so they were almost out of sight, but it would not be good cover for long.

"Oh damn, oh damn," Merriweather whispered. She made

a quick check of his wound, shoved a cloth from her bag against it, and shook her head.

"Not -- not your fault," he said. He clamped his mouth shut as he maneuvered enough to see over the slight embankment.

"If I hadn't sent the others on the way --"

"Wouldn't make a difference. We were headed for trouble, and you -- you knew it. Who do you think attacked us, clear out here with virtually no one around?"

She blinked. "He wouldn't. Not even Karto would --"

"Listen."

She held her breath. The whispered voices were unmistakable. They could have been anyone, except for Karto's tendency to snarl orders and curse his people --

Merriweather was so angry she almost headed straight up the embankment and would have charged them with nothing more than her pistol and sword. Oh, and the knives, but he feared that even she was not fast enough to take them all on. He grabbed her and hardly stifled a moan when she tried to fight.

"That bastard. That treacherous bastard --"

"Quiet," Mica whispered close to her ear. "He doesn't realize we know. He's taking care -- not be spotted. He fears we could still get away and he's trying to make -- make certain we can't name him."

"Yes," she said. She looked worried. "I don't see how we can get away, Lord Raventower. We have the stream at our back, ice covered and treacherous. No way to get across to the other side."

He nodded agreement.

"Gunshots weren't wise," he said. "Sound carries in ... in winter. Hope for help. Farmers, at least."

She nodded but didn't look hopeful at the thought. Mica didn't think it likely either. Still --

He thought the others were attacking when he heard the shouts and shots, but then he realized the impossible had happened and a battle had erupted on the other side of the road.

"Help -- help them," Mica said with a slap on her arm. "I'll be here."

She looked at him for a moment and then nodded and wordlessly scrambled up over the embankment and into the trouble. Mica had hated to send her into danger, but if they were to survive, they needed to take down the lieutenant and his people.

The battle seemed longer than he had expected, though he had trouble tracking time now. The world slipped away sometimes and came back with painful clarity. He heard shouts, though not Merriweather's voice. She wouldn't make unnecessary sounds. He had not sent her to her death, but if he had, then they would come for him soon enough.

Shadows passed over him. At first, he only saw a man and woman in uniform and felt his heart pound with fear. However, before he said anything, Merriweather rushed down the embankment and knelt beside him.

"Karto is on the run," she told him as she quickly checked the wound. "Two others are following him, so he won't be back this way. Duna and Leason here have told me the tale. Can you stand?"

"I'll need help to get there. To stay there. Tell me," Mica said, fearing he would be unconscious before he heard how they happened into this ambush.

Duna, who was taller than Mica and sturdy, helped him up. The man looked pale, but Mica thought that might be a show of anger rather than fear or injury. Leason, the woman, was shorter than all of them, but she had her sword in hand, and he thought she looked even more fierce than Merriweather at that moment.

Merriweather had waited until he was standing before she told him a quick account. "I had some friends in that group. You knew it," she said. "They'd been watching Karto. He'd volunteered for the duty, by the way, but all he'd known at first was that it was scouting trip into an area he supposedly knew. When he found out that you and I were along, his attitude changed. He'd been out here a few times since the war, though."

"Allies," he said with a sudden worry. "Atrians."

"Maybe," Duna dared to speak. He maneuvered Mica as gently as he could, but the movement was agony. The bullet was still in the shoulder. It would have to come out, and Mica shuddered at the idea. "My apologies, me lord --"

"No need to apologize. What -- happened here?"

"He waited long enough to make certain the two of you were out of range," Leason said with a scowl. "Then he turned on us. I think Karto was surprised to find we were ready for his treachery, though two of us were killed before we got away. We wanted to ride straight to you because it was plain that he wanted you two dead. I don't know why, Captain."

"Probably his orders," Mica suggested. "Meeting others."

"We were probably headed for more trouble than this," Merriweather agreed. "But we surprised him and took our own path, which was not wise -- but probably no worse than going with him in the long run. Damn him. Let's get Lord Raventower on the horse with me. You two take the other horses. They might come back."

"Might?" Mica asked. He looked at the horse they led him to. A tall, wide beast. Gray with a hint of white in the pattern; it reminded him of a foggy day. Riding the creature was not going to be easy.

"I shot Karto," Merriweather explained. She climbed up on the horse, her own face set with lines of worry. "If the wound is severe enough -- or it kills him -- we won't have more trouble. I don't think we'll be that lucky, though."

"Probably not," he agreed.

They got him on the horse. He was not conscious through part of it, but he came back once he was settled in place and Merriweather wrapped the cloak around him.

"No, lean back against me," she ordered when he started to sit up straighter. "I have you. But damn, where do we go? Are either of you from this area?"

"No, Captain," Duna said with a sound of regret.

"Too much open country," she said, and Mica felt her shift slightly, and he knew she looked around. "He has the better of us there. So do Karto's people because most of them are locals, too. We're at least a day away from the hills and better cover. We're too far from the last village."

"It's going to get colder tonight," Leason offered. She and Duna had mounted and were now flanking the horse that Mica and Merriweather sat upon. "It looks to me as though the clouds are already breaking up. We better at least find a farmhouse. He'll be looking for us to do that, of course, but what other choice do we have?"

"I don't want to get lost wandering around," she said. "But we need to get away from the trail and hope the snow covers the tracks well enough --"

"To Raventower Estate," Mica said. His breath caught as the horse moved and he hated the thought of the long ride ahead. He wasn't certain he would survive, but the others would find safety there even if he didn't. "Not as far -- as far as the hills. Best hope."

"He's right," Merriweather agreed though she sounded worried. "Let's head that way and at least get out of this area. We can make other decisions if we need to."

The other two did not argue.

They moved too quickly at first. Mica lost consciousness which helped in many ways, though he feared he would not wake back up and fought it for as long as he could.

When he did awake, he was on the ground.

"No --"

"Easy," Merriweather said. She put a cup to his lips. It was a strong liquor, probably home brewed, and must have come from one of the other two.

He sipped and coughed. His body felt like fire, from his shoulder to his feet. He didn't argue when Merriweather had him sip again. He couldn't say it helped, except that the world blurred around him a bit more.

He couldn't move his left arm and started to panic until he realized that the arm was secured to his chest.

"Duna took the bullet out," Merriweather explained. "We thought it best to get it done while you were still unconscious and before we went any farther. We've got you bandaged and ready to ride again. We can't be more than ten miles from the estate. Leason even went to ask a farmer, saying she'd lost her troop and needed to meet them there. We're on the right path now."

"G-Good," he said. "Let's go."

They got Mica back on the horse. The ride was nothing more than prolonged agony, but he held to the thought that they were going to people they could trust.

He hoped.

Gregorian had suggested he look in on them. Did his brother have reason to worry about what they might be doing?

No. Gregorian would have said so right out. His brother did not play those kinds of games. Get to safety there and then --

"We must -- must send a report to Gregorian," he said suddenly and seemed to startle Merriweather with the words. "Immediately, Merriweather. Karto may go straight to him --"

"Oh damn. You're right. There's no telling what he might do if he thinks he's going to be uncovered at any moment. A raven?" she asked.

"Pouch is still on my horse. I hope the animal turns up. I want the ravens back."

"Yes. Then we have to do this the hard way. Do either of you have pen and paper?"

Duna did. He handed it over, and Merriweather jotted something down sitting awkwardly behind Mica. "One of you will have to take it. Decide which one."

"Leason," Duna said. Mica saw him pulling a pouch from his saddle and handing it over to her. "She's a better rider than me. That's all the food I have left. We'll be at the estate soon enough, so don't worry."

"True. Maybe you should wait until we can supply you --"

"No. I'll go now," she said and took the note and more supplies from Merriweather. "Karto might not be heading for the city yet, but the moment he knows you two have reached safety, he'll be riding that way as fast as he can, wound or not. I might get a head start on him this way."

"Here." Mica had reached into his vest pocket and pulled out an envelope to hand to her. "That is a pass with Gregorian's seal, and it should get you through any kind of official trouble. There's a bit of blood on it. Tell him not to worry."

She took the envelope with a nod of appreciation. "Thank you. I'll do my best to reassure him. You three get to safety."

Then she turned and headed straight across country, away from the trail they were on.

Mica drifted in and out of consciousness for a while. The liquor helped numb some of the pain, or at least made him not care so much. It did not help him stay steady in the saddle, though.

Night came. They kept riding. Every sound startled him. Every wind-blown branch looked like an enemy coming their way. Merriweather and Duna remained mostly quiet, but he thought he heard hope in their whispered voices sometimes.

They bypassed a village and kept clear of the fields. The sun had gone down and the moon shined too bright against the white snow. The night felt like winter had come to his lungs. Each breath pulled ice down into him. Only Merriweather's warmth, where she held tightly to him, kept Mica from freezing to death right there in the saddle.

And they rode on.

"I think that must be it," Merriweather said suddenly. "There's a fence and a line of trees. Unless, of course, we completely lost our way and that's the damned Honorgate lands instead."

"No help there?" Duna asked. He sounded weary.

"No help. Might well run into Karto there, in fact."

"Ah. Never much cared for the couple Honorgate's I've met, so I'm not surprised. Maybe we need to find out --"

"It's Raventower lands," Mica managed to say. He'd shifted his eyes left and right, taking in the contours and the trees. "Follow to the left. Gate in a couple miles for herders."

"Damn. Good," Merriweather replied, and her arm tightened around him. "We're almost there, Your Lordship."

Almost didn't mean much to him right now. He watched as they rode along the fence, their horses slowed by the deep snow and the long ride. An owl protested and took off from a fence post. Deer darted across the field.

The fence turned and dipped down a hillside and there, at the bottom, stood the gate, along with guards holding weapons ready. They'd been remarkably quiet people since even Merriweather let out a little hiss of surprise.

Mica didn't follow much of what was said, but he understood there was some problem. He lifted his head and focused on the men on the other side of the gate. They were all bundled against the cold, and he didn't recognize any of them. From the sounds of things, though, they were no happier at being out on such a cold night as he and his companions. He could see a little cottage not far away. That would be the one where the sheepherder stayed.

"We don't let no strangers in. Them is the orders --"

"Where is Fopel, the shepherd?" he asked, his voice soft and gruff.

"I'm here," Fopel said and stepped out from behind the guards. City men, by the sound of their voices. Probably put here by Gregorian. "How did you know -- Oh Gods! It's Lord Raventower hisself!"

"Are you certain?" one of the men asked.

"Oh yes!"

"Yes," another of the guards said. "I seen him in the city a few times. Why didn't you say who he was, Captain!"

They were opening the gate. Merriweather gave a sigh of relief.

"I didn't know who you were," she explained. "And we've already run into trouble. His Lordship was shot, and we need to get him to safety."

"You must be Captain Merriweather, then. Let's get him to the cottage --"

"Too close to the gate," she said and sounded as though she regretted those words. "How far to the manor house?"

"About four miles. But if he needs rest, the cottage --"

"Is too close to the gate and we might well be followed. Don't let anyone in unless it is a woman with a pass from Gregorian, and then only let her in if she's alone. If she is not alone, stop her here and get me."

"Yes, Captain."

"Thank you. You're doing an excellent job. Be careful because there are enemies out there -- but you know that, don't you? That's why you're here."

"Yes, Captain," one of the men said. His voice hinted at something more. "There was a rumor that someone came over the fence on the northern border, Captain. I haven't heard a report on that one, though."

"Damn," she mumbled. "If it is Karto, he'll be between us and the manor house."

"Worse," Duna added, speaking for the first time. "He's in uniform. People might know him. They won't realize he's changed sides, he and his people."

"Good point," Merriweather replied. "Is there some way we can get to the manor house that will not take us too much out in the open?"

"Yes," Fopel said. "I'll show you, out along the fence. It's a longer way, though. It'll take us a few hours."

"Better long than stupid," Mica replied. He sat up a little straighter, and that probably helped Merriweather. He thought she might be trembling, but that most likely came from exhaustion and annoyance and not fear.

"Where are the Honorgate holdings from here?" Merriweather asked.

"The northern border, of course," Mica replied. "That's why I think the crossing into my lands is real."

"I am relieved to hear you so lucid, Lord Raventower," she admitted. Her arm moved slightly and held him a little tighter, as close to a hug as either of them had given. "You are feverish, though. It might be better if we take our chance --"

"No," he said. "A few more hours, Merriweather, and we'll be at the gate just a half a mile from the manor house. I don't think they'll expect us to walk up to the front door, you know. They're going to hunt everywhere for people skulking through the land and hiding in the bushes. Let them keep busy doing that, but let's not be where they are most likely to look for us."

"Yes," she agreed again.

Fopel led them away. The shepherd stayed on foot and declined to ride with Duna. "I can see the way better down here," he explained. "And look for signs, like rabbits and such on the move and what direction they came from."

That knowledge seemed to help. Fopel led them to bushes and into glades, away from the fence too often it seemed, but Mica didn't complain. People moved elsewhere. Fopel pointed them out once, and Duna dismounted to keep both the horses quiet and still. Merriweather pulled her flintlock pistol, and he felt her open the case that carried black powder and shot. He prepared to drop to the ground and hoped there was enough snow to cushion the fall.

The others rode away without seeing the group in the shadow of the trees. They were not, Mica was glad to see, heading for the manor house. Merriweather sighed with relief as well.

They waited for quite some time and then finally moved on.

Mica thought they must be getting closer. Was that a glow ahead? It had to be the house --

He was right. They came through a line of snow-laden pines and to the road that led straight to the main gate. Guards stood there as well, and weapons came up.

"Hold," Fopel said, though he didn't shout too loudly. Voices carried well in the quiet, chilly night. "It's me, Fopel."

"You got company," one of the men said. He came out, gun in hand. Merriweather twitched. "What's going on -- Oh. Lord Raventower. Is that the business tonight what got others sneaking around? In with you. Straight to the house now. There's been a lot of people about, and I get the feeling they'd rather you didn't get to the building."

"You are right, Stark," Lord Raventower said. He tried not to show he was wounded, but that was his pride getting the better of him.

"I'll stay and explain," Duna said. "And then I'll be to the house, Captain Merriweather. You need not worry. I know you can't fully trust me."

"Thank you, Duna," she said. They were passing inside the gate. The road here was lined with tall, stately pines, but guards moved to the left and right behind the trees, making certain there was no one hiding. "I'll see you at the house."

"We did it," Mica said as they rode on. It was just the two of them now.

"We did. You'll be safe now, my ... my lord."

She had almost said something else. Mica smiled despite how wretched he felt.

Mica remained conscious as they rode quickly toward the huge stone house. The windows blazed with golden light that escaped past the heavy curtains. Would anyone see them hurrying to that refuge? Mica wanted the door unlatched and the two of them safely inside. No one except Merriweather was with him now, though. Not even a raven to send for help.

The horse came to a staggering stop. Merriweather muttered a quiet curse. The door stood no more than ten yards away, but those yards were up a set of ancient steps and across an open veranda. Mica looked that way with despair.

"I can't, Merriweather. I can't walk that far. Can you get the horse up the steps?"

"I can try. If I get down, can you stay in the saddle?" Merriweather asked.

"Try," he replied. The single word did not sound reassuring even to him.

Merriweather started to get down. Mica found himself sliding down with her despite what he wanted. He couldn't really say what happened next. He knew she somehow got him to his feet and they began the laborious work of scaling an ice clad mountain that led, he thought, to the bright sun. One step and another --

Something rushed to them and took hold of his arm. He gave a startled yell -- or rather a croak.

"Fopel," Merriweather said with a sound of relief. "I have him. Get them to open the door. We're almost there."

Almost was apparently good enough for him. Mica closed his eyes and felt his body start to give way...

CHAPTER THIRTEEN

Later.

Mica rested in a comfortable bed, but not one at home. Candlelight wavered and sent shadows moving everywhere so that he was certain the enemy had captured him. Strangers stood over the bed and held him down.

"Sleep, Lord Raventower," Merriweather said.

He trusted Merriweather. He slept.

Sometimes it was not her voice that told him to rest or to sip a bit of broth. Sometimes he looked into the face of a stranger, and other times he saw Princess Jenlyn or even Queen Ylanda. He would not listen to those illusions, though he had no strength to fight them.

Rest. Wished Seldon was here to take care of him. It had been a long time since he'd had to deal with any sort of serious injury on his own. That thought caught his attention. He followed it. Had he become careless of himself and others because Seldon helped him?

Maybe. Mica thought about it a while longer, but even that disappeared into the fever-muddled maelstrom of his mind. Mica thought his hands sometimes moved, as though they built ravens. He wondered if he created one for himself...

Storms came and went. Snow danced across the window,

white against the gray of the outside world. Patterns of frost formed on the edge of the glass, a wondrous thing to watch as it moved slowly along the surface. He didn't like the people pulling the shutters closed or the curtains in place. They left them open most of the time when he protested.

"There are guards everywhere, Merriweather," someone said. "Let him have the window. He finds it fascinating."

"The fever has to break soon," Merriweather whispered, and Mica thought he heard fear in her voice for the first time.

She sat beside him. For a while, he found looking at her as fascinating as the window. Maybe more so. She had brought a book and read, and he wanted to ask her to read to him ... but at the same time he feared that if he spoke, she would become someone else. He watched her until he fell asleep again.

Sometime the next morning he woke up feeling different. Trembling, but more clearheaded than he had been for a while. He looked to the window and saw snow falling again, which was not nearly as entertaining as it had been now that he considered the poor people out there, guarding him.

"I'll get him to sip some of the tea," Merriweather said as she stepped through the door. She had a tray and sat it on the bedside table. "He doesn't fight me so much."

"Tea sounds wonderful," Mica said.

She yelped. Then she leaned over Mica and put a warm hand on his forehead. "Go tell them the fever broke."

He had the impression of a servant hurrying away.

"What --" he began.

"Drink some of the tea first. It's almost half honey, I fear, but you need the strength."

He didn't argue. He drank most of the cup of tea, the warmth pleasant. He ate a piece of bread and marmalade. Not as good as Gram or Ada's cooking, but still tasty and warm. His stomach grumbled. He wondered how long it had been since he'd had food since he felt so weak.

"What has happened?" he finally asked.

"Not much of anything since we got here. Four long days, Lord Raventower," she said and pushed hair back from her face. "You are never to get shot again. I won't stand for it."

He laughed a little. His shoulder ached almost to distraction, but he did not say so to Merriweather. She might insist that he rest, and Mica wanted to spend this time with her and to reconnect to the world again.

"That was far too close," she finally said after he had sipped a bit more tepid tea. It still tasted delightful. "There were times when I didn't think you would come through it."

"I must have thought the same thing," he admitted. "I remember I thought I was making myself a raven."

She gave him a startled, worried look. "Yes. You were apparently trying to put something together. I had never considered a raven. That you might -- you might --"

"I had never considered it, either," he replied and said no more since he could see the conversation bothered her. She had helped him lean back a little, fixing the pillows. They'd had him sitting up. He supposed he had breathed easier like that, but it was pleasant to lie down. "Thank you."

"Sleep for a while. Karto may have figured out where we are by now, but he's not getting in here."

He didn't doubt her, though there were things he wanted to ask.

When he awoke again, Princess Jenlyn sat by the bed. The fever had returned --

No, it had not.

"Ah," he said, blinking. "You really are here. Gods, and the Queen? I seem to remember demanding she be Merriweather more than once."

Jenlyn gave a slight laugh and patted him on the arm before she pulled the blankets up around him again. "You were a perfect gentleman, as always. If we hadn't been so worried about you, we would have been amused."

"Ah."

She put a hand on his fingers, startling him. "You must take care of yourself, Mica. I know you are going to want to push and do things, and though I suspect Merriweather could order you to go easier, I'm not sure you would listen to her."

"I would."

She smiled again. "Good."

"At least now I know why Gregorian suggested we look in on the estate. Everyone assumes that all of you are in the mountains somewhere. Are the children here, too?"

"Yes. This has been difficult for them," Jenlyn admitted. "We didn't tell them about you -- they've been upset enough. I must say that your staff here is exceptional, though. They've come up with games and events to keep them busy and away from the windows. At first, the children were more than a little rude about dealing with peasants, but they've since learned their manners."

"They're worried about their father."

"Yes. Which is why we have not told the children that you are here, wounded, and near death."

"Wise. Wait a few more days. I'll be better by then."

She agreed.

And he was. He felt better by the next morning and was able to use the privy rather than the bedpan. He didn't like to think about those days when he wasn't aware of what he'd been doing. Better now, though. Merriweather let him sit in a chair by the fire by the afternoon of that day, but only so long as he ate some soup with her.

He ate quite a bit, in fact.

She took the plates away and then came back with an envelope and handed it to him.

"This just arrived with a few new guards," she said.

Gregorian's seal on it. He pulled the paper open with

trembling fingers -- just weakness, nothing more, and held up the note. Then he gave a little laugh.

"Yes?"

"I simply cannot trust you out of my sight," he read aloud, and she laughed as well. "I am sending someone I trust to help out there. Stay where you are. We are waiting for the weather to clear."

"That sounds promising. And it means Leason got to him. She must have ridden like a demon."

"How are things here?" he asked. He waved towards the window.

"Quiet enough. There have been more attempted incursions along the borders of the estate, but no one has gotten this far. They are not Atrians, I think. And certainly not Atrian assassins."

"But those might be coming, too, if word is out that I am here, Merriweather --"

"We are not going for at least another five days and maybe longer. You are recovering, but we are not going to rush out."

He didn't argue. "We just cannot risk Jenlyn and the Queen."

"I know. However, leaving wouldn't help, you know. The Atrians would still come here first unless you purposely show yourself elsewhere and that just isn't wise right now."

She was right. Mica gave way.

The Queen sat with him for more than an hour that afternoon. He found it amazing that she took such time with him, but then he realized how worried she must be. She asked about the city and how things had looked last time he was there. Merriweather, sitting close by, filled in some of the facts for her. They reassured her that King Abertus was keeping close to the castle and not riding about and looking for trouble.

"He's too much like you, Mica," the Queen said when she stood. "Age has quieted his urges, but this war --"

"Gregorian is with him," Mica replied with a bright smile. "He'll do his best to keep the King informed and busy -- at the castle."

The queen gave a quirk of her eyebrow and then laughed. "Oh yes, I suppose that is a good part of his work, poor boy. Thank you, both for setting my mind at ease."

And off she went. Merriweather gave a sigh of relief. "Well handled, my lord."

"I was raised at court," he reminded her. "In the care of the King and the Queen, in fact. I do know them far better than a lot of people. Better than Gregorian does, in fact."

Merriweather nodded. They spoke about the court for a while until he grew tired and went back to bed. It had been a pleasant afternoon. They repeated it over the next three days, but by then he was starting to be restless.

It helped when a local found his horse and brought it to the Raventower estate, seeing the fine mount must belong to someone of importance. They rewarded the man for his care; the pouch still in place. He had his ravens again, though he had nothing to do with them at the moment.

Mica kept clothing at the estate, though he rarely came here. The tunic and pants were loose on him, but he was glad to dress and leave the room. They went down to the parlor, and there he got to talk to the children. They only knew that he'd hurt his arm and they weren't to be overly excited. That didn't hold for long, though they didn't throw themselves into his arms as they often had at the castle.

"Why can't we come and live with you?" Princess Tara demanded. She was the middle child and tended to be the spokesperson for all three of them. Prince Gregin, the oldest child, tried to live up to his place as his father's heir, but he was only twelve and given still to moments of childish delight.

"Everyone says the tower is probably safer than the castle. And it would be so much better than being clear out here."

"Though we have enjoyed being here," Gregin amended with a bow of his head to a servant coming by with tea and cookies. "I'd rather be here than the castle right now."

"But the tower --" Tara said.

"Is not a place for others," Mica said. He patted quiet Andra on the head. She stood by him, holding her doll. She'd always been a quiet child, and at seven she had become even more taciturn. He suspected she rarely got to talk between Gregin and Tara. "It's certainly not a place for children right now --"

"But what about that boy and his dog?" Tara demanded. "He lives there with you."

"He does," Mica agreed. "He also climbs into pipes and cleans them, and cuts food in the kitchen with his grandmother, and runs all kinds of errands that you two wouldn't like to do."

They wanted to argue but knew better on that point.

"But you took Merriweather, too," Tara said, her voice softer. "She was the only guard who ever treated us like we were more than packages to sit in the corner."

Well, there was an interesting point. Merriweather even gave a little nod. Princess Jenlyn, sitting across the room, looked bothered. Probably no one had noticed the change in how they were handled. He suspected Merriweather had been very proper when others were around.

"I'll see what I can do about your guards," Merriweather promised. "And we will see more of each other once the war is over."

"The war will never end," Gregin said, staring out the window.

Mica changed the subject. They talked about the projects the three children were doing, and how different the world looked away from the city.

"It will be better in the summer," Tara admitted. "I think everything will be better in the summer."

Mica agreed. A little later they took the children away. He sat back with a sigh of relief.

"You needn't have kept them so long," Jenlyn said as she and Merriweather both vied to fix his pillows and give him tea.

They all ended up laughing, including a servant who stepped in and took over, the man's eyes bright with humor.

"Thank you Onep," Mica said when the man put the cup of tea in his hand. "I don't think I'd survive the two of them."

"Maybe you should go back to your room," Jenlyn suggested. "You look pale --"

"This is a comfortable place to sit," he replied gently. "I want to sit and think for a while."

They both nodded and went back to their chairs and their books. Mica had one as well, but he'd barely glanced at it. The children had, oddly, made him think more about how other people were dealing with the war. He'd never thought much about it, especially since he had such trouble connecting with the emotions of others. That was why he liked his workshop so much. He tried to help others because he knew it was a good thing to do, but he did not always understand why they did some things.

He would never understand why some of the people of Sedina had decided to side with the Atrians. He tried to reason it out, sitting there by the fire. Profit probably was part of it. Profit and prestige in the new order. But they had to know that most people would despise them, right?

Power. That was the other part of the equation. How others felt about them wouldn't matter as long as they had the power to demand what they wanted. The Honorgates were a symbol of that attitude. Looking back over the years, he realized how much Lord Honorgate had worked at winning power for himself and his family, even when it lost him the respect of others. He had stayed within the lines back then, though. No one would have expected him to side with the Atrians.

Which brought Mica back to the realization of how little he understood people.

And how much he wanted to go back to his workshop.

Ten days later, on a cold winter morning, a sound startled him at breakfast. Merriweather had already pushed her plate aside and stood, giving him a quick nod.

"What is it?" Jenlyn asked, ready to send the children into hiding.

"Airship," Mica said. He tilted his head slightly, his eyes almost gone. "*Flash*. Gregorian did say he was sending someone he knew he could trust."

"Are you certain?" Jenlyn asked, getting to her feet. The queen looked worried, her hand holding tight to the edge of the table, though she said nothing.

"There it is," Merriweather said. She'd already gone to the window. "Definitely *Flash*. They're anchoring out in the garden. I suspect that's Admiral Rose and Greenwood coming down."

Mica started to stand, then changed his mind. He sat down. "Put two more plates down, if you would, Onep."

"Yes, my lord," the man said as though visitors dropped in from airships every day.

Admiral Rose was more than happy to have a nice warm breakfast and Greenwood seemed surprised to find himself settled at the table with with Princess Jenlyn at his side. Queen Ylanda greeted them, but she had always been a relatively quiet woman, and she waved away the formalities and went back to her food.

The children knew 'Aunt Admiral' as they called the woman, and though Gregin gave her worried looks, it was plain that the girls welcomed her visit. They asked for rides in the airship.

"Not today loves. I have to take Lord Raventower to look something over for us."

"That doesn't sound so bad," Tara said. But a look from her mother silenced the girl. Mica thought he might need to practice that look, though perhaps it was a magic power that only mothers held.

They did not talk business at first. However, the children were finally herded, reluctantly and complaining, away.

"They're getting to be a problem," Jenlyn said. "I can't blame them. If Gregorian could only visit -- No, I understand. What is going on?"

"We've had relative peace in the city," Rose said. She sipped at the tea with a momentary look of bliss. "A few incidents in town. Oh, and the General said that I should tell Mica and Merriweather that they were right. He's cleaned out the corners in the refugee camp by the castle. I assume you had Atrians there making trouble?"

"Apparently so," Mica agreed. "But you did not come all this way to tell us the news about the city."

"We have a confirmation," she said and sat the cup down. Onep filled it again, and Merriweather pushed the honey toward the admiral. "There are clockwork spiders, rather large ones, in the hills to the northwest."

"I feared as much," he admitted. "I am surprised to find you and *Flash* out here, though."

"We needed a test flight anyway," Greenwood said, finally a bit more at ease with the group since he had seen there was no formality here. "We took a circuitous trip, but people will report that we came here, and that we picked you and Merriweather up."

"Yes," Mica said, worried for a moment. "Ah. That should stop people from looking here again, once I am gone. Yes,

Flash is a good ploy for that work. Excellent."

"We'll shut down some of the rooms, your lordship," Onep offered. "Make it look as though there's naught here but a few servants for caretakers. There will be the soldiers still. We don't think, sir, that they realize how many, even though people have been stopped from reaching the building."

"The children are going to be a problem," Jenlyn admitted. "They're as much bored as they are frightened, and that is not a good combination."

"Princess, if I may?" Onep asked. She nodded. "We thought we might take them to stay out in the barn and the apartment there for a day or two. I've been told there are puppies and kittens. And since most of the guards stay there when not on duty --"

"Oh, excellent!" Princess Jenlyn said. She looked delighted and smiled at Mica. "I am in love with your staff. I would try to steal them away, but they'd be miserable in the city."

"As we've told you every time you stay here," Onep said.

Mica felt better about leaving them. He made a quick farewell to the children, who looked glum and afraid again. There was no time for reassurances, and he hoped that they were quickly moved out into the barn. Puppies, kittens, horses -- and soldiers. That ought to keep them busy for a while.

Damned this war.

He had trouble trudging through the snow to the rope ladder. Admiral Rose had gone on ahead, and Greenwood waited for the two of them to go up. They'd bade farewell to Duna who would stay and help with guarding the others. Merriweather had pointed out that they dare not take him along because there was still a chance, having been part of Karto's group, that he could not only give them away, but now the queen, princess, and the children as well. Duna had agreed and Mica didn't think he would try to get away.

Mica had a hard time climbing up to the deck, and his

hand trembled a little as he pulled on the belt and clicked into the lifeline. Rose gave him a nod and put a hand on his arm, steadying him as the wind bucked the ship a bit. Merriweather arrived a moment later and Greenwood right after her. They went straight to the control deck, which still showed some signs of repair but was in mostly good shape.

"Up anchor," Rose ordered before she was even fully in the room. "Sails unfurled. Let's get on our way. The course is still the same."

They moved with a sudden lurch that Mica did not like at all. "I need to go look at the engines --"

"No, you do not," Rose replied. "Krogor is working on getting the last glitches out."

He started to protest, but Merriweather stopped him as she leaned forward and stared into his face, making it plain she was not going to let him go. Then she looked at the controls. "We're heading toward the Honorgate lands. That might not be wise."

"But if they shoot at us, we'd have reason to bomb the hell out of their buildings, wouldn't we?" Rose said. "Because, obviously, it would be a hideout of Atrians. No, we won't -- but Gregorian thought we might want to take a quick look, you know. We flew over on our way there. I doubt they're expecting us back."

"I'm going out," Merriweather said. She did not argue when Mica followed her. He didn't think either of them would stay long in that frigid breeze that came mostly from the airship moving. Mica thought he already regretting leaving behind the manor house.

There were many people near the Honorgate house, but they all ran for cover. Merriweather pointed to one, though. "Karto," she said with a hiss of anger. "Well, not surprised."

"Gregorian will send in troops, but I hate that they are so close to my lands and where the others are," he replied. He kept his voice so low that he wasn't entirely certain even Merriweather could hear him, let alone those on the ground.

"They are safe enough, I hope," she said and moved him back into the control deck. They were past the building and without weapons fire from either side. "The rumors still say your manor house guests took refuge up in the mountains, so let the Atrians and their allies go searching through all the scattered estates from here to Windmere. Having them right next to an Honorgate holding is probably safer than many other places. Especially since we both made certain they saw us on this airship, and they know that we've left."

Rose, who had moved up beside them, gave a nod of agreement. "I was taking that rather august group to the mountain estate, but the weather turned against us. We had trouble enough getting to the Raventower lands and away again without much notice. We came in low and away from the Honorgate lands, practically pushed the group out into the snow, and then ran like hell again."

"Well done," Mica said.

"It was harrowing," Admiral Rose said. "I don't like having children on the ship. Or Queens and Princesses. You two retire to the cabin you shared before. We have some distance to go, and you both look as though you could use some rest."

Mica wanted to argue. He didn't.

They went to the little cabin that smelled faintly of the sea, still. Mica felt a dampness to the place, but the blankets were clean, and the room well-heated. They were as safe as they were likely to be for a while. *Flash* sailed on through the gray day. He and Merriweather slept through most of it.

CHAPTER FOURTEEN

They were both awake when Admiral Rose brought them lunch -- just sandwiches and some tea, but it was welcome. She sat on the bed by Merriweather and looked as though she was the one who should be sleeping.

"About halfway there. You both look better. Good."

The ship gave a slight bump, and they all three frowned.

"I need to look at it, you know," Mica said with a nod to the floor and the engine below them. "We can't go on sails all the way home if the engine gives out."

"You are not in shape to --"

"He'll just fret if he doesn't," Merriweather pointed out. He appreciated her stepping in. Admiral Rose had been his commanding officer for too long, and he had trouble dealing with her, even when he knew he was right.

"I suppose so," Admiral Rose said. "But --"

"I would rather fix this now, Admiral, then crash somewhere later. Or not be able to get away when an Atrian ship finds us."

"There are none this far inland."

"Yes, that's exactly what we thought when we headed for Windmere -- but there it was, coming up the mountainside to attack the train."

"You have a point, Mica," Rose agreed. She sipped tea and ate part of a sandwich. Mica said nothing more. Even though she had not given permission, he knew he had won the argument.

Rose watched him, so he drank his tea and ate his sandwich.

After the meal, she took him down to the engine room. Krogor's grunts made it plain the engineer was glad to see him. Mica promised not to do anything drastic, and in fact, Merriweather ended up doing most of the work at his direction. They made a good team, and after a few hours of testing connections and reworking gears, the ship did run better, if not at her best.

They had arrived at the suspect area around sunset. Too late, everyone agreed, to go flying around, or worse, hiking, to try and find the spiders.

Someone on the deck reported seeing a little movement just before they dropped anchor in an open field, but they couldn't be sure if it had been a spider or a deer. It did not come closer.

Greenwood assigned people to keep the watch all night and none of them for more than four hours out in the cold. If the spiders, or anything else, tried to climb up the anchor chains, everyone would notice the movement, but a guard would give them some extra warning.

The crew had pulled *Flash* down low to the ground so anyone in the area might not see them if they missed the ship flying in. Mica spent a few minutes after their light dinner (he was too used to big meals, he decided), to go watch the land. Merriweather stood with him. The night was cold with whispy clouds racing across the quarter moon. Wolves howled. The two of them soon went back in and Mica, at least, slept very well.

They were all up at dawn, sipping tea in the control deck,

and preparing for the journey into the hills. Rose had a map that showed the location of a few of the old mines in the area which was a much better idea than hiking all over. Mica didn't think he was up to any long walks. They moved from one area to another, Mica, Merriweather, and a few others going out to examine the locations.

It turned out easier to find the right set of mines than he had hoped. At the third mine, a guard checking the area before they flew off found something interesting near the northern line of trees.

"Same sort of tracks as we found down by the stream," Mica agreed as he knelt by the marks in the snow. "And I suspect this stream is the same one we crossed over last night. So, I'd say there are spiders in the area. This one probably came to the edge of the woods to check out the airship."

Probably not the way he should have worded it, and he realized as much when Admiral Rose helped him back to his feet and looked him in the face. Greenwood glanced around with a nervousness he never showed in the air.

"Are you telling me that these clockwork spider creatures have intelligence? That they can *spy* on us?" Admiral Rose demanded. She did not look away from him.

"Well, yes, there is that possibility," he admitted and wished this was one of those times that Merriweather could come to his rescue.

Rose let go of his arm and looked around the area, but not with the same worry that Greenwood showed. "At least that explains why your brother was so intent on getting you up here, even after he'd heard you'd been wounded. I have to tell you, boy, that I am not happy to learn this new aspect of the spiders."

"I'm not particularly happy to know it," Mica admitted. "But yes, there is a reason why Gregorian wanted *me* here enough to send an airship that might be much better used on shore patrol. I will tell you that the last group of spiders turned out to be less trouble than we expected, and even some help. These might be the same ones. I can't be certain yet."

"You did not build them," Greenwood dared to say.

"My father did."

Rose looked even less happy at that news.

They had no trouble following the path the clockwork spider left. Merriweather pointed out that it might be a trap, but that didn't stop her and Mica from going first. That seemed wise to Mica since he'd had some luck with controlling spiders in the past. Merriweather did take the time to explain how to kill the things -- or at least slow them down -- if they needed to.

"I've seen them pull themselves back together from anything but a shot to the headpiece," she warned.

"I want to go back up in the air now," Greenwood said. "Unless they can fly?"

"I'd like to say they can't, but then I didn't think they could swim, either," Mica pointed out.

They didn't ask any more question.

The countryside was covered in snow and so full of hillocks that Mica went up one side and slid down the other as often as he went straight. Merriweather tried to help, but there wasn't much use in it since she often slipped as well.

The clockwork spider's trail was plain though, and since they didn't know how far ahead the creatures might be, they went quietly.

Up another small incline --

And there was the mine, the opening still showing the timber used to shore up the rock and dirt. A spider stood just outside, the head twisting right and left, watching for the approach of something -- probably them.

It was not, he noted, like the others. This one was larger and the head more ornate. The metal glowed brighter, too, though that might have been because this one had not been sitting inside the walls of Raventower for decades.

Mica watched for a moment and then signaled the others to pull back. Merriweather kept her eye on the creature until the others were well back and then joined them. They huddled behind a huge pine and whispered.

Merriweather brought up the obvious point. "They aren't like the ones from the tower. I didn't expect another type."

"Neither did I," Mica agreed. He accepted a canteen from Greenwood and sipped, and then sputtered. It had not been water. "You could have warned me!"

Admiral Rose looked at her second with a raised eyebrow.

"For medicinal purposes, of course. Lord Raventower looked pale."

Rose laughed softly, took the canteen and sipped herself. So did Merriweather and Greenwood. If they passed it around a few times, would they all get brave enough to face the spiders?

"We are going to have to go into the mine," Mica warned. "He must be guarding something. And I want to know how many of them there are."

Admiral Rose, Greenwood, and the four others all loaded their flintlocks.

"I might be able to shut them down," he said as he stood again. "But be ready if I can't."

No one argued.

Mica and Merriweather walked straight to the opening. The spider held his ground, though his front legs raised in a sign of threat.

"Time will tell," Mica said.

The creature folded in its legs and the lights in the head went dark. Unfortunately, he was still right in the middle of the opening, and Mica couldn't decide if it was wise to try and move him. They had to sidle past the creature, Mica staying until last so that he might shut it down again if need be.

The spider remained dormant as he and Merriweather moved into the dark tunnel and the others followed. The light came from behind and below, and he could hear sounds ahead of them, the particular clicking noises he recognized.

In fact, when they came to an open area, they found spiders like the ones they'd left behind on the island by Headaway. Mica suspected they were, in fact, the same ones. There were also four other, larger creatures like the one at the door.

Mica looked back at the others. None of them were any happier than him. As much as he appreciated a good clockwork design, this --

Merriweather made a small sound of surprise. She was still staring at the spiders, of course. She would never have taken her eyes off them.

The spiders had been close together at first. Now the unnatural creatures began to move aside, and Mica saw what created the glow that lit the area. Lucky for him that Merriweather had hold of his arm because he had almost stood and headed straight for --

He knew it was an engine of some sort. Clockwork, of course, but so intricate, he could not take it all in. More than that, though, he realized that it was built entirely of sea metal. More than three yards wide and maybe seven yards long --the engine glowed with power.

He looked back at Merriweather. She only sighed and stood even before he did. She knew that he'd have to get closer to the device.

Spiders turned her way. Some of them clicked, but they did nothing unfriendly.

"The rest of you stay back," Mica warned His voice echoed through the tunnel.

No one argued. Merriweather, however, stayed with him.

Mica did not rush to the device. Though it did not appear to be connected to anything, that didn't mean it wasn't capable of doing *something*, and he didn't want to trigger it. Besides, Mica needed to know something important about the engine. A brush against the surface of one gear told him what he had already guessed.

"This one doesn't have a soul," he whispered to Merriweather. There was no reason to bring up that part about the spider-intelligence where the others could hear.

"Good. But what is it?" she dared ask. Her voice sounded remarkably steady. Merriweather only glanced at the engine, though. She was far more interested in the spiders who had pulled back and appeared all too polite, like servants standing at attention before their master.

Or just lining up to attack. Mica couldn't be certain which might be true.

"It's an engine of some sort," Mica explained, and loud enough for the others to hear now. Feeling more confident, he leaned close and stared into the heart of the machine. "Definitely my father's work again."

"I think they must have just put the device together recently," she said. "There are crates there to the side, and they don't look dusty."

He glanced the way she waved the flintlock. "Likely started after the spiders at the tower had gone to the island and put the submersible together. Then they came here and worked on this with their friends."

"Huh. But the spiders were shut down when we left."

"Dormant," he corrected. "They woke up again." He turned away from the engine and faced the group of creatures off to the right. "You know who I am."

"Yes," a few of them answered. Clearly spoke. Rose gave an odd sound, and he had to hope that she didn't simply shoot them.

"I want to take the engine away now. Can you build me a case for it?"

They went straight to work.

"Well damn," Rose said and even dared to come closer to them. "What is this all about?"

"I believe they have looked at the war and decided which side they are on," Merriweather answered. "Lord Raventower -- the previous Lord Raventower -- had been building things for the government to use in the war against Atria, remember. Even if they were a bit confused at the tower, they might have come to realize what is happening."

"You are assigning them human intelligence," Admiral Rose said. She frowned and looked at Mica. "Your ravens."

She had put that together. Mica gave a bow of his head in agreement.

"There were tales about your father before he was killed. I guess there was a reason the Atrians had him killed. Do you think you can trust his creations, though?"

He didn't correct her about the Atrian assassins. "I don't know, to be honest. But I can't leave the engine here. That is a hellish amount of power, Admiral Rose. I need to take it somewhere I can study the device and find out what we can use it for."

"Engine," one of the spiders said.

The answer still upset Admiral Rose, but Mica found it a relief. He'd have to talk to the creatures, but he'd do that after -- Oh, hell. He looked at Admiral Rose and prepared for what he feared was going to be a difficult argument.

"I need to take the engine," he said. She nodded agreement. "I need the spiders, too."

"That isn't going to happen--" she began and then stopped. She looked around the cavern. The spiders industriously worked at putting together a large crate. Mica thought some were attaching wheels, too. "Oh damn, Mica. I don't think --"

"I know. And for that reason, Merriweather and I will take the spiders and the engine and go somewhere else."

"You can't -- I can't -- hell." She stared at them for a while longer.

He said nothing more and went back to studying the engine. Lovely work. If he hooked it up to something, Mica had the feeling that it would be more powerful than anything this world had ever seen before.

"We can't take it back to the city, Lord Raventower," Merriweather said. The spiders were moving it into the case and were prepared to seal it closed.

"I thought to my tower -- ah, but how would I get it into my workshop? It won't fit down through the trap door and I doubt we could even get it up the staircase --"

"Not the city," Merriweather repeated. "There is too much of a chance that the Atrians would find out. Even with the spiders to protect it, I don't think we want to take that chance."

"You're right. But we can't stay here. The spiders have been spotted and it won't take long for others to move in, especially if they realize that *Flash* has been in the area. We'll have to head somewhere else. We don't dare go to my estate, right there by the Honorgate holdings. I'd say Windmere and Professor Blackwood, but we most likely wouldn't make it through the mountains in this weather. Maybe another mine, farther to the north? Southward? How far should we go --"

"I'll take you wherever you need to go," Admiral Rose said. She sighed. "I don't like them much, but you seem to have them in hand."

"I might not," Mica confessed. "But if we can find a place close by that you can drop us --"

"Not too close," she said. "And certainly not back at your estate."

"The island," Merriweather suggested. "The one off the coast of Headaway."

"Yes," he agreed. "The island is a good place for us to go. Get us close. We can get someone in the village to take us across if need be."

"We'll see how the weather stands," she said. Now that she'd made up her mind, the admiral was ready to move. "I suppose we better grab the ropes and start pulling --"

The spiders grabbed the ropes. Some pushed from behind.

"Well," she said, a bit more pleased.

They went out of the mine, the spiders doing the work, even awakening the guard with a tap on his head. Mica watched them and decided, by the time they reached the airship, that he could trust them.

The humans climbed up. Admiral Rose went to tell the rest of the crew about their unusual passengers. Greenwood stayed by the ladder and watched as the creatures climbed up, pulling the crate and engine behind them. Mica thought the man looked likely to kick them off in mid-flight once they were up really, really high.

"Down into the bay," Greenwood said with a sigh. There was barely enough room to move the crate on the deck.

Mica and Merriweather led the way down to the wider stairs. The bay was only one wall away from the *Flash's* engine, and he could hear Krogor working there, preparing to go again. Good. They had stayed here long enough already.

"Stay and guard the engine," he said to the spiders. "But do not kill anyone. Do you understand? Capture anyone who tries to get into the crate without me or Admiral Rose being here."

"Yes," a few of them said.

He had to trust them, he supposed. Unless he and Merriweather slept in the bay. It was cold and uncomfortable here. Mica wasn't ready to leave the room yet. He began to pry up the top of the case. A spider helped. He wondered if he ought to sit down and talk with them --

But the moment the top of the case came off, he was intrigued again. Merriweather said nothing. She had even sat down on the stairs, her lifeline still hooked into the pole. Probably wise. He almost fell when the ship shifted in the wind, but one of the spiders steadied him.

"Thank you."

"Welcome," the thing said, a swift bow and click of claws.

Damn. Too many interesting things going on.

They flew through most of the day then tied down on the back side of a hill during a brief snowstorm. Mica had been exhausted and aching by then, but he'd begun to understand the unique device they'd brought up from the mine. He found paper and drew some ideas of how to use it, but one that came to him most often was the one he dared not say aloud.

They flew through the next night and on the following early afternoon they reached the northern sea. They'd traveled wide to the west to avoid both the coal fields and the shoreline along the eastern coast, even though they had to skirt along another of the Honorgate lands. However, the weather remained cold and gray, and *Flash* kept to the lowest level of the clouds when possible. As they swept in around the islands, Mica finally pointing out a larger one that looked the most likely candidate for their last visit to the area.

"Let's make a thorough check before we leave you off here," Admiral Rose said. She frowned, and he suspected they might have a disagreement about Mica and Merriweather remaining behind.

Or they might argue about something else. Mica still debated if he should mention his singularly insane idea.

Rose went with them, and four guards down to the island and they climbed the precarious path that wound around the side. This rocky trail was not the same way they had gone before since they'd come in on the north edge of the island, but Merriweather pointed out where the other path intersected with this one. Before long they were down in the cavern.

"Damned cold, wet spot, Mica," Rose said as they stood on the edge of the rocky interior. He pointed out where the submersible had been docked, the chains and hooks still attached to the wall. Mica wished it were there now; he'd have had no trouble with what to do. "I don't know if this is wise, but we can't take the damned thing, and its guardians, back to the city. If anyone saw one of those spiders, Mica --"

"I know. It's all crazy." He ran a hand through his hair. "There's something --"

He stopped and shook his head.

"He wants to connect the engine to the controls for *Flash*," Merriweather said.

Mica turned to Merriweather, surprised by the statement. It was true, of course, but he hadn't said those words aloud. "How did you figure that out?" he asked while the Admiral sputtered and cursed.

"I saw your drawings. And I saw the way you looked at the wall between the bay and the engine room," she explained with a wave of her hand. "It was pretty obvious what you were thinking, at least to someone who has been around you for a while."

"That's insane!" Admiral Rose shouted. The word bounced around the cavern like an accusation.

Mica sighed. "You're right. Leave us here and --"

"Admiral, there is some old guy who just sailed from the mainland, ma'am," one of her people said, looking in on them with a bit of a frown.

"That'll be Ol' Foxlin," Merriweather replied.

"Yes, that's who he says he is."

"Please let him in," Mica replied. Admiral Rose nodded,

still too red-faced to speak. "We can arrange for supplies through him, Admiral. And a way back to the village. Once we get horses, we can ride back to Kamere, either with or without the engine, depending on what I believe I can do with it."

"Besides hook into *Flash's* system," Rose said.

He nodded.

The old man came into the cavern and chuckled at the sight of Mica and Merriweather, slapping them both on the shoulder. Mica managed not to show how much it hurt, but he was glad to see the man.

"Not surprised, I'm not," the man said with a bright smile. "Thought it must be ye' two what came back, being the only two with interest in this place. And ye' brought an airship this time. Wondrous thing, that, sitting there floating in the air like a bubble from a soap bath."

"Has there been anything going on here?" Mica asked.

"Not so we noticed, me lord," Ol' Foxlin replied. "Came over one day and saw the spiders be gone again, but we never seen them leave. Did you come lookin' for them?"

"No, I have them," he replied.

"Yes, thought you might. What will you do here, then?"

"We'll stay while he fits a new engine into my ship," Admiral Rose replied with a snarl. She lifted her hand before Mica could say anything. "No, you are right, my boy. As long as you don't blow up the ship, I'll be happy."

"I wouldn't do anything if I thought it would be a danger to the ship, Admiral Rose," he replied with a bow of his head.

"Admiral Rose!" Ol' Foxlin said with a start. "You be she? Truly? Why we never had such an important person here. And that be *Flash*, then? This is even more a wonder than I thought."

Admiral Rose seemed taken aback by the old man's sudden enthusiasm. Mica paid little attention. He had other matters to consider now. He spoke to Merriweather about them as they went back. It had been a useless hike, but the end result was good.

"My father did the design," he said as the two of them clambered over rocks, heading for the rope ladder. That was going to hurt again. Ol' Foxlin went with them and had an invitation to go aboard to see the ship. He'd be a legend when he got back to the village. "He created the engine to interface with a ship of some sort. Maybe an ocean-going craft, but the connections are much the same."

"What difference will it make from the regular engine?" she asked.

"Well, first of all, it won't need to be powered up. And it won't need any coal or wood to heat water. The engine will run without any input, which means it can go anywhere, Merriweather. It could sail beyond the seas and back."

"Ah."

"There are aspects of the machine that I don't understand," he admitted. "But the only way to know what it will do is to put it to work. Even if I tore the engine apart and put it back together again, I would only understand how it was built, but not what it can do."

"Do you think your father understood?" she asked. The airship was in sight. Ol' Foxlin was laughing with delight. A spry old man; Mica felt the ache in his shoulder.

"I don't know, Merriweather. There are times when I wish I could ask ... ask many things."

Mica climbed up the ladder, said good-bye to the old man, and left him in the care of Rose and Greenwood, both of whom seemed to enjoy the man's enthusiasm. Mica and Merriweather went straight to the bay. He began to strip more of the case from around the engine with the help of the spiders.

"You aren't going to move it?" Merriweather asked. She sat on the steps as usual, mostly out of the way.

"No. We're close to the ship's real engine, which we're not going to take out. I only want to bypass it for this test. I can't get started until she tells Krogor, though --"

Something hit the wall between them and the engine, and a moment later, the metal peeled away.

"I'd say they already had that discussion," Merriweather observed.

Krogor pushed his head in and nodded. He'd been over to look at the engine a couple times, but he'd said little. Now he gave a nod.

"Good," the man said. "Won't be much work."

Merriweather, who was used to the grunts and growls the man usually gave, looked suitably surprised and impressed by the words.

By the time Admiral Rose and her guest arrived, they had most of the wall down already. She didn't look happy, especially since the spiders were doing much of the work.

"We're going to fly over to the mainland and let Ol' Foxlin off there," she said, a bit of a smile on her lips despite the situation. "We can just use the sails for that. The winds are favorable."

Mica looked up from his work and gave a bright smile of his own. "It was good to see you again, friend. Maybe we'll have a chance to come to the inn again someday soon."

"Mayhap so," the man agreed. "But mostly you take care a' this war. I've no use for Atrians."

"We'll do our best. Thank you for being so vigilant."

The man bowed and moved away with the Admiral. She gave one last look of despair to her bay and engine room before she left.

"This had better work well," Mica said. "Or else she's going to be very upset."

Krogor grunted agreement.

The flight of the airship over the small straight to the

mainland would not have taken long, but Admiral Rose must have given the old man a slightly longer sight-seeing tour. Maybe she was looking for enemy craft, too. Mica paid no attention, though he was aware when the docked and he felt the old man go down the rope ladder. He thought someone else went too. They stayed there a bit before someone came back up.

Then back to the island.

Later Admiral Rose came into the room. They had the new engine stripped of the wood. Spiders and Merriweather were both crawling down into tight places and connecting cords and gears. None of them wore lifelines which had gotten tangled in the engine parts, but the weather seemed calm, and he hoped that they would not have any weather-related trouble.

"How long?" Admiral Rose asked.

"Tomorrow sometime," he answered and pulled back from work. His arm ached. He hadn't noticed until now. "We'll do a bit more of the connections tonight and then sleep for a while. I don't want to risk doing something stupid."

"And this is not stupid," Rose said with a shake of her head.

"This is a test," he said. "We have a bypass in place so that we can shunt the control back to the main engine at any time. I'll have that connected to a spot on the control deck, too. Torger will be here, and I will be on the deck. If either of us sees a problem, that person can shut down the new engine immediately."

"Good." She looked better about the idea. "Yes, that is good. Come away now, though. Dinner is ready. Then rest and go back to it afterward. I won't stand over you, Mica, and order what to do, but I expect you to take care."

"Dinner," he said and felt as though he didn't quite understand the word. Then the idea of food reached from his brain to his stomach. "Yes, that sounds wonderful. Thank you."

They ate up on the control deck. Greenwood still looked as uncertain as he had from the start, but he listened to what they had to say about the work that had been done. The bypass made him happy as well.

After a couple more hours of work, he and Merriweather went to their quarters. Mica took off his boots and laid down. So did Merriweather, though he thought she remained awake when he drifted back off.

He rested well since there was no trouble that night. The weather turned blustery the next day, though. This area got worse storms than in the south, and he hoped they could get away before anything worse hit. An ice storm would be more trouble than snow, coating the ship and weighing her down. He worked harder at connecting the new engine, but Mica thought they ought to use the old one and get back toward the southeast again, even if they risked being spotted by the enemy.

"Almost done," Krogor said with a shake of his head. "No use running now, me Lord."

"Oh, don't start that," Mica said with a shake of his head. "You were my commander long before I was Lord of Raventower."

"Not so long ago. You're not that old," the man said but grinned anyway. "Let's do the rest of this, Mica. Get it done. No use putting off the test, you know. I'd rather do it out over the ocean anyway."

"Ah. Good point," Mica agreed.

Krogor grunted.

They had everything hooked in before noon. Mica had run a narrow strip of metal up through the ship and into the control deck. He set up the bypass and tested it out. Admiral Rose stood over him and looked ready to do something daring.

"That's it," he said. He tapped the pole to the side of the room and got the return code from Krogor. "We are ready, Admiral. This might be rough. I suggest everyone settle inside."

That turned out to be one of the most important suggestions he'd ever made.

They used the main engine to pull away from the island, along the strait, and to the edge of the open sea. Mica, sitting beside Greenwood who piloted, nodded. Rose tapped the pole with the agreed code to switch engines.

The ship purred.

And then they *moved*.

Flash swept through clouds, over islands, out into the sea, and kept going. The gauges went off the scale as they gained speed. A soft, blue glow spread across the ship -- the same glow as he saw in sea metal -- and he thought the clouds sizzled into rain as they passed. He could even feel a little weight, as though the world pushed back at them.

The engine worked.

He used the bypass. They drifted to a slower speed but still moved forward.

"Well damn," Admiral Rose said. She sat back on her chair and looked at the rest of them. "That was more than I ever expected."

"The same," Mica said. He looked over to where Merriweather had taken a place on a bench. She grinned with delight. "I have no idea how fast we went. More than the gauges could read, and that also means I have no idea how far we went. I'll have to recalibrate everything, I think."

"Yes. We'll need to know. But damn, Mica -- we survived. Greenwood, turn us back to land if you would. I don't want to find us over Atria, which I fear might be far too close right now."

"Yes, good idea, Admiral," Greenwood agreed. He looked far happier than he had before the test flight.

The return was no less spectacular. Mica had an idea of how fast they traveled, but the only way to know for certain was to do a flight over land where they could tell by the map how fast they'd gone.

He checked the engine first, had some food, and then returned to the control deck. The others were ready to try again.

"There is our goal," Admiral Rose said with a tap of the map. "The village is almost 100 miles away. Under normal speed and with a good wind, we might make it in two hours."

Mica nodded. He had his watch out to time the voyage.

"I'm going to take us up so that we're just at the lower level of the clouds. They're relatively flat today," Greenwood said. "We shouldn't have trouble spotting our destination, especially since it is close to the foothills. If we find ourselves over the hills, we'll know we went too far. But being higher should keep us from being spotted -- and I really don't think we want anyone to see this."

"Yes," Admiral Rose agreed. "Take us up."

They drifted upwards, a leisurely little flight as they took their bearings with the map and compass. Rose nodded. Mica shunted the power back to the new engine.

They darted forward. The blue glow swept around the ship once more. Mica suspected that might be protection against the elements. They were moving very fast. He glanced at his watch every few moments as the minutes went by --

"Village in sight!" one of the women called out.

Mica hit the bypass. They began to slow.

"It can't be the village," Rose said. "We weren't traveling for long enough --"

"Close to one hundred miles an hour," Mica estimated. They slowed as they drifted over the foothills. "That is what I suspected."

"That's not possible. That's crazy," Rose said, but he could see a glint of joy in her eyes. "Do you know what this means? We can out fly anything, your lordship. We can go places and be back before anyone realizes."

"Oh, now there's a good point," Mica agreed. "As long as you can still use the regular engine in most cases, no one need suspect anything unusual. I trust that you have made certain of your crew, of course."

"Absolutely," she said. "Let's head closer to Kamere and then drop back to regular speed," she said. "People may hear rumors of a ship elsewhere, but if we play this right, they will not think it is us."

"I am going to work on the engine interface," Mica added. "We have an important tool here, Admiral. Used right, it might make all the difference in the war."

"Do what you can." She stood when Mica did and held out her hand. "Thank you, Lord Raventower. Thank you for all of us. You've given me hope of a faster end to this damned war. But you be careful. You have enemies -- and we need you."

CHAPTER FIFTEEN

Mica and Merriweather didn't leave *Flash* until early the next afternoon. They timed their ride back to the city to coincide with the changing of the army guards who arrived to keep watch by the Air Patrol's gate and along the road to the city. There was more cooperation between the two groups than usual, which Mica was glad to see.

He didn't think they fooled anyone by joining the group, but it did provide help if they ran into trouble. They did not. The wintry day seemed have sent everyone for cover again, and even when they reached the city, he didn't see many despite the hour.

"Worn down by the war, your lordship," one of the men explained when Mica said something. "Been quieter of late, and that's somewhat good. But it feels like the quiet before the demons leap up out of the land and destroy us all."

Some of the others nodded agreement. They rode together all the way through the gate and to the road that snaked up to the castle and the army camp beyond.

"I suppose I should go up and see Gregorian," Mica said with a slight frown.

"I don't think so, Lord Raventower," Merriweather replied

and surprised him with those words. "Chances are that he's not there anyway. But if he were there, he'd take one look at you and know you were seriously wounded. Chances are he wouldn't let you go home."

"Oh, excellent point, Captain Merriweather!" he replied and pulled the horse back when it tried to take the turn a few of the others were already heading.

"I've written a report to go to him," she said and handed the envelope over to a startled, and maybe amused, lieutenant. "Please deliver this to the General in person."

"Yes, Captain," the man said, saluted, and rode on. He looked back with a frown and stopped. "I'm sending four of the guards on with you."

"Thank you," she said.

Mica sighed slightly, though he did feel grateful that she'd stopped him from going to the castle. Gregorian, King Abertus -- even Seldon might not let him go again, and all Mica really wanted to do was reach home. Mica would not rest well except for there.

He had gotten out of the habit of watching for treachery while on *Flash*. Now he worried that they might find trouble anywhere along the road. He hated that feeling, but he saw it somewhat mirrored in Merriweather's face even as she glanced at the four who road with them, two ahead and two behind.

The ride through the city seemed to take longer than usual. He saw more damage and feared it had been done by locals rather than the enemy. Fools, he thought again. Just fools.

His spirits lifted when he finally spotted the tall, black hulking shape of his home, glimpsed past ugly factories that seemed to have inched even closer to Temple Square. A few people even wandered in and out of the temples, despite the snow.

Well, it was winter. Kamere had worse winters than this

some years, he knew. This one only seemed so horrible because of everything else that went with it.

Mica could not see the bay, even where there were breaks in the lines of buildings. The snow formed a curtain, and for a moment he feared the enemy would use that covering -- but no. The people of Sedina were ready for such a move.

Beyond the factory, they reached an area where the guards looked more nervous while he and Merriweather both relaxed. He found that dichotomy amusing. A few people shouted greetings, recognizing him even in the covering of his cloak. He happily returned the shouts and saw the guards look more confused. Mica would have thought he had a reputation for this sort of behavior by now. Even along here he found more damage, though. This was going to be a long and difficult war followed by an even more challenging recovery to erase all these wounds.

And the damned glowing woman stepped out of nowhere, crossing to his horse while Merriweather shouted for the others to just hold.

"I dare not interfere here again," she said. Mica had the urge to praise the gods, but he kept those words to himself. He watched her as she neared and realized that she was not entirely in this world again. Her hair moved, but not with the breeze that blew around them. A sort of fog seemed to envelop her, but the snow did not reach within that shell. "Listen," she said, her voice commanding. "Listen and do what must be done. Atric grows stronger."

She turned, walked into the shadows, and disappeared.

"Damn," Merriweather mumbled and started the horse on toward the tower, urging the soldiers to move as well. "Maybe that means we won't see her again."

"Maybe," he agreed. They passed by another set of buildings. Shadow Walk stood to the left, just ahead. "Bodies."

They found four bodies, newly fallen in the snow.

Merriweather sighed and left the horse in Mica's hands as she went over to investigate. "Feathers again."

"So, she killed them." Mica shifted uneasily and looked around. "They might have been waiting in the area for days, you know. Everyone would expect me to go this way."

"Which is why we have guards," Merriweather reminded him as she made a quick check of the bodies. "But these are Atrian Assassins. I've got the symbols."

He had seen her pulling them from the necks of the men and dropping them into her pouch. She came back to her horse and mounted.

"I'll send people to take the bodies to the General," she said. "I want the guards to stay with us the rest of the way."

Mica didn't argue. He could see the road to home from here, and Raventower stood over them, large and protective. He wanted within those walls, though he supposed that didn't mean he would be safe.

"There are two sides of this that bother me," Mica said as they rode on. "One, of course, is the continued attack by the Atrians. But the other is that our friend felt it was necessary to kill those men to make certain I survived. Why am I so important that the High Priestess of the Unknown Path feels she has to do something so strange to protect me?"

Merriweather didn't answer.

They reached the gate without incident, and went into the courtyard after an almost amusing pause because the men at the gate were new and actually didn't know Lord Raventower by sight.

Nyle came to their rescue.

"Open up, you fool. That's Lord Raventower himself!"

The guards quickly obeyed even before their commanding officer had arrived at a run. Merriweather directed the soldiers to take care of the bodies and left their four guards to say what had happened. Those four were still white-faced and all but trembling, so there was no use trying to hide it, he supposed.

Nyle walked them to the doors, smiling brightly. "Good to have you back home, both of you," he said. "It has been fair quiet here, your lordship. Except for the soldiers, but they're not a bad bunch. Some of them got a little out of hand, but your brother took care of that problem. The others are going to be happy to see you. We've all been right worried, hearing about trouble in the backcountry and all."

"There seemed to be less trouble in most places," Mica said. They stepped into the building, and he felt relaxed for the first time since he had left. "A few hot spots, I think, but mostly it was calm. I think the winter may be helping us there - -"

"Lord Raventower! Captain Merriweather!" Ada cried out in surprise.

For the next couple hours, they were plied with food, talk, and warmth in the kitchen. Mica could not hide from Ada and Gram that he had been ill. They fussed over him, which seemed sweet, but also confusing. He was grateful when Merriweather reminded him that they had better get some reports off to General Gregorian before he came looking for them.

They had a pleasant evening at the desk, though the ticking of the clock seemed louder than remembered. The messages went off with the guards, all of them carefully worded so they gave no secrets away about who stayed at the country estate or about what they'd found in the mine -- and how they'd used it.

Notes arrived Gregorian mid-morning of the next day.

So did Merriweather's mother. She at least had not brought a trunk full of cloth this time, though she did have rolls of lace across her arms. They had just been heading up to the workshop, and she followed, jabbering along without pause until Merriweather pointed out that she was listening for assassins.

The woman fell silent then until they reached the workshop. Tippet barked and still wore her ribbon. Mica saw Magina how noticed and smiled.

"Well, no trouble here, Jewel," Magina said with a bright laugh. "Good. Now what do you think of this lace --"

Gregorian's message simply asked for more details about some of the trouble they'd seen. Mica had not mentioned the sea metal engine in the notes he had sent the night before and he longed to talk to his brother about the find. However, he would not talk about it in something that might be intercepted and put *Flash* and her crew in even more danger. Besides, Mica expected his brother to arrive at any moment. Shipley had said the general had been coming by very nearly every day to look out over the bay.

Mica thought Merriweather ought to answer some of Gregorian's question, but she had not yet gotten free of her mother. He left those parts for her and glanced to where she kept guard. Her mother had the chair, and Merriweather was looking over a very fine piece of lace if Mica was any judge. Having grown up in the castle, he was not as uneducated about such things as others might believe.

"One last thing," Magina said. She'd said that several times already, but the tone of her voice this time drew Mica's attention. He looked over to find that she had gathered up the lace and had even stood at the edge of the steps. "I would like you both to come to my dinner gathering on the last day of the month."

Merriweather stared at her mother for a moment, shocked. Then she shook her head. "You are having a party during the war?" she finally asked.

"Not a party. We're having only a little gathering, mostly to share food and have one nice meal each month. It is important, you know, that we don't all feel as though there is nothing good left in the world. A tasty meal does a great deal to sooth nerves."

Merriweather nodded. She must have expected such an answer from her mother, but Mica found this to be a wonderful new dimension to the woman.

"It might not be a good time --"

"We eat early on those days. Four in the afternoon, so that people can head back home before too late. And if you mean it might be a bad time because the damned Atrians --"

"Mother!"

"I've said worse than that and I'll say it again. If you mean the damned Atrians might make trouble on that day, then we will not hold the gathering."

"I don't think --"

"Not many people have heard about your betrothal yet, Jewel," she said, and her voice softened slightly. "I'll only have one chance to have this show."

"Ah." Merriweather looked at him with a sigh.

"As long as everything appears to be calm, we should go," Mica offered. Merriweather nodded agreement, but from the look on her face, he thought she might be hoping for an actual invasion just to get out of the family gathering.

"Thank you both," Magina said and patted her daughter's arm. "I'll leave you now -- spider!"

Merriweather grabbed her pistol and threw open the case at her side, ready to load. Mica stood and crossed to be closer to the two so that his guard would not have to decide between protecting the two. He'd grabbed his sword.

He saw nothing. Then he noticed a little movement from ceiling to floor and gave a sigh of relief. "A real spider, Merriweather. Nothing to worry about."

He went to the desk and found a piece of paper, scooped the spider into it and carried the creature quickly over to the fireplace where it could scurry up between the rocks and into the chimney, a safe, relatively warm place during the winter.

He shook the spider towards the wall, but it leapt at him, bit his thumb and then leapt onto the wall like he had wanted anyway.

He yelped. "It bit me," he admitted and shook his thumb.

"Can I shoot it now?" Merriweather asked.

Magina laughed and headed down the stairs with her daughter, who clearly intended to see the woman back out of the tower.

"He's very kind, your young man," he heard Magina say. "Not many would try to save the spider, you know."

"He has a soft spot for spiders these days."

"Must be difficult since you apparently only want to kill them all."

The voices disappeared down the steps. Mica hadn't minded the visit, and even the idea of the dinner didn't bother him too much. He supposed it was a little thing to make someone happy.

He pulled over one of the half-finished insects and began to work with it, hoping Merriweather came back quickly. She did, but she was talking to someone. He sighed at the thought of more company until he realized the second voice was Gregorian.

"Mica," Gregorian greeted him. He looked tired. Mica imagined that was going to be a problem for a long time. "I'm glad you made it back. Honestly, though, you do seem to attract far too much trouble."

"Sit down. We need to talk."

"What did you find?" he asked, clearly seeing something in his brother's face. Mica had not thought he was that easy to read.

"We found spiders, of course. Some came from the island but also a few new ones. More than that, though, we found what they were working on. It is an engine, Gregorian. It is made entirely of sea metal --"

"Oh." That got his attention, and he sat up straighter again.

"No souls involved, unless they are so well hidden that I couldn't sense them. I don't think that's possible, though," Mica reassured him. "The design is clearly father's, but so complex that I dared not try to take it apart and see how it worked."

"What did you do with it?"

"We put it in the bay on *Flash*, along with the spiders who were more than cooperative."

"Good. Maybe we can find something to do with it." He looked at Mica. "What have you done?"

"We hooked it into *Flash's* system and used a bypass so we could switch from one engine to the other."

Gregorian stared at him as though he expected his brother to say it was a joke or something. Mica tilted his head and waited.

"That's insane. I knew I shouldn't trust you and Admiral Rose on the same mission. You two are crazy --"

"It is fast, Gregorian. Very fast. At least one hundred miles an hour and maybe more if we dared open it up all the way. I wasn't certain how much strain *Flash* could take, though."

Gregorian had stopped talking. He seemed to think through what Mica said before he spoke again. "How much can we trust this engine?"

"I don't know, but there was no sign of any trouble with it," Mica said. He sat back and tried not to wince as he moved his arm. His shoulder still ached. "I do intend to go back and do more tests, but we took the most important test right away."

"What can we do with it?" Gregorian asked. "Speed should be good for something --"

"If I may suggest?" Merriweather said.

"Of course. Stop being so formal," Gregorian said.

"I suggest we send *Flash*, by normal speed, inland again. Then use the second engine to curve quickly out over the sea and come in behind the Atrian fleet. We should be able to take down a ship or two and get away again. Do that a few times, and they'll believe we have far more airships than we do."

"Yes, that might work well," he agreed. He glanced at Mica and frowned --

"They are all fine, Gregorian," Mica said and even dared to pat his brother's hand. "The children are restless, but they always are in winter. When we left, they were going to move to the barn apartment for a while so that they could be with the kittens, puppies, and horses. They worry about you, though."

He gave a sigh of relief, as though he had thought there might be bad news. "And the Queen?"

"Honestly?" Merriweather said and smiled. "I think she likes being away from the castle for a while even in these circumstances. She's with her grandchildren, and they are not at court. You might have trouble getting all of them, including her, back in line after the war."

Gregorian laughed. He looked much better.

"Well, the news is not so good from here. We couldn't pin anything on Lord Honorgate, Mica. I'm sorry. We tried, but he claims not to have seen Payton and suggests you made that up, just to cause him trouble. Some of the other lords are wavering, even if they don't like him. So we let it go and have left him watched, but untouched."

"I had expected matters to go that way. And no sign of Payton himself, of course."

"A few sightings that may or may not be real. Nothing near Lord Honorgate again."

"We know that they're in contact," Mica said. He had no doubt of that part. "And I can't believe the two of them won't do something stupid again."

"True," Gregorian said and then sighed. "I have to get back, or someone will panic."

He stood and went to check the view from the roof. Mica didn't follow, and his brother didn't stay long there. Soon he came back and headed down the stairs. He looked far happier than when he had arrived.

Merriweather sat in her chair by the steps, but she gave him a nod. "That was more company than either of us needed. Can I get you anything? How is your arm?"

"My shoulder is sore," he admitted. "But it would be no matter what I do, and sitting here, pretending everything is normal, is helping me. I am glad we did not mention the injury to your mother or Gregorian."

"My mother might not have noticed. She hasn't seen you often. But I suspect you'll be seeing Seldon arrive not long after your brother gets back to the castle."

She was right, of course. Seldon came with the next changing of the guard, looked him over, gave him things to drink, and prepared to leave again with the guards going back to camp.

"I'd say you had a close call, Mica," Seldon reported. "But you had excellent care. Go easy for a while yet, though. Regain your strength. Well, if possible. I fear things are going to get out of hand again soon."

"I'll rest while I can," Mica promised.

The man nodded. He paused for a moment as though to say something more, but then he shook his head and went back down the steps. Mica felt sorry that everyone had to climb so far to find him -- but it did stop casual visitors from bothering them.

Ada brought dinner up to them that evening.

"No use you going down to the kitchen today, me lord," Ada said as she put the basket on the table. "You just take care and rest some. We want you well. We need you well."

Then she turned and left again before Mica could say anything.

The meal was lovely. Mica thought he would certainly put weight back on now that he was here, especially if his staff didn't allow him to do much more than sit at the desk and play with gears.

"You are lucky in your staff, Lord Raventower."

"Our staff," he said.

She blinked, then gave a little shrug. "Not quite yet, I don't think. Though if anything made me rush the wedding, it would be this food."

He laughed agreement. They talked about the engine, about the war, and for a while they even opened the shutters and looked out over the ocean as the sunset. Ships moved far out from the shore looking more ghostly than real at this distance. They reminded Mica, though, that they would not have calm for long.

CHAPTER SIXTEEN

They had two days of relative calm before a few skirmishes marked what Gregorian reported as the likely start of more serious trouble. The reports from Shipley had not been any better.

"I have to get back to my work," Mica said. He waved to the desk. "This is not it. I need to get back to *Flash*, Merriweather."

She frowned at first, but then she sighed and nodded. "I suppose you're right. Dress warmly."

He did. The day was breezy with light snow, but he didn't think the weather would get worse and he'd gotten somewhat used to the cold, even if he didn't like it.

When they came downstairs, Ada tried to talk him out of going but gave up quickly. "You both take care," she said as they put on their cloaks. "Take care and come back home quickly."

The worry on her face almost made him want to stay. He and Merriweather went out into the cold and rode away, once more with four guards to keep them company. Gregorian had given orders that they were not to leave Raventower without guards and even Merriweather knew better than to try and argue with them.

The streets appeared to be a little livelier today, though only a few people seemed sociable. Mica didn't blame them. It felt as though the trouble with the Atrians had already gone on forever.

That made Mica all the more intent on getting to the Air Field and back to work, not only on *Flash* but on any other ships that needed recalibration or new gears. Rose had sent him a single message since they got back and said all was well and to take care of himself. He suspected she was not going to be pleased to see him back, at least not at first.

The guards went with them all the way along the coast to the field. Mica did his best not to slouch or to show how his shoulder had started hurting worse with the bouncing. He knew that the wound was healing, and he could tell the difference from day to day. That did not make this ride any less annoying right now. He kept his temper in hand.

Besides, they could see down off the cliffs today and out to sea. Only a single ship stood out there at a distance. Closer, though, were the wrecks of several other craft that had washed up on the rocky shore below them. The sight of those battered pieces of wood and metal brought the war back to a larger picture for him. The battles were not just the city; the war reached out into the ocean and up and down the shore, where villages with little bays held off whatever the Atrians threw at them. Soldiers had spread out up and down the coast in a thin but vigilant line. There had even been a couple at Headaway, though they'd been helping at the coal fields during their brief flyover.

Mica stopped and studied a pile of wrecks. Some of the colors and shapes showed they were Sedinan ships, but most were from Atria. How much more could the enemy afford to lose on this coast, so far from home?

"Lord Raventower?" Merriweather said.

"My apologies," he replied. He turned the horse and rode on again, his mind troubled by both the waste of the war and the unreasonableness of the Atrians. The gate to the Air Field came into sight as they climbed the next rise. "There's been a lot more going on at sea than I had realized. I have a limited view from the windows in Raventower. It had mostly looked like a standoff from there."

"There have been more encounters the last ten days," one of the men offered. "While you were away."

Mica glanced at the sea again. "Preparing for something or are they getting desperate?"

"That's what we'd all like to know," the man answered.

"I'd been considering the war on land and ignoring the battle at sea," Mica said and thought about all those wrecks. "But this is just another reason why we need the airships."

The guards handed them over to the Sky Patrol who escorted them to *Flash*. Supplies and building materials were being handed up into the craft, and he could see work being done on the hull again. Reinforcement, he thought, which was probably a good idea.

Admiral Rose came out of the control deck just as Merriweather reached hooked into the lifeline. The older woman frowned and waved them into the room. Mica prepared himself. She had not been happy.

"You should not be here again so soon," she said before Merriweather had even gotten the door closed. "You need rest, Mica. I' not joking, boy. I will not be responsible for --"

"I am responsible for me," Mica said and kept his voice calm. He had already leaned over the controls and checked the changes they were making. "How are things looking?"

She sighed. "Sit down. I'll get Krogor, and we'll see if he can make words today."

Mica settled in the chair she indicated. Greenwood, the only other person in the room, gave them both a quick nod after she'd gone.

"I'm just as glad to have you back. There's not anything specifically wrong. Even the spiders are acting calm and all. However, you know how this works better than we do, and I don't want to mess anything up."

Krogor apparently felt the same way. They sat at the table and discussed the engine in more detail. Mica suggested some changes in the interface. They went down to take a look.

"Do you find this boring?" Rose asked. Mica turned and found she was talking to Merriweather. "I suppose for an army person --"

"I am Lord Raventower's guard," she replied. Then she unexpectedly smiled. "I am learning things I never knew existed. It's fascinating, you know. And I have found that I like flying, which shocks me. I was a 'feet on the ground' sort of person all my life. I wasn't even that fond of horses until lately."

"I'd rather be in the sky," Admiral Rose said. She glanced

upward as though she could see through the ship to the clouds above. "And Mica has given me a rare gift with this engine. The speed -- it still doesn't seem real, you know."

"I know. It will help us with the war, though."

"Tell Admiral Rose about your suggestion to Gregorian," Mica said. He had settled on the floor by the engine, a spider handing over parts.

Rose listened to the idea about circling around behind the Atrian fleet and hoping they thought there were more airships in the Sedina fleet. She sounded enthused afterward. Mica and Krogor got some work done, and Mica didn't even argue when Rose suggested he go back to the tower at a decent time.

Mica felt better as they rode away. Merriweather didn't say much on the return journey, letting him think through all the things he'd done on the ship, all the items Krogor had pointed out, and how helpful the spiders had been.

Merriweather hadn't threatened to shoot one of them, either.

For the next two days, Mica spent most of his time working with Rose on the ship. The rides to and from the tower seemed to be getting longer though, and a slight cold made him feel all the worse. If it didn't clear up either Rose or Merriweather wouldn't let him work anymore. Mica made certain he sat up straight in the saddle and coughed as little as possible.

He was not fooling Merriweather, though. He began to think she was as worried about his health as she was about assassins these days. When the weather looked bad on the third day, they stayed at the tower until it at least cleared up. That was his compromise, and she seemed to appreciate it.

They'd opened the shutter and looked out over the city just to make certain that there were no obvious signs of trouble today. Merriweather mapped out different ways to go when they saw fires or fighting. The day did look better. The temperature even rose a little above freezing. Though not enough to melt away everything, icicles began to appear on the edges of roofs where the snow had melted somewhat. The icicles, in turn, cast rainbow colors here and there and even the rubble didn't look so bad today.

"Time to go," Mica said as they pulled the shutters closed again.

His cold had mostly passed. He was tempted to stay, but --

They were heading out of the room when he heard an odd sound, like the whisper of his name, behind him. He looked back and then shook his head. It had been, he was certain, nothing more than the wind through the fireplace.

When he turned, though, he found Merriweather was staring as well.

"Did you hear something?" he asked.

"I thought -- like a distant voice," she admitted and looked at him as though she expected Mica to laugh at her.

"I thought I did as well," he said. That didn't reassure Merriweather at all. They both stood there for a little longer, but there was no other sound. He finally shook his head. "This is an old tower, you know. We've had quakes. It's bound to be a little unsettled -- and the truth is that if we're unsettled by odd sounds, we are probably never going to sleep again."

She laughed, looked once more around the room, and agreed. "We have work to do," she said. Merriweather headed down the stairs.

Mica followed but not before one last worried look at the room. The only sound now was the ticking of the clock.

Though the weather proved better during the ride, he was still happy to be climbing up onto *Flash* again. He noticed a group of people watching them, but they were too far away for even weapons, so he didn't worry. Merriweather had spotted them, and he heard her tell the guard to keep an eye on the group. Oddly, they did not protest that she was not one of them and couldn't give orders. Mica suspected they'd accepted her, and it wasn't even Admiral Rose's orders that made them listen. Merriweather had proven herself when she stood with them during this war.

"This way," Greenwood said, directing them to the control deck rather than the engine room. Mica feared that might mean trouble and he wasn't certain he was ready for something to go wrong.

Rose was on her knees at the controls, the board pulled out, many of the gauges unattached.

"We're trying to recalibrate for the new engine, Mica," Admiral

Rose said with a wave of her arm. She looked as though she might have been at work all night. "Krogor has gone from grunts to growls down there. Things are not quite working right."

Mica sat down on the floor by her. A few minutes later, he had taken over the job. The problem proved intriguing. It seemed that a direct link from the new engine to the controls made all the gauges go a little odd. Even sitting still, they read as though the craft was moving.

A few hours passed and Mica had a work around. The spiders made the pieces he needed, from bits of metal, and Merriweather even went to fetch them back to the control deck, so he wasn't going from one place to the other every few minutes.

"I know when anyone comes on the ship," Merriweather said when she volunteered. "And I trust you in the company of Admiral Rose and Lt. Greenwood."

They both smiled, and they all went back to work.

They had food where they sat. Mica even rubbed at his shoulder now that he'd crawled out from under the controls. A fine coating of dust covered his clothing, and he supposed his face and hair. Greenwood handed him a cloth, and he cleaned up before eating the bread, and cheese Merriweather passed to him.

"I almost have it," he assured them all. "I'm happy to see how well it is working, in fact. I thought it might take several tries before I could find the right model. There is an extension of power the engine always puts out, and I needed to --"

"Eat your food, Mica," Admiral Rose said.

He grinned and did as she said. It wasn't long before they were back to work and they finished just after sunset.

"We should take the ship out for a test," he said as he tapped the gauges. "Yes, now Admiral. In the dark -- that is the best disguise we'll have for the craft, you know. No lights. Head inland at a regular pace. Maybe even appear to have some problems. Then we'll head out to sea with the new engine."

Rose frowned. "I shouldn't make decisions like this when I haven't slept much in the last two days."

"Yes, you're right," Mica said and gave a bow of his head. "Merriweather and I will head back to the tower and maybe tomorrow --"

"Oh, sit down. We might as well take her out. I'll send the message off."

Greenwood cleaned up the area while she was gone. A few of the crew came in to sit the gauges. Mica talked to them about what to expect. and when Admiral Rose returned, she was clearly happy to see everyone ready for the test flight.

"Greenwood, you take the piloting controls," she said. Mica had expected her to take the spot, but she sat back in the command chair where she could watch everything. "We'll ease out and head due west. Make it look a bit rough, Greenwood. I've warned the others."

"Excellent," the man answered.

Restraining chains let go of *Flash* and they soon began to move off over the field. Greenwood added a couple lurches from the craft as they slipped away into the night.

"Running lights down fifty percent," she ordered after they'd been a few minutes in the air. "That should make anyone think we are slipping out of range."

Mica thought the readings looked good. They'd all hooked back into the lifeline now that they were in flight, and he stood over the controls, just out of reach, but watching them carefully. Merriweather kept out of the way, though she looked as excited as the rest of them.

They went out over the land for almost an hour, running dark, and the ship coasting along mostly on the sails rather than either engine. Farms and small villages dotted the area, and he suspected they might be seen by a few, but they'd only have to say they had trouble with the lighting.

Admiral Rose ordered the ship turned.

"I suggest you drop the sails as well," Mica said. They were far out over a huge lake that seemed to be mostly ice now. He could not even see a faint light of a cabin. This was an excellent place to make the transition, especially on such a cloudy night with very little moonlight.

"Sails down," she ordered, and it was relayed via the tapping of pipes that resounded through the ship. "Anything else you want to say, Lord Raventower?"

"I'm torn between good luck, and this is insane."

The others laughed. The message came back indicating the sails had been lowered. Admiral Rose sat back in her seat and looked over the gauges one last time before she nodded. "Transition and head for the sea."

Greenwood twisted the bypass controls himself, but he quickly had both hands back on the wheel. *Flash* moved with an even sweep from almost standing still to a rush out over the land that won cries of surprise yet again. Mica didn't think they would ever get used to it.

They'd swept northeastward and then curved back toward the land. Moving this fast did make spotting things difficult, but a cluster of small rocky islands let them know they were close to land again.

They turned, maybe too fast. The craft bounced somewhat, dipped toward the ocean, and then straightened as Greenwood got them back into control.

"Back to the normal engine or we'll overfly them," Rose ordered.

They cut back and slowed. It was a rougher transition. Mica studied the gauges and made mental notes on what they would need to change for this to work better.

"I thought we were going to be sailing home on the ocean for a moment there," Greenwood admitted.

"I had faith you'd keep us up. I know how much you hate the ocean," Admiral Rose replied.

"There is that point."

"Prepare weapons. Scan for ships. Make damned certain they aren't Sedina craft before we fire."

Mica stepped back and sat down. This part was out of his hands, and he had other matters to consider. "We need to disguise the ship in some way," he said. "*Flash* is too obvious, I think. But we can make just a few props to stick out from the rear when we come off the sea metal engine. Maybe sails in a different configuration and color?"

"Yes," Admiral Rose agreed, though her eyes never left the

view before them. "We might even rig up lighting that will make the ship appear to be a different color."

"Yes --"

"Ship seventeen degrees off the bow. Atrian configuration confirmed."

"None of our ships are trying to infiltrate the Atrian fleet, are they?" Merriweather asked.

"No," Rose said. "I was at a meeting where we discussed that possibility, and there was nowhere we could have the ships redesigned to Atrian standards that they wouldn't see the work done."

"Good," Mica said. His heartbeat was up though. He did not like war. "They will notice us soon, even without lights."

Flash sped onward using the original engine. He saw weapons come online. They were mostly cannons, like those up on the top of Raventower, though not with as much force as could build up in the pipes in the building. There were also people outside on the deck now, ready with bombs to drop as they came over the ship.

"Fire when ready," Admiral Rose said. Her voice had gone softer, too. Mica knew she didn't like war any better than he did.

Mica held his breath.

The first bombardment from the steam cannons hit square in their sails. Mica saw the main mast topple and fire kick up in a sudden surge. They had probably penetrated to the engine then, or maybe a cargo of oil. *Flash* sailed over the top, the fire almost high enough to hit them. More bombs dropped, and by the time *Flash* made a wide turn and came back, the ship had already started to go down.

"Second ship, ten degrees starboard," the woman at the controls warned. "We've been spotted."

"Take her. Prepare for a second attack," Rose said, and she sat forward a little, both hands tight against the arms of the chair. "I had hoped for a single ship, taken down with no one to say how it was done. If someone can name us as *Flash*, though, I don't think we'll survive long on the grounds even with a thousand troops around us. They'll know we shouldn't be here and that there is something special about the ship."

Mica agreed, although going after a second ship that had already spotted them was not going to be easy. That ship would have their own cannons aiming by now. Greenwood, his hands tight on the controls, headed straight in, despite the danger. Mica glanced at Merriweather and saw the frown on her face, though she said nothing.

"Fire when ready," Rose said, though he suspected those words really weren't needed. *Flash* had a crew that knew exactly what to do –

The ship gave a little shudder.

"Glancing blow," the man to the right said. He tapped a pole, got an answer in return. "Some splintering on the starboard hull."

"Thank you," Greenwood muttered. He did seem to mean those words and Mica knew why, though Merriweather still frowned.

"He has an idea of how the cannon is placed and the direction of fire," he explained, sitting back with her since he could do nothing now. "The cannon on ships aren't always placed in the same locations, and they're hard to spot, even when they let out steam. If you look, you can see they vented the steam in several locations. That's to throw us off --"

Another little shudder.

"Better weapons man than usual," Greenwood acknowledged. "Circling now."

And they did. *Flash* dipped low and turned. Weapons fired from their craft and Mica assumed more bombs were dropped from the deck. They swept low enough to see flintlocks fire from the enemy deck.

A moment later they were past the ship, and things began to explode behind them. Greenwood pulled them up on a steep incline, but something pinged against the craft. They went up though, and the ship below them became engulfed in flames and sea water, going down even faster than the first one.

Mica listened to the reports tapped out on the poles. Someone from the deck came in, her arm cradled against her chest and bleeding, though she gave a quick nod and looked steady.

"We lost Quaris and Drake off the deck, Admiral," she said. "Part of the lifeline system took a hit, and they lost hold. Quaris was already shot and might have been dead. Drake grabbed a bomb as he fell."

"I'm sorry for the loss," Admiral Rose said and meant those words. The others bowed their heads for a moment. "Get us clear of here, Greenwood. Fast."

They switched back to the sea metal engine and shot out over the ocean, circled back to land and all the way to the lake. Once there they settled in for some quick repairs to the hull to make the damage less apparent.

"The engine ran a little hot on the return voyage," Mica pointed out. "I'll look into some sort of cooling system. She ran well, though, Admiral. I'm sorry for the loss of the crew, though. I had hoped --"

"This is war, Lord Raventower," Admiral Rose said and touched his arm, drawing his attention back to her. "They are not the first we've lost since this trouble began. However, we just took out two good sized Atrian ships, you know. I can't say their lives were worth the win, but at least they didn't die for nothing."

"We'll get the ship working better," Mica promised. "I want this to work well, Admiral Rose. I want this war to end soon."

"As do we all. I suspect even the Atrians are ready for it to end, and I keep hoping they'll turn back home soon."

They spent a couple hours working on the ship's hull. Mica had gone back to the engine room and talked to Krogor about a cooling system. He wasn't certain how much the spiders understood. They had taken to simply latching on to the wall and waiting for orders. He found them fascinating but frightening too. Were they all the souls of men condemned to death for some crime? Could he really trust them?

Mica didn't dare think that way. The spiders were helping, and they'd be damned difficult to get rid of if they changed their mind. He had discussed this problem with Admiral Rose, of course. She'd watched them for a few days and finally had said it was a chance she would take.

But her people knew where to shoot if they needed to.

They made it back to the Air Field a couple hours before sunrise. Mica fiddled with things until the sun came up and then he and Merriweather rode away as though nothing important had happened.

Days might pass before the Atrians realized that two of their ships were gone. Rose might take the craft out again before then. Mica could not always be with them, and he had to let the crew handle *Flash* themselves. He'd done as much as he could to make it work properly.

At the gate leading back to the cliffside road, he looked back to where *Flash* sat in her cradle, the crew working on the hull and deck again. She looked small and almost helpless there.

He smiled as they rode away.

CHAPTER SEVENTEEN

T he next day they noted more trouble in town than there had been lately. Merriweather didn't even have to tell him that this was not the day to go back to *Flash*. Besides, he was glad to stay in his workshop again. Even making little insects felt good. He even began work on a pocket watch, the intricate design taking his mind away from all else for a little while.

Shipley came and sat with them for lunch that day. He was glad to see the boy who looked as though he'd been spending a lot of time outside, his face wind-burned and wild. Even Bear looked a little more wooly than usual.

"I gave some information to the General," Shipley said. The boy sounded calm at those words, which shouldn't have surprised Mica. He remembered how wary the boy had been of General Gregorian before the war, though. "It's got bad out there, me lord. I lost two friends this week. I think they was just stupid, but it hits bad."

"It does," Merriweather agreed. "I'm sorry to hear of your loss. Stupid or not, they did not ask for this war."

"True, true." The boy had shredded a piece of bread before he began eating it. Apparently, this was starting to wear on him. "I won't take Bear out with me these days, you know. It's too dangerous for him because he don't like no one to get angry at me. Besides, he marks me. Everyone knows about me and a big dog working for you."

"I'm sorry," Mica said.

"No, no. That's not so bad, you know. We has our chance to help, and that's good. I don't want Bear hurt, neither. I'm glad to leave him here. Ada and Gram have to bribe him with bones, though. They laugh. I think Bear likes it a bit. He enjoys the snow, and we go out together some days, but if I'm heading for trouble and know it, best to leave him here."

The boy was probably wise. Mica didn't like that he went out there to face danger, but Shipley knew how to handle himself. He wouldn't second-guess the boy, and he certainly wouldn't order him to stay in the tower and be safe -- even if he thought it would be safe here.

Mica went back to work -- and received an unexpected message. This one came under the King's seal, and for a moment he feared something had happened to Gregorian. Even Merriweather had paled and stood over his shoulder as he opened up --

"Ah," he said and put the paper down. His hand was trembling. "He's called a Council of Lords. I suppose I should have expected this sooner or later."

"Immediately," Merriweather said and brushed at her clothing. "You had better dress for the occasion, Lord Raventower. You'll want to make a good impression."

"Probably a waste of time," he said as he stood. "But you are right. I'd like to take Kandris and the carriage, but we'd probably end up with bombs again before we got there. And as much as I'd like an excuse not to attend, that might be too heavy-handed."

Mica dressed quickly in a good suit, but not the best since he'd be riding the horse. He was still thinner, and his shoulder ached if he moved it too much, but Mica didn't have any real trouble with it. Merriweather stood in the hall when he came out. She'd cleaned up as well and wore her dress uniform.

"You won't be able to come into the council with me -- well not right with me," he said as they went downstairs. Merriweather had already run down and ordered horses. They were waiting in the falling snow. "You can stand with the others in the gallery, though."

"Yes, that might be best," she agreed. "I will believe that no one will try to kill you there."

"Lord Honorgate will be attending, you know."

"True. Well, I'll keep an eye on him."

They rode quickly through town. Mica feared he had gotten too used to the ruins because he hardly glanced at them today. What had prompted the King to call this sudden meeting? Had something gone wrong? Nothing had happened in Kamere, but there could have been incursions elsewhere. They'd been beaten back before, but that didn't mean they would always win.

There was no use trying to guess what trouble necessitated this meeting. Mica and Merriweather rode in silence, though she seemed to twitch at every sound. No one tried to kill him, though, so he still didn't have an excuse not to attend.

The castle grounds were a mess, the snow churned into icy mud, the tents and huts looking worse than they had before. People moved sullenly out of the way, though a few, seeing it was him, did greet Mica with some pleasure. They had food, at least. King Abertus had opened the stores, but they would not last for long.

Mica parted with Merriweather at the door to the council chambers where other soldiers greeted her. He slipped away and tried not to feel odd that she wasn't at his back this time. This was clearly not a place devoid of enemies. Lord Honorgate already sat at his chair across the table, and Mica couldn't guess if his face was red from anger or drink.

The others hadn't had as far to ride, most of them having been at their city estates. Mica arrived last, and he expected some fuss over it, but before anyone could say anything, King Abertus and Prince Gregorian entered the room.

"Thank you for your prompt arrival," the King said and signaled them to sit.

Gregorian stood by the King's chair playing the part of a guard. He had taken to standing there since he married the princess, and no one had taken much note of it. Now, however, Mica saw how many of the Lords and Ladies looked from Gregorian to Mica -- and a few to Honorgate. Mica also noted the half dozen empty chairs of Lords who were not in the city, and he hoped that meant they only saw to the care of their lands. Two of them were coastal lords, and they would have their hands full.

"I will not keep you long," the King said. He looked tired and worn -- more so than many of the others. Honorgate certainly didn't look as though he'd missed a day's sleep or a meal for that matter. "We must talk about the possibility that our allies will not be able to help us."

"You've had word from the south?" Lord Chimso asked. They were free to speak here in council. Unlike other Kings in the past, Abertus did want to hear their ideas.

"Some word and none of it good. General Gregorian?"

Gregorian bowed his head and took over that part of the conversation. Mica knew much of what he said already since he and his brother talked often. He took that time to watch the others, though he did not stare. It had not occurred to him until now that some of these people might be in league with Honorgate. Mica had so little contact with them that he never thought --

Ah, but Gregorian did have that contact, living here at the castle. If the general mistrusted someone, he would have told Mica already.

"Prince Kistrin has gone to the south," the King said when Gregorian finished outlining the few facts they knew about battles along the southern border and trouble that might be related to their own Atrian invasion. "So far there is no word back from him. We have reached out to some of our other allies, but I fear nothing will come from those areas, either."

"What can we do?" Lady Vosetin asked with a worried shake of her silver-haired head.

"We are gathering more troops from the hinterlands and the mountains of Sedina," Gregorian explained and at least tried not to look as though he wanted to do something else. Mica knew that Council meetings were not his brother's favorite pastimes. "They are coming from the outer areas, even through the snow. This has allowed us to reinforce the fishing villages. Those fine communities did well to hold off the enemy this long, but they are losing too many people in the battles. We'll have trouble if the Atrians are reinforced and try to land somewhere outside of Kamere. And if they come for Kamere, we'll have trouble enough holding them back as well."

"You are saying, essentially, that we need more help," Lady Vosetin said. She looked troubled. "And there is nowhere to find it, is there?"

"There is still help we might get," the King said. "And that is why I've called you here rather than simply send you reports on the status of the war. We may have to buy mercenaries from Argine and farther south. They will not come cheaply, you understand. There is a war down there as well, and the mercenaries are going to be able to pick whomever they want to serve."

Lords and Ladies moved uneasily in their chairs. They knew how this was going to go. Mica sat back and began to make a few calculations of his own.

"I don't know what the damned Atrians want here," Lord Tulane snarled. "They've no reason to be here!"

"They want a richer land than their own," Mica answered and thought about the situation. "Besides, this is the land of their ancestors. I would not be surprised to find out they believe this land should be theirs by right. That's often a good excuse for war."

Some of the others mumbled agreement, and no one brought up the god of war.

Lord Honorgate leaned forward, though. His eyes narrowed as he stared at Mica. "You are a fool, boy. Do you really think this war is that simple?"

"Of course not, " he replied and did not lose his own temper, though he saw Honorgate inched closer to being enraged. Mica had done his best not to address the man at all, but he realized this conversation was inevitable. "I'm certain there are many intertwined matters involved in something this momentous and more than a sudden longing for ancestral lands. If you have other things to add, please do tell us. I'm sure we'd all like to know."

The man came half out of his seat before Lady Pelgin caught his arm. He dropped back down with a snarl and leaned over the table toward Mica who really didn't know what had set the man off this time. Mica often didn't understand people, but from the looks of others around the table, no one else understood Honorgate's reaction this time.

"How dare you," the man hissed. "How dare you accuse me of

--"

"Of what?" Mica demanded, interrupting the man before he got going. Mica had listened to enough of Honorgate's tirades in the past. "Of knowing something that I don't? Perhaps you have studied the history from five hundred years ago better than I have. Maybe you've heard more things here in the city since I have not been around much of late. I would be happy to hear what you have to say, Lord Honorgate. I would be glad to listen to anyone with answers that might help."

The man began to sputter, cursing beneath his breath, but loud enough for the others to hear.

"No matter," King Abertus said and drew silence, even from Honorgate this time. Mica wondered why he had let the confrontation go on so long, except that it did put Lord Honorgate in an unpleasant light. "The past link between Sedina and Atria is not our problem right now, even if that might be the reason for our current troubles. Back to the matter at hand: we are going to need funds to buy mercenaries, my lords and ladies. I am *requesting* donations. If they are not adequate, I will *require* the nobility to add funds later, and some of you may not like to find how I assess what you give then if you do not give now."

Blackmail, Mica thought. He almost smiled. "I'll pledge ten thousand gold crowns," he said. The others looked at him, shocked. Did no one remember that he was rich?

The others added their pledges, though none as high as his. Even Honorgate added his own amount, though Mica suspected they'd be hard pressed to get anything of him. No matter. They all signed and sealed their donations, and the paper was finished with the King's own seal.

"I will not keep you," King Abertus said and stood. The others rose hastily. "Let us hope the war ends soon and we do not need to hire the mercenaries."

Everyone nodded agreement.

Honorgate was the first to leave, but not without a snarling curse at Mica before he headed out the door. That won looks from the others -- most often the sorts of looks parents gave after their child has been rude. Mica wondered if they would lecture him.

Mica wanted to have a word with Gregorian, but he realized he didn't want to be obvious about taking his brother aside for a private talk. Though he despised the usual political games that were played here at court, he did know the basics of what not to do. He had wanted to tell his brother about sinking the two ships, but obviously not in front of everyone else.

At least not in front of Honorgate.

He sighed and headed out of the room, not at all surprised to find Merriweather waiting for him at the door.

"I saw Lord Honorgate leave. He went out alone, and I can't say there was anyone who looked particularly ready to follow him. He was a bit angry."

"You saw what happened."

"Oh yes. He was ready for any excuse to have a go at you, Lord Raventower." She shook her head and stopped before they exited the hall into the main part of the castle.

The place looked busy as Lords and Ladies gathered their people, palace staff rushed about, and dozens of priests and priestesses added to the chaos. Merriweather stopped and shook her head.

"We have to be brave, Merriweather. Though I had hoped to have a few moments with Gregorian." He looked back over his shoulder. Gregorian talked to General Dohark, an ancient man who mumbled and repeated everything three times. He still held the title of General only out of a kindness and because, in his day, he'd been a formidable leader. Gregorian always tried to be polite to the man, but this clearly was not the day for him to listen. Even as Mica watched, though, a few more people crowded in to take his time.

"I think we need to rescue him," Merriweather said. "No, not directly. You'd only annoy everyone if you went in and drew him out. Let's be a bit more cunning in this, Lord Raventower."

"You've spent a lot of time at court," he said.

"Oh yes. I know how to handle things. Tidgren!"

The tall soldier spun around at the sound of his name and hurried towards them.

"Your Lordship," he said with a bow and gave Merriweather a curious look. "You want something."

"Go tell General Gregorian that someone is waiting for him at his office and needs to talk to him right now."

Tidgren ran a hand over his shaved head and then gave a decisive nod. "Only for you, Merriweather. Besides, the general is likely to reward me for saving him from that mob."

Tidgren walked away. Merriweather waited a moment and then signaled Mica to come with her. They did not head straight for Gregorian's office, though.

"We don't want to be that obvious. Look at Lady Pelgin. She's watching us," Merriweather said with a slight snarl. "I don't think she noted what Tidgren is doing, though."

"Do you think she's working with Honorgate?"

"I don't know. I don't trust any of them," Merriweather admitted.

Mica wanted to say that was a rather harsh attitude to take towards the nobility, but he realized that wasn't what she meant. Merriweather didn't trust anyone.

Mica had made his way towards a hall that would have taken them to the archives, and Lady Pelgin lost interest in them. Mica supposed they never considered that Gregorian would have a way to his office that would not take him out into the public areas.

The guards at the private hall started to move to stop them, then stepped aside in haste without even a question of what they were doing. Mica wanted to believe that they were so quick because they recognized a Lord coming their way, but he rather suspected that they didn't want to deal with Merriweather.

As they approached, yet another guard gave a quick knock on the door and opened it so they could go quickly into the office.

"Ah, it is you," Gregorian said and looked relieved. "I had hoped so. *Flash* went out last night. Any news?"

Mica and Merriweather took the chairs in front of the desk. Mica had thought to make this quick, but he didn't suppose it would hurt for his brother to take a few minutes to sit down and hear something that he supposed was going to make him happy.

"Two ships," Gregorian repeated at the end of the tale. He had sat forward and looked from Mica to Merriweather. "You are telling me that you took out two ships so far out at sea that we haven't even heard about them yet."

"Somewhere southwest of the Rock Pile," Merriweather replied, giving the common name for the mass of small islands they'd used as a reference point.

"We might have gone looking for more, but the new engine began overheating, and I didn't want to risk having a problem," Mica added. "I'm trying to design a cooling system, but I don't know if I can test it in time --"

"Two ships," Gregorian repeated and sat back. "I had my doubts about the use of this engine, you know. I couldn't imagine the speed."

"It is -- incredible," Merriweather said. "But I don't suggest you take a flight until after the war, General. I don't trust it much either, but I was able to see what it can do now."

"I did not want to mention this anywhere there was a chance news could get back to Lord Honorgate," Mica added. "You are the better one to tell the King. If I went, I would only draw attention, and I suspect that a technical explanation will have to wait since even I don't understand how the engine works. That study won't happen until after the war. What should I know about the trouble?"

"We had another invasion yesterday, halfway up the coast at Fintail --"

"Damn. Nice people there," Mica said with a shake of his head.

"Good people. They did their duty with the army and beat the Atrians back. The trouble to the south might be worse, but we are hoping that Argine will be able to keep that war confined and little of it will spill over into Sedina. It does present a problem, though. As the King said, mercenaries are going to go at a premium. Prince Kistrin and his private guards are there more to map out the possibilities rather than hire anyone just yet. We're holding our own, but we want the option handled if we need it."

Mica nodded and shifted slightly. He figured he might as well approach what might be a more delicate to discuss than the enemies.

"How low is the treasury?" he finally asked.

Gregorian gave a quick smile. "Not as empty and the King implied. Most of it has been shipped inland and hidden, to be honest. We will use it as needed."

"Then why this?" Mica asked, confused by the reason for the Council Meeting.

"Because many of the lords were already arranging to leave the country -- yes, the country, not simply to go hide in their estates. Only those directly involved in the war already were allowed to stay on their estates, along with a couple of the older nobles. You wouldn't have heard since you live here. Of course, there are complaints every time you leave Kamere. They do watch you."

"I can imagine."

"The King let it be known that you are working specifically for the crown. No, I didn't tell you about all the pettiness that has been going on at the castle. You'd be bored."

"The call for funds was to get the Lords involved," Mica said.

"Right. They've contributed their quota in soldiers, of course. Most of them have shipped in grain from their estates to help feed the army and the city. However, many of them would rather leave the unpleasantness, as Lady Pelgin calls it, and come back when civilization returns."

"Are they helping by being here?" Mica asked.

"No. And the King agrees. He won't let them leave the country, but he has made arrangement for most to go to their estates if matters turn worse. We know they will fight for their individual lands if they find themselves besieged there."

Mica agreed though that would mean the country itself would have no united front. He could see the problem, though. Even though they'd already had a long war with Atria, the battles had rarely touched their shores and never devastated Kamere to this degree. They simply were not prepared for it.

"We should have some quiet," Gregorian said. His finger began to trace spots on the map laid out on his desk. "We've held them out of Kamere and this is where they most want to be. Finding a landing somewhere and battling their way up and down the coast and through the land? No, they don't have that kind of resources. We have held them out of the coal fields, but they have more massive fields of their own. They're trying to stop us from getting shipments out, but that's mostly just to inconvenience us."

"Can the city hold out?"

"We have wood for heat, at least," he said with a sigh. "The Atrians would have done better by not destroying so many of the buildings. We are building a new train line that heads west from the fields and hooks up with the one to the mountains so that we can bring coal from that direction rather than straight down the coast. That line should have been built years ago. It goes through Honorgate land, and he is not daring to complain this time."

"Can it be trusted through his land?" Merriweather asked.

"No. But we will have troops to travel on every train," Gregorian said with a snarl. "We're taking what precautions we can, and we'll cut through the least amount of his land that we dare. I will be quite happy when we can remove the bastard from power and not have to worry about him any longer."

"What can I do?" Mica asked.

"Learn how best to use that engine. See if you can salvage the submersible and find a way to use it. Find out why assassins are trying to kill you," Gregorian said. He stopped and looked his brother fully in the face. "*Don't get killed.*"

CHAPTER EIGHTEEN

The weather grew marginally better over the next few days, though no one trusted it to stay that way. The sun melted some of the snow, which would have been nicer if the snow melt hadn't congealed into slabs of ice each night. They had no new attacks and news of two Atrian ships sinking out at sea did improve tempers in the city.

During the better weather, Mica tried sending his ravens out to scout the ocean for sign of other Atrian ships. They had no luck, and the sudden onset of bad weather proved too difficult for them to fly. Best to keep his ravens close, Mica had finally decided, and to use them to reach Gregorian. They could fly to the castle even in bad weather, but only because there were places to land and rest along the way, and to beat the ice off their wings.

The Atrian craft continued to sail near the bay, while the Sedina fleet had been pulled down south. They prepared for an assault, but waited for the best chance to win. A few of the smaller Sedina ships darted in and out of the bay -- daring sailors -- and kept the Atrians from gathering in force. The Sedina airships did their part as well, and the airship battles were often spectacular.

Merriweather stood by the window looking out at the city and the corner of the bay. She sighed.

"No invasion?"

"No, Lord Raventower."

"Then I suppose we had better prepare to leave," he said and forced himself to stand and step away from the desk. He pulled the lid down over his work. "I'll go change into something more suitable."

"I will not."

"I hadn't expected you to," he said with a bright smile.

They went to their suites, and Mica quickly changed having already arranged the clothing. The idea of a dinner gathering left him uneasy. He'd never been sociable, but he supposed there was no harm in doing something nice for Magina. Even Merriweather had agreed this was a little thing.

She'd gotten into her better uniform. Mica had suggested she wear her medals, but she'd laughed. "They wouldn't know what they meant anyway," Merriweather said as they went down the stairs. "I thought about a dress, to be honest, but a uniform might work better to get us through the city if there is any trouble."

"Excellent point," he agreed.

The others worried about letting them ride across town, as though the two of them had not made far more dangerous journeys of late. A group of soldiers would go with them through the worst part of Kamere and then would head up to the army camp.

"Amazing how often soldiers need to go across town whenever Merriweather and I step outside," Mica said, looking at the young, nervous soldier who had ordered three others to get ready to ride. "I would almost suspect that General Gregorian had left standing orders not to let me out of your sight."

"He didn't say that sir," the soldier replied. "Well, not exactly like that, anyway."

So, they rode out with the guards who took them all the way to where the road divided, one path heading to the castle and the camp, and the other to the estates of several of the cities rich, both nobles and not. The guards went on to the castle and the army camp beyond while Mica and Merriweather turned to the left-hand road and entered an area with spacious houses, often on lovely tracks of land. The estates had spread across the hillside with the castle casting light like a candle above them.

There were, of course, guards patrolling this area, so they didn't need the extra guards who had brought them to the road. The area was in better shape than most they'd gone through. On the lower levels, though, he found a number of abandoned vehicles that had been pulled off into fields, waiting for the war to end. No one had gas or coal to run the steam engines. They were, he felt, the sign of the technology they were about to lose if they did not move quickly.

And the Glowing Lady stepped out of the shadows again.

"Listen," she said, her voice fainter than before.

And she disappeared.

"Didn't she say she wasn't going to interfere anymore?" Merriweather asked. Her hand moved back away from her flintlock.

"I can't say she actually is interfering since nothing she's said has helped," Mica replied as they rode on.

"That's a bit of logic I hadn't considered. Maybe the 'interference' part was in regard to the dead Atrian Assassins we found. Let's hope that we don't need her to help that way again."

"I would like to believe there will be an end to that sort of behavior, but I'm sure what first triggered her arrival," Mica said. They passed more guards; Merriweather was always recognized, even if he was not. "Why does she come to us out here and not in Raventower?"

"It might help if we knew what she was talking about," Merriweather replied. She had slowed. Apparently talking about the glowing lady was better than heading for her family home. "Why does she appear to you?"

"Us," he corrected. "I haven't seen her when you aren't with me."

"That's because you don't go anywhere without me."

She had a point.

"I don't know what is going on with her," Merriweather said after they rode on a few more yards. "I am getting tired of her unhelpful statements. I'd rather fight a battle than deal with that sort of mystic nonsense again."

"Don't curse us, Merriweather. At least wait until we're on our way home."

"The battle might well be during dinner if my brothers are as rude as usual," she warned. "There is a reason why I don't spend any time there, you know. My brothers and their dimwitted wives are almost always around the house. Mother will not let their children come to her official functions, though, so we'll be spared that problem."

"Ah," he said. "So not much different from the formal dinners at the castle huh?"

"I've been to both. You're right," Merriweather agreed.

This did not sound promising, but Mica supposed there was no use saying they should turn around and go back home. One dinner; he had survived those events at the castle on the days when he had been ordered to attend. He supposed there would not be so many people here and that meant not so many noises and movements. All he had to do was keep his focus mostly on the food or on Merriweather.

They reached the Merriweather townhouse in the next curve of the road. The building was large and handsome and fronted on a majestic park filled with snow laden trees -- and soldiers. The guard kept a camp there, which probably made the Merriweather place a very safe location.

The livery man came and took their horses. Tynus, who had once delivered Merriweather to Raventower, sniffed a bit in derision and led the animals away. Mica wished they'd ridden Kandris after all, to see if the man would ridicule at that mount.

"This is it," Merriweather said as she straightened her jacket. "I hope mother appreciates what we're doing for her."

The doorman held the door with another delicate sniff and a stiff bow of his head. Servants could be far more pretentious than those they served, and Mica thanked the gods that his staff was so pleasant. A night in someone else's care would make him appreciate home even more.

The maids looked at Merriweather with such distaste that he feared there were enemies until he realized that they disapproved of the clothing she wore. He heard the word 'uniform' whispered, much too loudly. Merriweather must have had a lot of experience with them because a glance their way mostly quieted all the servants.

"I hope you are ready for this, Lord Raventower," she said.

Oh, and what a change his title made to these people. Whispers stopped. Heads came up. They almost crowded around him in their haste to ask if there was anything he needed.

Merriweather rolled her eyes at the show, and he almost laughed.

"The others are already at the table," the butler said. He had not exhibited the same distaste as the others, and Mica thought he and Merriweather might get along. "You timed your arrival well."

"Thank you, Walson."

"Your mother would like to introduce you. I'll get her."

Merriweather straightened her jacket again, but there was a brighter gleam in her eyes this time. Mica suspected this might be a bit more fun than she was letting on. Magina arrived at the entry and smiled, signaling them straight into the dining hall.

"Our last two guests have arrived just in time! You all know my daughter Jewel, and this is her betrothed, Lord Raventower."

Yes, this was fun in an odd way. He had never seen so many shocked faces, including the servants.

But there were also problems. The Merriweathers clearly had no idea about the trouble with the Honorgates. Lucky for them that Lady Honorgate, and not her husband, sat at the table. The woman looked at him with one eyebrow raised, but the fact that she did not go into an instant tirade appeared promising.

Honoria had the place next to the woman.

They stared at each other for a moment. Honoria looked away first. Another win.

The rest of the group consisted of Merriweather's three brothers -- one of whom he'd already had a sword fight with -- and their wives. Burnis, Cherick, and Torlin looked nothing like their sister, and the three wives might have been triplets since they wore the same hairstyle, the same jewels, and had the same pouting, pudgy faces. Torlin did not wear his guard uniform and looked more than a little annoyed that his sister did wear hers. Mica was also introduced to a cousin, Eustacia Merriweather, who batted her eyelashes at him and made certain he saw the flash of the jewels she wore when they were introduced. Not the subtlest of women, he thought.

They sat down. The first course arrived immediately, and Mica thought everything had been timed so that there could be little discussion. The meal proved to be quite good. Magina explained how they hoarded food for the dinners. Baron Merriweather nodded now and then and spoke mostly to his eldest son about some problem with the cloth factories. Mica answered anything directed at him, but he had the feeling the others were trying to guess his new role in their lives before they leapt into the attack.

There were too many courses, and he felt obliged to eat some of everything, though he did not drink much of the wine. The brothers should have done the same. By the time they were sipping their after-dinner drinks and nibbling at some cake, Burnis Merriweather had started to get a bit loud in his discussion about the war.

"Useless army," he said with a snarl. "Can't even fight the damned barbarians. They let the rioters run loose through the city, too. We should drive the poor into the sea, you know. They're just Atrians in disguise."

Burnis was staring at him. Mica ignored the man and talked to Magina about cooks for a moment. Even Baron Merriweather gave him a nod of appreciation that Mica did not pick up the fight. His role as protector of the poor was known to everyone in the city and Merriweather's uniform said all they needed to about the army.

"Oh, it's so delightful that you even know about such things about cooking, your lordship," Eustacia said and batted her eyelashes again. "You are so refined and such a gentleman. I can't imagine how you and Jewel ever made such a bond! She was always such a rough child so I, at least, was not surprised to see her join the army where they required action and not thought."

The three brothers laughed agreement.

"And you three know nothing about how the army works," Baron Merriweather said. "You are children, though, so I suppose I shouldn't expect better from you."

They were not children, and the slight did not go unnoticed. Faces turned red, but they'd apparently learned not to speak back to their father. Magina sighed and shook her head, and when Eustacia looked ready to say something again, Magina tapped the woman on the arm and silenced her.

Eustacia pouted.

They talked a bit more about inconsequential topics like the weather and gardening, though Mica knew very little about the last. He wondered if Ada and Fern might like a garden, though. He'd have to ask. When Burnis, who seemed to be the spokesman for the three brothers, brought up the war again, Baron Merriweather turned to his daughter.

"That reminds me, Jewel, that I don't believe I have congratulated you on your new rank. The jacket looks good on you, though I think we can do a bit of tailoring."

Merriweather laughed. "Thank you, father."

He sat back and considered her for a long moment. "I know the King had a moratorium on creating new Captains, so you must have done exceptionally well. Well done."

Mica suspected this might have been the first time her father had said anything like that to his daughter. The boys had fallen silent again.

The conversation picked up as they moved to the parlor. Baron Merriweather and Mica even discussed some of the aspects of the war. Mica thought the man looked a little happier for the discussion. He imagined that talking to his sons had become something of a chore.

Mica had to concentrate, though, on the conversation at hand. Other people talked around him, and it proved difficult not to let his mind wander. He did hear Lady Honorgate say something about her husband moving most of their portable wealth to their northern estate even before the war.

Was that what he was supposed to have heard? Mica couldn't see how it could help much, but he would pass the information on to Gregorian.

He'd dared a glance at Honoria. She'd seemed quiet during most of the meal, though she sometimes chatted with Burnis's wife. Now she had settled in a chair between Eustacia and Merriweather, with Mica on the other side of his betrothed. Lady Honorgate sat across the room with Magina, while the brothers and their wives clustered in a group from Mica to Baron Merriweather. Looking at that group, Mica was reminded of a bunch of chickens with the males puffed up and crowing while the women pecked and clucked and generally didn't say much at all.

The conversation between Merriweather and her cousin proved to be far more entertaining, especially with Honoria literally in the middle of it. He had never seen his sister caught so much between being amused or appalled.

"There is the jewelry from your mother and grandmother, Honoria," Merriweather said. "I would like you to have some of it, of course."

Mica hadn't noticed the conversation change, and he turned back on this one.

"No, thank you," Honoria replied. She even sounded pleasant. "I have no need for such pretty things."

"Oh, but priestess," Eustacia said, a hand solicitously on Honoria's arm. "Oh, but you should. I know you're allowed jewelry. And a few sparkles will always help someone who is so plain otherwise."

"That's interesting, Eustacia," Merriweather said with a tilt of her head and mimicking her cousin's tone. "I always wondered why you covered yourself in jewels."

Honoria bowed her head and Mica could tell she had come close to laughing. Everyone else had gone silent at the words. Eustacia transformed from bright red to white and back again before she forced a laugh of her own.

They somehow got past that moment. Helsta, Burnis's wife, said something about it being so nice to get away from the children and how difficult winter was on them, especially now with the war. Female voices rose in a chorus of agreements, and Mica couldn't say he had ever been so happy to hear about children, colic, and the trouble with bedtimes.

The men began talking about hunting, a conversation Mica barely acknowledged with a few nods. Hunting had never been his sport, though he did admit to enjoying a ride through his estate in the spring. That seemed to remind them all that Mica was a Lord. He thought some of the wives were giving Merriweather looks of jealousy. He hadn't thought how they might feel trapped with their hunting husbands and bands of children, though he knew they wouldn't have willingly given up either.

They'd have to be leaving soon, and he couldn't say he was

entirely sorry. The gathering had been entertaining, but this was not something he would want to repeat very often. They had attended as a kindness for Merriweather's mother, and she was all smiles still, despite the occasional bad manners and snipes from nearly everyone, including Merriweather herself. Mica had the impression that Baron and Baroness were used to that sort of behavior from their children.

He wondered if a tap on Merriweather's arm would be enough to --

Bells rang outside. A moment later they could hear the shouts from the army camp across the street.

Merriweather quickly rose to her feet. "Stay where you are. I'll see what the word is. Be prepared to move to a safer place in the house. This room is too full of windows. Lord Raventower, you stay with me."

Thank the gods for that, he thought. The wives looked panicked, and their voices rose in cries of worry about their children. Baron Merriweather ordered everyone silent, and that seemed to quiet them for now.

Mica went with Merriweather out of the room and into the hall filled with worried servants.

"Get ready for everyone to leave," she told them. "Walson, go out the back with a few of the boys and get the horses and carriages ready. They may not be safe to take, but if they are, we'll send everyone home."

"Yes ma'am," Walson said with a quick nod and obviously wanted that answer. He hurried away, and Merriweather sent the others off to get cloaks and other things ready so that people could leave without delay. She handled the servants well. They didn't even seem to question that she had taken over, so he had the suspicion that most of them had been here before she went to the army and simply knew better than to question her.

Mica couldn't blame any of them for the haste they made to get the guests away, though he knew the three brothers and their wives lived in homes barely a mile away in a semi-circle around the larger townhouse. They could have walked there if need be, though considering how drunk the men were, and how given to panic the women appeared to be, he thought it might not be such a good idea. He hoped the danger wasn't too close. Mica would do his best not to be trapped here with the others. Honoria had been polite and not said anything to him at all tonight. She had spoken to Merriweather, so maybe the slight had not been noticed. Besides, even the Merriweather's must have heard about the trouble there had been between the two until recently. Had Magina hoped to reconcile them or was their word that the long-time battle had come to an end?

Mica wasn't certain the trouble between them had ended, but he appreciated that his sister did not bring up black magic during the dinner. He might mention to Gregorian to thank her. He didn't dare do so himself for fear of how she might interpret the words.

Mica went with Merriweather out of the building and into the street where soldiers were lining up. A captain stepped aside and crossed to her, nodding in greeting.

"There's an invasion on the north side of the bay, Captain Merriweather," the man said. They could not see the bay from here. "At least two ships rushed the land with steam power and one stuck fast before the soldiers streamed off. That's all I've heard. We're too clear the streets, so if you are heading home, I suggest you do so quickly."

"We have people who need to get to their places. Lady Honorgate and Priestess Honoria especially. If they go out my brothers and their wives will have to go, too, but they live close by. I've had their horses and carriages readied. All but Priestess Honoria will be on the hill, so they should get home quickly."

"Yes, if they are going to go, send them off now. I doubt the trouble will reach this far, but the Atrians are closer to the hill and the castle than they have been before."

Merriweather nodded and went back into the house, Mica at her heels. She got the others moving, though not without the expected wails and cries of despair. These people loved drama far too much. Eustacia took the chance to be the first to escape, making certain her carriage got out ahead of the others. Eventually, Merriweather and the servants bundled the last of the sons and their wives into their carriage. Of course, they had all come in their own livery. It was all show, and there was still wailing and shouts.

"I would think they would wear themselves out," Mica admitted as the carriage pulled out of the way.

Lady Honorgate, going past, gave him a nod of agreement.

Honoria walked behind the Lady and his sister paused beside them. Mica held his breath and bowed his head to her, not daring to say a word.

"It is a day like this when I am grateful that we were spared the horror of a normal family," she admitted.

And then she was down to her carriage and inside.

"I will not laugh. I will not laugh," Merriweather muttered, but she had to bow her head.

Baron Merriweather moved to stand beside them. "Thank you for getting them off so quickly, Jewel. We've had to deal with them at the house, panicked and bored, during one attack. You would have thought the battle had been created solely to inconvenience them."

"Unfortunately, there are more than a few people who feel that way," Mica offered.

"Yes, there are. I'm embarrassed to call those three my sons sometimes, though. I keep hoping they'll grow up, but I don't see it happening. I guess I'll have to live with it. I should like to get together again without the rest of them, though. It is an unexpected pleasure to talk with you, Lord Raventower."

"Ah. Not nearly as crazy and eccentric as you expected."

The man started to turn red and then laughed brightly. "You are right there. Take care going home."

"Thank you for attending," Magina said. She had her arm in her husband's, and they looked far more content than Mica had expected. "I know this isn't the sort of thing either of you enjoys, but you gave me great happiness tonight. I do grow tired of Eustacia's catty remarks, and it was a joy to see her put in her place. I know it's petty, but after all, I've put up with from her -- I do wish she would go to the estate with her mother and sisters. I suppose, though, that she couldn't rule there as she does here. They're all too much alike."

"We will not be taking dinner with your aunt and cousins," Mica said.

And that won laughter again.

"You two be careful," Magina said as their horses were brought up. "I'll see you soon. I received some new lace yesterday --"

"I'll come to the house and look it over," Merriweather said. "I don't want you traveling through the city just to show me some cloth, mother. Safer for me to make the trip. Besides, I'm not certain Lord Raventower could stand any more lace."

Magina gave a little laugh of her own. "Yes, I suppose so. Come by when you can. Do be careful."

CHAPTER NINETEEN

The Atrians had attacked at dusk as the enemy rushed off the ship and onto land. Darkness came soon afterward, and allowed them to hide better as they moved through the area. Before Mica and Merriweather had gone very far, full night had fallen, though the snow caught the ambient light of the moon and made the area brighter than it would have been otherwise.

Anxious voices filled the night, and neither could make sense of anything said. Mica had to trust the guards who moved along the street, all of them heading toward the shore. Merriweather had asked the news before they had gone too far, but there was nothing new from the initial report.

"I want to find the best way to get back to Raventower," she admitted. "Or maybe we should go to the castle?"

"Raventower, if we can," Mica replied, which didn't surprise her. "The castle wouldn't be much better than your home during a crisis, you know, with all those people stuck there."

"True." They pulled aside as another band of soldiers followed by three private carriages headed up toward the townhouses. "We might skirt along the west edge past Temple Square and not take the main road. We'll see when we get there."

The main road would be the quickest, of course. However, if the fighting was anywhere near that area, going through the back streets and circling through the industrial area, and perhaps past the middle-class housing, might be better. Mica would leave the decision to Merriweather; he trusted her instincts.

A lot of people had come out of their buildings to see what was going on. Mica could not imagine what drove them to do something so stupid. The guards warned them to get home. Most, it turned out, were servants sent out by their employers to learn what they could.

"That should be criminal," Mica said as a young man was sent back to the building nearby. "They have no right to risk the lives of these people just because they employ them. I'll have a word with the King."

That won quick looks his way. Someone recognized him. The name Raventower circulated up and down the street, an odd echo that startled him.

"They're grateful you even consider them, Lord Raventower," Merriweather said. "And it is a good thought. I know the King would not approve. He does not realize most of what goes on outside the castle, though."

"The war has made him more aware," Mica said. "And some of that is because Gregorian and I bring these things to his attention. I'll pass this on to my brother if I can't get to the King soon. Aside from putting them in danger, it does interfere with the work of the guards, so King Abertus might get cooperation if he words it that way."

Merriweather nodded agreement. She looked back but her parent's house had disappeared around the curves. He thought she might have sighed with relief. Her brothers and their wives would not have come this far, but they had caught up with Honoria's carriage, which had been slowed by all the people on the street. Unlike the others, her driver did not shout at people to clear the way.

Mica wasn't certain Merriweather even knew whose carriage they had reached as she spoke. "Lord Raventower, I have no idea how I was born into such a strange family or how I turned out so different from my brothers."

"Don't talk to me about odd families, Merriweather," he said.

Honoria, who had been looking out the carriage door to judge the traffic, glanced his way with a frown that changed to a nod of agreement. They even kept pace with her carriage all the way to the turn for the castle where she went up that road. None of them said anything, but it had felt extraordinarily calm, even in the midst of the madness of war.

They'd left everyone but the soldiers behind as they headed into the city. Mica could hear the battle in the distance: flintlock weapons thumped and sometimes an occasional shout closer. Fewer citizens moved in this area, and those they saw seemed more afraid than curious. Some had already hidden behind trolleys and abandoned wagons.

"Go home!" Mica ordered when he found such a group, children and all, huddled there. "Get to your homes. The battle is nowhere near here. If you don't feel safe in your homes, go to the castle. Hiding like this will not help. Either the Atrians really will get this far and be quick to find you, or else the soldiers might mistake you for Atrians!"

The men seemed to have gathered up their courage at those words -- or else the new fear of what he said overcame the other worries. It hardly mattered. The adults ran toward the castle, children in their arms. He hoped they found somewhere safer.

Merriweather still hadn't decided which way to go when a group of soldiers riding fast overtook them, and then came quickly to a stop. Gregorian rode with them, and as the soldiers fanned out into key spots, he stopped and stared at the two in shock.

"What in the name of all the gods are you doing out here?"

"We told you about the dinner at the Merriweathers," Mica reminded him. "And don't get that look. We were there long before the trouble started, and we headed home as soon as possible."

"Yes. Well." He started to look around, ready to move on.

"Lady Honorgate and Honoria both attended the dinner as well."

"Dear Gods and Goddesses --"

"There was no bloodshed," Mica assured him. Merriweather had grinned but looked away at a sound from the direction of the bay, reminding Mica that they should not stay here long. "Two things to tell you, though. First, Lord Honorgate had sent most of his portable wealth to his northern estate, and he did so before the war -- which I take to mean before Kamere was attacked."

"Oh, not much a surprise," Gregorian said with a snort. "I am not surprised to know that he was aware of trouble long before it hit the shores, although, like everything else, we'd be hard pressed to prove it, wouldn't we? The man is an eel."

Mica didn't argue, though he wondered if any of the soldiers riding with Gregorian might disagree with those words. He hoped Gregorian was careful about whom he rode out with on nights like these.

Sounds came, but farther away this time. Gregorian gave a signal, and two men rode off, scouts to see what was going on down a side road. It probably didn't hurt for Gregorian to sit here a little longer and wait for information to come his way.

"There has also been an increase in smuggling along the western rim of the northern sea, up in the area of the wild land," Gregorian said. "No, you wouldn't have heard the news -- it hasn't been so much that we are worried, and the troops up there said it can't be more than a couple small ships now and then. I suspect there is probably a connection since that is the other side of our fine Lord Honorgate's land. They're continuing, despite the ice settling in. That means someone is making it worth their while. No sign of what they are bringing in --"

"Maybe they're actually taking things out," Merriweather suggested. She looked more than a little uneasy about being in one place, though.

"His riches?" Gregorian asked. "Maybe. I'd be quite happy if he joined his wealth somewhere else. What is your second point?"

"The King needs to order the people on the hill not to send out their servants when they hear there is trouble. It is needlessly putting those people in danger and making the work of the guards all the more difficult. Having that many people milling about could make it far too easy for an entire group of Atrians to join the throng."

"Yes. Good point. I'd heard there was some trouble, but I think the soldiers downplayed it because it would sound bad if they couldn't even deal with a few servants."

"They deal fine with the servants. They shouldn't have to, and it is dangerous for everyone."

"Yes. Okay. Anything else?"

"Oh, we did see the glowing woman again. All she said to do

was to listen, so that was no help. I had almost forgotten to mention it," Mica admitted. "And that's just a sign of how odd my life as become."

"It would be helpful if we had an idea of what she wanted," Merriweather added. "And it is also important to remember that she's killed several people without any real sign of difficulty. I'm glad we're on the same side -- if she is, in fact, on any side."

"Yes," Gregorian said. He had signaled his people to start moving again. "Be careful around her."

Gregorian looked directly at Merriweather with those words. Mica hoped she remembered them.

"Is it safe to take the road home?" Mica dared to ask as Gregorian gathered his people together again.

"I believe so at this point, but take care," he said. He did not say he would send guards with them, but then the road was full of soldiers anyway. "The main attack has been pushed back. They were mostly trying to scavenge food as far as we can tell. Two other ships had moved down to the fishing cove, but they didn't try to land. Instead, they went out over the statue which did not pull them down, unfortunately."

"That is bad," Mica agreed. That news suggested a truth about the statue that he had avoided saying and didn't even want to consider. If it had any sort of intelligence..."Maybe they got through by chance. Some other ships have managed to get across without a problem."

"That is true," Merriweather said and sounded as though she wanted to believe those words as well.

"They dropped a few things into the water," Gregorian added. He looked troubled this time. "We suspect they were bodies and not entirely certain they were dead. Some may have been people captured from the city."

"Damn," Mica said. Worse and worse, if they were making sacrifices to the God of War. The Atrians knew, beyond a doubt, that the statue sat at the bottom of the sea and right where it was, too.

Which again suggested why they wanted Raventower which would give them the closest base to drag the statue back up..

Before Mica could ask more, two scouts came back and gave a quick series of signals.

"Go home," Gregorian said. "I think the way should be clear but be careful."

Gregorian and his men took off and apparently headed for the northern bay and the trouble there, though from the sounds of it that battle had mostly eased anyway. Good. He didn't want anything serious.

Soldiers passed them on both sides all the rest of the way home. There were few signs of people past the Temple Square, which only went to prove that the poor often had more sense than the rich. The poorer part of town had gone to ground, he realized. On a night like this, anything could happen to someone unwary of the dangers.

Fewer soldiers patrolled this area as well. The quiet was almost unnerving, and he was more than happy to turn up the path to Raventower itself. He could see the light there, glittering from the campfires within the courtyard.

Snow had frozen along the path and melted into glassy mirrors along the incline. They both dismounted and led the horses on foot for the last ten yards, He could hear the voices at the gates now, and knew they'd been recognized. Soldiers moved out from the gate and guarded them the last few feet, which seemed a kindness on a night like this when even the call of a dove startled everyone.

Nyle came to take the horses.

"Quiet here, me lord, though we had a bit of worry when the ships appeared off the shore. Odd things there."

"Gregorian told us," Mica said. He glanced towards the ocean which he couldn't see much from here. He didn't say anything because he wanted inside and away from the madness of the night.

The dinner gathering had been pleasant, Mica realized. There had been antagonism, but even the bad manners had been seemed normal and mundane little matters to handle. He was glad they'd gone and sorry the evening had ended in panic --though maybe that was better than to have lingered for small talk.

The soldiers appeared to be uneasy, and the rest of his staff looked quiet and grim, but nothing had gone wrong here. He and

Merriweather spent a few minutes in the kitchen and ate a couple cookies (though the gods knew he didn't want to eat anything else), which helped to calm the staff. None of his people were usually given to excessive worry, but the ships off the side of the tower had unsettled them. Mica wondered if he had been home if they might not have taken the incident better.

At least they would not be going to more dinner gatherings, or any other social events, for a while. Was that really better? Back to dealing only with the war? He thought Magina might be very wise in having her gatherings to remind people that there was more to the world than what they lived through this winter. Spring would come again.

Mica and Merriweather went up to this workroom, and he settled at the desk. Roe must have kept the fire going strong the entire time they were gone. The room felt pleasantly warm and the lights bright. Mica pushed back the covering on his desk and began to move pieces of metal around without actually putting things together.

The backpack with the wings that he used to fly -- or at least glide -- sat by the desk still, gathering a bit of dust. Mica worked on it for a bit. The blades needed adjustment, so he fiddled with those, while Merriweather moved through the room as though hunting for assassins in every corner. She seemed far too restless.

Merriweather had checked the windows and climbed up on the roof and back down again. She took her chair to the spot by the stairs, but she didn't sit down.

"I am going back downstairs to talk to the soldiers for a moment," she said. "I trust you'll be safe here."

Mica gave her a nod. She still paused, but with a growing frown, she turned and hurried down the stairs. He almost warned her to be careful.

The quiet enveloped Mica this time. He'd been spending too much time with others, and while he didn't mind having Merriweather in the room with him, all the others around were starting to bother him. He didn't want people in the courtyard or on the roof. He didn't want soldiers in the streets everywhere he passed

--

Mica wanted the Atrians to go away. If tonight's attack had been a raid for food, they clearly had some problems on the ships. They'd run one ship aground and the second must have been close enough that the first could be used as a bridge to reach it. They could not have gotten much food, though. Mica feared matters were going to get worse if the Atrians got more desperate. Could they buy the enemy off if they gave them food enough to get home? Ah, but how could they guarantee that they would leave?

He played with the pack for a bit more and then put it aside and picked up gears and couplings. Pretty little things. Perfection. A few bushings and mainsprings, some clicks, rivets, and wires....

A sound. A whisper as though someone spoke words he could almost hear. Mica came out of his chair so quickly that it fell over. He righted it out of habit, but his hand was on the knife he had taken to wearing of late. The sound had stopped after what seemed to be a sigh. Sound from the window? It hadn't sounded like it. More like it had come from the clock.

Mica crossed to the device. He still clicked on, minute by minute, since they'd first wound it up. No more clockwork spiders or anything else as dire had appeared. Payton had said there were more secrets in Raventower and every time he heard such a sound, he feared the man might be right.

"Lord Raventower?"

He looked back with a start to find Merriweather entering the room. Tippet had barked, but he'd not paid attention. That had been rather stupid.

"Sorry," he apologized. "I thought I heard something. I fear I am just a bit uneasy today."

He crossed back to the desk and turned the chair so that he faced her. She eyed the clock with some trepidation, but she turned away and faced him.

"Is there any other news?" he asked.

"Nothing too troubling," she said, glanced at the clock, and then back at him. "The guards at the gate had noticed some people interested in watching Raventower but given that we had an infestation of clockwork spiders, I can't say they don't have a good reason."

"True, especially since you and I half expect some other sort of infestation as well."

Merriweather gave a reluctant nod of agreement. "There is confirmation that the raid was quick, and they grabbed whatever food stuffs they could find, mostly from the army camp that had been near there. The army had expected a serious attack and left the camp, but the Atrian attack appeared only to keep the soldiers busy elsewhere while they raided."

"They are getting desperate," Mica said.

"Which will make them dangerous in whole new ways. Maybe we'll get lucky, and there will be a mutiny on the ships. Maybe any other craft heading our way will be headed off, sunk, or turn back rather than get caught in this mess. Unfortunately, I don't think we'll get lucky enough for any of that to happen and help us."

"I am going to work for a while, Merriweather. I need some normality before I try to sleep tonight."

"Yes, Lord Raventower," she said. She sat back on the chair. "Yes, I think sitting here calmly for a while would be very nice."

They both knew they wouldn't have many chances like this for long.

CHAPTER TWENTY

T wo days later the Atrian's attempted another invasion from the north, and this one brought a far more serious battle. Mica and Merriweather could not see the trouble, even from the roof, but they received reports during the day, some of them from Shipley.

"Battles all along the coast, me lord," Shipley said. He held his hands to the fire and still looked pale with cold. "From that village, the one you talk about sometimes, the fishy one --"

"Fintail," Merriweather offered.

"That be it. From Fintail to the Air Field. I heard tell that all the ships what could take to the air have."

"I believe it," Mica said. "A few are over the city now."

"I noticed," Shipley said with a little shake. He had no use for things that flew and found the idea that Lord Raventower and Captain Merriweather were apt to take off in an airship at any time rather disturbing. "They didn't attack the Air Field this time, me lord. Wise, probably, considering how they failed so bad the last time."

"True. So, the fighting is north of the field?"

"North and south," the boy said with a shake of his head. "After the bands of our men went north, some few Atrians climbed up them cliffs, me lord. They held the place while more comes down from the airships."

"Damn!"

"Yes, me lord. I hear it be bad up there, the fighting. I seen a lot of wounded carried back into town."

"Gregorian? Where is he?" Mica asked.

"I can't rightly say, sir. I think he went north before the other attack, but he'll be fighting for the city now, won't he?"

"He'll be fighting where he can do the most good," Merriweather corrected. "And wherever it is, it will be for the city and all the rest of the country."

"Yes, Captain. I suppose so." The boy stopped and shook his head. "I just don't know what to expect. What if they come to the bay now, too?"

"There are still plenty of soldiers to hold off any attack there," Merriweather assured him. "We wouldn't leave so easy an area unguarded, especially at a time like this."

"Go get some food and rest, Shipley. I might need you to go out again later." Mica put a hand on the boy's shoulder. "Thank you."

"I wonder if I should be fighting with the rest of them?" he asked suddenly.

"You are already helping in ways that others can't, Shipley. You're helping both Gregorian and me. We have soldiers, my friend. We do not have enough people who are knowledgeable enough about going out and finding information for us."

"Yes, me lord. I guess so."

He left looking unsure, and Mica hoped the boy did not run off to join the battle.

Mica looked at Merriweather and gave a shake of his head. "You and I --"

"No," she said. "Just no, Lord Raventower. What you said to Shipley applies to you, too. You have abilities that no one else in the country has, and you've already used them to help in the war. Besides, think what it would be like down there with all those poor people dying around you."

He had not thought of that part and gave a shudder of near panic. All those life lights trying to reach him, looking for a way to catch on to him --

"No, we will not go," he agreed.

They sat out a long night, watching fires on the far north of the city, but not able to see anything distinct. Airships battled over the bay, though, so maybe the Atrians had thought to bring in troops that way. They'd have had a hard time finding a safe place to put the soldiers down, anyway. He thought one tried, but at best they might have gotten a dozen people on the ground before the craft was shot down and exploded.

The next morning a high wind and snow rushed into the area. The airships retreated before the gale, and he saw one -- Atrian he hoped -- go down in the ocean near the ship anchored there. After that, the snow blew so hard for a few hours that it was impossible to see the sea or the city from the windows in the workshop.

Mica had given up trying to work on anything. Gregorian had not sent any messages, though Mica had dared a raven when the weather calmed, sending it off to the castle in hopes that his brother would arrive there sometime soon and send back word. Right then that was all he could hope for on this miserable day.

By chance, he found that the bell he had sometimes used to call down to the lowest level did not work. He had thought to have tea brought up rather than making Merriweather go all the way down there with him. A little tea by the fire, a bit of quiet -- he needed that while he worried too much.

"Well damn," he said, looking at the cord. "I don't know when that happened --"

"Probably when the last group of assassins was in the building," Merriweather suggested. She had brought the ladder and looked down the hole as best she could. He didn't think there would be anything to see, but it gave her something to do. "Or maybe it was the spiders? I don't recall you using it since then."

"Neither do I," he admitted and put the ladder back for the soldiers on the roof. He supposed they ought to build another. "I've always tried not to get used to ringing it for my every whim.

"I don't trust this," Merriweather said, not surprising him. "We need to be able to alert the others. Let us go down and talk to Roe and Nyle if we can pry them away from the guards."

Once she'd settled Mica safely in the kitchen, Merriweather went outside and came back with both to the kitchen as well. They discussed the bell, and afterward, the two men went off to check the entire building again. Mica supposed it needed to be done and he almost suggested he and Merriweather join the search, but he wanted to be back at the workroom in case the raven returned.

Heading back up the stairs, he had another thought.

"I am going to have Nyle cut off the gas into the line to the building, and we'll use the lights until we run it out," he said, tapping the last pipe as they headed into the room. "I realized how dangerous it is to have this running through the entire building -- how easy it would be to use it against us."

"Candles and oil lamps? Do you have enough, or should I suggest the army find us some?"

"I don't think it would be wise to use the army for such work, Merriweather. Some people would take exception to it."

"And that would bother you, wouldn't it?"

"Very much so. I believe we have enough on hand anyway. If we run low, I will apply to the King, like all the rest of the lords."

"That's better?" she said, a little surprised.

"Not better, but normal."

She nodded as they took their places. Mica thought she understood. Right now, any sign of normality would help them keep some trouble away.

"We will have to conserve," he said. He looked at the bright lights from the chandelier that hung in this vast room. "I will probably have to stop working so late at night. I don't suppose that's bad."

Merriweather had not scolded him about working so late the way Ada sometimes still did. He should have, though, considered her in all of this. While she had done well keeping to his hours, that didn't mean she wanted to or that she should.

And a raven arrived.

He leapt up and got it from the case. With the windows closed there was no way for it to come straight into the building. The raven still had a coating of snow when it came out onto Mica's arm, his beak clicking and sounding very annoyed. The wings were so cold that Mica thought his fingers might freeze to the metal.

"Prince Gregorian sends his regards, says they fought back the Atrians. He says to get some sleep. He asks if there is anything he needs to know tonight."

"Nothing," Mica said. He put him back in the cabinet. "Go back and tell him so."

The bird gave a click of his beak and headed back up to let himself out into the night. Though he hadn't used them often, the guards on the roof had gotten somewhat used to the ravens coming and going. Mica feared they were starting to think the birds were something more than simple clockwork creatures. There was no hope for what they thought, and Mica would live with the results after the war.

"General Gregorian is wise," Merriweather said, a touch of laughter and relief in her voice. "We could both use with some rest, Lord Raventower."

He almost argued, even though he had been thinking along those lines not so long before. Mica nodded and began to close things down, pulling the lid across his desk. Thinking about sleep had made him tired.

Merriweather stopped at the edge of the stairs and looked around. He wondered if she'd heard a sound again, but he hadn't this time.

"Sea metal," she said suddenly. He frowned. "Make small lights of sea metal that can be either strung in the stairwells or carried. Maybe both. I understand that you distrust the metal now. It bothers me on some levels, too, especially having seen the statue."

"Yes." He tried to keep his voice steady, but he still couldn't think about what he'd seen without a slight shudder.

"However, you used the metal for years before you knew, right?"

"Yes."

"Do you know of anything that has gone wrong because of something you made?"

"Aside from the souls?"

"Are they wrong?" she asked. They'd reached the hall and stood there, neither going to their rooms. "They are strange. They are scary. However, I have seen them at work now, and all I've seen is that they help you."

"And what if I --"

"Don't be ridiculous," she said. "If you started to do evil, I'd settle the matter myself."

He couldn't be entirely certain she joked. He wasn't certain he wanted her to be joking. The answer made him smile.

"I'll think about it," he said. Then he gave a shrug. "I suspect you are right. It would help to have lights. Better lights than we have now, in fact."

So, the next day he spent most of the morning putting together little globes of light. Roe and Nyle shut down the tank they had buried at the side of the tower and started bleeding the gas lines dry. A Raven sent off to Gregorian returned to say that he would come for the tank that night -- yes, they could use it elsewhere.

"He also asks that you keep a close watch on the cliffs beyond Raventower," the raven reported. "He says they found Atrians climbing there, but they were several miles south and where the cliffs are less dangerous. The General is heading south to see what areas need reinforcements."

The situation had to be serious for Gregorian himself to head out so far from the castle. Mica looked out the window towards the sea, with the cliffs edging in along the right side.

Few people went climbing there, and even nesting birds were wary of the narrow juts of rock and dirt that crumbled at the slightest provocation. Merriweather watched as well and then stepped back.

"I'll put extra guards to watch that area in particular," Merriweather said. She gave the raven a long look and then walked away.

Mica put the raven away and went back to work on the lights. Shipley even did a quick check of the shore, picking up a little bit of metal here and there, Bear with him. He also made a note of anything unusual.

Mica went up to the roof with Merriweather and the guards to look at those cliffs, though. The day had turned winter cold again, with a blanket of gray clouds out over the ocean and whitecaps dancing up on the rocks. The cliffs stood like claws reaching out into the sea, and even as they watched, a huge boulder broke loose from halfway up the nearest one and dashed its way down to the water, taking several more rocks and a train of dirt, snow, and ice with it. The crash sent a fountain of water up almost half as high as the cliff again.

"Well," Mica said, pulling his cloak tighter. "Maybe we should hope they'd try to climb up that way."

Merriweather agreed with a nod and glare. "I've arranged for the guards to change every three hours from now on. It's too damned cold up here for them to stay too long. They'll stop seeing things."

"Goggles will help, too," he said and wondered why he hadn't considered it before now. "I'll see if any are to be had in town. But shorter times up here are wise. Fresh eyes will help."

The guards, he noted, ignored the conversation, but he thought he saw a hint of relief in all their faces. The days were not only cold, but the wind also came straight off the sea with no obstructions. At least down in the courtyard they had the wall around the area and some tents and blankets.

Merriweather stared at the cliffs again. "They'd be fools to try this close to the city. There's a reason we don't even build out that way."

"True. Except for a few hermits living in shacks and a guard post -- and that post gets moved every two years or so as the ground around it becomes untenable. One good quake and those cliffs would come down -- and leave behind new cliffs, just further inland and no better for it. That's happened every couple hundred years. I suspect the Raventower peninsula was created by such an action. Let's go, Merriweather. I have lights to make."

She gave him a proper bow. "Of course, Lord Raventower."

He could see the smirk as she went to the ladder, the first down to make certain nothing dangerous had gotten into the room in the few minutes they'd spent on the roof. He came down after her and chanced to see a couple of the guards grinning their way.

The large room felt warm, the fire burning brightly. The lights were already off, and Mica knew he'd need some time to get used to the dimmer illumination. However, he already felt better for having the dangerous gas line shut down. He even thought he might take out the pipes entirely and start over after the war.

And there was a thought he'd not had for a while. *After the war.* There would be a time when they'd be thinking about things other than the Atrians. He looked forward to those days.

"Note from Admiral Rose," Merriweather said and handed over the envelope. Shipley had run the messages up and headed back down to help Roe and Nyle. He never shirked work, and he was quick to learn things.

He opened the seal and read what he had expected to find. "Admiral Rose says she would like my help with some trouble on *Flash.* Since she's not specific, they either really do have trouble with the new engine or else she wants me along when they take the craft out again. I'm betting the last. She wants me to come as soon as possible."

"That sounds like trouble," Merriweather said. She looked around with a show of regret.

He felt the same way. They'd not had enough calm time in the tower. He wanted to stay here and work on lights and insects. He wanted --

He sent the raven back to the castle with news of where he and Merriweather intended to head as soon as they could get the horses ready.

Merriweather stood. He did as well and closed the top of the desk. He tried not to sigh as he followed Merriweather down the steps.

"We are going to help end this war, Lord Raventower," she said without looking back at him. "We are going to convince the Atrians that this is a dreadful idea. We're going to find a way to destroy that statue so that they never have a reason to come back. By summer, this will be done."

"Do you really think so?" he asked. Down one floor and another, and another again before Merriweather answered.

"Yes, I think I do. The Atrians came in winter because they thought that gave them an edge against us. They were right in some ways. We're used to closing down and settling in for the winter, while they have snow almost year-round in most of Atria and know how to deal with it instead of hiding. What they just didn't realize is that a preference to avoid snow doesn't mean we couldn't handle it if we had to."

"Excellent points, Captain Merriweather," he said. She'd cheered him up a bit, even though summer seemed a long way off. "I'll tell the others we are going and not to expect us back tonight."

"I'll order the horses ready and sort out what guards are going with us."

They both went about their work. They were getting more efficient at it now that Merriweather trusted the people in the tower -- and trusted him not to do anything stupid.

He met her at the door, waiting until she arrived before he went out. The gray clouds had given way to light snow as he'd expected. The wind blew off the sea, so they'd have it to their right through most of the ride. That was only slightly better than straight in the face. He felt sorry for the horses, though.

"Would you consider riding Kandris with me?" he asked.

"I don't think that would be a good idea," she said and sounded as though she regretted it. "The soldiers will be on their horses. I fear those animals might not react well to Kandris."

Mica had stared off at the clockwork horse that stood in the far corner of the courtyard. She was right. Horses had reacted badly to Kandris out on the road.

"We need to get the horses to spend more time with him," Mica suggested. "Just in case we need to take Kandris for some reason."

"I'll talk to the quartermaster when we get back," she said.

Their horses stood ready by the stables. Far too soon, they were heading back out the gate and into the city. The buildings blocked much of the wind for the first part of the journey, but soon they had to traverse the section between town and the Air Field. The wind off the right sent icy sprays of seawater up over the edge of the land. To the left, the hills curled up and down, hiding the army camp though the towers of the castle still rose upward in one area, bright like candles against the falling of night. One set of guards had left them at the north gate, and another two rode with them on to the Sky Patrol gate. Merriweather spoke with them before they reached their destination and were passed through into the care of the other group.

Four members of the Sky Patrol rode with them out to *Flash*. The airship still sat in the cradle where they'd last seen it, and there had been considerable work done. They'd reinforced the hull, and as he climbed upward, Mica saw the mostly hidden spots where the new hull would move forward on one-half and backward on the other half. The new shape would make Flash look much larger, the needed camouflage for when they attacked again. The material looked was only a thin wood and would not stand up to much of an assault.

Rose waited at the top of the ladder, and from the look on her face, he knew the problem was with the engine.

"I didn't want to send for you, but Krogor says you are the only one who can handle this," she said and started for the bay. "A member of the crew tried to destroy the engine this afternoon."

"Damn. An Atrian?" Merriweather asked as they reached the door. She looked back toward the sea.

If an Atrian had done the work, then they knew about the engine, and that could cause a problem.

"I don't think she was an Atrian or an Atrian spy," Admiral Rose said with a sigh. "She was a good kid, but some of the other crew said that magic bothered her. None of them realized how much until she came into the bay and attacked the engine with whatever tools she could find. She didn't survive. Some backlash, we think. The spiders didn't kill her."

"I am sorry it happened," Mica said and even dared a hand on her arm. "That's something none of us considered."

"I've talked to each member of the crew this afternoon. The rest of them are shocked and dismayed, but mostly that they had no idea what she was going to do."

Mica had reached the door and went on down to the bay. The engine glowed fitfully and might not be safe to keep it aboard if there was a problem with the power.

Krogor, working on the other side with the regular engine, looked over and didn't even grunt. Mica began to look the sea metal engine over, the spiders moving to stand by, ready to help with the work.

When he looked back, Admiral Rose was gone. He hadn't

noticed her leave. Merriweather sat on the steps watching him.

"I think I can fix it," he said stepping back to stand by her. "She managed mostly to dent a few pieces, but as far as I can tell, nothing is cracked or broken. I might have to forge a piece or two, but I hope not. If I do, I'll either have to take material back to the tower or get Nyle and some of his equipment here. The second isn't practical, and the first sounds like trouble if people realize what I am working on."

"True," Merriweather agreed. "We might be able to get some of Nyle's tools here without too much notice, but it is still going to be risky."

"I should have brought my tools," he said. "The spiders don't seem to have the delicate pieces that I need. We need to go back, Merriweather. Go back, get the things, return and do this right --"

"You stay here," she said and stood. He looked back at her, startled. "I'll tell Admiral Rose where I am going and be certain there are guards on you the whole time. People she trusts. You can feel when someone comes onto the ship. I expect you to be careful."

"Merriweather --"

"I can travel far faster if I am not looking for people trying to kill you. What do you need?"

"Take everything under the cover on my desk -- tools, pieces of metal, gears, even the unfinished insects. It's possible I could use some of those pieces to replace others here."

She nodded. "Just remain here. I won't be long."

But she would be. Even at top speed -- which he hoped she didn't try in this weather and through town -- she would be more than two hours.

He went back to the engine, trying to focus on what he would need to do. Krogor continued to work on his side of the enlarged room, and at least he didn't feel alone. Mica knew when Merriweather left the ship by the slight twitch it gave. Even in the cradle, the craft still reacted to the pull of someone on the ladder.

The door to the room opened only a couple moments later, and he'd hoped that Merriweather had changed her mind. Instead, he found Rose and Greenwood coming down the steps. He greeted them and then he realized something.

"Tell me she did not send the two of you to play guard?" he asked, so appalled that he could do more than wave his arms, as though to make them go away.

Admiral Rose gave a short laugh. "She asked us to find people we trust. Well, Greenwood and I are the most trustworthy people on *Flash*, don't you think?"

"But -- but --"

"We aren't going to be doing much until you get the engine repaired or decide it can't be," Greenwood reminded him. He stood with his back against the door while Admiral Rose sat on the steps, much as Merriweather had before.

Mica couldn't order them out and decided he might as well tell the Admiral what problems they faced.

"I meant to say you'd done an excellent job with the hull," he said. "As long at the Atrians don't realize --"

"We had the material delivered, but the crew did the work, mostly at night and in the snow and fog. I doubt anyone realizes, even the others at the field," Admiral Rose said. "Let's hope it counts for something. What is going on here?"

Mica pointed out the trouble and why he needed the more delicate tools. He also told them that what he did might not help, but he would do his best.

"I would love to know where my father worked the metal for this," he admitted. He looked at the spiders. "I might find out later, but right now it will be enough to get it working again."

"I agree," Admiral Rose said. She didn't really look at ease, though she tried. "I don't like being sidelined when we could do help."

"Once Merriweather returns with the tools, I see no reason why you couldn't take *Flash* up with the regular engine if you think that best."

"Huh. I hadn't thought of it," Admiral Rose admitted. "I've already begun to think of the ship as something used outside the normal range of airships."

"It might be rough up there, though," Greenwood added. "Which could create trouble for Lord Raventower while he works. I suggest we stay at port unless we have to go."

Rose agreed leaned back. "I don't have the knack of relaxing much anymore." She looked up at Greenwood. "And that's why you suggested that the two of us come down here to keep Mica company, isn't it?"

Mica listened to the two discuss the matter as he went back to work on the engine, gently working a few pieces free and trying not to think about the woman who had been killed. He could not tell what had happened and that meant he couldn't decide how to avoid the same fate. He felt no trace of her soul in the engine, at least.

Every time the ship twitched a little in the wind, he looked toward the door, even though he knew it was too early for Merriweather to return. Rose noticed, of course.

"Well," she said after maybe the tenth time. "I had heard you were engaged, and I didn't know if I believed it, Lord Raventower, since you never mentioned it."

"It did not occur to me --" he began.

She lifted a hand and smiled. "We have not been in much of a sociable situation. I didn't realize who your bride to be is until now. You two make a good pair."

"She's gotten far odder since she began spending so much time with me," he said. "It helps."

"I'm sure it does," Rose said and laughed. Greenwood had finally put it all together and seemed pleased as well. Maybe having the two of them together made sense to everyone else.

Mica was no less uneasy about Merriweather being gone, but he did appreciate that the two of them did more than simply stand guard. They talked, asked questions, and kept him busy. Busy was better.

The ship gave a more violent twitch. Rose signaled Greenwood who went out. Not long afterward, he came back with Merriweather in tow.

Mica smiled and watched as his guard looked from the admiral to Greenwood and back.

"Oh, don't tell me you two --"

"We've already covered that, Captain Merriweather," Rose said. She gave Greenwood a nod, and he left, but she remained. Maybe sitting there did help after all.

Merriweather brought the case she was carrying down the steps. Over the next few hours, they took apart most of the top of the engine, laying the parts out on the floor where they both sat down and began to work.

The heat from the steam engine kept the area warm. Mica knew that they wouldn't power it down because of the enemies close by, but also because in this weather suddenly heating the pipes again could be dangerous. That made working far easier than it would in the summer when there was virtually no way to cool off such areas.

His mind wandered a little bit as he thought about a cooling system for the entire ship.

"Lord Raventower?" Merriweather said.

"Ah. Sorry. I think I see the answer to an entirely different problem." He took the pick she had been holding out to him for some time and focused back on the work at hand.

One of the others arrived with a note for Rose. She read it and frowned. The crewman left, but Admiral Rose continued to frown.

"A problem?" Mica dared to ask.

"There appears to be a line of airships not far from shore. We don't dare remain tied down here if they head our way."

"If we can get this back together, we might be able to circle around and give them a surprise," Mica said and went back to work.

"Is there a chance of that happening?" Admiral Rose asked.

"Actually, yes. We're down to the last few pieces. I've been able to replace two parts of the sea metal with material I had on hand. It is not a perfect fit, but I think it will hold for a flight or two until we can forge something more suitable."

"You see ways to redesign some of this, don't you?" Merriweather asked.

"A few refinements," he admitted. Then he smiled. "This is the sort of thing I'm good at, you know. I can build things from scratch, but Admiral Rose already knows that I spend a good deal of time refining bits and pieces of the interface on *Flash*."

They went back to work, Mica focusing on the engine, checking and double checking each piece as he fit them back in. The spiders had been remarkably silent and mostly still, and he wondered if they had a sense of how the engine should work. Could he count on them from stopping him if he did something entirely wrong? It might be something to test -- later. After the war. In that summer world that Merriweather had mentioned earlier.

One piece, another. Only three left but Mica felt less assured about these parts. He didn't mind being daring, though not with the lives of others.

Krogor had been puttering around on the steam engine. As Mica put the last of this one together again, he came over to inspect the work.

"I expect you to say something if you see a problem," Mica said. He twisted his neck. Too many hours working on this. He feared the dawn could not be too far away.

Krogor looked it over again and then gave a shrug. "I should know?"

"I don't like it all to be in my hands," Mica said. Then he shook his head and straightened. "But there isn't another choice, is there? Admiral, I suggest we take her up and inland. Make it look as though we fear to get caught in a battle just now."

"Yes," Admiral Rose said. She stood and twisted a bit to ease kinks of her own. The steps could not have been all that comfortable. "Another test flight for us, I guess. Let us hope she still works as well."

Mica rechecked both the interface and the cutoff that would switch between the two engines. Merriweather went up the steps as Admiral Rose left and looked outside before she came back down with a shake of her head.

"Cold out there. Snowing and dark. If the Atrians dared, this would be a good time to make their move, at least against the Air Patrol. I don't think even they would dare fly over the city in this."

"We won't be long in port then," Mica said. He gathered up tools and put them away in haste. Bells started to ring, and the pipe let out a few taps. Krogor answered with a bang of the wrench in his hand.

"Going now. Go up. I can watch here," the man said.

"I should --"

"No," Krogor said. "You go up to the control deck. Watch the readings."

Mica wanted to argue, but he knew that the man was saying. Both of them should not be here in case anything went truly wrong. Krogor was the engineer, and he had the right to make the decision on which one should go.

"Yes. We'll go," Mica said. Merriweather looked relieved. "Cut the engine out if there is any fluctuation, Krogor. Don't wait for the order. You know that, right? If the engine starts going dark and light or changes color --"

"Yes," he agreed. "Go. Not much time."

Mica headed for the stairs, hooking back into the lifeline which they'd all taken off while they worked. Merriweather went ahead and opened the door to the bitterly cold, winter night.

Mica looked back once and then hurried after her. Mica knew he'd done the best he could, and he had to trust himself on this one.

CHAPTER TWENTY-ONE

They walked through an icy hell from the engine to the control deck. Merriweather pushed the door open and hurried into the room, Mica close behind her. People were working hard at their stations, and Admiral Rose only gave the two a nod.

"Take your places," she ordered. "We need to go now. The sun is coming up."

The snowfall was not as thick as he had feared. Mica looked out the window at the world around them, all white and gray, but he could clearly see at least half a mile from the ship. He could not see what might be lurking out in the ocean, though.

"This is going to be rough," Greenwood warned. "More so than usual, I fear. We haven't tried out a flight with the new hull additions, and the wind is not in our favor at the moment. It will help when we turn inland, but we need to go north first and get clear of any other of our own ships."

They would not be switching to the sea metal engine for a while. Mica sat back in his chair and simply watched what the others did. Merriweather had taken her usual place on a bench and was, he noted, carefully watching gauges. She was probably learning enough about airships to qualify for the crew before too much longer.

Admiral Rose ordered the release of the lines. The ship bobbed upward and sideways. An alarm rang as they hit part of the cradle. Messages passed via the pipe and by some of the crew who streamed in and out of the room with reports.

"A dent only. We're going," Rose said and sounded relieved.

The engine had begun to purr. Krogor kept the steam engine in excellent condition, and Mica knew the craft would do well even without the new addition. He relaxed. The wind buffeted them from the right. The land, though mostly flat in this area, still presented a few obstacles like buildings and tall trees that made going up higher wise. The winds, however, grew worse as they climbed.

"Inland," Rose ordered. "Take us inland, Greenwood, before we crash."

He began turning the ship, a slow move -- but with the wind at their tail, they ran far better, even without sails. There was no use putting any up in this weather to have them get encrusted with ice and possibly tear. Besides, they'd have to go down again before too long if they started the other engine.

Admiral Rose didn't appear to be in any hurry to do so. They sailed over snow-covered land and villages hazed in wood smoke. Greenwood found a frozen stream, sparkling as the sunlight slowly penetrated the snowstorm and followed that natural path inland. He didn't seem to need any orders from Admiral Rose, and Mica realized she trusted her first officer and pilot to handle the course on his own.

"We're out of sight of villages, Admiral," one of the others said. "We look clear."

"Turn and prepare," she ordered and shifted slightly in her chair. Mica could see the glow of anticipation on her face.

The craft did a tighter turn than usual. The winds were not as high here, so far from the shore, but still enough to make *Flash* seem to protest and fight them. Mica had already sat forward, looking over the gauges and waiting to see the changeover to his sea metal engine.

Not quite yet. Mica looked up with a start as he heard an odd metal scraping sound and saw the nose of *Flash* start extending outward. He'd forgotten the disguise.

"We put the new hull plates on at night and mostly in the dark," Admiral Rose said. "And worked through the foggy mornings when not even another ship at the port could see what we were doing. I'd put out word that *Flash* needed more hull repair than we had first expected. Everyone assumed that was all we were doing, even when we worked late. We've never had the extensions fully unfolded. That should be it."

Even from inside, Mica could tell that the ship looked different. "Good work," he said.

"Let us hope that everything works," she replied. "Let us see what we can do."

She gave the signal. Mica slowly cut power from the steam engine to the new one --

And they were flying very fast again. Smoother, he thought, than they'd had the first times they'd tried it out. The refinements to the interface worked better. They raced through the clouds and out over the ocean beyond the edge of the storm. He couldn't say how long they'd been flying, but the sudden open sky and clear waters startled him.

"Circling around," Greenwood warned.

They sailed back into the stormy weather. Ice, snow, and water rushed over them obscuring the view, though Mica could see the turbulent sea as they passed back over.

"Cut power. Hold as best we can. A report, Lord Raventower."

"The engine is starting to grow hotter. I suspect we have reached the length of time we should probably run it without taking a break. The interface worked very well. We are now on steam engine power once more, and the change was smooth."

"Can we -- dare we -- stop the engine quickly?" she asked.

"We could try. The ship would still have momentum, though. If we decided to stop *Flash* at those speeds with the sails and dropping anchors -- well, there would be damage to the structure, I'm sure. Better to use the engine to overshoot or get close to anything you want to attack and then move in at normal speeds."

"A ship that fast might scare the hell out of the Atrians, though," Rose said. "It might even be enough to get them to back off."

"True. But it would also make the enemy very interested in how we managed it," Mica said and shook his head. "But they are bound to wonder at some point."

"No reason to rush it," Admiral Rose agreed after a moment.

"Surprise will help. And letting them worry about what is really going on will be better than letting them know right away. They are a superstitious lot from all I've heard. We might be able to use that, to our advantage."

"Ghost ships," Merriweather dared to say. "There were always tales of those craft on the Middle Islands after the Atrians had held it for a while."

"Yes," Admiral Rose said as he looked at Merriweather and smiled. "We might need more of a disguise, my friends. Ruined sails, the signs of battles in the new outer hull --"

"Yes," Greenwood agreed. Others nodded as well. Mica thought it funny how so many of her crew seemed to be open to crazy ideas. He did wonder about the woman who had attacked the engine, but something like that might happen on any ship.

"Shall we head in?" Greenwood asked. He glanced back at Admiral Rose with a bit of a frown, as though he had expected the order before now.

"Food first. A little rest. The storm is going to rage on. We might as well hold off out here on the edge for as long as we can and give Mica's engine time to rest before we put it back to the test again. Mica, I want you to sleep."

"I don't need --" he began. He saw her face. "Yes, of course, Admiral."

The others laughed.

He went down to the room a little later and slept well enough with Merriweather keeping watching. After a few hours, Admiral Rose finally sent word that they would head inland again within the hour. Mica stopped to check on the engine and then learned that he and Merriweather were to dine with the admiral in her suite.

The room was tiny but elegant and took Merriweather by surprise. The food was only slightly fancier than what they usually ate on board, but the location was a pleasant change. There were only four of them at the table: Rose, Greenwood, Mica, and Merriweather.

"We've been circling," Rose said, her finger tracing a circle on the table. "There are no signs of any ships or islands in the area at all. Not even a stray seagull as far as my people could tell. We've mostly been using the sails to help save the steam engine power, but now we need to head back. Our disappearance, even over land, would be noted before too much longer. I thought the storm, though gave us some time to rest."

"And we all needed it," Greenwood added. "The crew has been working for days. Most of them have now had some rest. I even sat with the engines so Krogor could rest, though I don't think he really did."

"He'll hold up," Rose said. "I wasn't certain I would, though." She shipped some juice and sat the cup aside in the little indentation where it wouldn't bounce around in case of a sudden wind. "I hope there was no battle back on land while we were gone. As much as I would have loved to go racing in, guns blazing, I don't trust the engine that well. Besides, I have faith that the others can handle that trouble. We, my friends, will watch for any lone ships and do our best to take them out. The sea ships might have even tried to make a landing, but Gregorian's people will hold them off."

"He was heading north," Mica said.

"Yes, I heard. The General lets me know what's going on, which is more than I can say for the others. He would not have gone so far that he couldn't get back quickly, and he wouldn't have taken many of the troops with him, leaving the city under-defended."

"True," Mica said and felt better for hearing those words, though at the same time he hated how Gregorian kept throwing himself into the battle. Mica sipped some of his juice and forced himself to calm again. "From what I could see, the clouds are still heading inland off the sea. We should be able to come in quite close to shore without being seen."

"Exactly," Greenwood agreed.

"Then I think we are ready to get to work," Admiral Rose said. She rang a bell and crew came and cleared away the table, though Greenwood grabbed one last piece of bread before it disappeared.

"I would have thought we would go back sooner," Mica said as they stood.

"I considered swinging back around and going as soon as the engine cooled," Rose admitted. She must have gotten some sleep because she looked more alert. "My worry was that the Atrians will have tried for the city again -- but the chaos of a battle would have made it difficult to use our speed to an advantage. If the Atrians are true to form, they'll have attacked and pulled back when they realized they still couldn't win through."

"And if they have won through?" Mica asked.

"All the more reason for us to surprise them."

They all agreed.

The flight back went fast and smooth, and no Atrian ships crossed their path. They flew *Flash* slightly south of the city and came in over those claw-like cliffs. The snow still fell here, and it was impossible to see the city, though Mica spotted the outline of Raventower.

Back out to sea and back in again, running only a little faster than usual with a spurt of power from the sea metal engine and then gliding silently forward without either engine running.

This was not a good idea.

One of the Atrian airships appeared before them, and much farther out at sea than they had expected. It might have had some damage *before* they collided.

Greenwood signaled for the regular engine and started maneuvering the moment a shape vaguely appeared before them. They went upward at so steep an angle that Mica felt himself pushed back into his chair. *Flash* swerved to the left, but they were already hard up against the other craft and hit with the sound of wood and metal torn apart.

And they were going down.

"Power the new engine!" Admiral Rose shouted. "Keep us out of the water!"

The Atrian ship -- Mica could see that it was not Sedinan -- should have pulled them down since it had hooked into the side of *Flash*. Mica wasn't certain if they'd done so intentionally or not. Mica dared to glance out the window and saw there was some hope, though.

"1 think their nose is hooked into the damned shell that extended out," Mica said. "Can you pull it back in?"

"Boarding party heading our way!"

Mica wasn't certain anyone heard him and now probably wasn't the time to try and direct them to it. Crewmembers had moved out onto the deck, but those at the controls remained at their posts. Admiral Rose stood and started for the door and then changed her mind. Merriweather moved to that position, her sword in hand, ready for anyone who tried to get in.

"Give the warning of quick ascent with the new engine," Admiral Rose ordered. "Then prepare to try and pull the shell back and see if we can knock them free like Lord Raventower said. Make damned sure all your lifelines are hooked and that you are braced!"

Horns sounded through the ship. Mica could see the edge of the battle by the glass window and out the smaller window in the door. The fighting looked brutal, and for one moment it looked as though a group of Atrians would reach the door --

And then *Flash* surged upward. The people fighting on the deck began to slide. The *Flash* crew had their lifelines in place, and he hoped none had been cut.

The Atrians didn't use lifelines even on their own ship. As *Flash* went up at least a fifty-degree angle, it pulled the other ship with them. They were moving so fast that most of the people had no chance to catch hold of anything. Mica saw bodies tumbling away across both decks, though the Sedina crew had their lifelines.

The ship went too high and too fast. Mica had sense enough to cut back to the other engine as his ears popped and he felt slightly lightheaded. *Flash* leveled out with a slight thump. The clouds were below them, and lightning played across the surface.

Rose went to help with the control to the shell which had, he was sure, stuck. Mica tried to see if there was some way to get the ship free --

"Stay down!" Merriweather shouted. He thought she meant it for everyone and saw that an Atrian had reached the door. Mica could see a bomb in his hand and a look of unholy glee on his face.

Merriweather did something that made him yell in protest. She yanked the door open, but at the same time she leapt outward and shoved.

She lost her footing and went down. The man flew backward, collided with the edge of the other ship -- and the bomb exploded.

Parts of the Atrian craft came apart, and the rest tore free. Even above the wind, he could hear the cries of fear as the other airship dropped downward toward the clouds and the sea below.

Greenwood began taking *Flash* down as well, though not at as steep an angle. Mica pulled himself to the door, but Merriweather was already back on her feet and heading in. Together they got the door closed. He thought there might be some fighting out on the deck still, but he didn't think the battle would last.

"Merriweather--" he began.

"It worked," she said.

He nodded and went back to his position. The sea metal engine still read too hot and seemed to be taking longer to cool down. He would likely have to go to the bay and take a look, but right now he sat back in his chair and pretended that he had not broken the rules by rushing after his guard.

Admiral Rose said nothing -- and he thought she had been going for the door as well, now that he recalled the scene.

Merriweather sat on her bench and rubbed her shoulder, but she didn't look severely injured. Good. *Flash* flew onward, though not as well as he would like to see. They were heading a little north of east and would see land again soon. Right now, though, the sea appeared below them, waves reaching upward into the wind swirled snow. They were, he thought, close to shore.

"We shouldn't use the new engine again soon," he warned. "I might have to go down and check it out."

"We are still in the air," Rose said as she sat back. "I'll take that as a good sign, but I want reports on damage. Go check the engine. I want to know when we dare use it."

Mica stood, Merriweather with him. They made a quick trip along the outer deck, which showed damage and blood, but people were already working at getting it back in order -- first by putting the railing together for the lifelines. That part of it was gone worried him, but they skipped over that area and hooked in again quickly.

People had died here. He had a sense of that, but there were no life lights because there were no bodies nearby. Mica thought the crew must have quickly taken their own dead to somewhere safe if they hadn't fallen into the sea with the Atrians. He was grateful that he didn't have to deal with that problem right now. His greatest fear at being involved in a battle was not fighting the enemy, but rather dealing with too many of the dead, enemy or ally. Merriweather would understand and so would his brother -- but he doubted even Admiral Rose would again accept him so easily if she sw tht interaction.

The thought frightened him. He had to fight that fear away.

Only a few yards stood between the control deck and the door to the bay. They had to push hard to get it open and inside the found a rush of steam, although not enough to be dangerous. The steam had risen and escaped out the door, but down lower they found only damp heat. Water dripped off of everything, and Krogor looked as though he had bathed in his clothing.

"Cracked pipe," Krogor said. "Almost fixed."

Mica nodded and went to check his engine. The sea metal glowed with an almost reddish hue, but even as he watched, the intensity -- and the radiated heat -- began to lower. Spiders stood by in a line, and Mica suspected they were worried. Unfortunately, unlike his ravens, these clockwork creatures were not as apt to talk much.

Mica checked the repair work and saw nothing had come undone. The temperature continued to drop. He thought the engine might be functional again within the half hour, but he hoped they would not use it again today.

Mica and Merriweather went back to the control deck, and only barely in time. Another Atrian ship suddenly came out of the clouds, swung around and came at them. Mica threw himself into his chair and kept an eye on the gauges, but unless they were suddenly going to run, there was little he could do.

They did not, at least, run into this ship. *Flash* took damage again, but it was the other craft that backed off and disappeared into the clouds and snow, heading back out at sea.

While the others concentrated on the battle, Mica watched Kamere, which had appeared to their right. There had been trouble here, and he tried to get an idea of how the fight for the city had gone. Mica did not see any Atrian ships in the bay, but one was in pieces and battering up against the cliff between the Air Field and the city. He suspected some of the buildings had taken damage from an airship, especially since one such craft was down in the water nearby. There were fires in the city again, widely scattered.

"Another ship coming in," Greenwood warned. "Any sign of the rest of the Sky Patrol?"

"Two down. I think the rest are still chasing some of the craft off from the shore," Rose replied. She'd been watching the windows on all sides and now sat back again. "Prepare for battle. This looks like the last enemy in this area."

"Let's hope so," Greenwood said. He watched the other craft so that he could keep their already damaged side away from their guns.

Weapons fired with one solid hit in the aft area, though the other two missed or did only glancing damage. *Flash* swept past the other craft. The Atrian ships were large, slow, and stocky. They could not turn as quickly, so they tried to ram them. Greenwood had not expected the move since it would likely do damage to their craft as well --

He still maneuvered them mostly out of the way, but the Atrian ship clipped theirs, and the jolt sent the woman at weapons bouncing hard against the controls. She fell back with a moan, holding her obviously injured arm.

The Atrian ship cut across their bow and would be able to fire --

Merriweather unhooked, moved to the chair and stood to the side.

"Lord Raventower -- send power to the weapons," she said as her fingers moved quickly over the controls. Mica understood. Power already fed into the weapons system, but only a fraction of what the steam engine produced. Now he opened the shunt all the way, just like on the submersible. Dangerous -- the amount of steam power that could build up quickly might rupture the system which had not been built for it. However, if they waited, they wouldn't get a chance at a shot and that Atrian ship would have the advantage.

Before Admiral Rose could even comment, Mica had shunted all the power and Merriweather had fired -- a direct hit through the hull and into the heart of the ship.

"Well damn," Greenwood said.

The enemy ship spurted fire and went down. Unfortunately, there was another coming straight at them.

"No, not you either," Merriweather muttered. She had to work around the woman with the broken arm, but that didn't appear to be much trouble for her. Nor was the fact that the other ship tried to evade. They must have not expected to be seen so soon or for *Flash* to recover power fast enough to fire on them at that distance.

Merriweather fired again, even as both the Atrian ship and *Flash* tried to evade.

She hit -- not once but twice. That airship was going down as well.

"No more?" Merriweather asked. "I was just getting the knack of this."

Mica had already shunted the power back to the engine. They'd been doing little more than drifting, and apparently one of the helium banks had begun to leak since they had started to lose altitude. With the engine engaged, they could fight the descent while the bank was repaired. He heard the tapping of those orders passing back and forth around Admiral Rose.

In the silence afterward, Admiral Rose looked from Merriweather to Mica and back again. They had, in effect, taken command out of her hands. Mica tried not to wince at the thought, but Admiral Rose appeared more startled than upset.

"Thank you, Captain Merriweather," Rose said she finally said. "Your quick thinking likely saved us."

"You cannot keep her," Mica said.

That won a little laughter. One of the crew helped the woman with the injured arm out of the control deck. Admiral Rose waved Merriweather into the place.

"Just for now. We have backup for the spot, but we are short of crew overall. I would appreciate if you would help out."

"Glad to," Merriweather said. She did glance at Mica. "I just consider it part of my job to make certain Lord Raventower is protected."

That brought another round of laughter.

"Take us back out over the sea, Greenwood. Lord Raventower,

how is the second engine looking?"

"It has cooled considerably," he said. Mica realized his heart had been pounding too hard and he took a deep breath and sat back. "I would not trust it for anything longer than ten minutes because it will reheat quickly again."

"Good to know," Rose said. She sat back as well.

"The damage to the aft of the ship is not extensive, but it is going to be a problem," Greenwood said. He turned the ship in a wide, slow arc that gave them a view of the city. Mica saw no other airships hanging over Kamere, and nothing left along the coast within their sight -- which was getting better because of the lessening snow -- and even the ships in the sea appeared to be pulling back. It looked legitimate for them to go in that direction before anyone got a closer look. "I believe our disguise is still intact enough that no on either side realizes who we are yet. I suggest we get clear before any of our own craft get close, though.

"Five minutes, second engine," Admiral Rose said when they had lifted up into the cotton-like interior of the clouds. "Does that sound reasonable, Mica?"

"Yes ma'am," he replied and put his hand on the control. "Ready."

"Greenwood?"

"Steady. Watch for any trouble from the damage and cut the engines if we lose stability. We'll still be moving fast, though."

Mica kept his eyes on the gauge because he didn't trust the engine not to overheat again -- but they made some distance over the sea again, dropped below the clouds, and found themselves completely alone.

"We'll do what repairs we can," Rose said. "As best as we can out here. We might have to tear off the extra shell."

"Maybe so," Mica said. "But there might be a way to do repairs quickly and with no risk to the crew."

"Spiders," Rose said and must have considered the possibility already.

"Spiders," he agreed.

"Let's see what we can do."

The three of them went down to the bay. Soon the spiders

crawled over the hull and did repairs to Mica's instructions. Rose watched as did Merriweather, of course. A few others gathered.

"I don't much like the looks of them," Greenwood said at last. "But I'm starting to think they're more helpful than I would have expected. And I suppose, as long as we have the engine, we'll have them."

"I think it wise to keep them around," Mica said. He pulled his cloak tighter. The night, the cold, and the damp started to wear him down. The adrenaline rush of the battle had long passed as well. Now he only felt cold and shaky, but like the rest of the crew, he kept at his work.

No, not like the crew, he reminded himself. Neither he nor Merriweather had been assigned to this craft, but that didn't mean he had no interest in seeing *Flash* flying properly and able to make it back to port. He remembered being on board as a crew once when Lord Chimso took a tour of the Air Patrol. The man had demanded to know everything, complained when he didn't understand, and had gotten in the way of even common work. Praise the Gods and Goddesses that they had not run into danger with him on board. The man had written a scathing report about *Flash* for the council, but Mica had been ready for it and had sent Gregorian a list of things he knew the man was going to mention simply because he didn't understand them. He had made certain that Gregorian did understand and could explain to the others.

The Air Patrol got more funding rather than less.

They'd proven themselves in this war, both *Flash* and all the rest of the airships. Mica thought, oddly, that his father would have been happy.

With the repairs done, they turned back to Sedina, made good speed for four minutes and then slowed and limped to the Air Patrol field, looking as best they could like an airship that had been in battle, took damage, and now came back to port.

Some people might wonder where they'd been or what had happened. It wouldn't matter. They'd done very well, and he better understood the limitations of the engine.

He feared they would need it again too soon.

CHAPTER TWENTY-TWO

The road remained empty as he and Merriweather headed back to the city. They probably should have taken a guard, but the Air Field was short of soldiers. Merriweather kept to the side by the cliffs, but she watched both sides with a kind of intensity that made Mica reluctant to speak at all. He supposed there could be enemies anywhere.

A sailing ship sat on fire about a mile off the coast, the black smoke mingling with the gray clouds. The two crossed debris that must have come for an airship. A few bodies laid in the snow as well, and the closer they got to the city, the more destruction they found.

An entire company of guards kept watch at the North Gate and ordered them to dismount before they neared. Merriweather didn't even snarl at the order.

"Oh, your lordship and Captain Merriweather!" The man in charge waved away the others. "I'm sorry --"

"No, you are wise," Mica replied.

"Well done," Merriweather added. "We're heading for Raventower --"

"Then I'll send four guards with you," the man said and shook his head as though he expected them to argue. "I insist. This is not a night to trust that you can get through without trouble. We've had Atrians drop in from airships, and I can't believe that we managed to find them all. Since they're already after you, Lord Raventower --"

"Please get your people ready to go," Captain Merriweather interrupted. "If we find other soldiers heading for Raventower, I'll send them right back."

"Thank you."

Mica didn't worry too much about shorting them if trouble came this way. The man in charge even asked for volunteers and got more than they needed. Horses arrived, already saddled for the men. The delay could not have been more than ten minutes.

Waiting had felt like a very long time, though, as they stood there in the cold wind and the last of the snow. Mica could see stars off over the ocean as the storm's trailing edge finally came through the area. They'd flown to that far edge hours ago. The moon rose, too bright; the illumination outlined every damaged ship in the ocean and all the ruined buildings in the city. The castle even looked to have taken some damage in one of the spires, but nothing serious could have happened, or else someone would have mentioned it by now.

They rode on into Kamere. Mica said nothing as the weight of the day hit him. He had never liked battles, and Mica hated far more having such an important part in one. Even so, he was glad the engine had worked so well.

Mica couldn't say he trusted the engine, though. Or the spiders. What had made him think the creatures should stay on the airship? What if those people were not safe?

He started to pull back and turn.

"What's wrong?" Merriweather asked with a nervous glance around.

"Nothing. Everything." He felt like a fool. "I had second thoughts about some of the stuff we left behind, but I think it will be safe enough for tonight."

"Safe enough all the time," she said and surprised him. She knew he meant the spiders. "Admiral Rose is no fool. She won't take chances."

Mica nodded agreement. The soldiers were curious but asked nothing. Mica glanced back and wondered if he should have gone to the castle -- but once again he chose not to. Gregorian and the King both knew where to find him and Rose would send her own report.

They rode on through the empty streets and past ruined buildings; the only sounds he heard were dogs barking and the screeches of cats and rats. The war felt too close, even with no enemy in sight.

"Is there any news we should know?" Merriweather suddenly asked. Mica suspected the silence wore on her as well.

"We heard there was a nasty battle to the south," one woman said with a nod in the direction they were headed. "But General Gregorian himself was there, and the Atrians were driven off the cliffs and into the sea. We had some battle around the bay, but we held them off here, too. They tried to drop more of their men into the streets, but even when there were no soldiers to catch them, there were still locals. Did no one warn them about Shadow Walk?"

That won a bit of laughter all around, even from Mica.

"We're still worried about some infiltrations," a young man added. "But the big drive didn't work. They have to run out of people sooner or later, especially if our Air Patrol and the Navy can keep them from getting reinforcements. I don't know why they haven't left already truth be told."

"Something more is driving them," the woman said. "This whole business about the God of War -- bothersome, that is. And trouble for us. I think religious fanatics are the worse, your lordship."

"I agree, especially in this case," Mica replied. "But they will run out of men, food, and weapons. And airships. We took down a few tonight."

"I seen two go down in short order to one ship," another woman said. "Just took them down. It were a wonder to see, sir. Cheered us all greatly."

Mica smiled at Merriweather. They couldn't say they were the ones on that ship or that Merriweather had shot them down -- most people thought they were on *Flash* and wouldn't have recognized the ship in her disguise.

Merriweather, though, sat up a little straighter. Mica realized he had as well.

"The King has ordered that we not allow any strangers down into the city," the first woman said. "We aren't getting many along the road anyway, but if any traders or farmers with crops arrive, they're to be taken straight to the castle. I'm not sure that's at all wise either, but it might be safest for those travelers if they are legit. Any stranger is likely to be mistaken for an enemy."

"And even if they aren't, there are people who would rob them of their goods," another added in a softer voice. "We're going to be a long time recovering from this."

They all nodded and fell silent as they neared the Temple Square. There they saw their first group of people, and they might only have been pilgrims come to pray to some god. The soldiers warned them off, and they disappeared again. The soldiers kept close watch now, though.

The open area between the temples felt alien. Mica was used to seeing people here at all hours no matter what the weather. Now, though, the place was deserted and the sound of their passage echoed in the silence. Mica wanted to see someone at the doors to the temples, beckoning for the faithful to come for prayer.

The early attack on the temples had seemed a waste of

Atrian resources, but now, seeing the place that was usually vibrant and alive, Mica thought he saw the reason for the attack. That did not even take into account that the God of War was no longer welcomed in the Sedina. Sedina -- the land of justice. They followed Dina and the Temple of Justice above all others.

The God of War would have a hard time finding a place here.

"They struck at the heart of the city with their blows, and I don't think we even realized," Mica said aloud. "This is the place we must bring back."

"I agree," Merriweather said. Then she snarled. "Damn."

The Glowing Woman stepped out of the shadows again.

"Stay where you are," Mica warned, but that was to the soldiers. They were all jumpy, though they must have heard about these encounters by now. Oh yes, and heard that some people died, as well. It probably didn't matter that those people had been Atrians.

The woman moved closer to Mica. So did Merriweather which won a glance from those strange eyes and perhaps a little hint of humor. It was hard to tell since she seemed far more ethereal this time. Her clothing moved in a wind that was not here and the white around her appeared to be cloud-like and was not the snow of this place.

"Listen," she said. Her voice was a faint and unearthly whisper and somewhere close by a dog bayed in answer. "Trouble is coming. Listen. Don't let them have Atric."

She did not step back into the shadows this time but simply disappeared.

"Oh yes," Merriweather said with a sigh. "So helpful as usual."

Soldiers shifted uneasily. They looked around, but the woman was gone, and Mica didn't intend to stay out here in the cold any longer than was necessary.

"I wish I knew what she meant," he admitted because the silence was worse.

"What is Atric?" Merriweather asked with a sigh. "Something related to Atria, I suppose, but it's not a term I've heard. If the damned assassins would stop throwing themselves out of windows or over cliffs, I'd even ask one."

That brought a little, nervous laughter, but it was a reminder, too. The soldiers turned their worry back to the enemy army and their assassins. Mica was glad to see it because if they were attacked, it wouldn't be just him who was in danger.

They were well into the area dominated by factories when he shook his head and looked back to Merriweather again.

"Why does she only appear on the streets?" he asked.

"Maybe there is some sort of pattern to it," Merriweather suggested, which was something he had not considered. "We should go over maps, just to be certain."

"And why me? Yes, you are with me each time, but she always walks up to me, and it's been plain that she's trying to tell me something."

"Like how to let the spiders loose," Merriweather muttered. He hoped the others didn't hear that one.

Why him? Mica rode on in silence for a while. Was it his ability with life lights? With souls? Did that draw her to him?

Oddly, he didn't think so. Mica wanted to go to people from the Temple of the Unknown Path and see if they might help him out. Maybe there was some code he just wasn't catching. Some significance in what she said that went beyond the mere words.

They'd gone past the factories and into the slums. Mica only noticed because of the soldiers grew more nervous. He and Merriweather, though, were far more at ease here than they had been in the better parts of town.

Amusing, he supposed. He could see Raventower ahead

of them now, not far away. There would be warmth and quiet. He suspected the Atrians would not attack again too soon, so maybe they could stay inside, and he could make butterflies again.

Or was that childish? Maybe so, but he so desperately wanted to have at least an hour of such time that he began to press for the horse to go faster.

Movement at the opening to Shadow Walk stopped everyone, with the soldiers reaching for weapons. An old man stopped out of the darker shadows, one hand on a cane and another lifted to show he had no weapon.

"Lord Raventower, sir. We hears you are about tonight. Bad night for it, me lord."

"Yes, it is Dosa. You shouldn't be out here."

"Won't be for long." The old man did not try to come closer. "Just thought you ought to know that all is quiet here, me lord. We took care of what Atrians came our way and stacked the bodies out for the soldiers who took them off. Would have left them for the rats, meself, but that would ha' been a worse mess for us."

"That's true. I'm grateful you've done your part, Dosa."

"Go on home, me lord. We don't let none come any closer to Raventower if we can stop them. And tell Gram and Shipley that we keep watch on their place. They should stay on with you, though. It ain't safe since some knows they work for you and even if they don't like Atrians, they ain't always wise about their attitude toward you."

"I cannot be loved by all," Mica said with a smile.

The man gave a cackle of a laugh and disappeared back into the dark.

The soldiers were not so worried now. Despite their earlier joke, Mic thought it must have been a bit of an eye opener to realize that even the people of Shadow Walk could help. Mica hoped it somehow changed opinions. They would need cooperation after the war.

After the war ... he kept thinking those words. He had to believe in them.

Just as they reached the curve in the road that would take them either up to Raventower or down to Fisherman's Row, a strong wind blew off the sea, so cold and hard that it startled the horses and brought everyone to a stop as they tried to get the mounts under control again.

Mica glanced down the road to the cove -- and cursed.

"Merriweather! There are a couple small boats heading for the shore down there, and I can't believe they are ours!"

"Damn! Don't these people ever sleep? You -- up to the gate and say we have an invasion at the cove. You, back to the city and round up anyone you can."

Mica watched the area below. The guards on the shore had just spotted the ships as well, and the cry went up. Soldiers came from the buildings where they had been staying -- slowly, pulling on their cloaks and boots, but preparing for the trouble.

Soldiers from the Raventower courtyard swarmed down the hill and went past in a rush.

"Why does trouble follow you, Captain Merriweather?" one shouted and others laughed.

The men who lived in this area were down helping the soldiers.

Mica started to turn his horse that way as well.

"No, Lord Raventower," Merriweather said, startling him as she cut across his path. "They'll do their best to hold off this group. You and I need to get to the tower and prepare to hold it if necessary."

The Atrians wanted Raventower. She was right. He silently wished good luck to the soldiers and followed her up the road instead.

CHAPTER TWENTY-THREE

They rode quickly up to the gate where a few remaining soldiers let them inside. As they reached the safety of the courtyard, Mica heard shouts from down towards the bay, but that could have meant anything at all.

"Half of you down to the base of the hill and make certain no Atrians come up this way," Merriweather ordered. Mica saw a moment's pause as though they decided if she had the authority to order them. They chose the right answer, and a few hurried out the gate.

The courtyard seemed empty with most of the guards gone. Kandris stood by the far wall, but he had begun stamping his feet, a sign that he knew trouble was near. Mica wished he had time to reassure him -- but Merriweather headed straight toward the building.

Nyle and Bear stood on the steps outside. Mica learned that Shipley had climbed on the wall that stood over Fisherman's Row, but he came down at Merriweather's shout. Mica gave a sigh of relief to see him land safely inside the wall and not go tumbling off the far side.

"We're going in and sealing the door," Merriweather said. She shook her head at Shipley's sound of worry. "No, it doesn't look bad, but there's no reason to take chances with

Lord Raventower's life. I don't like to see them coming into the fishing cove. There might be assassins."

Mica had thought the same, and he didn't argue about getting inside. Roe stood at the door and held it open for them, shaking his head with worry.

"Good to have you back, me Lord and Captain Merriweather, even if you did bring trouble with you," Roe said as he shoved the door closed. He and Nyle put the heavy bar in place.

"Not with us, I hope," Mica said as he put his cloak on the hook by the door. The thing felt heavy with snow and ice, and he hadn't realized the weight until it was gone. "But the trouble is close behind. The others are asleep?"

"Not so you would notice," Roe said with a laugh. "There hasn't been much sleep since they attacked the city, Lord Raventower. I hope this isn't more of the same."

"It isn't that much trouble," Merriweather assured him. "We saw only a small force, and I suspect they were going for Raventower, but they won't get it."

They found the others in the kitchen sipping tea and eating bread and cheese. Mica had never seen the group look so tired and worried, but when he and Merriweather appeared, their attitudes changed.

Nyle grabbed tea, but he went back to the door where he could at least listen to what was happening outside. Mica appreciated that he took the position. Unless Mica went upstairs or to the roof, there wasn't much they would know about what happened outside, though one of the men on the roof might bring them news.

"We're glad to have you back, Lord Raventower," Ada said. She sounded far too serious. "It's good to know you are safe, both of you. We worried, what with everything going on out there, and knowing airships had been shot down."

"I suspect the greater part of the trouble has passed, at

least for a while," Merriweather offered. She looked content with the cup of warm tea in her hands.

Mica could feel snow and ice melting down the back of his neck and into his clothing. He brushed at the cold spot with some annoyance and would be glad to get up to his room and sleep for a while.

Nyle came to the kitchen, and from the look on his face, Mica knew he wasn't going to get to rest soon.

"There's trouble at the gate, Lord Raventower," Nyle said. "I dared a quick look and then closed and bolted the door again. I don't know that we have anything to worry about, but better to be safe."

Mica nodded agreement. "The rest of you should be prepared to go to the back rooms and lock the door between the kitchen and them."

"Nyle and I will be with you two," Roe said. "We already decided, all of us."

"I would rather --"

"You'll have to order us," Nyle said and met his startled look with a steady stare. "And even then, we won't obey. We have convinced Shipley that he and Bear can help more down here. If things get out of hand in the tower, he and the dog are to do their best to escape and get help from wherever they can."

Shipley gave a grim nod, proving his agreement to the plan. That meant the boy and dog would be heading into the slums and Shadow Walk, the closest area where they might find allies.

"Well damn," Mica said. He pushed his hand through his hair. "People always told me I'd have trouble with my staff someday."

That brought the laughter he had expected. When he stood, Merriweather and Roe did as well, and Nyle moved toward the opening that would lead upstairs.

"We talked it out, long before this trouble," Nyle told him. "We had to be prepared, you know, whether you were here or not."

"Yes. Good work," Mica admitted, and Merriweather gave a nod of agreement.

They made quick work going up the stairs. Roe and Nyle had been busy, he saw. A good many of the gas pipes were already gone, leaving behind the bare walls, which looked much better. If he ever put gas lines back in, he would hide them somehow --

Not something to worry about right now.

"We need to watch for assassins coming up the walls," Merriweather said as they reached the workroom. She went to the right and threw open the shutters. "Damn dark out there. Going to be hard to see. Roe, you take one side and Nyle the other. Lord Raventower and I are going up on the roof with the soldiers for a few minutes."

The two men nodded and clearly didn't think twice about her orders. Nyle had crossed and opened the other shutter. Neither opened the window beyond, though.

Merriweather started up the ladder, and Mica followed without comment as well. Even from the roof, he could clearly hear the trouble below, though.

"A few got in the gate," one of the soldiers said. "They've held back most of the others, though, and I don't think any of the first group survived. We've watched the tower walls, Captain Merriweather. Nothing we've seen so far."

Mica stared out over the battlements toward the sea. The first light of day pierced some of the usual morning fog off the ocean, and he could see the shape of other small craft coming their way. The first two had only been the start of many.

"I think they expected to make landfall before they were spotted," Merriweather said. She squinted and shook her head. "I'd say at least eight more and maybe a few we didn't see that have already reached the shore."

"Rowboats, fitted out with sails?" Mica asked. "So that they would make the least amount of sound?"

"That's what I would guess. Do we use the cannon?"

Mica looked over at the weapon and out at the sea and the spread of the boats. "I don't think so. They are too far apart to do any good. Look there -- an airship is coming in. Must have been on patrol. They'll have a better chance of hitting them."

Merriweather gave a nod of agreement.

"We signaled to the castle about the attack," one of the soldiers said and pointed to a lantern on the floor beside him. "They'll have relayed to the army camp, so help is on the way. I would guess any soldier between here and there that saw the light might be heading our way as well."

"Good." Merriweather sounded remarkably calm, and Mica decided to mimic her attitude. He was too tired to decide if he should be enraged or afraid right now, so setting both emotions aside seemed the best idea.

The trouble at the gate remained intense with shouts, cries, and an occasional gunshot. Mica could pick out some of the trouble in Fisherman's Row, which would be a dangerous spot with more of the ships moving in. The airship, though, had begun dropping combustibles into the ocean. Oil, he realized, that lit and spread across the water, catching several of the boats. He looked away, not wanting to see the screaming men trying to escape that death.

The battle in the village had grown in the last moments. He saw a fire in one of the buildings and hoped it didn't spread up through the rest of Fisherman's Row.

More soldiers rushed into the fray, and he suspected another group had nearly reached the gate to Raventower, too.

"We may have problems," Merriweather admitted and leaned so far out over the parapet that Mica almost grabbed her back in fear. "A few of the Atrians probably got past the soldiers on the shore. I expect them to try to climb the hill behind the buildings and try to reach Raventower from there."

"I don't think they'll get that far, but even if they do, they will have to climb to the tower, over the wall, into the courtyard and still have to fight their way to the building."

"They might get to the cliff and climb around to the seaward side -- but I suppose that's not much better and a lot more dangerous with the wind kicking up."

"They want the statue," Mica said, though softly. "I think that's their primary goal now. They must know they can't take Kamere, but maybe the Atrians can hold on to the village and the land peninsula long enough to do whatever it is they intend to do to get to it."

"A larger ship coming in, Captain," one of the men said and pointed.

She and Mica crossed to stare out over the ocean. The ship was, Mica, though, one of the largest he'd ever seen. He'd not been paying much attention to the craft out there and wondered when this one had wandered in so close to Kamere.

He didn't like the looks of it. "Cannon," he said. "It's going to be difficult to get the power built up, though, Merriweather. We used the gas line to heat the water faster. I think I have better work for Nyle and Roe."

"Yes," she agreed.

He went to the trap door and opened it but didn't climb down. "Nyle, Roe! We need steam to the cannon!"

"On our way," Nyle said. He closed up the shutters on his side, and Roe did the same. They both glanced back at Mica, but they didn't stop to ask the news.

As they headed down the stairs, Mica pulled back up and crossed to Merriweather. "I need to divert the steam from the usual cannon to the one on the east. We have never fired that one, Merriweather. I suggest you let me --"

"Just get the weapon powered and loaded," she said. "You know I'm the better shot."

"True." He didn't like to think what would happen if it didn't work properly, but he said no more. The soldiers kept their distance, but they didn't stop watching the enemy and reporting so Mica knew the soldiers at the gate had finally beaten back the enemy and those on the road kept any others from getting closer. The fire in the village seemed to have been confined to one building, and the light illuminated the cliff so well that it would have been impossible for anyone to climb there without being spotted. Mica stopped worrying about anything on that side and turned his attention to the ship coming closer. Several of the small boats still burned in the oil, but the airship had pulled back at the sight of that larger craft, knowing it would have an array of cannons to aim at them.

"We could hope that they come close and get caught by the statue," Merriweather said looking back at him.

Mica had been studying the readings. The steam pressure began to rise, though slowly.

Mica looked at Merriweather and shook his head. "We'd have to believe that the statue would work against them. I'm not so confident of that possibility."

She grimaced and nodded agreement.

They turned their full attention back to the cannon. The body of the stone raven that stood at this corner had unfolded to reveal the weapon. Mica looked it over and decided it would work. Merriweather tracked the large ship, though the gauges were slow to respond.

Down in an area even below the kitchen, Nyle and Roe would be hard at work. The system still worked, even without the gas heat. A large, shallow pan filled with water was lowered to the heat. The water rose rapidly in temperature and turned to steam. The pan then lifted with the lessening of weight and tripped the spigot for more water. With several of these pans moving in rotation, an almost steady flow of steam rose upward into the narrow pipes. The problem was that the pipes were cool and the steam at first condensed and warmed the pipes but lost the power they needed. Gradually, though the steam rose upward floor by floor in the narrow confines of the main pipe, and pressure began to build. A slow process if they had to start from scratch, but since they used steam to heat some of the building, the pipes rarely got too cold.

When they needed higher pressure, though -- and without the gas fire -- people had to shovel in the coal. Roe and Nyle would be hard at work not to let the heat lessen.

The pressure did not rise as quickly as he would have liked.

"It's going to be a long time between shots," he warned. "We're at 75% right now. How does it look?"

"The ship is getting closer. That's good. And bad. I can see their cannon pointed this way. Do we trust that they want the tower so badly that they will not destroy it?"

"No, I wouldn't go so far as to trust my life on that idea."

"Prime the bomb," Merriweather ordered

Mica did so and stepped back, watching as she adjusted the cannon one more time. She glanced back at him. "I assume that this one has been made to the same specifications as the other."

"Yes."

She nodded and went back to work aiming the weapon.

The fog grew worse, and added with the smoke off of the water, making it harder to see. Some fog crystallized into frost and snow. Dangerous, slick stuff on any surface. Mica wondered why Merriweather waited --

And then she fired. The explosion of steam from the gun warmed the air and dissipated too slowly. He could not see if she had hit --

Oh yes, she hit. The explosion was initially small and then

tripled in size a moment later.

"That was lucky," she said. "Must have had something dangerous on the deck."

"Airships!" one of the men cried out and pointed.

The light from the fire had illuminated the airships which moved not far behind the sea vessel. Mica had already gone to grab the next bomb. They only had two left, but that hardly mattered. The airships had caught the wind and were heading straight in.

The pressure barely rose above the sixty percent mark. Mica feared if they shot now, the bomb would drop too close to the tower. Merriweather took the shot before he could say anything, and the bomb sailed out and impacted with the nearest of the airships, driving a hole into the deck and pulling down some of the sails. The airship somehow managed to turn away.

"No time, no time," Merriweather said and stepped back from the cannon. "They're heading straight for us."

"Ladders dropped. They intend to try to take the tower from the roof," Mica added.

Merriweather drew and loaded her pistol. "You need to go down --"

"We don't want that door open now," Mica replied, and she didn't argue

"One of our own is coming in!" a soldier shouted. The four of them had pulled their flintlocks and loaded, moving up beside Mica and Merriweather. He had no such weapon and regretted it now. He'd only be of any help if the enemy got close enough to drop down on them and he'd rather not be in that position.

The Sedina Airship -- *Air Flower*, he thought -- had swung in from the west of the tower, circling around and back at the enemy. Weapons fired on both side, and one of the Atrian craft took enough damage that it began to wobble but hadn't gone down. The ladders had deployed, and Atirans would soon be on the roof.

Mica knelt on the roof and pulled off the cover to a smaller passage. There was one weapon he could still call upon.

"Ravens!" he shouted. He heard a rustle of metallic wings and stepped back. All six of the birds swept up and onto the roof, and before Mica could even give orders, they were into the sky and attacking the people on the ladders.

A few Atrians still got through, landing in the limited space of the roof. Merriweather got between Mica and one man, severely wounding him and grabbing the dropped sword to hand to Lord Raventower. He gave a nod of thanks and fought off a second man -- and tried to prepare himself for the moment when someone would die. Too close here. The life lights would come to him. They couldn't hide what would happen from the soldiers.

He wounded another man and wounded him again. The fool smiled thinking that Mica wasn't proficient enough to kill him. The man had not counted on Merriweather. She didn't kill him either, though. She got under his guard and shoved him off the roof.

Another ship came closer, the ladder filled with Atrian soldiers. Some more of the Sedina army came up through the trap door, though. He would rather they hadn't opened it, but he realized they needed the help.

"Going to be crowded down here," Mica shouted with a nod to the rope ladder dangling and empty now.

Merriweather nodded.

Mica caught hold as the ship started by and scrambled upward with Merriweather at his feet -- and then others came up as well, and they were Sedinans. A couple ravens flew by. For a moment he had the odd feeling that some real ravens had joined his creations.

Shots were fired from below but not from above. One of the soldiers fell and Mica hoped he survived -- he had not been high and being already wounded might save him from immediate attack. More Sedina soldiers swarmed up on the roof as he reached the top of the ladder and threw himself onto the deck, automatically reaching for a lifeline and cursing as he remembered that the Atrians didn't use them.

Merriweather arrived right behind him. The others followed, and by then the crew that was left on the ship -- there must not have been many -- came out of the control deck.

Merriweather shot the first one, someone else killed the next. Mica rushed the door to the control deck, Merriweather at his side.

"Try not to fire guns in here. We can still survive this!" he shouted.

Four people ran the ship, though there were spots for four more. The captain of the ship, a wraith of a man with scraggly gray hair, stood and raised a flintlock, aimed straight at Mica.

Merriweather fired first.

"Sorry," she said. "I forgot. No guns."

She quickly dragged the captain out of the room and to the deck. He had not quite died yet, and Mica gave her a nod of thanks.

By then others had grabbed at the men who had controls. The pilot tried to turn the ship towards the city, but Mica got the controls back in hand as the others fought behind him. He tensed, expecting deaths. However, Merriweather and the others didn't want a battle in here and the fight dragged out onto the deck.

Merriweather came back in. A small cut bled on her arm, but she took the weapon's position. "You can fly this?" she asked.

"My father's design," he reminded her. "Not as refined as the later ones, but basically the same. I'm going back to the tower. I want all our soldiers to get off if they can."

"I don't think that's --"

"They are nothing more than targets right now, Merriweather."

"What are we going to do?"

"Take down the other Atrian ship and maybe others if we get the chance."

Mica fought the airship back up and away from the direction of the slums where it had almost crashed. He felt them slide along the edge of one factory and knew the craft had taken damage. No matter.

"Get them ready, Merriweather."

She gave a sound of agreement and reluctantly left the weapon's station. And him.

Mica heard her yelling out on the deck and felt the shift of weight as people moved towards the ladder. He had to fight the controls and cursed the Atrians for not waiting for a better design or at least having lifelines.

He didn't think there had been more than eight of the soldiers who had climbed up with them. He hoped that the soldiers left at Raventower had taken care of the Atrians so they were not shooting at the ship and the people they dropped off. If there was a problem, he expected Merriweather to come back and tell him.

Curve around, slow -- the Atrian airship pilots had to be exceptional to keep this hunk of metal in the air. He cursed his father for not doing a better design from the start. He got them to the tower, though, and felt the weight shift as the soldiers disembarked again.

Merriweather came back and took her place.

"We have the ship to ourselves?"

"Yes, Lord Raventower. Shall we fly away to some exotic

island?"

"Oh, don't tempt me."

She laughed.

The last of the Atrian airships came into view as Merriweather sat at the weapons.

"If we shoot the other ship down, it will fall on Raventower, Fisherman's Row, or Shadow Walk," Merriweather said and drew her hand back.

"Then we have to lure it elsewhere. Still another ship out there, Merriweather. Let's go for it, at least until we can draw this one away from the city.

"I don't think the Sedina airship realizes we've taken over."

"Ah. Well, I'll try to avoid that one."

"Excellent plan."

When the Sedina airship came at them, they backed off as they headed out to sea, rather wobbly which was not entirely his intention. He hoped they didn't look worth fighting. The second Atrian ship followed. Did they realize the change in crew? He suspected they did.

"Turning now, Merriweather. Take what shots you can."

"There are only two shots loaded," she said. "I'll make them count."

And she did, though she had to wait until the enemy were well within range -- which meant their own borrowed craft was within range as well. One shot scored across the front of their airship, sending huge splinters into the air. Mica hoped the weapons had not been damaged and Merriweather --

Merriweather took two shots, in quick succession, and both went through the body of the other craft. The Atrian airship plummeted to the sea.

"I don't have much control. I'm going to come in, north to south, over the tower again. We'll have to jump. I intend to lock the controls into place and the airship will go on, I hope to the cliffs beyond."

She looked at him, started to say something, and changed her mind. Instead, she watched while he brought the ship around again, cut the engines and let them drift. He shoved the controls into place and Merriweather handed him a dagger.

"Push that in to hold the controls there."

He did so and hoped that it held.

They didn't have much time. Merriweather went to the door and held it open. The tower loomed just ahead. Mica didn't wait -- they needed the best chance they could get to land on the tower.

"Get halfway down the ladder," he ordered.

"You should --"

"Go!"

She snarled a curse and obeyed. He followed. They were not centered on the tower, unfortunately, which gave them less of a window for the jump. The soldiers were aware of what was happening, though, and he realized that they caught the ladder, as though they could hold the ship by sheer force.

Maybe not stop the craft, but they could slow it. Right then the ship was mostly floating on the hydrogen tanks, and though she was heavy, she was not being propelled by the blades from the engine or from steam itself.

No time to think --

Merriweather leapt from about ten feet and he hadn't time to see how she landed. He had to jump from about six feet higher and at the last moment feared he would tangle in the ladder --

Landed amid a stand of soldiers who had purposely put themselves in his path. Damned good of them since he came close to hitting the tower's parapet with his head.

They'd let go. The airship sailed on.

"Thank you, gentlemen," he said as he stood and brushed at his clothing. They were looking at him rather oddly, he thought. "That was well done. It all went better than I had hoped --"

Merriweather appeared in front of him and grabbed him by the collar of his shirt. "Are you insane?"

"Really, Merriweather, when are you going to stop asking that question when you clearly already know the answer."

She sighed and let go of his shirt. The airship had just collided with the cliffs and slid down to the ocean.

"I think we should go inside before you come up with any other wonderful plans, Lord Raventower."

He didn't argue.

CHAPTER TWENTY-FOUR

The battle still raged, though off to the north and away from the city. Mica and Merriweather retired. They had no choice. Both had gone far beyond the limits of when they should have slept. Mica barely remembered going to his room, kicking off his boots...

He slept for a few hours: deep, dark sleep without even a dream or nightmare, which he considered a blessing after what they'd gone through the last few days. Only towards the end did he have the odd feeling of someone talking to him, a whisper of words that he could not quite make out.

Mica awoke to find the room empty. The shutters were still sealed tight, the magic embedded in the window beyond still strong. He could see a faint line of light along the edge of the window frame, so either he'd only slept a few hours or slept more than one day. He couldn't guess which.

Mica stood, wincing at bruises and stiff muscles but surprised to find nothing worse. He pulled out clean clothing from the chest, cleaned up, and wondered if he had beat Merriweather up for a change.

He should have known better. When he opened the door, he found Merriweather at the stairs and talking quietly with Shipley.

"Lord Raventower," she said when he stepped out. "I do hope we didn't wake you."

Those might have been the voices he had heard, but he really doubted it. "No, not at all. Is there a problem? Never mind. Silly question. What is the problem now?"

She flashed a quick smile. "The battles have mostly ended, your lordship," she said. "Gregorian sent a message and suggests we get the submersible to land now, if possible. He fears that the Atrians may have seen it during their invasion of Fisherman's Row. He thinks it would be better protected on land."

"Yes, he's right," Mica agreed and wondered why he hadn't thought of that problem. "Let's go down and have something to eat. What time is it?"

"Just before noon, me lord," Shipley said.

Mica did not ask which day. Not in a good mood, he realized. Mica tried to overcome how he felt, at least for the length of their meal. They had so few nice times these days, and he knew that his moods affected how the others looked at the trouble around them. At the moment, there was less trouble than there had been in days.

By the time they reached the table, he had already begun thinking of ways to get the submersible the rest of the way to the shore. That improved his mood as well.

The first plan he considered might work the best, but it did have certain ... drawbacks.

"I have an idea for bringing the submersible to land, but it would mean getting at least some of the spiders back from Admiral Rose --"

The others turned to him.

"No, that is probably not a good idea," he said, reading the looks on their faces. Even Merriweather looked as though she might have taken action against him this time.

"I have other ideas," he reassured them all. "Shipley, is the base of the catapult still on the beach?"

Shipley swallowed a piece of bread quickly. "The one they used to lob bombs into the city?" he asked. "Yes sir, mostly. Most of the splintered wood got carted off, but the bottom part is covered partly in metal, so no one's bothered much with it yet."

"Good. The next question is how to secretly build a crane that can take the weight of the submersible. Granted, she's small, and most of the time I hope to have her on the surface and floating to the shore."

"Can you get her interior clear of water so that she can float?" Merriweather asked.

"I believe that's not a big problem, but the ballast tanks are full."

"And you intend to empty them," Merriweather said with a sigh.

"It won't take much once she's already on the surface."

"And a target."

"I plan to do all the work at night, and with luck, we might even have snow or fog."

Merriweather went back to her food. The others asked a few questions. Mica talked to Nyle about the sort of crane they would need. They'd used the same type of equipment to fish *Flash* out of the water, and if he could have, he would have borrowed one back. They were his design, though, and if he could get the material, they'd be able to put something together in a day or two.

If Gregorian wanted the work done faster, he'd have to supply metal, wood, and people to do the labor. Mica said as much in a note he sent back to the castle, though he tried not to sound as though he demanded the help.

Gregorian showed up later that afternoon while Mica and Merriweather were out in the new forge, trying to sort metal. He came through the gate with six soldiers and a dozen prisoners. They also brought their own equipment with them. Mica, who still worried about the prisoner's connection with Payton, looked surprised. Merriweather had already put a hand on her sword.

"They've been cleared," Gregorian said. He looked at Merriweather with one eyebrow raised, but her hand remained where it was. "We've tracked most of Payson Honorgate's movements with the prisoners. He'd only had a couple days with them."

"Good," Mica said. The men looked ragged but willing to help.

"The six guards stay -- no, don't argue. I have an entire patrol of twenty outside the gates. These six are here just to watch the prisoners unless there is an attack."

"Better still," Mica said. "This will still take me a couple days, though."

"I expected as much, but I thought we had better get to work since there is a chance had they spotted the thing. I don't believe this it is something we want to fall into their hands?"

"Atrians, traveling to Sedina under the water where we would have even less warning of their approach? No, not a good idea," Mica agreed. "Granted, now that they know it can be done, I expect they'll start working on plans of their own. I just don't see any reason to give them a head start with a functional model."

"Yes. True, all of it."

"Let's go have tea. No, come on. Nyle --"

"I'll show the men what we need," Nyle said. He didn't seem worried about working with them.

"Thank you."

"My pleasure, Lord Raventower."

The exchange won odd looks from a couple of the prisoners. They must have recognized him before now. Was it only the politeness of the exchange? He guessed that might be so. Other lords rarely thanked the people they ruled over. Mica had seen that too many times.

Gregorian appeared anxious, but he slowed when he saw Mica limping. Merriweather wasn't much better.

"Are you two doing okay?"

"Jumping from moving airships," Merriweather said with a shake of her head and a wave of her hand toward the debris that was not quite visible from here. "I don't recommend it, General Gregorian. In fact, I don't recommend going on an airship with your brother. He tends to do odd things."

"I'll remember that warning. Lucky that I'm in the Army and not the Air Patrol," Gregorian decided.

Ada and Gram greeted the General with bright smiles as they got him some tea and cakes. He'd been by while they were with Rose, Mica learned. He even seemed far more at ease now at the huge table.

Sweet cakes appeared. Tea followed.

"I don't know how your people manage such good food under the circumstances, Mica," he admitted. "I've had soldiers asking to be reassigned here, and they've admitted it isn't because they enjoy how often you seem to come under attack. Apparently, that is worth it for the cakes and other sweets that come out of the kitchen. The quartermaster insists that he's not providing anything to you, either. He even made me look at the supplies, just to be certain his name was clear if it every came up."

"We always stock in heavy in the spring and summer. Usually, during the winter, I provide some food to the poor, you know. We've done that this year, but most of those people are up at the castle right now," Mica explained.

"We've hardly dented the supplies," Ada said with a wave towards the rooms behind the kitchen. Mica knew that the last several rooms on the corridor, carved into the native stone, were filled with non-perishable foodstuffs like wheat and barley, while other rooms had shelves of bottles filled with prepared fruits and vegetables. Ada and Fern had been working at setting things aside from late spring through early fall.

"I hope that things will be better soon," Gregorian said. "We are holding them back. That's the best we could hope for right now. If allies arrive -- but we can't count on that. What are your plans?"

Mica had the paper in his pocket, and together they went over the notes on the crane. Gregorian promised to send some metal scraps. Mica said they'd be working through the night, especially moving the base of the catapult.

"It's close already," he said. "All we need to do is get it there at the edge of the bay as the tide goes out and we'll be able to move it on the wet said with less trouble. How does the weather look out there?"

"Cold. Clouds blowing in again," he said with a snarl.

"Excellent." He smiled at Gregorian's snarl. "No, really. Visibility could be down if we have either snow or a warmer storm and fog. I'll take either, though I'd prefer fog."

Maybe the gods had listened to him. When he went out a couple hours after sunset, the fog was so thick he couldn't clearly see the ocean from the edge of the road.

Gregorian, fearing that the Atrians would use the fog to make an attack of their own, had lined the shore with patrols. They helped as well, each group, in turn, taking their part to move the huge base a few yards farther down the shore. Mica and Merriweather had both helped all along the path. It was not Mica's way to stand by.

Despite the cold, he was sweating and miserable by the time they reached the area of Fisherman's Row. Merriweather had kept with him, helped when the base stuck, but mostly kept to the work of guarding. When they reached the edge of the fishing village, the others collapsed onto the sand and Mica would have done the same, but he spotted Shipley and Bear coming down the road.

"You had a few locals watching you, me lord," Shipley said. He pulled his cloak closer -- a better cloak than the boy used to have. Mica suspected Ada had made it for him. "Can't say there was anyone what worked for the Atrians, though. The locals, they didn't seem to think it odd at all to see you out there movin' a block of wood and metal, either."

"I don't know what I'll have to do to surprise them in the future," he said with a shake of his head.

"Don't even think about it, Lord Raventower," Merriweather replied. "I really don't want to know what you could come up with if you actually *tried*."

Others laughed, even the prisoners and soldiers who had been working so hard.

"Let's get this covered over with the nets," Mica said. "Then back to where it is at least a little warmer."

The fishermen had left their nets a bit lower on the beach than usual, and well within reach so there wasn't much trouble to pull them over and pile them up on the slightly raised wood. Mica had already taken the time to examine the surface and knew exactly what he needed to attach the new crane.

He looked out at the ocean, measured where he remembered the submersible to be and nodded. If this went well, they could have it out of the water and up to the building where the locals kept some of their fishing equipment. Mica hoped to do so tomorrow night.

He never really expected things to go smoothly, but it was a nice thought.

They went back to the tower and had a nice warm meal, and then he went to bed and slept until noon when Shipley came to get them up. He might have slept a few hours longer, but there was more work to do today, and he needed to go talk to the men of Fisherman's Row. They'd have the duty of watching over the little ship once they brought the craft to shore.

They were more than willing to do the work, too, though he saw a little bit of discord between the locals and the soldiers. He supposed it wasn't a surprise. Most of the young men Gregorian had assigned to this patrol appeared to be from a group of villages to the west, and they all knew each other. Not being people who lived near the ocean, they didn't understand the culture here and sometimes ridiculed what they saw.

"We don't need this kind of trouble," Mica said, having pulled one young man aside. He'd gone red and angry at being reprimanded. "We don't need to fight each other --"

"They stink --" the man said.

"And what do you smell like when you come in from the barn, boy?" Merriweather said, stepping in.

The boy glowered.

"You want me to send you to General Gregorian? Maybe you are an Atrian spy, trying to make trouble," Merriweather said and looked him over. "Your hair is light enough --"

"I ain't no spy!" he said, his face gone white. "I would never help them --"

"But you are," Mica replied. "You help the Atrians every time you make trouble here. You know that, right? You've heard how their spies are trying to turn us against each other?"

"I would never --" He stopped, and a bit of sanity overcame his anger as his face cleared. "I never thought about it that way, I guess. We always made fun of them when they brought fish to market --"

"You don't like fish?" Mica asked.

"Uh --"

"Maybe you can get someone to take you out and fish before you go back to your village," Merriweather said, and this time she smiled. "I think you might like to find out how much work it is."

The boy stared out at sea. He turned quite pale this time, especially watching the roiling waves made worse by an offshore storm.

"Don't make trouble," Merriweather said. "And stop the rest of them, too. If I hear that you are insulting and harassing these fine men again, I'll send you all to Gregorian. Even if he doesn't think you are Atrian spies, there are far worse places to serve. Believe me."

"Yes ma'am," he said and hurried away.

"Well done," Mica said as they walked on down toward the shore. The day still held a hint of fog. Mica didn't want anyone watching too closely at what they did.

Several rowboats went out, including one that carried he and Merriweather. The larger sailboats remained pulled up on the shore and were mostly undamaged since it was no use taking them out in the bay and making them little more than objects for target practice.

The others began to throw in small nets and drag them out again with a few fish. Soon their hulls would fill, and they'd have to head back in. Mica didn't have much time. He and Merriweather had done their best to work out where to find the little craft.

There it was, too. While the others threw nets around them, Mica lowered a hook and heavy chain. It took several tries to catch the edge of the submersible, and he had to hope it would hold. The fishermen threw their catch in around them while Mica secured the second hook a little farther along the edge of the craft. Soon they were rowing back to shore, Mica and Merriweather playing out the heavy chain that reached all the way to the coast thanks to Nyle's hard work. They'd brought the huge chain down in a wagon, and the locals had moved it to the rowboat in the pre-dawn light.

Mica jumped out of the little craft and into the knee-deep

water and while the others pulled the rowboat out of the waves, he dragged the chains forward, keeping it low in the water. He tripped, though purposely, and caught the end of another heavy chain and hook buried in the sand. He latched the two chains together and then moved away and off to help the others.

They had not been too noticeable, he thought. And the base remained hidden beneath the larger nets. The chain he had hooked to was attached to the base.

Now they had a tie to the submersible, but it was going to take a bit more work to get it out of the water. At least she wasn't very deep.

They went back to the tower where the two of them rested for a few hours. The sun went down on a bitterly cold and windy night, so they did not have as much luck as they'd had before now.

Then Mica reassessed that idea.

"The waves are pounding against the shore, the tide is up --" he all but yelled to the others as they started fitting pipes together, pushing the first few far down through the center of the stand. Others were digging out the chain. "This is going to be easier than I hoped!"

"Easier?" Merriweather said and looked incredulous. She had already slipped twice on the sand.

"Won't have to clear the ballast! Didn't want to have to dive down into the ship and hope I could get the release to work. But with the ocean moving this powerfully toward us, we should be able to reel it in like a big fish!"

Merriweather still looked doubtful.

The work was not easy as they turned the crank that pulled the ship, inch by inch, closer to the shore. Mica joined in the work, trading off with others. Four did the work at a time, but it took hours. Mica began to fear that they'd either have to drop the ship where it was, at least partly out of the water, or else he'd have to go out and climb in to see if he could clear the ballast after all. The tide was going out --

And a massive wave caught the submersible and rolled it several yards forward. It was all but on the dry land.

"Get the wagon!" he yelled.

Kandris stood behind the fishing shed, already attached to the wagon. Mica had considered using oxen, but they would have had to come all the way from the Air Patrol Field and would have drawn notice.

The wagon did not want to move on the sand, but they maneuvered it to where crane pulled the submersible up -- painfully slow -- and down into the wagon. Kandris couldn't pull the heavy wagon out of the sand, and they ended up with wood under the wheels until they hit the stone pavement and went upward, the clockwork horse's metal hooves having no trouble on the ice, though almost all of the humans slipped and fell at least once. They didn't have far to go.

Mica had wanted to take the craft up to the Raventower courtyard, but Gregorian and Merriweather had talked him out of it. Better, Merriweather had pointed out, to have the craft closer to the water, in case he could fix it and put it back out to sea.

They maneuvered the wagon around to the building which was only barely large enough to get the wagon and the ship inside. The door was turned away from the sea and the back wall reinforced against the sea and wind.

Kandris backed the wagon in, and they released the metal horse from the reins. The clockwork creature turned around and looked inside just as Merriweather and Mica did. Mica found that amusing, despite being so cold that he could barely stand.

Mica climbed up on the wagon and began to examine the ship.

"Water inside," he said, pointing to the window. "Not full,

though. When we abandoned the craft, the entrance must have sealed shut fast. Lucky there. We can roll her on her side, open the seal, and let the water out."

"Right now?" Merriweather asked.

"Tomorrow," Mica said, though he did want to have a go at it. The rounded craft would not be hard to turn.

"Then let's get up to the tower, warm up, and get some sleep. We'll be back down here soon enough, I think."

He agreed. They rode Kandris, there in the dark with no one to see them. Warmth, food, sleep -- the others following behind them were muttering much the same things.

At the top of the hill, Mica looked back down. The others had taken down the crane and hidden the evidence of what they'd done. He could see the building, but not the submersible. Overall, it was a good night's work, and he didn't think the Atrians had any idea of what had happened. The little toy ship was safe for now.

CHAPTER TWENTY-FIVE

Mica wanted to go to the shed first thing the next morning, but Merriweather talked him out of it before they even went downstairs.

"We don't dare rush down there. The crews on those ships would have noticed some of the activity the last few days. If you go straight there, they'll be more curious. The submersible is draining -- I asked. The guards turned it on the side, and they said most of the water has drained out along a crack by the window. The interior is now more frost than water, so they're heating the shed. Give it a little more time."

"Yes," he agreed and coughed. "Besides, being warm is going to help us. What a miserable few days, but at least we got the work completed."

"True," she agreed. "Let's go down to breakfast. The others will want to know how we did since neither of us could hold a conversation last night."

"I don't know that I can now," he admitted and followed her down the steps. "You're right. This is not the day to go rushing back to look at the submersible. I don't know if I could make any sense out of it, even knowing what it does."

"One would need a working brain for that, Lord Raventower. I don't think we could find one between the two of us."

She made him laugh.

The scents from the kitchen revived Mica. Ada sat him down and fussed over him, which drew smiles from Mica and the others.

He did not go back to the workshop since the kitchen was far warmer than the upper rooms. He felt oddly at peace here, and he hadn't anywhere else for a while. It might only have been exhaustion, but whatever the cause, he felt better for sitting at the table and not worrying about the war for a while. Merriweather did get his small tools and the pile of parts for insects, and he happily worked at the clockwork creatures.

Merriweather received reports from the guards. She let him know that there was nothing serious going on.

"The Atrians are interested in the shore, as we suspected, and they even launched a smaller boat to take a closer look. Gregorian had it attacked, but they didn't make too much fuss over it, and the boat went back to the ship. Best to let them get less curious. I doubt they'll keep the watch up for more than a day or two."

Mica thought Merriweather might be hoping for such behavior, even if neither of them believed it. He said nothing, though, and sipped honeyed tea while he played with the wings of the insects, letting his mind go blank for long stretches of time. Peace. He'd even take this counterfeit version for an hour or two.

Gregorian arrived at the tower just before noon the next day. They were all huddled in the kitchen. Even those who had not gone out to work on getting the ship from the ocean looked as miserable and cold as the rest of them.

"You all look like you're still half frozen," Gregorian said as he took his place.

"More than half," Mica agreed. He still had a bit of a cough but waved away his brother's concern. The tea was helping. "But we got her out of the water and hidden. I was going to go down and look today, but Merriweather wants to go check on her family." Merriweather gave him a bit of a glare at those words and Mica tilted his head and smiled. "Oh, that's not it? Then maybe you really are going to look at some cloth your mother wants to show you?"

She snarled and threw her hands in the air.

"I brought the change of guard for the men here," Gregorian said. "If you are going, I suggest you leave now and ride with them."

"I --" she began. She stood. Then she shook her head. "I don't like leaving Lord Raventower alone, sir. There's no telling what he might do."

"Odd, but I feel the same way when I leave the two of you alone," Gregorian replied.

"I'll stay inside," Mica offered. "I'll make insects."

"Thank you. I won't be long, I hope."

She turned and walked away, without even looking back though Mica did see a twitch of her shoulders as she went up the steps and out of the area.

"You would think that she doesn't trust me," he said.

"I can hear you!"

And they laughed. They heard Merriweather go out and Mica did hope that she didn't take too long to check on things. He would worry. Mica had thought to go with her, but he knew if he had suggested it, she would have decided not to go at all. They all fussed over him because he had a touch of a cold.

Mica worried when she simply walked from upstairs to downstairs. Riding clear across town --

As it happened, Mica had things to keep him busy. He might even have thought it purposeful except that Gregorian hadn't known she was going to head out today. However, he had some notes from Rose covering problems with her new, odd engine.

The two ended up talking about it anyway. He trusted his staff who heard more than any of the lords anyway. Gregorian trusted them as well. He never seemed to consider that they needed to be careful.

"I understand the basics of how it works," Mica said and then shook his head. "However, the amount of force the engine creates when we switch over pushes us to at least a hundred miles an hour. You don't want to be heading upward when that happens, by the way. And you better hope there is nothing in front of you. I think, with a bit of practice, we could learn how to pilot in those conditions. Greenwood, who is the best there is, was intimidated at first, but by the end, I think he was willing to work with it. The spiders that come with the engine caused some consternation, but since they went out on the hull and fixed damage -- while still in the air -- I think the crew was happier with them by the time we landed."

"What about the initial trouble, though -- the damage to the engine --"

"Something Rose will have to watch for, of course. The admiral believes the woman reacted to the idea of magic. It's happened before."

Gregorian nodded. He drank more of his tea. Nyle had remained at the table with them, and Mica suddenly realized it was not because the man had nothing better to do.

"Merriweather put you in charge of watching over me?" he said.

Nyle smiled. "Yes, at least after the General leaves."

"Ha," Gregorian said with a slight laugh. "Nice to know that she considers me competent enough to hold off the kind of trouble that you attract."

"I would think so, too -- but notice that Nyle is sitting here, even with you in the room."

Gregorian looked over at the large smithy. "Ah. Good point."

"Is there more I need to know?" Mica asked because it was not like his brother to simply lounge around drinking tea.

"We've noticed the movement of the Atrian ships, a little jockeying for positions. We thought they might be going for the submersible until we intercepted a note to prepare for the statue. Which means, apparently, that if they get it up, they intend to bring it to land. I don't like the sound of that, Mica."

"If it were just a statue --" Mica said and then shook his head. "But it isn't. I wonder if we could make a wall around it. We've enough rock and debris along the northern shore from The Claws."

"Or bury it beneath rock?" Gregorian suggested.

"We couldn't take ships out to drop the material on it -- but maybe we wouldn't have to. Could we catapult it from the shore? The problem is deciding how much we would need. The statue has magic -- I'm sure of it even though I haven't said so aloud --"

"I know. We've been avoiding it as much as possible. I would much rather destroy the thing."

Mica agreed. "We probably need to talk to people from the Temple of the Unknown Path and hope they are far more helpful than their High Priestess."

Gregorian nodded agreement. They had more food, sitting there at the kitchen table rather than going up to the workshop. Mica felt better sitting here with the others -- and closer to the door, so he knew when Merriweather returned.

Gregorian didn't seem to be in any hurry to leave. "Important people know where I am and can reach me, including by the flag system we set up on your roof. Did I mention that?"

"No."

"One of the men suggested it a few days ago. The same

sort of things they use out on the ships."

"Oh. Good idea."

"We have lights at night, but those aren't nearly as effective during the day. But still, important people know where to reach me. For as long as I am here, the hordes of castle courtiers cannot constantly bombard me with questions about matters they can handle without me. You and I have just discussed something I dare not bring up in the castle at all for fear of who might walk in --"

"Or listen in?" Mica asked.

He gave a glum nod of agreement. "I want to trust the guards in the castle, but right now I'm paranoid about everyone. I know people have listened to the supposedly private conversations with the King. King Abertus is not happy about that part. I can't begin to guess what is going to happen with that after the war."

"After the war seems an odd term these days."

Gregorian agreed with a nod. Then they spent a long time talking about how the war appeared to be progressing. Before long, Mica realized that his brother was not nearly as worried as he had been even a few days ago.

"The report from the Navy is encouraging," Gregorian admitted. "We've broken the main supply line. They're still getting some small craft through to reinforce their people, but they can't maintain a sustained effort for much longer. Add to that the fact that we have turned back every invasion and destroyed more of their craft than they've destroyed of ours, and I see hope that this will end, and not too far in the future."

"I think all that holds them here now is that damned statue," Mica said. "I am not entirely sure why. Do they know about the magic? I think they must, which still makes me suspect the magic has to do with the time when the statue was created and then thrown into the sea. I've been studying some material from that time, but it isn't easy, especially when I'm constantly interrupted. Ha! Something we have in common, I suppose."

"True, though at least you get pulled aside to do things like help Admiral Rose. She came as far as the Army Camp to see me yesterday. The woman says you are a genius and you take insane risks. She likes you."

He laughed, but he supposed the risk part was true.

"The problem we will still have, though, is one of trust," Gregorian admitted. He sat back and frowned. "This is one I cannot discuss with others, even the King at this moment. We know there are enemies planted in the city. They are, of course, among the poor because outsiders would stand out among the higher classes. Of course, that doesn't mean people -- like our dear Lord Honorgate -- can't side with the Atrians. The worse problem we are going to face, though, is going to be one of trust."

"And yet the poor, and that's whom you have to suspect, have remained loyal and fought as hard as anyone else," Mica said.

"I'm sure that's annoyed the Atrians, too," Gregorian replied with a bright smile. Then it faded. "It doesn't count for much with some people, though. There have been several lords who have told the King that he needs to run the poor out of the city before we can be safe."

"I -- are they --" Mica couldn't seem to find the words to express the anger he felt at hearing such a thing.

"Don't worry. King Abertus is having none of it, and they know better than to talk to me. Their fools besides. Whom do they think does the work here? It certainly isn't them."

Mica nodded and took a deeper breath before he answered. "They'd be fools to do it, even if they could," Mica said.

"A few are putting up the pretense that the poor would have a better life living on the land rather than in the city. King

Abertus asked the last one -- no, I will not tell you names -- if he was going to provide the land for them to farm. Those lords haven't been back with any new quaint little ideas yet."

"I don't understand how people can be so blind," Mica admitted. "People accuse me of hiding in my tower and not dealing with the real world -- and in some ways people are right -- but I still understand how that world works better than they do."

Someone pounded on the door. Nyle went to check and came back a moment later with a folded note.

"A soldier said some man delivered this at the gate for Lord Raventower and then hurried away."

Mica took it with a frown and then nodded. The address on the outside said Lord Raventower. He knew the writing. "Merriweather," he said waving it before he opened the note.

He stared at it, reading the opening several times --

My dearest sweet Mica...

"Mica?"

"She's in trouble."

Gregorian stood and leaned over his shoulder. "Oh hell. Just that greeting says she's in trouble. Read the rest."

Mica forced his emotions under control. He put the note on the table because his hand had begun to tremble. "My dearest sweet, Mica -- I'm sure you won't mind, but I'm slipping off to spend a few days with my cousin Satin. Please remind the Ravenstower Cook that I won't be there. All my love, Jewel."

"Well damn. That is serious. And it is her handwriting --"

"Code. Some secrets here."

He hadn't noticed that Gram, Ada, and Shipley had come to the table, all of them white-faced with worry. Nyle stood close by, all of them ready to move. They cared for her -- and even Gregorian looked willing to bring the army out.

Mica forced himself to calm. Several breaths. Then he

looked at the note again. "Of course, she gave us hints. This is Merriweather. First is Satin. She's never mentioned a relative by that name. Next is Ravenstower rather than Raventower. She would not make that mistake."

"Yes, and the word tower is slightly smaller besides," Gregorian agreed and stood to lean over his shoulder. Look at the word after it. Cook looks more like rook --"

"Raven's Rook?" Shipley asked suddenly. "There was such a place, me lord. Used to be part of the slums, it were, and filled with apartments. A company come in and cleared them all out and made it a factory. Hired back many of the people what used to live there to do the work, though, so it wasn't all lost. Closed down now during the fighting though."

"Made some fancy cloth, they did," Gram agreed. "Shiny like --"

"Satin," Gregorian said.

"And she would know all of this," Mica added. "It might even be one of the family businesses."

Gregorian gave a grunt of agreement. He went back to his chair and sat down, which surprised Mica.

"We need to do this carefully. Someone delivered the note; those people will be watching to see how you react. We don't dare rush off with the army, but as it happens, the guard is going to change within the hour, and that will be an easy way out for you, Mica. Shipley, we'll need you to pinpoint the building and find out who has her and how many there are. You can leave now, but don't head straight there. Meet us back on the main road. Don't come back here."

"I'll be wise sir," the boy said. "We'll get her back, me lord."

He gave a whistle for Bear, and the two went off before Mica could even think to say anything more.

"Roe and I will go out, too," Nyle said. "We'll go out with the soldiers as well. I'll go see to the uniforms for all three of us."

Gregorian nodded. "Ask for a map of the city as well."

Nyle came back with a load of wood for the fireplaces, and buried in it was a package with the map and three army jackets in cadet black with silver buttons. The day was still light enough that someone watching could have noticed such things, even if most of the soldiers wore cloaks with hoods. He had brought weapons as well.

The worst part came then: the simple act of waiting with nothing they could do except to look at a map and guess the general area of the building. Mica thought that Gregorian tried to keep him busy. His brother planned his battles, and every time he watched Gregorian's finger trace a new path through the streets of Kamere, he knew there was thought behind the movement.

The soldiers prepared to march out as the others came in. Mica, Nyle, and Roe slipped out of the tower door, all the lights dark behind them. Gregorian had already gone out and ordered the men to mount. No one made any extra notice, though they knew that three of them were not their comrades. There was no doubt they recognized all three.

They went down the road, around the curve -- he glanced toward Fisherman's Row but saw only normal movement there.

The weight of his flintlock felt odd. The sword sheathed into the saddle while he rode glinted in the sunset light. He hadn't known the day was so late.

If something had happened to Merriweather --

No. If the Atrians wanted her dead, they would have killed her and sent back the body. She had a use for them, and he knew what it was, too. Word had gotten out about their betrothal. Lord Honorgate and his companions were going to try and use that against him.

Mica's hand touched the flintlock. There would be a

problem if people started dying around him. That would not stop him from doing what he needed to do to get Merriweather back.

CHAPTER TWENTY-SIX

They passed Shadow Walk just as the weather began to turn bad, though Mica had seen a lot worse lately. A cold, icy wind blew at them, and snow began to fall once more. He thought he heard a collective sigh of frustration from everyone around them. They knew there was going to be some sort of trouble -- Lord Raventower did not ride out in the guise of a soldier for no reason. So far, though, he and Gregorian had said nothing about the trouble.

A few people passed them. Mica kept his head bowed, wondering if any of them were spies. He knew a few faces and trusted those, as much as he trusted anyone right now. Everyone seemed in a hurry to get home before night closed in and before the storm fell upon them as well.

He could have wished for the High Priestess Ledea to appear in the form of the Glowing Lady. Maybe she would have given him some true answer this time. He needed to know what to do because if they made mistakes --

Mica bowed his head, taking soft, quick breaths. Nyle rode beside him and glanced his way but said nothing. He did not doubt that Nyle felt worries as well.

Shipley appeared at a curve in the road. Gregorian told all but four of the others to ride on while he stayed back with the four soldiers, Nyle, Roe, and Mica.

"We don't dare take too many in with us," Gregorian explained. "We have a problem. Captain Merriweather has been taken captive, and we mean to have her back."

The soldiers looked startled by the news, and all of them gave quick nods of agreement.

"What have you found, Shipley?" Mica asked.

"The building, like we thought, me lord," he said. He had a hand on Bear's head and gasped slightly, having run some distance. "Not many there, sirs, but he has a dozen or so Atrians in the building across from it. I think he expects them to be found and him to get away if there is trouble."

"Him?" Gregorian said.

"Didn't see him, but heard him with two bad boys he has out front to keep the watch. He talked funny, though he knew the words." Shipley knelt and began to draw in the snow. "The road here goes right past the front, and you'd be seen afore you could dismount. Walkin' up ain't no better, not from this road. But there be alleys that will take you to the back of the building. I can show you them ways. You can ride most of it."

They followed Shipley into the hollows between the buildings, some so narrow that riders had to dismount. Finally a horse refused to go on. Gregorian looked back and signaled them to retreat.

"Back a couple yards," he said. "We'll leave the horses there."

"Yes, General," Shipley said. He was hardly a shape in this darkness where Mica thought the sun must never reach. The buildings overtopped each other, leaned inward, and in many places even blocked out the snow. "We're close now."

The rest of the walk went quickly and silently. Some of the buildings here were not abandoned, but there were few doors or unblocked windows on this side. Mica suspected it was to keep thieves out since it would be hard to spot them breaking in.

They were shabby buildings of cheaply made brick, too much of it crumbling away. A good-sized quake could bring down large sections of this area, and Mica feared even the wear and tear of a few more years might do the job on its own.

Something to study later.

Something to keep his mind occupied during this walk. He feared what he might yet find. He had to keep that image from his mind.

They stopped. Shipley waved to a building that had taken some damage from a bomb, though not as much as some of other others. There were signs of people having moved in this area, and the stairs to the door --

Mica caught Gregorian by the arm and signaled the others back. They retreated to the shadows again.

"Yes, I saw it too," Gregorian whispered. "The stairs are mined. Anything might set the explosives off."

Mica had dropped down on his heels and studied the wooden stairs from underneath. "Looks like it can be disabled at the top of the stairs. I am going to need something back at Raventower."

He'd started to back away, and Gregorian caught his arm, but when he saw Mica's face, he merely nodded. "Be damned careful. Take Shipley to see you out and back again. I'm going to deploy my men down the street, but I'll wait for you to return."

"Thank you," he said and started away with Shipley and Bear at his side. Gregorian had not asked what he was going to go retrieve. Just as well.

He took his horse from where they'd left them and pulled the startled Shipley up into the saddle. "Bear can keep up with us. I'm not going to race so fast that I risk getting us killed on the ice."

"Yes, me lord," the boy said.

He suspected Shipley had never been on a horse before. He could have left him at the edge of the alleys and found him again when he came back, but Mica simply did not want to slow down. Besides, Mica thought Shipley might be a good guard while they rode. He was not paying enough attention to the world around him now, though he did try to keep his head lowered and the hood in place. Shipley and Bear were a kind of disguise as well. No one would expect a Lord of Sedina to be riding with a beggar boy at his back, even if they did know Mica.

Up to the gate. The guards were surprised to find him, and he wasn't certain he hadn't been spotted. Should he have been more careful?

No time. No time to worry about it.

He put the boy off of the horse and swung off, throwing the reins to the nearest man. "Stay here, Shipley."

"Yes, me lord."

The boy looked stunned, and he eyed the horse with a little worry still. Bear was still prancing through the snow, having enjoyed the run. Mica raced up the steps and into the building. Ada appeared --

"I need something from upstairs," he said and didn't even slow.

Mica was out of breath by the time he reached his workroom. Merriweather's chair sat by the steps, and he glanced at it with a moment of despair. His hand touched his chest where the note still rested below the jacket. Wise Merriweather. Smart Merriweather. Whoever held her (he had a good guess), knew they were betrothed. A sweet address to her husband-to-be would not have seemed in the least bit out of nature for such a relationship.

He still hadn't completely gotten his breath back when he grabbed the backpack from where it still sat by his desk. It felt heavy in his hand. He'd repaired the damage from the flight to escape the clockwork spiders, but he had not tested the device out since then. No matter. If he judged this right, all he needed was the wings and not the engine. He slipped the straps over his shoulder and tightened the belt across his chest, and then headed back downstairs.

The weight on his back made him awkward, and he slipped on a couple steps coming up hard against the turn in the wall. With a snarl, he reminded himself of every time he'd warned others about racing down the steps. He said some encouraging words to Ada and Gram and then was back out into the snowy evening.

Shipley didn't know what the pack meant so he wouldn't lecture Mica. He didn't want to think what Merriweather would say when she realized -- providing he survived.

Mica did not intend to stop and explain any of it to Gregorian, either. He pulled the boy back up into the saddle before him, though he felt a bit awkward with the backpack. They rode away, though Mica was wise enough to go slow down the path from the tower.

"I need to get into the building on the right of Raven's Rook, Shipley," he said. He kept his voice calm. "I don't want to be seen doing it, so we'll need a back door.

"Huh," the boy said. "No doors on the back, nor the side. But low windows, locked -- but I can take care of that problem."

"I had hoped you could."

"You learn things on the street," he said with a slight shrug.

"I'm grateful for your help. I don't want to make a lot of noise. I don't want to blunder in and make this worse."

"We'll get her back," Shipley said. He seemed to mean those words.

They reached the area where they left the horse again. This time Shipley took him to the right, snaking their way past buildings and across piles of trash. A dog barked and growled, but a sound from Bear put it on the run. Nothing else dared even make a sound before the huge animal.

"This," Shipley whispered, tapping the brick of the building. Mica wasn't certain how he knew since all the buildings looked the same to him. "This way."

The boy moved carefully around the side of the building and climbed along a ledge that was hardly an inch wide, his feet finding holds in the broken brick around it. He checked one window, wood covered, and then another, and another. This time he pulled something from his boot and worked at the lock, barely a soft scratch of sound. The window slid upward, and the wood popped out, though the boy caught it as he climbed inside.

Mica handed up the pack and then hoisted himself into the window. Bear stayed outside looking mournfully up at them.

"Squatters here, me lord," Shipley whispered and nodded toward a hint of light. They had a fire going -- dangerous inside a building like this. "Best avoid them."

"I will," Mica put his pack on and then put a hand on Shipley's shoulder. "Go tell Gregorian that I am going to the roof and for the love of all the gods, don't shoot me if he sees movement up there."

"Roof," Shipley said and then gave a shake of his head. "I heard about them wings. Sir --"

"Go. Tell Gregorian that I will let him in the door -- or if he hears trouble to come in as best he can."

"Me Lord --" the boy began, his voice almost rising. Then he stopped. "Yes, sir."

Shipley went back out the window. Mica pulled it closed and shoved the wood back into place. He couldn't tell how long this would take and he didn't want anyone to wonder who had wandered in here, whether they worked for the

Atrians or not.

Just in time. Mica heard the sliding step of a couple people, neither trying to be quiet.

"You're daft, man. Look. Windows all closed. Not breeze."

"I felt it," another said, his voice surly. "Felt it in me bones. It be death come for us, boy. We're doomed --"

"Well, death can't come too soon if I have to listen to this again tonight. Just go back and drink your grog."

Mica wondered what the two men would do if he stepped out of the shadows right then, all dressed in black and hooded. He thought the wings might be an interesting added touch. Mica waited instead, hardly daring to breathe. They didn't sound as though they worked for the Atrians, but he wouldn't take the chance.

Besides, he needed time for his eyes to adjust. He stood in a long and narrow room, a doorway where the two had gone lit by the fire beyond. The fire did not appear to be too close, so he inched that way, hoping to see a stairwell.

He found it, with the squatters in a room across from the steps, the doorway standing open to where they sat, but no one lingering close by. They were all huddled by their meager warmth. He smelled fish now, too. That was a common food for the poor, and he saw that they had a few on spits over the fire. They were intent on their food, so he inched to the steps, studied them for a moment and then moved up two, skipped the one with the crack across it, and up another two. The wood made sounds, but he was quick, and if anyone came to look, he didn't see them, and they didn't see him.

Three more floors up. There were squatters on the second floor, too, but they had moved off to another room, and Mica went past without a problem.

The next -- he could see through to the building beside him where part of the wall had caved away, and he saw movement there, a floor below where he stood. He moved towards the broken wall to get a better look and to see if there was any guard on the roof of Ravens' Rook.

He watched the one man inside the building as he paced, mostly in the shadows. Payton Honorgate, of course. He'd suspected as much when Shipley said the man spoke the language but sounded odd. Payton had acquired an accent.

Rats ran everywhere on the last two floors and even some on the roof. They squealed and yelled at his presence, but so far no one had come to look. Mica wouldn't have either.

Down on his hands and knees, Mica crawled across the roof and looked over the edge. The other building stood a floor shorter. He had thought so, though he'd had a hard time telling from the narrow alley. The wind was not quite at his back, but close enough that he could use the extra lift to his advantage.

He unfurled the wings. They caught the breeze and twisted a bit. He didn't dare use the blades since the small engine made an odd noise.

Mica pulled the hood and goggles over his head and stood. No time to waste. He backed up to the far edge of the roof he was on and then ran and leapt.

He saw Gregorian in the area below, shaking a fist at him. Oh, not a happy man down there. Good thing Mica wasn't in the army, or there might have been an ugly court martial before they were done.

And then he landed on the ice and snow that spread across the other roof. The pitch was not steep and that left layers of ice in puddles everywhere. A slip put him perilously close to the far edge, but he yanked the wings shut and threw himself into a roll to the side.

Stopped. Mica could hear no cry of alarm as he unhooked the pack and shoved it aside. He listened for a moment longer, thinking there might have been a voice or two out on the street. There were guards there -- the bad boys, as Shipley was apt to call them, the ough gang members from Shadow Walk or the areas around it. Tough young men and easy to hire, but not as good as trained guards.

Mica crawled to the edge and looked over just to be certain. The two guards stood snarling insults at each other and the weather. The snow began falling harder again, and the wind rattled off the roofs all around, making the perfect cover for what he needed to do next. He could not be silent in it, he feared, but if the wind kept up, he might go unnoticed.

Mica prayed that he didn't mess this up because Merriweather would be annoyed. He didn't want to annoy her.

Mica wanted her back and safe. That seemed a very odd feeling because he realized she was the first human he had ever, truly felt close to. He was friends with his brother, but they'd never been family.

He had to fight the trap door open and used a blade from the wings to dig through the wood along the edge, finding it both locked and iced over. He didn't care that the cold metal, large and unwieldy, cut his fingers.

The door swung upward at last, and Mica threw himself over the edge and into the darkness.

CHAPTER TWENTY-SEVEN

The stairwell inside this building was worse. Part of it had been ruined during the bombardment of the city. Mica studied the first of those obstacles, seeing the scorch marks of a fire that had not spread far. He supposed the fall of snow had put it out, probably toppling down from the roof.

Soot, ice, and snow made everything more treacherous. Mica had begun to tremble, but that did not come from the cold. He fought the reaction back with a surge of logic: he could not do this well if he thought about Merriweather and panicked. He must focus his concentration on each step.

He studied the array of broken wood and dangerous nails before him and worked out his next four movements with exact precision. Mica caught part of what had been a railing, pushed off and slid down two feet, kicked gently away from a broken wall and swung himself out over the broken beams before he dropped three feet or more, to what he hoped would provide solid footing.

The wood beneath him creaked, but it held.

Mica worked out the next three movements, which were, unfortunately, a little more elaborate and prone to make unusual sounds. Wood cracked as he caught hold of part of a wall, the noise like the clap of lightning and thunder from someone right beside it. He feared making any more noise as he drew closer to the others. Mica stopped and listened, hearing distant voices. Nothing that sounded like Merriweather, though. He desperately wanted to hear her.

Careful, he told himself. He dropped and grabbed frantically at the slivered wood of the wall when the step beneath him gave way. Carefully, he moved his feet downward again to the next step. The wood beneath his fingers sent small wooden spikes into his hand, but Mica kept his balance and didn't tumble down the broken stairs to the next level.

Rats ran, but then they'd been running everywhere already, and if anything, the creatures covered some of his noise. Mica stopped for a moment and tried to get an idea of what might be waiting below him. He sensed movement, but he had to go down yet another floor. The stairs here were not broken, but he mistrusted them and moved with most of his weight pressed hard against the wall as he sidled downward for half the steps.

The lights grew brighter, but there were dark shadows as well. Mica went to his knees and carefully moved from one step to the next, his back to the wall, maneuvering as carefully as he could.

Listening. Voices. Some were Atrian, the words guttural and harsh. Mica knew some Atrian, but everything echoed oddly around him, and he could make no sense of it. He wanted to know what they wanted.

He desperately wanted to hear Merriweather.

One step and another. Mica had to move sideways on his knees, but he hoped that would keep him from being spotted even if someone happened along. He didn't think though, that there were guards at all inside the building. He supposed, given the state of the stairs, that they would not expect anyone to come in that way. The Atrians had the back door mined and the front door guarded.

Mica thought he might surprise them and for a moment he considered rushing in --

No. He had no idea how many there might be.

By the time he got to the bottom step, he had found there were broken walls and doors between them. Weaving equipment provided many obstacles as well. He could see nothing clearly.

Mica paused by the one doorway where he heard the voices -- at least three. Everyone appeared to be concentrated in the far corner, and there might have been another shape on the floor by the wall. He willed that shape to move and thought he saw a slight twitch. It might be Merriweather. He let himself believe so and then he hurried away, heading for yet one more stairwell and the door to the outside.

They had the wires hung over the doorknob, and it was easy enough to unhook them so that when the door opened the explosives did not go off. When he carefully opened the door, he was surprised to see Gregorian standing close by the stairs and looked at him with shock. Either his brother was too angry to consider what might have happened or else he had complete confidence that Mica would not let the bombs go off. Either way, he thought Gregorian might be a bit too reckless right now.

"Up," Mica said with a wave of his hand. "Fast! They might feel the draft, but they're a floor up!"

They all came up, quick and quiet, and slipping into the shadows. Shipley and Bear did not come up. "I'll go bother the bad boys," Shipley whispered. "Keep them busy like and noisy."

"Thank you," Mica whispered. "Count to 200."

Shipley nodded. He and Bear headed for the edge of the building.

Mica pulled the door shut but did not set the explosives

again. He quickly laid out the problem with the floor above them, especially the looms that made hazards on the way in.

"But we have surprise on our side," he added. "That's going to help. I could tell they're relaxed up there. We just have to be fast. Be careful."

"My men already know they are not to use the flintlocks unless I order them to shoot," Gregorian said. "How fast does Shipley count?"

"Good question. Let's get up the stairs."

He and Gregorian took the lead. That was probably not wise, but Mica was well past any sort of reasoning. Soldiers followed, and Nyle and Roe came last. He wished there were more of them. He wished they could have come through the wall and attacked without any delay --

He heard the dog barking, a deep, fierce sound. Voices rose outside the building. That would draw attention to the front of the building and the windows there. They still would not expect trouble to be coming up behind them.

No time to make more plans. No time to think about what they were doing.

Gregorian caught hold of Mica's arm as though, at the last moment, he thought to hold his brother back. Mica shook his head, and Gregorian released him, and the general stayed at his side. That might be wise because if anyone died here --

No, don't think about that, either.

The shouts outside grew louder, and the dog had started baying. Mica heard someone in the room mutter a curse.

Time to move.

The looms provided a bit of cover, even if they did slow the group as they rushed in. They helped to hide how many there were, too. An Atrian shouted a warning and others came their way, but Mica moved to the right and around another four looms before he could clearly see the far corner of the room.

Merriweather sat on the floor, tied up in the corner. Payton Honorgate stood over her, his sword in hand, ready to move --

"Stop now, Payton, and you might survive," Gregorian warned. He did have his flintlock in hand and aimed straight at the man.

Payton snarled and threw his sword away -- but in the same moment he drew a dagger with his other hand and leapt straight at Mica who had come closer.

Mica was ready for the attack, though, and a kick sent him stumbling backward. Payton gave a yell in Atrian and changed direction, heading past Merriweather. He grabbed a chair and threw it at a window and leapt out even as Gregorian fired.

Mica rushed to the window, fearing that Bear and Shipley would go after him, but they were in a fight of their own. Nyle looked out and cursed and threw himself out as well -- but he went to help Shipley.

"Did I wound the bastard?" Gregorian asked.

"I don't know. I don't care," Mica said.

He turned back to Merriweather. She mumbled things he could not understand since she had a gag in her mouth. From the look on her face, he might not want to know what she was saying anyway.

He let Gregorian take care of the rest of the battle while he knelt and undid the gag and untied her arms and feet.

"Thank you, Lord Raventower," she said. She looked more embarrassed than angry now. "They were waiting just as I came through the Temple Square. They knew who I was."

"What did Payton want from you?" Gregorian asked as Mica helped her to her feet.

"I am really not entirely certain," she admitted. "Aside from being a link to Lord Raventower, maybe just someone from Sedina he could rant to. The man is a fanatic, but we knew that much, right? I heard a great deal about Torger and

Atric. I think the last might be some follower of the god who maybe led the refugees to Atria."

"That would make sense," Mica said. "Good."

"Still not much help." She limped a little over to a corner where she recovered her own weapons, including the corset with the lovely knives. Two of them were missing, and Mica suspected she had put up quite a fight. "He seemed to think he could convince me, or bribe me, into getting him into the tower somehow. Barring that, he hoped to buy his way in with me. I had the oddest feeling about him. I do not think he can be the one in charge."

"No?" Gregorian said. "That might make sense. Everything we've seen out of him has been erratic. Any idea who could be the one?"

"Maybe someone on the ships," she said. "Someone who doesn't have direct control over him."

"I don't know if that makes him any less dangerous."

She rubbed at her wrists and frowned.

"Are you all right?" Mica finally asked.

"Yes. A bit bruised, but nothing worse. Your hands are bleeding."

He looked down at them, surprised. Then he remembered the metal from the blade and the slivers of wood. He decided not to mention either. She'd want to know the whole story, but he hoped to be back to the tower and to safety before then. One of Gregorian's men arrived with bandages, pulled a few slivers, and wrapped the hands up, mumbling about getting better care later.

The soldiers had taken the Atrians so much by surprise that their own injuries were minor. Roe had gone to the window, probably to chase down Payton, but apparently knew it wasn't a good idea.

"Shipley's alright," Roe said and gave a wave to the boy. "Round the side, Shipley. We're heading out!"

They were. Gregorian had done a quick search, found nothing of interest, and ordered his men back out. He designated two to remain and guard until they could remove the explosives from the stairs and do a full search. He'd send people as soon as he could find them.

They started toward the back door while Gregorian and his men took care of the prisoners. An Atrian had died, but he'd been back in the corner and Mica never even noticed. A bit of luck there.

They passed the prisoners, one of whom snarled something in Atrian at Merriweather. Mica didn't think she understood what he said, but she kicked him anyway.

Her mistake. Mica heard a slight snap and saw her almost go down on the next step forward.

"Damn!"

The Atrian laughed, and then stopped when her hand went to the blades on her corset. Oh yes, they'd seen her use those weapons. She limped away, her face red rather than white, but the foot obviously causing her some pain.

"Not broken," she mumbled to Gregorian when he crossed to them.

"I should take you off duty for a few days --"

She looked at him as though he was crazy. Mica thought he must have much the same look. "Even if I had broken my foot, do you really, truly want to put some other poor, unsuspecting person in charge of your crazy brother?"

"I think I should resent that," Mica said. "I prefer eccentric."

"I'll compromise: crazy and eccentric brother. I heard someone come down the stairs, even if the Atrians were too stupid to notice and Payton too concerned with telling me how a person in the army should follow Krogor. You flew to the building, didn't you?"

"Just from the roof next door."

"Well, that's better than I expected. I thought you'd jumped from the roof at Raventower again."

"Ah. I hadn't even considered it, though that might have worked --"

"Crazy," she said.

He didn't argue. Instead, he swept Merriweather up into his arms and carried her down the stairs.

She didn't complain, either.

CHAPTER TWENTY-EIGHT

Mica carried Merriweather out of the building, down the outside steps, and continued down the alley. Gregorian had shouted orders at several people and then rushed to join them. Roe, Nyle, Shipley and Bear followed behind the four soldiers who stayed close to guard General Gregorian Raventower.

"I'm sorry Payton got away, but this could have gone much worse," Gregorian said.

Mica noted that Merriweather had turned a bit red again.

"You can put me down," she insisted.

"We're not far from the horses," Mica replied. He had managed not to slip on the ice yet. She wasn't a small woman, but he had no trouble.

"You're actually enjoying this, aren't you?" she demanded. She'd started to squirm but stopped as they had reached the horses.

"I am thinking about the tale we can tell our children," he said and won startled looks from her and his brother. "The story of how their mother was captured by the evil traitor and was completely unharmed ... until she kicked a poor, helpless prisoner."

"Huh," she said as he helped her up into the saddle.

She *accidentally* kicked him in the chin.

Gregorian laughed. "You should have known better, Mica."

He agreed with a grin of his own. It hadn't been much of a kick, at least.

They left some of the horses under a guard for the soldiers in the building. Gregorian wouldn't leave them without a good way to escape. The rest of them led mounts out but stayed on foot, remembering how narrow some of the passages coming in had been. One soldier had an extra mount for Mica.

Shipley led them back out through the maze of alleys, and none of the paths looked any safer for having already captured the enemies. Payton Honorgate had run, and they knew he had allies. The soldiers spread out before and behind them, moving silently as they went through one passage and another. At least they were somewhat out of the wind here, Mica thought. He still led Merriweather's horse, though she was perfectly capable of handling the animal herself. He wondered why she didn't ask for the reins.

Glancing back, he had one good idea of why she was so quiescent about the situation. He noted how she twisted and turned at every sound, playing the part of a guard on a slightly higher elevation than him.

"We're being followed," she said once, though softly. "I don't think it's more than two, though. Might even be locals who are bound to be curious about what's going on."

Gregorian nodded, gave a few hand signals to his men, and kept moving. Two more guards slipped to the back of the group. They did not slow.

Mica found himself trembling in the aftermath of the confrontation. They'd gotten lucky. If Payton had been less of a coward, he wouldn't have run, and Merriweather would likely have been dead. If the Atrians hadn't been so assured of their trap, the battle would have been fierce. If ... if ... there were too many chances that might have gone a different way, and he had to push all those other possibilities out of his mind. They'd done this part. Now he needed to focus on the next step.

This was not a safe night. Not at all. Payton knew how few of them were in the group. If Payton had many followers in the area --

Mica tried not to think too much about that possibility, either. They'd done well so far.

Shipley pointed straight ahead. They could see the main road not far away. While they went straight, Shipley and Bear took passage to the left, an opening so small that Bear could barely squeeze through. They were gone before Mica could ask what he intended. The look on the boy's face had shown worry, though, so he knew, without the others saying anything, that they were in trouble.

He handed the reins to Merriweather at last. She frowned but nodded and must have realized that she'd only slow them if she came off the horse. Gregorian gave more signals and Merriweather nodded as well. Mica didn't catch them all, but he knew that the general expected trouble at the street.

Mica's worry began to shift quite suddenly from Merriweather to Gregorian. He hadn't thought much about his brother rushing out with him to save the Captain, but now he fully considered the insanity of the top military officer in Sedina being on the street with so few soldiers.

If Gregorian had been killed back at the building -- if he were killed now --

The Atrians were going to target Gregorian. They would likely target Mica, too -- but then they'd been doing that from the start, and he didn't think so much about it. But Gregorian --

There was not a damned thing he could do now, of course.

Mica hadn't seen his brother look quite so intense as he did right then. Gregorian did not get many chances to direct expeditions like this one, he supposed. The general oversaw the larger war, and though he was often with the troops, the amount of involvement would rarely be as personal as this had been.

Mica thought he understood his brother better.

No Atrians waited at the edge of the alley and the street. The road had a slight covering of snow, too -- no one had come this way. That did not make it safe.

Gregorian frowned and spoke softly. "They're going to expect us to go to the castle, I think. Raventower is closer, though."

"Maybe we should split up," Merriweather suggested. Mica had been about to say the same thing, but he was glad that it came from her instead. Gregorian might take her more seriously.

"I don't think that wise," Gregorian admitted after a moment. "We're already too few, and if one group is picked off, the other will be all the easier to attack. Together and straight to Raventower. We have more soldiers there and on Fisherman's Row. We might also run into a patrol along the road."

No one argued. The group mounted the horses and hurried out and around the corner. Raventower stood to the left, a faint shape through the falling snow, but a good sight. They were not far --

Trouble coming their way. The Atrians burst out of a passage between two buildings, fifty or more and all with swords in hand. Payton, he noted, was with them but not in the lead. Not a brave man.

Mica almost said so to Gregorian -- and then remembered that Payton was Gregorian's father. He kept the words to himself, especially since the battle was already upon them.

"Back!" Gregorian shouted. "We can outrun them!"

That was true. They rode horses and the enemy on foot. Though the Atrians were better trained for winter conditions, they could not move as quickly as the horses.

They did not have many flintlocks, apparently. A couple shots followed them, but Mica didn't see anyone hit.

"More trouble ahead!" one of the soldiers shouted.

Horses came to a skidding stop. Gregorian looked around and pointed to the area across the road. The building there had been gutted by fire, but it did provide some cover.

The horses didn't want to go inside the ruins, but they found a passage mostly clear to the left and got the animals at least off the road. Nyle and one of the guards stayed with them, in hopes they'd all be able to ride away again.

The sounds grew too loud. Too many of the enemy rushed their way. The Atrians saw the signs of where they'd gone -- they couldn't hide them. Mica helped Merriweather to the first bit of cover. She dropped to her knees and began loading her flintlock.

"They were very pleased to get my weapons and especially the powder and shot," Merriweather said. "Which made me all the happier to get it back."

"Short on firepower," Gregorian said as he loaded his own weapon.

"That was my impression, sir," Merriweather said and began loading the second flintlock. Calm. Steady.

The second group had arrived, and though not as large as the first, combined they presented a formidable wall of fanatical faces. Mica pulled up a handful of clockwork insects and held his sword with the other hand. It wouldn't be long before the attack came.

He swept a glance over the group. No sign of Payton who must have stood behind his allies. He wondered how the Atrians felt about such a leader --

Not the one in charge? Merriweather had said so, and he trusted her observances --

Movement swept through the group, an odd shift to their left. More shouts and yells. They would sweep in on them at any moment. Too many --

No.

The Atrians scattered as a wave of locals rushed into the street from the alleys around them. They carried makeshift weapons, and by numbers alone, they fought back the Atrian forces.

Shipley. Shipley and Bear fought in the midst of the trouble, a blade slashing at enemies and Bear grabbing legs and pulling others down. Mica had never seen the two look so fierce. Gregorian shouted for his own men to get out there and help.

The attack had been so unexpected, and the chaos so complete, that Mica still could not find Payton even as the last of the Atrians escaped. He expected the man had run long before now.

Dead had fallen in the road. Still not close to him, and he didn't know how they were going to get through there.

Shipley and Bear arrived, though, while the locals were still chasing the others off. "This way, this way," Shipley said and pushed past the horses and into an alley that led them away from the battle. Nyle, Roe, and the General's men joined them. Mica got Merriweather onto a saddle. She did not kick him this time.

Mica learned that going away from the battle was good for many reasons.

"I got the locals first," Shipley said, walking by Gregorian who led his horse as did everyone but Merriweather. The area here was dark, dank, and mostly deserted. The buildings on this side of the road had been falling to ruin for decades. Even the people of the slums usually avoided the area. "But there were more of the Atrians coming from everywhere. I found one group of your soldiers, sir, and they was going to Raventower to get more. I warned the locals to get clear and let the soldiers do their work when they got there. I hope they listened; there's no easy way to tell locals from Atrians, you know."

"You did damn good, Shipley," Gregorian said with a hand on the boy's shoulder.

"Thank you, sir," the boy said and seemed to mean those words. They went on in silence for a few more yards. "We can't go much farther this way. We'll be back on the road soon and make better time. The buildings fell over along the way here, and there be no passages for even those on foot, at least none fast enough."

"Back to the road then," Gregorian agreed.

Every step took them closer to Raventower. Mica could see the shape more clearly now, and he would be glad to get there. He looked back at Merriweather and found she had her flintlock in hand and remained ready for trouble.

They came back out to the road just as the band of soldiers reached the spot. Looking at their numbers, Mica feared they might have left Raventower without adequate protection, and considering how much the Atrians wanted that building, that might be far from the wisest decision.

Gregorian, though, must have seen the same thing. "Fifteen of you back with Lord Raventower to guard the building!" he shouted. He waved his hand at a group, and they cut themselves out from the others. "The rest of you with me!"

They parted company. Mica's people, including Shipley who rode with Roe, came with him. He feared Bear might have trouble keeping up with them as they raced toward the road up the hill. They made it to the gate, though he could see that one group of Atrians pulled back when Merriweather shot in their direction. Besides, Mica and his group would be inside the gate and have it closed again before they could get close.

Once they were inside, Nyle leapt from his horse and shoved the gate closed and locked. The soldiers still there had taken positions on the walls and were ready with firearms. There were not many of them, but Mica had the feeling they would have held out well enough anyway.

Home. Safe.

Nyle and Roe took care of the horses. Merriweather came off her mount and took a limping step forward and gave a nod to Mica.

"Not broken, but I did twist it a bit. I'll be fine."

"Inside," he said and waved toward the building. He was having trouble even thinking clearly now. "Inside and rest for a while."

She nodded agreement. Mica had to use the knocker and identify himself to Ada before she unlatched the door. They were quickly inside, though, and the door secured behind them. The kitchen had never looked like a happier place, especially after Nyle and Roe joined them. Ada and Gram had kept working through the day and presented a plethora of dishes for the meal that evening.

Gregorian even arrived just as they were preparing to eat.

"Ah. My timing is getting better," he said and took the chair by Merriweather. He looked worn and wet. "Payton got away, of course."

"Of course," Mica replied. "I can't say I really care much right now."

"That's been the general opinion," Gregorian said. "We foiled a couple important plans, by the way. The Atrians had been slipping a few soldiers in nearly every night for at least ten days, probably more. They were going to draw the army out by pretending to be only a few and then fall on them and hope to destroy a major part of the city's defenses. It might have worked, too. However, Payton saw his chance to grab

Merriweather and thought he'd have a way into Raventower through her. That, at least, is what we suspect happened based on what we've heard from the few prisoners we've taken. The man really is a fool."

"I guess I'll count it lucky then," Merriweather said with a shake of her head, "rather than stupidity on my part. I thought I'd pass as another soldier on the road, you know. They've been safe enough since there are so many patrols. I planned to join up with another -- I'd just left one behind -- and ride on to the tower. Payton had good timing in that part."

Gregorian nodded and smiled as Ada put a plate of food in front of him. "Thank you. I am famished."

They ate and discussed a few other things, but it always came back to the trouble at hand.

"Your friends were very brave, Shipley," Gregorian said. "And I know they took a chance because Payton could easily burn down the slums if he gets his way."

"They know," Shipley said. He'd given Bear a piece of bread dripping with gravy, and the dog watched him attentively for more, his head all but resting on the tabletop. "But we'd talked, some of them and us, afore. No use, they say, waiting around and seein' who wins. Lord Raventower, he always helped when they needed it. So they come to help him, sir."

And not to help either the General or the King. Gregorian understood the implications. He gave a quick nod of understanding.

They had an excellent meal. Mica realized that nothing had been settled, though. They had, by chance alone -- and Payton's stupidity -- managed to foil one problem, but others still festered. More trouble would soon be on the way

CHAPTER TWENTY-NINE

Battles continued all through the next few days as the soldiers did their best to flush out any more of the Atrian soldiers. The locals helped as well, and the notes from Gregorian said that even certain lords and ladies found themselves impressed by their bravery and loyalty.

So maybe something good would come from this before they were done.

Winter fell upon them once more with a rush of wind and a fall of snow that covered all signs of battles. Mica had known the weather was changing, but even he looked out the workshop window with surprise at the white world that lay below the tower. The others had mentioned snow at the morning meal, but he hadn't fully comprehended the extent of the storm until he went all the way down to the door and looked out.

Snow stood halfway to his knee and piled up higher where the soldiers had shoveled it aside in other areas. It still fell, and he could not imagine how much more they might get.

Mica closed the door, gave a nod to Merriweather, and headed up the stairs. They might, in fact, have some quiet today.

Merriweather had been using his cane and moved easily

now. Neither of them was in a hurry, and she crossed the room and stood by him when he opened the shutter to look out again, as though he would see something different from here.

"I think this might be good," Merriweather offered. "I'm not sure. I can't say I like snow much at all, but --"

"I agree," Mica said. The fire cackled behind them, warmth at his back, while the window seemed to leak cold. Even so, he could not stop himself from staring. Part of it, he realized, was how calm the city looked. Nothing much moved today, except what he took to be patrols moving along the main roads. He hoped they would not be long out in the cold.

"That's General Gregorian," Merriweather said with a nod to a group that appeared to be heading for the road up to the tower. She gave a little sigh of relief. "Not in a hurry, though, so it can't be trouble."

They watched until the group came safely through the gate. Mica thought about going downstairs, but Gregorian seemed to have headed straight up to see them.

"Bad news?" Mica asked.

"Not for us," Gregorian said with a bright grin as he sat down and waved Merriweather to do the same. "After the confirmation of seeing Payton involved with the Atrians, the King agreed that we needed to look more closely at Lord Honorgate. A raid at his townhouse found an altar to Torger and correspondence between Lord Honorgate and his son -- and between him and government officials in Atria. Rather damning stuff to leave sitting around. He's disappeared along with Payton, and Lady Honorgate seems to have gone to one of the family estates."

"So, he's been found out for certain," Mica said.

"Among the notes were some plans on how to take over the country. There were also a few names of allies within the government."

"Better and better."

"It's not anything we can use to drive the Atrians away from the shores," Gregorian admitted. "But it does mean we'll curtail their work behind the lines. Anything helps. There were some papers in a kind of code. I brought copies. I thought you might like to go over them, Mica."

"Oh yes," he said and was even enthusiastic about the work. He took the package from his brother.

For the next two days, Mica sent back translations of the code that included things like locations of stockpiles of weapons and explosives, both in the city and beyond. Gregorian was more than happy.

Payton had remained in the city and was stirring up enough trouble that Mica thought it might be wise to come up with a plan to catch him. He thought, in fact, that he had the perfect bait. He told the plan to Gregorian via a raven.

Gregorian arrived at the tower a few hours later.

"Your idea is insane," he said as he entered the workshop. He lifted a hand before Mica could say anything. "However, considering that we think Payton and his father both might be crazy, it might actually work."

"There is more going on than you've told me," Mica said, looking at his brother.

"A series of small acts of sabotage and two attempted assassinations. Mayor Corinth might not yet survive, though Seldon is helping him."

Mica hadn't spent much time with the mayor of the city. They did not get along, a problem that had only been intensified by the trouble with the clockwork spiders. Ignoring each other had mostly worked to their advantage.

Gregorian had apparently grown weary of the games since he so openly endorsed the idea of behind Mica's plan.

"Merriweather and I will start work tomorrow morning," Mica said with a glance out the window and a frown at the cold. "I will let Shipley start spreading the word that we are going to fix the submersible and use it to destroy something in the water off the coast."

"And you think that will draw Payton to try and stop you before you can launch the craft."

"Payton, Lord Honorgate -- I suspect any number of the Atrians will get worried since the statue is apparently something they really want," Mica said. "Oh, they wanted to take the city, beyond a doubt, but since they haven't retreated, even though they've lost all chance of that first goal, I have to believe that the secondary one is still an important focus of their invasion. I don't have to tell you that two of their ships have been inching closer to that area. Merriweather and I have been watching them. I'm not certain if they have any idea how to lift the statue, but you know it is possible that they don't need a plan."

"Pardon?" Gregorian said with a frown.

"The statue has some kind of magic. It may even have intelligence. It might be that the statue will help them, either to get it up or just to use powers we have little protection against."

"No. They would have done it by now," Gregorian said, but there was a hint of worry in this face.

"Not if they aren't certain what they will find," Mica replied. "It occurred to me, Gregorian, that Merriweather and I are really the only *living* people who have seen what is at the bottom of the ocean. They may only know that the statue is there. They may have some strange idea that it will imbue them with the power to defeat us, but I don't think they realize that power is something tangible, not just a gift of their God."

"Damn," Gregorian said. "I don't like to think -- do you really believe this thing is intelligent?"

"I don't know. It's something that came to me in my sleep last night. Not the kind of thought I would normally have, but it has stuck with me all day and prompted me to say we need to move before the Atrians do."

"Ah. Merriweather? You saw it, too. What do you think?"

"The statue was not natural," she said. Her voice had dropped a bit softer than usual, and she shook her head with worry. "I don't know if Lord Raventower is right, but it is not something I would take a chance with, General Gregorian. I would like to find a way to destroy the damned thing, but I think we need to remove the Atrians first."

"And start with Payton or Lord Honorgate, or both," Gregorian said. He stopped and shook his head. "Father. Grandfather. I will have to come to terms with that someday, I suppose. But not now during a war where they are doing all they can to destroy the country."

"And I will have to deal with the reality of my own father's legacy," Mica added with a nod. "And the mother we share -- but at least we don't have to deal with either of them in person."

Gregorian nodded, stared at the clock for a moment in silence, and then shook his head. He looked back at Mica. "We want Payton and Honorgate out of the picture anyway, so I'll agree to the plan. I can arrange for the types of guards you've asked to have on hand, but we can't continue to do this for more than two or three days."

"I'll get Shipley out and to work right away, then," Mica said and stood, anxious to get started. "Merriweather and I will start with a trip to the building and look over the craft. It is possible I might truly get it working, you know, but that is not going to be my primary goal."

"Keep watch on him," Gregorian needlessly said with a nod to Merriweather. "Once he starts working on something, he does tend to stop paying attention to other things, like people who might be trying to kill him."

"I will, sir." She stood when Gregorian did, and they

started for the stairs. "Is there anything more?"

"We're having trouble on the castle grounds again," he admitted. "Not in the castle itself, but around it. I think that either Honorgate or Payton might be directly involved, but so far, we have not been able to find either of them. It's annoying and it could get worse before too long. Everyone wants the war over. They want to go home. The castle grounds are not a pleasant place to stay in winter, for all we're doing our best to help them there. Most of them know it, but even they are restless. We have many injured men with their families, too. It's a damned mess."

"Let's see if we can't get some of it cleaned out, then," Mica said. Merriweather went down the steps first, Gregorian next, and Mica last. Mica did not turn back when he heard that odd, whispery sound behind him, but he saw Gregorian glance into the room. Gregorian said nothing. Mica supposed they were all getting used to the strange sounds.

"We had expected a quick win, you know," Gregorian said as they went down the steps. "Not that we've done badly or that the war has been too long, but we had expected that if we defeated the Atrians on the shores, then they'd retreat back to their ships and head home. It's happened before."

"But this time even sinking many of their ships hasn't chased them off," Merriweather said with a shake of her head.

"Right. Rose has sent some airships out. They have not found any more supply ships coming in, but the Atrians still act as though they expect help to arrive. Your observation about the statue makes me worry that is exactly where they expect help. But even if not, we need to get this settled for our own sake."

Before the hour was out, Shipley and Bear went on their way to Shadow Walk with a bit of gossip to spread while he asked the usual questions. Merriweather and Mica went down to look at the submersible. He made notes, and they went back to the tower again, leaving the ship carefully guarded for the night.

Mica had hoped to see an attack on the ship that night, but it didn't happen. He and Merriweather went back the next day and worked for several hours. Nyle brought them food and did not leave again, helping with the work as well.

At a better time, and in better weather, Mica would have enjoyed those hours climbing in and out of the little craft. There was considerable work to do, unfortunately. He had hoped that the small ship had not taken so much damage, but gauges and parts of the interior had been corroded by sea water. The outer hull had a few dents, but so far he could not find anywhere that it was actually holed except for the crack by the window.

Gregorian had been right about one important fact: the more he worked on the ship, the less he concentrated on the real problems around him. Merriweather worked with him, and Nyle even came the second day from the start. Those two watched for danger.

They knew they had danger. Four of the six guards sent by Gregorian had been picked from a group already suspected of backing the Honorgates. It was possible they might act to try and kill Mica, but he counted on them trying to gain the repaired submersible first -- and he, alone, could fix the vehicle. They even gave out reports, directly to the guards, on how they had all the essentials repaired, even though that was far from true. Mica did not want them to have the craft in working order, after all.

There were other guards in the buildings nearby -- men who had taken up residence there in the guise of fishermen. At least they were safe and warmer inside, Mica thought. The weather was turning on them again, and he suspected that they might as well give up for the day --

A dog barked in the distance. Once, twice, and then three

times in a row.

Bear.

"That's it then," Merriweather said and loaded her weapon, though she sat it carefully on a shelf to her side so the weapon would be unseen at first.

Mica had his sword at his side and two flint locks by the door. He nodded to Nyle who went and loaded them as well and brought one back to him.

There would be craft coming in along the bay, mostly hidden in today's the wind and snow. Mica should have realized they would want this kind of weather. Mica moved to slightly behind the craft and to the left. Merriweather was already to the right. He signaled Nyle to draw closer to the submersible, which would provide some cover.

Mica banged on the craft a couple times. Three times more. Repeated it. That would be a warning to the guards outside the door -- the ones they trusted -- in case their people had missed the dog barks.

Mica could not tell what was going on outside their hut. The time waiting proved worse than Mica expected. He tried to study the pattern of bolts along the edge of the submersible and then pulled his attention away from that with sudden worry that he would get caught up doing something so useless and create a problem for others.

A few shouts outside. No sound of weapons fire yet, though. No sound of actual battle, even. Good. Their people had to be careful.

The door opened, and the guards whom they had suspected of being traitors were the first ones in. They looked almost as smug and Payton who stepped up to the opening and smirked. He had been living rough lately, but the idea that he was winning apparently made up for being so miserable.

"Finally, all the trouble in one place," Payton said. "You are fools --"

But the other soldiers had arrived from the fishing village, and the shouts from outside drew Payson quickly into the fray. The fighting proved worse than Mica had expected. Payton had brought too many with him, and those people seemed intent on making certain Payton got away, even if they died. Mica saw three different men charge straight into the line of fire to protect Payton who ran back to the rowboat not far away. The damned man was going to get away gain!

Or not. Merriweather and Mica both stepped out and moved forward while Nyle and others did their best to protect them. A sword cut at Mica's arm but did not stop him. Merriweather, though still limping somewhat, moved forward without slowing. The cold, bitter wind off the sea blew in their faces, but Mica refused to lose sight of Payton who was struggling into the boat when they both fired.

And both hit.

Payton slumped forward against the side of the rowboat. One of the men inside grabbed him and pulled upward. Payton's legs moved as he attempted to climb over the edge.

"Bastard is still alive," Merriweather said with a hiss of anger. She started to reload the weapon, but a glance around changed her mind. She threw the gun aside and in three quick moves, she pulled blades from their pockets on her corset and threw them at the approaching men.

Two went down with knives in their throats. The third took the blade in the shoulder, but Nyle killed him a moment later. Merriweather had grabbed hold of Mica and began to pull him away from the bodies. It probably looked as though they were trying to intercept the rowboat which had started to head south along the shore and angling towards the spot where the statue still laid beneath the covering of water, and that couldn't be chance.

"Oh damn, oh damn," Merriweather whispered as they reached the rocky ground and could not follow. The storm,

Mica noted, had suddenly calmed. Unnatural, that glow of green in the air, the feel as though the world itself held her breath. Nyle and a handful of soldiers stopped beside them. The battle behind had ended-- either over, or just no longer of interest to either side in the wake of this new strangeness.

Mica and Merriweather moved out into the water, knee deep as the waves stilled. The clouds glowed green all around them, and thunder sounded like muted laughter. The rowboat had begun to move unnaturally fast, especially since no one rowed. It swept forward, straight for the whirlpool that suddenly appeared.

Payton stood, though unsteadily. The rowboat had started to turn, and he faced them now, no more than 100 yards away. A maniacal grin crossed his face, and despite the blood on his chest -- one of the shots must have pierced his body -- he still raised his arms high into the air.

"To Victory!" he shouted.

And then he threw himself into the sea.

Lightning rent the sky, the bolt striking into the water as well. The small rowboat swirled around disappeared under the water, the men shouting in fear. The water swallowed them all.

The sea glowed bright blue, and lightning struck again.

"I'm pretty sure than can't be good," Merriweather said.

They all backed away. Quickly.

CHAPTER THIRTY

The blue glow died away with bright concentric circles that had spread outward at first and now moved back toward the center, slowly leaving behind the dark and turbulent waters. Mica and Merriweather stood at the edge of the waves, ignoring the cold. He wasn't certain what would come next or what the enemy might do, but they waited.

The storm returned, though it seemed as though the air itself tasted odd now. Snow fell mixed with chunks of ice the size of his thumb that hit with bruising force. Lightning crossed the sky and back again, though at least it didn't crash into the sea.

They backed away toward the shore, neither saying anything. Neither did Nyle who took hold of their arms and hurried them to higher ground. The soldiers had begun to whisper among themselves, and their faces appeared pale from more than the cold.

Mica paused to look in at the submersible. It hadn't been damaged as far as he could tell. He wasn't certain he really cared right then.

"Get this area cleared and all but four of you go back to the army camp," Merriweather ordered to the soldiers. Mica suspected they were so rattled that they didn't understand even her simple commands. "Gardner, I'd like to put you in charge here. Put the Atrian bodies on the far side of the building and send our dead and wounded back to the castle. I don't think anyone is going to be out making trouble in this weather."

She spoke so calmly and with such authority that the others nodded and began the work. Mica felt a little better for hearing it, too. Calm. Things were odd, but nothing horrible had happened. Not yet.

Nyle spoke with the locals, and Merriweather handled the soldiers. Mica stared out at sea where some Atrian rowboats made it back to their larger craft. He could see them rowing away, though the storm obscured most of the scene.

Mica felt unsure of what to do now. He didn't understand any of what had happened.

"Back to the tower, Lord Raventower," Merriweather said with a touch on his arm. He'd still stared out at sea, but not truly seeing anything there.

"Yes. Good." Mica turned and took several steps with her at his side. Merriweather had the cane again and limped a little worse. She was watching everywhere, and he realized what a fool he had been to stand there and not even think about Atrian assassins. "Merriweather, I don't know what to expect next."

"I imagine not. I would like to think that Payton is dead and that's the last we'll have to deal with him. But what we saw --"

Mica nodded and said nothing as they climbed the road, Nyle catching up with them before they'd gone far. The soldiers had pressed on ahead and turned the corner to head back to the city, the castle, and finally the army camp beyond. Merriweather had not sent a written report. Gregorian would want answers and Mica didn't think either he or the Captain would have any for him except for the bare basics of what had happened.

The weather did not improve. The falling bits of ice began

to form into a slick layer that covered road, rock, walls and even the previous snow, as though entombing everything in the frigid facade. The three had a hard time on the last yard or two to the gate. Roe let them in. The tents inside were overlaid with ice, and the fires sputtered in the onslaught, but the people here coped with it.

Shipley and Bear arrived just behind them and squeezed through the gate, the dog making odd bell-like noises as he moved since so much of the ice had stuck to him. Best to get them all inside the tower and stop standing around as though Mica expected something to change.

"I seen what happened," Shipley said as they neared the door. "I can't decide if it all went well or if it went worse than anyone could ha' guessed."

"That pretty much sums it up," Merriweather agreed. Thunder shook the world around them.

They hurried into the building and down to the kitchen. Bear crossed to his rug and laid down with a sigh of relief. Ada, Gram, and Fern got them tea. They said a little about what had happened -- no one wanted to upset Fern -- but the two older women could tell that they were not happy with the results.

Everyone could tell the weather had turned bad, even from here. The building trembled with the thunder directly overhead, and Mica could hear what sounded like hail pounding against the wooden door and shuttered windows of the main floor above them.

"Merriweather, get the soldiers into the main hall," he said. She frowned. "Leave the ones guarding the walls, but the rest who are just waiting for trouble can wait in here. They'll be better for it. Nyle, Roe -- get the fire going."

"I'll make tea," Gram said. "A huge pot of tea."

Everyone began moving again, which seemed somewhat better. Mica thought about going with Merriweather, but just sitting at the table seemed as much work as he could manage. His fingers didn't even want to play with clockwork pieces. He had to write to Gregorian. Had to tell him what happened to Payton.

Tell him what had happened to Gregorian's father.

That had been playing at the back of his mind. He logically knew that Gregorian was no more attached to Payton than Mica had been to their mother. Both those parents had chosen a path that led to treachery. Just the same, Mica could have wished --

"Another package came for you earlier, me Lord," Gram said and pushed the leather case over to him.

"Thank you." Something, maybe, to distract him.

The soldiers already started coming in and sounding better for it, though the noise took him by surprise. Shipley and Bear had but themselves at the steps that lead down to the kitchen so no one would get past. Nyle and Roe moved up with the boy, and if there was an assassin in the group, he wasn't going to have an easy way to reach Mica.

Merriweather came in, noted the package, and sat down. "Something else from the temple?"

"Yes," he said and belatedly started to open it. Mica couldn't imagine that this could be important. Nothing had helped so far, and he thought they might have to change direction. Go after the statue. He'd shied away from that idea before now, but nothing else seemed to work.

He pulled a massive, ancient tome out of the leather case. It must have been hundreds of years old, he realized. Priceless, too, he supposed and paid the book a little more attention. The circular design on the cover was inlaid with gold, some of it flaked away but --

"Ah, now," Ada said and leaned forward to get a look after she'd poured him more tea. "Now there's something I never thought to see again."

"The book?" he said, startled.

"No, me lord. The design there."

"You've seen it before?" he asked.

"Yes, sir. You're sitting on it. It's there under the rugs."

Mica looked over at Merriweather. She stood and called for Nyle and Roe.

"Clear the table, if you would," Mica said. This had to be a mistake.

They moved away the heavy table and moved the rugs, Ada frowning as the dust that raised and muttering about a good cleaning come spring. The floor, he realized, was surprisingly flat under the several layers of covering, not at all like the bedrock he'd seen at the castle, which wasn't worn flat in some places, even after centuries of use.

The last rug came away. Ada had a broom and swept aside some dirt and dust, so vigorous in the work that Merriweather sneezed.

Ada had been right. The symbol carved into the floor was the same as that on the book cover. In fact, comparing the two, Mica could see that some of the book's design had been worn off, but it was clear on the floor with inlaid stone making the three concentric circles and the lines that radiated out from them.

"Like the assassins' symbols," Merriweather said with a snarl in her voice. Then she tilted her head. "But not quite. Those aren't daggers."

"They look like rays of sunlight," Mica said. He'd knelt and brushed his hand across the design. "Good work. I've never seen anything this old that was as well done. It must have been here when --"

He stopped.

"Lord Raventower?" Ada said.

"We have been fools not to realize." He looked up at Merriweather who still frowned. "They pushed the statue of

Torger into the sea. They would not have pushed it far. Raventower was built over Torger's temple."

"Well damn," she said and knelt as well. "I guess that explains why they want the tower but not you."

Mica gave a distracted nod and began studying the floor for other signs. He supposed that the other rooms beyond the 'kitchen' had been there when the tower was built. They'd have to check everywhere for other signs --

A guard came to the entry and handed over a paper to Shipley, and he handed it to Merriweather. She sat back on her heels, wincing slightly since she still had trouble with her foot, and read quickly.

"General Gregorian wants us at the castle as soon as possible, Lord Raventower," she said with a worried frown. She handed him the note, but he didn't bother to read it. "From the timing, I suspect there are a lot of questions about what happened down in the bay."

"Yes, a lot of questions," he agreed as he stood. "We can add ours to theirs and be no closer to an answer. The rest of you cover the symbol back over, if you will. Don't worry. We've lived here a long time without it being more than something pretty under the rugs. And despite the problem with my parents, I really don't think there's been much trouble at Raventower down through the years."

"True, sir," Nyle agreed. "We have never been a superstitious bunch anyway. I suggest you take Kandris, sir. I wouldn't trust any other mount on those streets in this weather."

"Merriweather?" he said, leaving it up to her.

"Yes, he's right," she agreed. She didn't even appear upset by the idea.

"I am going to bring the ravens as well. Leave the guards here Merriweather. They couldn't keep up with us anyway."

She wanted to argue that one but didn't. They both went

Raventower & Merriweather 2: War/405

up to the workshop and Mica brought out the ravens, putting them in a pack that he tossed over his shoulder. They were restless which might just have been because they hadn't been out much, or it might have been something to do with the statue. He didn't ask.

Merriweather went to the window that had a view over the bay and opened the shutter slightly. "There is still a slightly blue glow in the water."

"Sea metal glows blue," he reminded her with a wave of his hand to the desk. The cover was pulled down, and they could not see it, but he felt the touch of power from there. "We had better go."

Back down the steps. Mica retrieved the book that had been lately handed to him, put it back in the protective leather case, and handed that one to Merriweather to carry. He wanted his hands free.

Nyle had gone out for the clockwork horse. Kandris stood by the door, stamping impatiently against the ice. They had a blanket across the back and tied down, but not a saddle. They needed nothing more. Mica mounted without a problem, and Nyle helped Merriweather up behind him. She took a firm grip around his waist.

"Lock up tight, Nyle."

"Yes, Lord Raventower."

He turned the horse and headed for the gate. The men there stood huddled in cloaks. He could see the trail where the messenger had brought the note in, but not another out. He hoped he at least took the time to warm up. They should have told him to stay.

The wind off the ocean felt bitterly cold in one moment, and too warm in the next. Lighting still stabbed across the sky and he thought maybe being on a metallic horse might not be the best idea after all. He urged Kandris a bit faster, despite the ice beneath the snow. Off the hill, at least, he thought.

Mica glanced down Fisherman's Row as the horse took the turn in the road. He saw no one around except for a few huddled at the building with the submersible. Far down beyond the buildings, the sea spiked up and down, but not like the rolling waves they were more apt to see. Clouds swirled over the water, so close that it seemed sea and clouds touched in many places.

"Oh yes," Merriweather mumbled at his back. "We'll be able to explain this."

He thought the Atrian ships were even pulling up anchor and getting out of the immediate area. He could see a bit of steam rising from the engine of the closest. They had not bothered with the elaborate set of sails and seemed in a hurry.

They saw no one at all on the streets. The area around Shadow Walk, where they'd often seen at least one person watching, appeared to be abandoned. Nothing moved along the path that skirted the rest of the slums. The ruins from fires stood out more starkly against the white snow, a reminder that the few days of hostilities had changed a great deal in their city.

No one moved in the temple square, either. The wind blew hard and cold through the area, lifting the snow into a white mist. They did not feel any more of the warmer winds off the ocean. Mica regretted it, and Merriweather pressed closer to him in the bitter cold.

On through better parts of town and --

And they found Atrians. Mica didn't think they'd been planning on an attack of any kind. There were shouts of surprise and weapons out. The Atrians had blocked the road to the castle and perhaps had even been heading that way.

"Down," Merriweather ordered. She slid off and drew her sword. Mica did the same. No time for flintlocks --

As soon as they were down, Kandris charged straight into the Atrians. Mica saw him knock two down and stamp over them -- they were not getting back up. The horse spun, bit the shoulder of one Atrian who screamed and fell, and charged at a group of four more.

Mica and Merriweather didn't waste time. They fought past the horse and the enemy. Kandris backed up, holding the Atrians at bay. He shoved Mica backward with a sideways nudge of his metallic shoulder.

"He wants us to go," Merriweather said.

"I don't want to leave him here --"

A look from Kandris, the bright glow of his red eyes, changed his mind. He backed up. Kandris charged the enemy again. Merriweather grabbed Mica's arm and pulled him up the road towards the castle. He looked back, but Kandris was not having much trouble with the enemy.

Then the weather changed again, the wind howling too loud to hear even the battle close by as snow and ice came down like a curtain between them. They had reached the hill heading up to the castle, and the road wide here and relatively easy to follow, even in this damned weather. They trudged on through the snow and the ice, up toward the gate they could not clearly see through the storm. The snow fell harder.

It felt as though something strange had happened in the world. Not anything aimed directly at the two of them, but still dangerous and unpredictable. The lightning had not come closer, and the thunder seemed muted, but sometimes it felt as though some giant moved through the world and everything trembled.

They reached the gate, stumbling up against it, both of them too cold. Mica tried to shout, but the sound of the storm covered any sound they made. There was really no hope of getting to cover anywhere else, either. Snow and ice weighed them down. They couldn't get back down the road to any place --

Kandris rushed up the hill and hit the gate with such force that it snapped open, winning cries of shock from the inside.

Mica had started to step forward, but Merriweather cut in front of him and parried the blade of a soldier who rushed their way.

"Back down, you fool!" she shouted. "Lord Raventower!"

The man backed up in haste, his face white beneath the hood he wore. He looked from Mica to the horse and back to Merriweather. "Gods," he whispered. "What is happening?"

"We don't know. Beware. There were Atrians on the road. Can you get the gate closed again?"

Kandris, apparently taking this as orders for him, shoved the gate closed and stood against it. Nothing would get through there. Mica wasn't certain the guards appreciated the gesture, though, from the worried looks they gave the horse. That might have been the splatters of blood, even around his mouth.

They still had to get all the way to the castle. The path was snowed over, the huts and tents buried in snow and ice, and the shouts and cries of people almost lost in the wind. Mica feared he might even be seeing a few life lights drifting through the snow and hoped none found him.

They pressed on, forcing their way toward the bright light of the building ahead of them. Up the steps and another door -- but the guards here knew them and got them inside.

Bright. Warm. Mica could hear the prayers from the temple people echoing all through the building. He wasn't certain if that would make them any safer. Something had changed in the world when Payton threw himself into the ocean, and Mica had the feeling that even the Atrians were not prepared for this one.

CHAPTER THIRTY-ONE

Gregorian met them at the door, looking as though he'd come running. "I had no idea the weather was going to change this drastically. You should have gone back --"

"There was no time to turn around," Mica admitted. He stripped off his cloak, the ice clicking as it fell off and hit the floor. The steward gingerly took both their cloaks as though winter might be trapped in the folds, and he didn't want to release it inside. Mica hoped they dried before he and Merriweather had to go out again. "I felt as though the weather followed us and appeared worse behind rather than ahead, though neither was good."

"You made it, praise the gods."

And the prayers grew louder at that moment, as though in agreement. Gregorian gave a start but then turned away, signaling them to come with him as they headed for his office.

"What is the problem?" Mica asked.

"Oh, many problems, I fear. The weather only makes matters worse. I've had reports about what happened at the bay. Damn, I wish I knew what it meant."

"I'm sorry about your -- about Payton," Mica said as they reached the private hall to his office.

Gregorian glanced his way and then put a hand on Mica's arm. "We have made ourselves, all three of us. Of the three parents, Payton had the least influence, you know. Livinia had her hand on Honoria, but our sister has started to fight her way out from under that cloud. Did you know she sent me a rather amusing report about the Merriweather dinner gathering? You'll have to read it sometime. Later. Much later, when we can appreciate the humor."

"And what about Greyland Raventower?" Mica dared to ask about his own father.

"I liked him," Gregorian replied. "I still miss him. He knew I wasn't his son and he never treated me badly. He was odd and grew stranger towards the end -- but when they said he and mother had been assassinated, I didn't cry for her."

Those were the most truthful words Gregorian had ever said about their family. The admission helped at such an odd time.

"Thank you."

"Yes, well." Gregorian led them down the hall to his office. "Best to get that out of the way."

The King sat behind Gregorian's desk, which did not surprise Mica. The man had been reading notes, but he unexpectedly stood and moved out of the way to give Gregorian the chair. That seemed odd, but then everything was strange these days.

"Mica, first I need you to look over these notes. They're part of the papers we took from the Honorgate estate. Not the coded ones that I copied over for you, but some letters."

He took the papers before they even sat down. Some of the letters had yellowed somewhat with age. Several appeared to be notes about supplies stockpiled in a small farm near the coast.

"I am a Lord in the Council," Mica said when he looked back up. "I've seen Lord Honorgate's writing many times.

These letters were not written by him."

"So, it is true," the King said. "I didn't doubt you, Gregorian, but we needed someone else to verify. I don't know who --"

"My mother is friends with Lady Honorgate," Merriweather pointed out. "And I do recognize her hand."

"Ah." Gregorian sat back, surprised. "She is either in this with her husband, or she's been handling the matter from the start without him. I would rather think the second, you know. Lord Honorgate is a drunk. No one would trust him with such delicate matters."

"Yes," Mica said. "That does put a different color on everything. I could never understand how Lord Honorgate handled the dangerous conspiracy with the Atrians, to be honest. Unless his drunkenness was always sham, but I never had that feeling."

The King nodded. He didn't look any happier. "We have been watching Lady Honorgate and her daughter, of course -- but mostly to see if her husband contacted her. We were not looking specifically at what she was doing."

"There are more problems," Gregorian added. He finally waved the others into chairs, several of which were arrayed around the room. Gregorian looked to have been busy lately. "Very many problems. What do you make of what happened at the bay?"

"I don't know," Mica admitted. "Whatever it was, the changes came quickly -- the blue light and the lightning make me believe that there must be magic involved, though."

"Which is what we believe," Gregorian agreed and sat back in his chair. "I've asked the High Priestess of the Unknown Path to join us. Her group has kept entirely to themselves at the far end of the castle, but I think it time that we discuss these matters, instead of sifting through a few clues that seem to make no sense."

Mica winced at the idea of facing that woman again, though maybe she would be better in the flesh. Merriweather had grimaced as well, but she made no other sign of her own emotions.

Someone knocked at the door; not the high priestess, but Seldon came in.

"I heard of your perilous ride," he said. "I thought I ought to look you over before matters got worse. Oh, and I heard you hurt your foot, Merriweather. Let's see to that as well."

"Don't argue," Gregorian said and gave the Priest a nod of appreciation.

The man sat on the floor and worked at Merriweather's boot, which apparently embarrassed her. Mica was grateful for the care the priest gave her, though. He didn't want her to suffer, and he certainly didn't want her to be slowed if -- when -- the next trouble struck.

Another knock. This time a woman with long silver hair came into the room, gave a nod all around and settled into the chair without a 'by your leave' to the King.

"I have come as you requested," she said.

"And you are?" Gregorian asked with a glance at his brother.

"The high priestess of the Temple of the Unknown Path," she said with a frown. "You asked for me to come and speak with you."

"You can't be," Mica said and won a look with a raised eyebrow. "You can't. I've met the High Priestess out on the streets several times over the last few days. Merriweather and I have both seen her. She's taller. Dark hair -- glows and isn't entirely there --"

"Oh, now that is interesting," the woman said and leaned forward, her eyes wider as she stared into his face. "And she claimed my place, did she?"

Mica started to say something. Reconsidered the wording.

"She told us that she ruled the Temple of the Unknown Path."

"Oh, there is the problem. To rule is not the same as presiding over the temple, you know. If she had given you a name --"

"Ledea."

That did startle the woman, but not in fear. "I should have realized. Ledea is the most powerful goddess in our pantheon."

Merriweather made an odd sound. Mica might have echoed it before he cleared his throat. "But we've always been told that you cannot name your gods --"

"We can't name them. That doesn't mean we do not *know* who they are. It would be unwise to toss around the name of the gods and goddesses of magic, don't you think? Not the sort of thing that you would want people without training to know. We've always felt it would be better if the names were not known outside the temple. However, if she came to you and even gave her name --"

The shadows moved behind the woman's chair.

"I did appear to them."

Ledea stepped out into the light. The High Priestess looked at her with a little shock before she bowed her head. Mica wanted to stand and bow, but he didn't think his legs would work at all. Merriweather had started making several odd sounds, and he looked at her with worry this time.

"I was rude," Merriweather admitted. Her voice grew a little louder. "I threatened a goddess --"

"Yes, you did," Ledea agreed as she stepped forward. Did the room somehow get larger? The walls didn't seem to be where they had been and were, perhaps, not as distinct as they should be. "You were quite brave," Ledea added. She appeared to be more solid this time, and even more aware of the world around her. She even put a hand on the High Priestesses shoulder.

"I didn't know what you were!" Merriweather protested.

"This is true," Ledea said with a slight smile. Her hair moved, and there was the faint whisper of a breeze and a mist that moved along the edges of where they sat so that the walls no longer appeared to be there. "But you knew I was not normal. You knew I was dangerous, but you were determined to help Lord Raventower. We have other matters to discuss. Far more important matters. The gods normally cannot move in your world, my friends. We have tried to warn and persuade, to nudge just a little without upsetting the balance -- but now something has happened, and the risk to the entire world requires that we step forward and try to change the path."

"We?" Merriweather said with a slight frown.

"Payton?" Mica said at almost the same time. "Is it what he did that has changed things?"

"Yes, as you've seen already with the unsettling of nature and the new storms. Payton Honorgate was not dead when he leapt into the water. He willingly sacrificed himself to Atric."

"Who is Atric?" Gregorian dared to ask. Mica glanced his way. His brother appeared steadier than any of the others, including the High Priestess and King Abertus.

"Atric was the last High Priest of Torger," she said, glancing again at Merriweather. "He was an ambitious man, though. Those who reach the highest position in the temple hierarchy share some of the powers, as gifts, from the gods they serve. Atric knew how to hide his true self, even from the God he served. When Torger reached out to give him a gift, Atric grabbed hold of the God and took more than was intended."

"But that didn't change things, did it?" Merriweather dared to ask. She seemed to have gotten back some of her color and her nerve. "Not like what is happening now unless that part of the history was completely wiped away."

"No, it did not change much," Ledea agreed. "Atric was the chosen, after all, and already held his place of power. We tried to limit what he could do, though. Torger, Eligeius and I were a trilogy in those days, closely linked."

"You were linked to the God of War?" Mica asked.

Shadows moved. A man stepped forward this time; tall, handsome in a way that could make any mortal feel inadequate.

"Eligeius," Ledea said with a nod of welcome. "I had hoped you would join me."

"Lord Raventower asked a question about knowledge that has been lost to this world," Eligeius replied. His voice held an odd, echoing sound, very different from Ledea's. "Am I not the God of knowledge?"

He said those words with a smile. Mica felt as though they were in danger just by being in the presence of these two, but he also knew that they would never have another chance for answers. He wanted to ask questions -- many questions and found it difficult to know how to phrase any of them.

"What can you tell us?" he said, having found nothing better to ask.

Eligeius and Ledea both smiled. If the storm had been raging in this room, it would have dissipated in that warmth and power.

"I will answer your other question first," Eligeius said. "The answer pertains to everything else. Torger, Ledea and I were a trilogy of gods, ancient as the land. Torger was not the God of War before Atric's reign. He was the God of Protection, both in life and in the journey to the afterlife, which was a good God to ally with magic and knowledge."

"Atric took immortality from Torger, along with other powers," Ledea added. The snarl in her voice filled the room with a power that made Mica shudder a little. She shook her head, and Mica felt as though she pulled a little of herself back once more. When she spoke, her voice sounded far calmer. "Atric lived for hundreds of years, and during that time he worked at changing the perception of 'protection' to that of 'war' which had been part of a larger picture -- to protect the lands of the people from enemies. Atric wanted to raise an army and rule the world, to gain power even the gods would envy."

"He also had learned that part of Torger's realm, the part where he helped the recently dead to their afterlives, was something he could touch and eventually control. He found he could take the souls of people and use them to make himself more powerful. He built a statue, not to Torger, but to himself, and there he sacrificed people."

Mica had begun to feel a new worry, but he could not bring himself to ask. He thought he didn't want to know --

Ledea watched him. She gave a little nod, as though she understood. Maybe she knew what he feared -- and it hardly mattered at all anymore, did it, what he did with souls?

"When we understood what was happening, we came back to the world, which we had created so long ago," Ledea said. Her hand moved as though to caress something much loved. "Yours was one of our first, and best; a creation we had made from pure love and joy. Before this world, one God would build, another would tear down, and chaos kept us from becoming anything at all. We decided we wanted to be more. We formed what we are now so that we could cooperate, diversify, build and create -- and so we built and did not destroy."

Mica had never thought much about how the gods got to be the gods, and he supposed this was the sort of lesson that some people would have spent their entire lives trying to learn. The High Priestess appeared to be ecstatic, but that might only be the presence of her goddess. The King had gone still and silent. Gregorian nodded as though everything made sense.

"That brings us to now," Eligeius said. "Or close to now by a few hundred years. We tried to stop Atric from doing worse than he had already managed, even though we knew that manifesting in the world might do harm. We worked through the local people as best we could. They didn't like what Atric had done, and in the end, it was they who worked to destroy him and the statue. They killed Atric and his followers were exiled. The land became Sedina and followed the new goddess of justice, though they accepted others as well."

"We thought Atric was gone," Ledea said.

"Oh, but he had always meant to be part of the statue, hadn't he?" Mica asked and leaned forward. "A clockwork creature, where his own soul could reside because he knew his body must fail eventually."

"Yes," Ledea replied. "We didn't notice, such a little dark thing there in the bottom of the sea. Atric remained quiet, questing farther and farther with his mind, for he was still too closely related to the gods and could move in ways that humans cannot. At last, he found the link between Torger and me, and though that link he could touch the realm of magic. Even then he moved carefully. He had learned patience in his long life and longer exile to the metal shell he now wore."

"The first noticeable change came almost a century ago when ships began to sink as they passed over that area," Eligeius explained. He sat on the edge of Gregorian's desk, for all the world like a lecturing professor. "He began to feed on new souls he dragged down and used that power to build up more magic. This was helped even more by the Honorgates, who are descended from Atric's line."

"Lady Honorgate --" Gregorian said and waved towards the desk.

"She married her cousin, you know. The same line," Eligeius said. "And her part of the family had been far more devout than the other lines. She brought her son up in the followings of Atric, and he was, in fact, a high-ranking priest -- which made his willing death all the more powerful."

"My sister and I are of that line then, too," Gregorian said. He clearly didn't like the realization.

"All the world is related in blood," Eligeius said and leaned down to look Gregorian in the face. "You choose your own way. Humans always have."

"I tried to help by going to Lord Raventower," Ledea said. "I know that what I told him was cryptic and he might not understand -- but to do more at that point would have given power to Atric. We tried to be circumspect and to keep this in the hands of humans."

"I had influenced a priest to do the translations for very early works," Eligeius added and nodded to the case Merriweather had put by her chair. "I had hoped to give you an easier answer than the one that required us to speak to you. Atric knew what I was doing and moved to make certain the work stopped by bringing Payton back to Sedina and made certain he was in the right place to kill the priest. Payton took advantage of the moment to check the archives on the chance he might find something important about Greyland Raventower's work. He was not much interested in the clockwork and steam engines, you know. He only wanted the tower so he had the temple in his hands. Your mother had seen the symbol when Payton showed her whom he served. She knew it from the bedrock of your building --"

"Oh," Gregorian said.

"We found the symbol under the kitchen table tonight," Mica confirmed.

"Should have seen that one coming," Gregorian mumbled. He seemed more at ease now. "What put the Atrians on the move, though?"

"Atric is quite tired of sitting on the bottom of the sea."

Ledea shook her head, and Mica had the impression that she hated what Atric had been doing. "He has concentrated his essence in the head of the statue, the symbolic brain, and kept it alive. The rest of the body had begun to corrode away which is part of the reason he's moving now. He needs more sacrifices to grow strong enough to move, though, and he can only do that on land where there are more victims. He used a considerable amount of his power to put Payton in place and to give him the charisma he needed to start a holy war. The Atrians want to get the statue back to land -- back to the spot where your tower stands. And so, here we are."

"What happened to Torger?" Mica asked.

"I have been doing what I could and protecting those I hoped would help me defeat Atric and regain some of my lost powers."

Mica looked to the right.

Seldon stood.

Merriweather was making more odd sounds. Mica thought he might make a few as well.

"Atric helped me in some respects," Seldon said. "By stealing some of my powers, he left me able to hide what I truly was and to walk among humans without fear of what my presence on this world might do. I have always found it amusing, though, that no one wondered at how easily and often I could do healing magic. Humans have a wondrous ability to simply accept what is before them."

Ledea reached out to Seldon. Eligeius did as well, and Seldon -- Torger -- touched both their hands. A moment of peace had filled the room before Seldon pulled away. Seldon looked back at him. Mica could not think of this person he'd known all his life by any other name.

"Your father was my chosen priest, though he didn't know it," Seldon explained. He moved to stand between the other two gods, and energy swept in around them. This was a powerful triad. "I had gifted him with powers and began to lead him towards understanding, which is not an easy thing in people who have come to distrust the God Torger. Unfortunately, your mother and Payton Honorgate had already joined in an allegiance, and she corrupted part of his work. The assassins were an entirely human intervention to handle the problem he'd become and very likely a wise one."

The King nodded his thanks for that understanding.

"I saved you, Mica," Seldon continued, "and planted the powers your father had held as a seed within your soul. I hoped we still had enough time for you to grow old enough to understand. I stayed with you. Your ability to deal with souls is essential for your battle with Atric. He has long ago lost his true body, you know. He is only a soul now, but a very powerful one."

"You've helped me from the start," Mica said.

"Yes, as best I could. You chose your own path. I would not have pushed you into this trouble. However, once you had started to feel the awakening of your powers, I made certain I stayed close. The sea metal, Mica -- you always tried to find out about the magic in it. There is a reason why others who study it can find nothing. It only works for you -- and your late father."

"Ah," Mica said and thought this made sense.

Seldon looked weary. "This has been difficult since I had to bury every impulse that would show me for my true self and would also change your world. Gods cannot go there without making changes."

"And we are not there now," Merriweather said. Her hand was remarkably steady as she waved it toward the wall that seemed ghostly at best.

"Not on your world. We took another dangerous act, but we trust all of you," Ledea explained. The glance she gave them, a sweep of her head around the room, felt like a blessing. To have her trust gave them strength. "We took you into our realm. Your presence here could create problems if you chose to do so. Do you want to make that choice?"

No one did. Mica may have been the most emphatic in his choice, but they were all too aware of how badly things could go if they acted unwisely. Mica could feel the power around him, but he need only think about Atric to realize how little he wanted to play such a game.

"What am I supposed to do now?" Mica asked.

"We cannot say," Ledea replied. She saw the look on his face and lifted her hand. "No, we cannot say because we can no longer see what is happening. You, Lord Micalus Raventower, are closer to the truth of what can happen than we dare be. This is in human hands."

"What happens if we make the wrong choice?" Merriweather asked, always practical, even in the face of this madness.

"Atric has gained power," Seldon answered. "He is sapping more of my essence. If this continues, then I will cease to be. Atric will move into the realm of the Gods -- and if he does so, then nothing you know will remain the same."

CHAPTER THIRTY-TWO

C oming back to the world was like suddenly waking from a dream. Mica blinked. Ledea and Eligeius were gone. The walls were back where they belonged.

Seldon stood before him. "I leave this in your hands."

He opened the door and walked out past the guard. Apparently, no one beyond the room had sensed anything different. Mica had started to stand. He changed his mind and looked to his brother instead.

"Well, damn," Gregorian said. "This just gets worse, doesn't it? Now we not only have to worry about saving Sedina but apparently the whole world and even the realm of the gods."

"We don't have much time, either," King Albertus added. He shook his head and then looked back at them. "Was that real?"

Mica stood this time. Merriweather got quickly to her feet as well.

"I need to find answers," Mica said. He felt steadier than he had expected, especially the way his mind still bounced and swirled and tried to make sense of any of it. A hint of mist still lingered in the corner of the room, a remnant from another place. "I am going back to the tower and studying everything that has already been sent to me. I'm going to go over everything we learned about Atric. There has to be something we can do."

The others agreed. Maybe they were happy to put the matter in Mica's hands. Mica wasn't certain what they would do if he failed, but at least he'd likely not survive to see the aftermath, given how dangerous the situation had become with this latest warning. Not a pleasant thought, but probably the truth. Of course, if they didn't do anything, or if they didn't move fast enough, or if they did the wrong thing --

Everything would change?

Mica left the office. He wasn't certain he'd bowed to the King on his way out. He knew he hadn't asked permission to go. Merriweather kept at his heels, unusually quiet, even for her.

They went past dozens of others who mumbled about the weather and had no idea the real troubles they faced.

They reached the outer door, retrieved their cloaks, and Merriweather put a hand on his arm. "What do you plan?" she asked.

"I plan to go back to Raventower. I can think more clearly there. I don't know what we are going to do, Merriweather, but I suspect that it will have to be daring."

The weather had tamed somewhat while they were in Gregorian's office -- and elsewhere. He and Merriweather stepped out into a hard snow, but the wind had quieted. Lightning no longer lit the sky. Kandris stood at the bottom of the stairs, stamping his feet impatiently and shaking snow from his silvery body. Snow and frost covered any of the blood still on his body.

Mica didn't remember much of the ride back to Raventower. He barely noticed when they passed through the temple square, and of giving a nod towards the people who stood at Shadow Walk and Fisherman's Row, and of going through the gate. Mica probably said something to Ada when she came out to welcome them back, but Mica only truly took note when he found himself sitting at his desk and working on the pocket watch again, putting the pieces together. He worked through to the end and held the watch up to the light, watching the hands move even if he had not set the time.

Merriweather sat at her post by the steps. He had the impression that the night had gone late, but the clock was too far to see in the dim candlelight. Even Merriweather's face remained hidden in shadow.

"I think I have a plan," Mica said.

"I thought you might, Lord Raventower. And I assume that it is going to be both daring and somewhat crazy."

"I don't think you need the *somewhat* qualifier."

"Ah."

Mica signaled her over to the desk, drew out a piece of paper, and began making notes on what he thought they should do. She added notes of her own. The plan became no less insane, but they worked it out anyway.

He slept for a few hours. Words whispered to him. He listened this time...

Early the next afternoon they headed back to the castle. Mica had no trouble finding Seldon who was out in the castle's courtyard helping to treat people who had suffered injuries over the last few days. Seldon looked no different as he gave a friendly nod to Mica.

"I have an idea," Mica said. He put the paper in Seldon's hand and watched as the man -- the God -- looked it over.

"You'll need the sea metal engine," Seldon said tapping the page. "But yes, it is possible."

"I'm going to talk to my brother now." Mica took back the paper. "Then I will need to go to Admiral Rose. I'll have to tell her and a few of her people."

Seldon nodded agreement. He went back to his work.

The meeting with Gregorian and the King didn't take much longer. The two looked over the plan, a flickering of their eyes showing a touch of concern, but they were probably well past shock by now.

"Can you arrange this diversion with the fleet?" Mica asked.

"Yes," Gregorian said, and the King nodded agreement. "But what if the Atrians don't do as you expect?"

"Then we come up with another plan. The same applies if this one doesn't work. I suggest, King Albertus, that you prepare to tell people to leave the city and that Gregorian starts working up plans on how the soldiers could help. Let's hope it doesn't come to it, but better that they escape rather than fall to Atric who will steal their souls. Go to the mountains. Find another way to fight back."

"Yes." Gregorian stood and held out his hand. "Good luck, brother."

Mica took his hand and smiled. "Good luck to all of us."

The ride along the shore to the Air Patrol Field turned out to be the calmest and most relaxing time Mica had spent since this entire madness began. Six guards trailed behind them, and Merriweather still watched the shadows for any sign of trouble. Snow fell, but there was a sense of peace, a gift before things went worse. Mica didn't even mind the cold, though he hoped to survive to see the spring.

Mica shook those thoughts away. He was still refining the plan. He had to approach it as though he knew it would work. To act in any other way would likely doom them. He dared not hesitate.

Admiral Rose looked worried when Mica said they needed to talk alone -- just her, Krogor, and Greenwood. They both listened to the tale with growing disbelief, their cups of tea forgotten on the table. Voices spoke somewhere else. The wind moved the airship slightly.

"I'd heard about the strange weather down in the city," Rose said. She sat back. "We had a little of it, but nothing horrible. I knew something was going on, though. Mica, if Merriweather wasn't here to confirm the story, I don't think I would have believed you."

"I thought you trusted me," Mica replied.

"I thought so, too," she admitted. "But you have managed to come up with something even I think I should question. This is crazy."

"Yes, it is," Mica agreed.

"The plan," Greenwood said with a shake of his hand. "You can't really think --"

"Seldon has already agreed."

Greenwood fell silent. He also paled.

Mica looked to Krogor. The engineer stared at the table for a moment longer and then looked up.

"It is a good plan. I'll be ready. There is no shame in helping the gods."

"Ah. Yes," Rose said as though that part only now occurred to her. "What do we do?"

"Gregorian is arranging his part. First, we need to collect more spiders and take them back to the tower."

"Let's go then," Rose said. She stood.

"May I suggest limited crew?" Merriweather asked. She'd been quiet. "I can handle the weaponry if you'll allow me. Do we need more than a pilot and engineer?"

"If we want sails -- ah, but we won't, will we?" Rose frowned. "Going out to the island to get spiders is not as dangerous as the later work, though. Let's keep them at least that long."

"We don't know what Atric can do, to be honest," Merriweather admitted. "He is probably very much aware that we've had direct contact with the other gods now. I think the fact they took us out of our realm may have helped because he won't know what we were told that we can use against him. He's not moved against us yet, but that doesn't mean we are safe company."

Admiral Rose stood and looked at her. "There is no safety in numbers for this battle," the woman finally said. "You are right. Greenwood, arrange for the crew to leave the ship. And you --"

"I'm the pilot."

"I can pilot her myself, you know."

Greenwood looked up and shook his head. "Not as well as me, and you need a good pilot for this. Besides, we need you to watch everything else, Admiral Rose. The rest of us are going to be preoccupied, you know. And there's no telling what this Atric might try to do to stop us."

"Yes. Well, at least you're not telling me to get off *Flash* with the others. Kroger, if you would rather not --"

Kroger grunted, and that ended the conversation.

The crew left the ship, though many of them were reluctant and the looks they gave Lord Raventower showed that they knew who was behind this current business, even if they didn't know the plan. Mica didn't think they realized the ship would leave without them, though. He and Merriweather were the ones who threw off the ties, and *Flash* began lifting before the crew had crossed to the land-based quarters. Mica saw the group turn back in disbelief as the airship rose into the cloudy sky.

They moved carefully despite that they probably would not keep the secret of the engine much longer. Greenwood piloted them inland for more than twenty miles before he gave a nod to Mica. "Ready," he said.

Merriweather sat at the weapons station, ready for any trouble.

"Do it," Rose said. She looked around and shook her head. "Damned quiet without anyone else on board. Let's make this fast."

"Yes. Fast is the word," Mica agreed. "Prepare to engage the other engine."

Greenwood had apparently got a feel for the change and the power because the flight went as smooth as it was fast. Mica enjoyed it.

They overshot the island and curved back around over an ice-covered ocean that looked desolate and far too cold. Snow had fallen on the land, and the rocks glinted in the faint light, showing a layer of ice as well. Smoke rose from the distant chimneys in Headaway and Mica doubted anyone even saw their arrival.

Mica put out the anchors -- heavy work and the wind was brisk enough that they needed four to hold steady. Greenwood went with Merriweather and him down to the land. They'd lined up close to the cavern, so they only slid and fell a little on the ice.

The spiders in the cavern took notice the moment they arrived, a few rushing straight at him. He kept from saying the 'magic words' though. They needed to know if they could trust any of the creatures.

"I need help," Mica said. "It is the same battle that my father prepared to fight. Atric is attacking us."

Some of the spiders stopped moving. Mica almost thought he could sense shock in the way their heads turned, and lights flashed.

The others kept moving. Merriweather and Greenwood waited for his signal, but Mica wanted to give the spiders every chance he could --

When one grabbed his leg, Merriweather had to kick it aside and kill the creatures. "I just can't trust you."

Mica drew his own flintlock. They managed to destroy four more that had kept coming at them. Two others fell to the attacks of other spiders.

"Will you come with us?" Mica asked. "Will you trust me?"

One spider came closer. Mica lowered his weapon and ignored Merriweather's sigh of frustration.

"Command," the spider said, a rusty noise, the word clearly difficult.

The voice reminded him of the way his ravens had sounded when they first started speaking. The remaining spiders were cooperative. They built the wooden cases, pulled them up the hill to where the airship sat tethered, and then climbed into the boxes and allowed Mica to seal the crates shut.

Greenwood and Merriweather went up first and hoisted the wooden boxes up and stored them in the bay with the engine. They had a dozen more spiders. Mica hoped it would be enough.

They would know soon.

Mica climbed aboard, helped to winch the anchors up, and prepared to return to Kamere. The weather turned worse as they neared the city, but that didn't surprise any of them. Greenwood had no trouble bringing them around to Raventower.

The guards on the tower at least recognized *Flash* and didn't try to shoot them down. The dangerous winds off the ocean proved difficult enough as they lowered the crates to the roof, though. Mica followed them down with Merriweather only a moment later. He gave a wave to Roe and Nyle out in the courtyard where they watched. At least there would be no surprise when the two of them came down the stairs to the kitchen.

Rose took up the single anchor they'd used to hold in place and headed back to the control deck. In a moment, *Flash* moved off again.

Merriweather stood at the side of the tower and stared off

at sea, bringing her hand up to shield her eyes. "I saw the signal flag. They're ready."

Mica gave a look at the other ships; the Atrians had moved a little closer to the bay again. They would not have much time, so it was just as well that everything was already in motion. No time to sit and rest now. No time even to go down to the kitchen for a quiet meal.

And that was good because if Mica sat and thought about everything...

"Whatever you do, do not open the crates," Mica said to the guards, pointing to where they had stacked a dozen boxes by the wall. "Even if you hear voices from them."

"Voices," the young woman to the right said. She looked at the crates, which were clearly not large enough for humans. "No sir, we will absolutely *not* open them."

"When my two men come to open them, I suggest that you go back inside," he added, but he didn't take the time to say more.

He started down the stairs. Merriweather stayed a little longer, but he didn't know what she told the soldiers. Maybe it helped that she had Captain's rank and could order them to do what he had suggested. Maybe they would not obey either of them, having been put on watch by General Gregorian.

Probably it would not matter either way.

Mica went down the ladder and crossed to his desk. There he pushed back the cover and swept everything into a pouch: insects, tools, pocket watch and dozens of small pieces that had not been made into anything yet. He couldn't be certain what he might need.

Merriweather stood behind him, and when he turned, she gave a grim nod.

"At least this will be over quickly now," Merriweather said. She glanced toward the shuttered window but did not cross to open it. "The Atrians must have seen us arrive. They'll know we plan to do something."

"And I hope that works in our favor," Mica replied. He hooked the pouch onto his sword's scabbard which might not be wise if he needed the sword. He suspected he would not.

He took two ravens and gave another two to Merriweather. She put them in her own pack.

"You know you don't have to --"

She looked into his face and her head tilted. "You know you can trust me, and this is not something either of us will back away from now. We have a job, Lord Raventower. Let us both hope that the plan goes well."

They did not speak about what would happen if things did not work.

They stopped for tea and cakes with the others. Mica lined out what Roe and Nyle had to do.

"Be careful," he said at the end. "Let them out as soon as Merriweather fires. I don't know that I really trust the spiders, but they are weapons we need right now."

A few minutes later, muffled in cloaks, Mica and Merriweather moved down the road to Fisherman's Row with a band of soldiers on patrol. They chose a building with a good view of the bay and slipped inside. The room felt warmer than outside -- barely.

Atrian ships had already moved into the bay. The Sedina craft swept in for the attack and the battle, by *chance* moved the Atrians closer to the statue, and the Sedina fleet might destroy the enemy this time.

"Well," Merriweather said watching the fray. "We may have to change our plans."

"I expected the Atrians to put up more of a fight. If they don't --"

"There are the Atrian airships finally. This should make a difference."

It did. Mica watched in worry, fearing a Sedina ship would

still go down, but after a few more worried shots, the Sedina's used their small steam engines to maneuver back out of the area, finally leaving the Atrians with a clear run to the statue.

"Well done so far," Merriweather said. She pulled her cloak closer. Now if they do what you think they will --"

"They came to Sedina with the intent of bringing the statue to the surface," he said. He couldn't see the area clearly from here. "I have to believe that they will be both prepared to do the work and that Atric will want to help them. Better they do the hard work than us."

"Not safe, letting them have their hands on it," Merriweather said and then raised her hand to stop what he had started to say. "But still our best chance. While they're busy with the statue, everyone else can prepare for other trouble."

"Including us."

"Especially us."

"The last ship has gone around the curve."

They didn't have far to go to the building with the submersible. Captain Merriweather ordered the last guards away, and they were glad to go, even if they did give the two some worried looks. Mica had begun to drag the wide door open, and Merriweather helped. He didn't know if the Atrians could see what they were doing -- likely not since even the airships had swept in with the Atrian ships, and he doubted anyone looked in this direction with their prize so close at hand. A single Sedina ship had moved closer to the bay but still kept their distance from the Atrians and their work.

At least he'd had a chance to work on the ship after they'd brought it up to the shore. Though far from completely fixed, it was useable now, especially for the short distance they would be taking her.

Mica and Merriweather climbed into the craft. He sealed the door behind them. Not everything worked -- but he'd made certain of important controls as well as the weapons. Merriweather checked them all over with a nod.

"I don't think it will be too long," Mica said. He hated that they couldn't see what was going on, but he trusted --

First came the explosion of one bomb, then another, and another in a line between them and the sea. Sand and water flew up battering the building before the backlash from the multiple blasts tore apart the building --

If the gods were truly on their side --

Water rushed up the shore and through the rough canal the bombs had made. Though not deep, the water moved swiftly, and the submersible rolled forward, almost stuck, and then bounced back into the shallow sea.

CHAPTER THIRTY-THREE

Mica quickly moved the submersible forward, the steam engine pressing as much against air as water. He feared getting stuck in the shallow water where the Atrian airships would have easy target practice. The sea shelf fell off quite close to the shore, though, and the craft plunged downward at an odd angle. Mica straightened them and pulled his hands back from the controls.

"Well, that worked," Merriweather said. "Gives me hope for the rest of the plan."

The idea seemed even more insane now that they were taking the first steps. Mica concentrated on moving closer to the statue, though he began to make small circles as soon as he could see the tell-tale glowing blue. He could see that the Atrians were already at work with hooks trailing from ships.

"As I thought," Mica said. "The statue is helping. They're already lifting it upwards."

Merriweather looked over the weapons. "Are you ready?"

He watched the glow of blue start to shift upwards. Whatever fish and other creatures that had still been in the area began to rush past them like a stampede. Debris rose in a swirl of sand, rock, and seaweed.

"Going up. Get ready."

Mica took them to the surface. He did not stop to remind her where to fire. The sight of the statue, half-risen out of the sea, sent a shiver through him. The statue's eyes blinked, and the head slowly turned toward them. Mica tore his gaze away from the glowing blue creature draped in seaweed and decorated with shells and starfish.

Mica locked the controls into place and threw himself into the small corridor. He shoved the first projectile into place and prayed that it did not get stuck like the last one. Study of the ship had convinced him that too much heat had caused the previous malfunction. They wouldn't have time to build up that much temperature in the tube this time.

"Ready!" he shouted.

Merriweather already had her target. She fired almost immediately. Mica threw open the tube and stepped aside, letting the steam escape into the interior, raising the temperature for them by several degrees.

"Hit in the neck!" Merriweather yelled.

They had four more bombs. They fired them in quick succession, even while the Atrian ships and airships turned their attention on the submersible.

Sedina craft moved in as well, though; ships swept into the bay, and the Sedina airships came up out of the south, having gone wide of the city and around in a curve. They dropped out of the clouds and began to attack the dozen Atrian ships in the bay.

The spiders, though, probably took the Atrians most by surprise.

"There they are," Mica said as he threw himself back into his chair and raced the submersible towards the statue, and as close to the peninsula as he dared. That put them the farthest from the ships and with the statue between them. He couldn't say this was safe, but it was still better than anywhere else out here in the ocean.

Besides, they were not alone.

The spiders had leapt from the tower into the sea -- that had to have been an impressive sight. Now they swarmed up the body of the statue. Mica thought Atric might have twitched.

Holes had opened in the neck, the marks of four explosions that had torn apart more than half the metal between the shoulders and the head. Merriweather's precision had been perfect. Mica didn't think anyone else could have done so well.

Through the splashing sea, he watched the spiders leap onto the chains the ships had dropped to Atric to get him out of the water. It did not take much to disengage the ones on the body. Then they swarmed upward and began tearing away at the metal that still held the head to the body.

"We need to get out there," Mica said. He knew they would regret leaving the warm interior of the little craft, but there was nothing more they could do from here.

Merriweather unstrapped, heading out ahead of him and up the ladder. She stopped and looked back at him. When he gave a reluctant nod, Merriweather shoved the hatch open.

They both scrambled up onto the wet, slick outer surface. Waves rushed over the top, drenching them. This was beyond cold. The water seemed to freeze around his eyes, and he had to take one hand loose from the hold to rub at them, trying to see if all was what he expected to find.

The body of the statue came free and crashed into the sea. The water, in turn, washed up over the craft while Mica and Merriweather held tight to the hooks that would secure the craft at a mooring.

"Could have timed that better," he mumbled, his teeth chattering.

He thought guns might be firing in their direction, or maybe just at the spiders. The head floated on the water now, only a couple chains still attached to the Atrian ships. Two of the larger spiders were still working at getting those connections free, but the others had formed a chain that led from the head to the submersible.

Impossible to walk across it, but they could hold on to the legs and move from one spider to the next. Mica waved Merriweather ahead of him, and she didn't argue. He couldn't decide if she was brave or just so cold that she no longer cared what they did. He'd almost reached that level himself.

Except that this he thought the plan might be working. The spiders even helped more than Mica had expected. As soon as he and Merriweather were in the water, the spiders pulled the two swiftly along and to the head.

Probably not the safest place to be, Mica knew. He could hear the soft growls of anger and knew that Atric hadn't been destroyed -- but he had expected as much. They'd been told the essence of the ancient High Priest had settled in the head. The shock of what had happened wouldn't hold him back for much longer, and Mica knew they had to move fast.

Very fast.

Merriweather grabbed hold of the statue first, but Mica wasn't far behind. He felt a tingle -- unpleasant, but not terrible. Not yet.

The battle raged on around them, airships and sea ships firing at each other. Neither side aimed at them though -- the Atrians didn't want to risk destroying the last part of the statue, and the Sedinans had been told to concentrate on the enemy.

This still felt like a precarious position, not counting on whatever power Atric might still bring against them. Mica scanned the skies. They had little time.

Flash came over the top of Raventower and chains dropped as the craft neared. The ship's canons fired at anyone who came near. The spiders worked swiftly, anchoring the four hooks into the edge of the head. Ravens swept down from the tower and out at the nearest of the Atrian ships, attacking the crew and driving them away.

Merriweather and Mica began climbing up the chains without trying to help. They needed to get to the deck to be safe. With the head attached, *Flash* was already heading for a small opening between two Atrian ships, which made it difficult for either to fire without risking the other craft, though that wouldn't stop them for long. Merriweather made it to the deck first. Rose hauled her up and then grabbed Mica even as the Atrians started firing at them.

"Tell him to go!" Mica shouted as he and Merriweather hastily put on the lifelines and hooked into rails.

Rose shoved a flintlock into Merriweather's hands and hurried to the bay door where she shouted the order.

The sea metal engine took over, and they moved very, very fast; faster, Mica thought, than they had before. The Atrian and Sedina ships disappeared behind them in a roar of wind. They gave away the secret of the engine, but it wouldn't matter if they didn't deal with Atric.

The blue glow of the engine enveloped the craft as they went out, faster and faster until they could see nothing but open sea all around. Nothing marked this place, and no eyes would see what they did here.

He did not have to look to know what Atric was doing. The head drifted upwards as though powered by his own airship, the red eyes glowing with power.

"Did you really think destroying the body would help you?" Atric demanded. The voice sounded deep as a bell so that the world around him trembled with the sound. "Fools. You cannot hope to defeat me."

Merriweather was already at work, tossing fishing nets over the head, the ends with massive weights attached. Atric snarled and turned his attention to her for a moment, but Mica moved and released the chains that had been holding the head to the ship.

The head began to fall, Atric surprised by the sudden change. He heard the deep laughter and saw the head start to get control --

Then it hit the water, and the explosives in the weights went off.

Mica did not have to give any orders. They headed upward as fast as the engine could take them, the swirl of clouds surrounding them in a mist that made it impossible to see from one side of the ship to the other, though looking over the edge of *Flash's* deck, he could see the glow of bright lights. Atric's life lights were following them upward, trying to reach the one place where he might yet reside -- Mica's body. Mica had been given the power from the God to fight this enemy.

He hoped his insane plan still worked.

Mica could no longer tell which way they moved. The wind lessened here. If there had not been a deck beneath his feet, he couldn't even have told up from down.

Atric still surged onward, a flash of angry lights rushing up to the railing. Merriweather came to stand to his right and Rose to his left. Greenwood remained at the controls, but the last two came up to the bay doors to watch this battle that was between him and the enemy of Torger.

The audience was all in place, and the villain had finally come to the stage.

The life lights grew larger and brighter than any Mica had ever seen before. They moved in a spiral, and he thought he could see tiny flashes of lightning moving from one to another. The lights shifted, though not coming towards him. For a moment he saw a face with the scowl of someone who counted himself better than anyone he had ever known.

Then the lights swept in at Mica and from the start, he knew he had little chance of holding this almost god out. He fought the life lights back, one, then another, but they swarmed in again. He touched on a life he did not want to know; such a hunger for power that there was little else in the thoughts.

Mica represented an unexpected link to the god Atric had betrayed. Mica was what he wanted to be -- human, powerful, rich -- able to kill the others at will. Mica still fought back. If he could hold the lights off long enough --

But Mica hadn't enough power of his own. The lights came into him, first one and then another, bright and burning, but confused still, uncertain what it meant to be a human again after all this time. He would do better in this body than as the statue. The fools had helped him!

Mica felt his own control slipping. He turned to Merriweather and lifted his left hand, nodding --

Merriweather stepped forward as she raised her flintlock, aimed, and shot him through the heart.

A moment of fire but not really pain. Mica died too quickly to feel anything more. Odd that his soul seemed stronger when his body fell. He shoved at Atric, pushing the frantic creature back out. There was nothing more here Atric could take.

Mica had been unique, with the gift that had drawn souls just as Atric had done the same. Atric had squandered almost all his power in the fight with Mica. He tried to reach Merriweather, but Mica held him back.

With a howl that ripped through his soul, Atric leapt out of the dead body, leaving Mica alone to die. The move had been made in panic because Atric had already used far too much hoarded power, and Mica knew that the would-be God no longer had a chance of survival.

Except if he figured out the last trick, and Mica knew they dared not let him.

Dying had not been so difficult.

Coming back was far harder. Mica became aware of a hand over his shattered heart, of pieces reknitting themselves, and of pain that tore through his body as though the bullet had ripped through every inch of him. He wanted to cry out and dared not. Mica blinked. Krogor stood between the railing and the spot where the other crewman from the bay knelt over him.

Seldon.

The magic took forever from the perspective of Mica's mind. Twice he almost let go. Seldon worked harder, tried to block some of the pain and gave Mica strength that was not his own.

Howling. Mica could hear howling, and the wind grew stronger again, the clouds agitated.

"No more time," Seldon whispered and helped him to his feet.

Atric had become one of the recently dead, and like all of those, he was drawn toward Mica once more.

Confusion showed in the swirls of colors as Mica moved to the railing. Rose caught his arm, her face white. He gave her a distracted nod.

Atric's lights moved. Smaller now. Circled. Formed a face.

"You cannot -- You died --"

"I brought him back," Seldon said and moved up beside him

Shock. Fear. Mica reached into the pouch where he had put bits and pieces of things, his fingers brushing against clockwork insects, the reminder of his own odd humanity, a link to who he wanted to be and the future he fought to gain.

"No," Atric said, the word echoing around them. "No. To do that would change too much."

"I knew better than to face you myself," Seldon said, his voice loud and echoing in this place. "I dared not let you touch me. I will not make that mistake again, Atric. And now you will get what you deserve."

Panic and fear gave Atric a moment of strength. The lights

started to coalesce into something dangerous. Mica brought out a handful of insects and threw them into the lights. They did the job better than he had hoped.

Atric panicked, and at that moment, Mica gained the control he needed. He pulled the pocket watch out, reached into the air and took hold of the lights. They burned his hand, the rage still too strong.

"You cannot bring someone back from the dead! It would change the world!"

"You haven't been paying attention," Mica said. His voice sounded oddly normal as he waved a hand to the clouds of white fog around them. "We are not in the world."

If Atric had gotten free here in the realm of the gods, there would have been no chance for any of them to survive after all. The realization of their location had surprised Atric, and Mica took hold of him, one light after another and shoved them into the most basic of clockwork creations -- a pocket watch.

"Back now!" he said, breathless from the work. He put both hands around the watch and willed Atric to stay inside.

Seldon and Krogor rushed back to the sea metal engine. Rose went to the control deck and shouted instructions to Greenwood before she came back to Mica and Merriweather.

Dropping now -- very definitely dropping and fast.

"Get -- ready," Mica yelled above the wind as they grabbed hold.

Merriweather and Rose prepared the next pieces of the trap --

Down. Slowing. Mica could smell the sea before he saw it, and they came, finally out into a surprisingly bright sunlight. He kept one hand clamped over the pocket watch and drew a small sharp piece of metal from the bits and pieces of things he carried. When he opened the clock's lid, the inside sparkled as the life lights tried to escape.

He glanced around. Nothing but sea everywhere he looked.

Mica shoved the spike into place, stopping the minute hand from moving. At the same time, Merriweather held out a case of lead. He shoved the watch inside, glad to have Atric out of his hands. Then they put the lead into a case of sea metal, and another covering of lead. By then the combined cases weighed too much to hold. They knelt by the railing, attached two anchors, and shoved it all overboard.

He watched the splash as they sailed over the spot. Rose yelled for Greenwood to circle. They went around the area -- once, twice, a third time.

"When I spiked the watch, I trapped him in a moment of *now*," Mica said aloud with a glance at Rose. Krogor had gone back to the engines. Seldon -- Seldon just wasn't with them any longer and Mica wasn't certain where the God had gone and if he would survive. Mica hoped so. "The clock is made mostly of sea metal. It will not give out. The other cases trap Atric from any feel of the world beyond the watch, even if he found a way to get around the idea of time."

"We did it?" Merriweather asked. She sounded, probably rightfully so, shocked and looked pale.

He turned and smiled at her. "Yes. I think we have. You did your part very well, my love."

"Thank you, Lord Raventower."

She gave a bow of her head ... and then she slid down to the deck and wept.

CHAPTER THIRTY-FOUR

They turned back to Kamere, heading into a storm that had apparently grown worse after their escape into another realm. Mica and Merriweather had taken their places on the deck. He hoped that Merriweather had calmed now. He wasn't certain what had upset her so --

Oh, then he realized he was a fool. He looked down at his jacket and the spattering of blood. She had, truly, killed him. She'd had to trust Seldon to bring him back. The world itself had depended on what she did, and she did it quickly and without pause -- but the actions had not been easy for her.

Merriweather had been the one who saved the world.

Mica turned his attention back to handling the engines. The sea metal engine had lost power. He suspected taking it between realms must have drained too much, and the engine might not recover, but they were still making a good speed back towards the city.

"Steady, Raventower," Rose ordered.

He gave a start. His mind still wandered.

"My apologies," he said and looked at the gauges. Everything ran well enough.

He'd died. He remembered that part vividly, including that odd time between life and before he accepted death. A God had brought him back to life. He had trusted Seldon to do so; it had been part of the plan from the start. Mica had not realized the trust Seldon had put in him, though, until that moment. Mica could have done what Atric had done and grabbed a piece of the god for himself.

Mica had known so at the time. He had also known that if he had acted as Atric had so long ago, he would be changed. Mica wanted his old world back, not to trade it for some new one -- and he had never sought after power.

Rose shifted. He paid better attention again, trying to wall all those thoughts behind the need to get through this last part. They would be nearing Kamere. He didn't think more than a couple hours had passed, but how could one be sure when they'd gone to an entirely different realm and back?

"Land in the distance," Greenwood warned.

Mica tapped the poll and switched between the two engines. They'd still be going faster than normal as they glided in, though. This could be dangerous especially given the amount of trouble he could see ahead of them.

The storm at least had started to dissipate. The winds were not as strong, and Mica could see the sky through the breaks in the clouds. Airships swarmed everywhere, and at this distance, he still could not even make out friend from foe.

Then Mica realized many of those ships were heading out to sea, while others headed northward. *Flash* swept past them all, headed inland over villages, and then back again, slowing finally to a pace that matched the others.

"I wish Seldon had stayed help out," Mica said. "A little extra protection would be nice about now."

"We don't need Seldon," Rose said. "I'd just as soon not have a god on the ship. Besides, we have Merriweather at the weapons."

Merriweather gave a quick bark of laughter, more herself again. Good.

Two Atrian airships held on over the bay, but as *Flash* turned to do battle, they parted in two directions. Greenwood automatically turned toward the one that had gone towards the city, circling around and forcing the Atrian ship out towards the ocean again before Merriweather shot it down.

Mica had been paying more attention to the battle in the sea, though. Two small Atrian ships were already on the run, even using their steam engines which was a clear sign of worry.

No wonder. Spiders had attacked the other ships. Mica could

see where they'd literally torn several of apart, just as they were now doing to yet another. The Sedina ships had pulled back, doing nothing more than block the escape of any but the two that had already gotten out.

"Well," Rose said. "Nice allies. I'm gaining a warmer feeling for their spidery little hearts."

"We can leave them to patrol the coast for now," Mica mused. It was, he thought, the first normal statement he'd made since they started back, and he saw Rose give him a nod that seemed more relief than agreement.

People stood on the streets below as they went over the city and north to the Sky Patrol's grounds. The other airships were coming in as well, an unusual sight. They'd lost too many of them, but it was still a wonder to see the remainder all anchor at their moorings and drift down to the cradles.

With only the four people on board, they needed some help from the ground crew, but it wasn't long before Mica and Merriweather were bidding goodbye to Rose, Greenwood, and Krogor. Admiral Rose had even brought him a clean tunic and jacket. He had changed there on the control deck while the ship was secured. A small scar showed on his chest. He hoped Merriweather did not see. He changed quickly and left the other shirt and jacket behind. Moments later they were at the railing and preparing to go down to the ground.

"Watch him," Rose told Merriweather with some worry.

"Well, that is my job."

There was a certain amount of chaos on the Air Field with all the crews back and celebrating the win. Merriweather somehow got them horses, though. It wasn't until they were riding the stretch between the field and the city that Mica finally came to realize that the war was likely over. He looked out at the ocean and could barely see a ship in the distance, and from the shape, it was one of the Sedina craft, not Atrian. The enemy had seen the statue destroyed, and Mica suspected they would not be back.

He tried not to think about what that meant for Merriweather's future.

The guards at the north gate were in a better mood. The shouts

Mica could hear in the city already showed life returning. He was not surprised to see a line of people already leaving the Castle grounds, dragging their belongings with them as they headed back to their homes. Mica had thought about going up to see Gregorian, but the road was packed.

He could head home instead. Gregorian knew where to find him.

Many people had gone no farther than the temple square. Celebrations there were already underway, with singing and even lines of dancers. Priests and Priestesses must have hurried down before the others, because the temples -- even the damaged ones -- showed bright, welcoming lights. Mica worried that the celebrations might be premature, though he couldn't imagine what would bring the Atrians back again so soon.

He and Merriweather went unnoticed past the crowds, wrapped in their cloaks and heads down. They were not the only people on horseback.

Tired.

Mica saw Seldon.

This was not someone he'd expected to see again. He slid from the horse and Merriweather gave a sound of surprise, though maybe only because she recognized the God as well. He'd been walking along with the others but moved aside to greet Mica and Merriweather.

"I had not expected to see you again, sir," Mica said and wondered how one really did talk to a god. He had to settle for the politeness he had always shown to Seldon. "When you weren't on *Flash*, I feared -- assumed you had gone back to live with the others."

Seldon gave a brighter smile than Mica had expected. "I intend to stay a while longer. I cannot go back to being Torger, you know. That being is tainted, and I fear that if I returned and tried to be what I had been, I would be corrupted too. I have spent a lot of time with humans. I understand them better, now. I think, as Seldon, I can still be a protector."

"Yes sir," Mica agreed, unreasonably glad to know Seldon was still here.

"Who knows? Someday there might be a temple to Seldon here," he added and smiled again as he looked around the area. "Both of you go back to Raventower and rest. You have done well."

Seldon walked away, talking to others as he passed them. Mica noted how people looked happier to be with him.

"Back to Raventower," Merriweather said and mounted again. He did the same. "Rest would be good."

Mica agreed. He sat up straighter now and waved greetings to those who called out to him. This was what he had helped save, and it was time to bring back the joy.

Seldon had done that for him, just as he did for the others he talked to.

They went past the ruined factories, the slums, and Shadow Walk. Nothing seemed much different here. A few of the locals had already made it this far and were hurrying to get back to their homes, or maybe to grab some better place and hold it against the original squatters. Mica thought about what he could do next spring that might help.

Gregorian and a few guards marched up the road from Fisherman's Row. Just as well they hadn't tried to get to the castle then.

"There you are," Gregorian said as Mica and Merriweather dismounted.

"What are those ships doing?" Merriweather asked.

Four of the larger Sedina ships circled into the bay. Mica almost protested, fearing that they would be pulled down. They didn't know for certain --

"They're preparing to bombard the area and break up the rest of the statue." Gregorian looked back. People moved away from the shore. "I don't think there will be damage to the buildings, but if there is, I'll send some of my crews in to rebuild yet today. Oh, and you'll be glad to know that the spiders pulled the submersible out of the water and carried it off up the shore, apparently to get it out of harm's way."

"Did they? Good," he said. He still had odd feelings about the sea metal, but at least he didn't fear using it. The statue would be the last of it anyway. "Yes, destroy the rest of the statue."

"The work is in the hands of the Navy," Gregorian said. He looked back. "But they won't take long."

The ships sent four volleys of explosives, hardly seconds apart, down into the depths below the peninsula. Mica winced and worried about his home.

The explosions sent cascades of water up into the air, along with glittering bits of the metal. The ground shook, and Mica looked with worry up at Raventower. He saw the building sway slightly and his breath caught, but then everything stilled, and he saw only a slight hint of dust.

"That's it then," Gregorian said. "Good work, Mica. Both of you did a good job --"

"Sir," Merriweather began. She looked troubled. "The war is over --"

"I think so. But that doesn't mean there are not still Atrians in the area, and those are going to be even angrier than before. I have decided that you are going to be spending considerably more time at Raventower, Captain."

She smiled. "Thank you, sir."

Gregorian did not ask how their part of the battle had gone, not with others present. He did understand that they'd won, though. They parted company with the idea that there might be peace for a while. Even the soldiers up at the courtyard seemed to understand that the war had ended. He thought they seemed reluctant about leaving Raventower, though.

Ada and Gram had a meal ready when they came in the door.

"Shipley seen *Flash* come back over, me lord," Gram said and waved up at the ceiling and the sky several floors above them. "So, we just gets ready for the two of you to come home. Sit down now. About time you had a real meal."

And a celebration. This was the way life should be. Gram had decided that living in the castle wasn't so bad, and she and the boy would stay on. Bear looked happy on his rug. Fern laughed with them, a rare occasion where she didn't shy away from anything emotional. Nyle and Roe began talking about how to rebuild the smithy now that the soldiers would be leaving.

A return to life as it should be, though with one change. He'd begun to notice the glances towards one person at the table.

"Captain Merriweather will be with us for quite some time, according to my brother."

"Good!" Ada all but shouted.

Fern came over and hugged Merriweather.

After the meal, he and Merriweather went up to the workshop. She took her chair by the steps while he crossed to the cabinet and looked within. Only two ravens had returned, and he feared they might be the only ones left. He hoped that the others had found peace.

"I'd like to open the shutters," he said.

"Yes. The sunset should be lovely," Merriweather agreed. She opened the one overlooking the city. He opened the one that looked at the sea. The glass had cracked and would have to be replaced though he could feel the magic still intact.

The ships had moved away. The view showed only the peaceful sea, a few clouds low on the horizon, and the sun casting light and shadows everywhere. He had not expected to see such a scene of peace. It took him by surprise.

"Yes, that's better," Merriweather said. She went back to her chair, and when he turned, he found that she watched him.

Mica went to the desk and poured out the pouch full of bits and pieces, his fingers pushing them into little piles. He did not sit down.

"There is something more I must do," he finally said.

She looked at the clock. "Yes, I know."

Mica crossed to the clock, opened the door to the inner works, and reached in. With a slight jerk, he pulled the heart out of the clockwork and held it in his hand, listening to the steady ticking like the beat of a heart.

"It's time," he said. "It's time for you to go, father. The work is done. Thank you for the help you gave us."

He reached in and broke the small piece of sea metal.

The life lights were surprisingly bright, and for a moment Mica thought they might try for him. Instead, he felt a sudden sense of peace as they drifted up and away -- gone in a heartbeat.

"Well done," Merriweather said softly. "Both of you, well done.

Mica slept well that night, without a whisper of words to awaken him. Life had changed, but for the better. He knew it.

The next morning at breakfast a note arrived from Gregorian with only a single line:

The King has a job he would like you and Merriweather to do for him.

THE END

###

PREVIEW: RAVENTOWER & MERRIWEATHER 3: MISSING

Chapter One

Something howled through Mica's nightmare, a loud wail that rose and fell and returned once more to send a shiver through him. Something wrong, and he didn't even know what to do to fix it this time. Did he hear the whisper of a lost god? Of his dead father, freed from the clock where he'd stored his soul for so long? Were they coming for him, all the dead he'd seen, touched -- given over to clockwork creatures? They'd stayed of their own accord, hadn't they?

The howling could be anything. The howling could be --

Mica opened his eyes.

The howling could be the wind of a fierce winter storm as it rushed past the window of his tower bedroom. Home. Safe and home in his own bed. The dawn had come, and for a moment he could pretend that all was well.

Mica turned slightly and stifled both a moan and muttered a curse. Every part of his body ached today. There were pains he could not even name, and they were persistent enough to wake him entirely on this miserable cold day. He could not fall back asleep, no matter how he pulled the blanket up higher around him or how tightly he closed his eyes against the growing gray light that filtered in around the edges of the shutters. He really needed to fix that problem.

And the wind still howled.

Mica cursed again and sat up, grabbing his night robe and

pulling it tight around him, hoping to block some of the breezes that leaked in around the window. The steam heat worked, at least. When he'd first returned to Raventower, ice was apt to form anywhere but the kitchen during winter.

Today Mica could go and take a shower with water heated by the steam system that heated the room. He could go down to the kitchen and find out what wondrous things Ada had made for his homecoming. He didn't have to go out into the cold.

Merriweather would be there. She had, he suspected, already gotten up and gone down to check things out. That got him moving out of the bed, feet on the nice, though cold, carpet. He pushed aside the shutter just enough to see what he had expected; snow fell in a white sheet that blocked the view of even the courtyard below. Ice had cracked as he moved the outer covering with a slight bell-like sound. It all would have been pretty if it hadn't been so cold.

A good day to be home.

Mica didn't take long to shower, avoided trying to count bruises and cuts, and dressed in warm clothing. The battle with the Atrians was at least over for the moment. Maybe even for the entire winter -- that thought put him in a better mood. By the time he'd done dressing, Mica had gotten used to some of the pains and thought he could present himself as something less than an invalid limping along and cursing the world.

As he had expected, Merriweather's door stood open and her room was empty. He tried not to be embarrassed. She was, after all, a soldier, and used to early hours. He was a clockwork scientist with a dubious link to the realities of daily life.

Mica stopped at the stairwell and looked up and down. One flight led up to his workshop, a place he'd missed dearly of late. He almost went there, just to tinker around for a little while - but the idea of breakfast drew him downstairs instead, one limping step after another while he tried not to moan where anyone might hear him.

The lower of the old tower's floors smelled of everything he had hoped: exotic spices, baked goods, fruits, and herbs. Ada had the food ready almost before he sat down. The older woman smiled brightly at his arrival. Merriweather already sat at the table, her fingers wrapped around a cup of tea, and the others were there as well -- Nyle, Roe, and Fern, plus Gran and even Shipley. Bear, the huge, long-haired dog, stretched out atop of the steps leading down to the kitchen and kept well away from the heat of the hearth today. He probably thought longingly about romping in the snow.

They had an excellent breakfast, all of them pleased. No one spoke about any type of work, except that Ada and Gram talked about cooking more food. Neither Mica nor his friends could not see the wreckage of the city from here which meant they could avoid the memory of the war for a little while longer. Mica appreciated the break from the constant feel of disaster lurking nearby. They couldn't even see or hear the winter storm, although sometimes the hearth gave a little huff of sound as a bit of wind found its long way down the chimney.

Reality came back to them before the meal was finished. The knocker pounded. Nyle waved the others to stay seated and went up the steps toward the main floor and the big door. Merriweather looked likely to follow him but changed her mind.

"We have an entire company of soldiers out there," she said when Mica looked her way, curious at her sudden trust. "Nothing bad is going to get through to knock on the door."

A cold breeze blew past and a moment later the door closed again. Nyle came back with an envelope and dropped it in front of Mica by his teacup. "Looks like it is from your brother."

"Yes," Mica agreed, studying the seal with some trepidation. *Official.* Not even something come by one of Mica's clockwork ravens, though then that might not have been possible in this weather. It had looked like a major storm.

The last thing Mica wanted to face this morning was some official missive from General Gregorian Raventower.

"You might as well read it," Merriweather said with a sigh -- so he wasn't the only one with feelings of distrust toward the inoffensive beige paper and blue wax seal.

He broke the seal and pulled the paper open.

The King has a job he would like you and Merriweather to do for him.

"Damn." Mica read it over again as though the words might change. Then he passed the paper to Merriweather who took the paper with two fingers as though she feared the note would bite.

"This can't be good," she mumbled after she'd read the words. "I should hate to think that King Abertus believes we're actually competent because of the last few days."

That won a slight laugh from Mica and grins from the others. He wanted to pass this off as just a minor problem, and something they need not worry too much about -- no. Gregorian wouldn't have sent that note today, and especially in this weather, if it were a minor problem. Gregorian knew what hell Mica and Merriweather had gone through already. This had to mean something dire.

Gregorian did not order them to come to the palace immediately, but the implication that they should hurry was there in those sparse words. The King wanted their help and the King did not deal with minor matters.

When Mica looked at Merriweather, he would tell that she felt the same way. He nibbled at his toast and marmalade, barely noting the taste. Was this something more with the war? They had barely gotten past the battle with Atria, but that didn't mean the enemy had entirely given up. Though, with their god gone -- if not destroyed -- they might have trouble getting the drive they needed for another try at an invasion.

"I'll arrange for our escort," Merriweather said as she stood, though with obvious reluctance. "I'll come back in and have more tea before we leave. Finish this fine food."

"Oh, but do you have to go in such bad weather?" Ada said with a shake of her head.

"We're asked to the palace," Mica said. He tried not to sound annoyed and depressed. "This has to be something important. Gregorian wouldn't have sent for us in this weather otherwise."

Gregorian didn't say why they were wanted which was another worrisome piece to this note. Mica took up the paper and read it over again as though he might have missed something in the single line. He hadn't, so he put the note away in his vest.

Roe and Nyle got up and went on about their business, Roe even daring a hand on Mica's shoulder when he started past. "It's good to have you back, my lord. Whatever this new trouble is, do be careful. Things aren't altogether settled."

"We'll be careful," Mica promised and smiled.

Damn, he just wanted to stay home.

Mica felt the cold brush of air as Merriweather opened the door and stepped outside as the cold rushed into this warm haven. Even Bear moved out of the draft. They would be taking horses in this weather, Mica supposed, and not a lovely comfy carriage where he could stretch out a bit and cover up in blankets. They would also have the guard. He thought about taking Kandris, his magnificent clockwork horse, but the metal would be cold as ice in this weather, even though the cold would not affect the animal.

Ada fussed over him as she always did and managed to lighten his mood. Merriweather came back, trailing some snow after her even though she left her cloak at the door.

"They'll be ready." She sat down and nodded her thanks to Fern who poured her warm tea. "It's going to be a cold ride, but the guard tells me they've heard of no serious trouble in the city."

"Good." Mica sat up straighter, ready to put on a show for the others. He would not go out there looking sullen and bad tempered.

This was only a ride through town and talk to the King and Gregorian. They'd dealt with misplaced gods and haunted statues. He had become the High Priest of Torger -- or maybe he was the high priest of Seldon, since that was the God's current incarnation, and someone he had already considered a friend all this life before he had learned the truth.

What could the King want with him now?

Merriweather stood. Mica sighed and did the same, knowing it was time to face the storm. Maybe the weather would be too daunting, and they'd have to turn back? He could hope for that answer and a delay in facing more trouble. Mica still hadn't gotten up to his workshop, and as they headed out of the kitchen, he looked upward with a sigh of regret. Tippet would be up there, still waiting for him. He thought Fern kept the little clockwork dog company when he wasn't around, though. Ada had hinted at it in the past.

Mica and Merriweather pulled on winter boots, long hooded cloaks, and wrapped themselves in scarves and donned gloves. He gave one last wave to the others who had come to watch, and then followed Merriweather out into the white world beyond the door.

The wind howled around them.

"I suppose we really have to go, don't we?" Mica asked as they carefully headed for the horses that the soldiers held ready at the bottom of the stairs.

"I would be glad to go alone and come back, my lord," Merriweather said, all proper guard again.

"What? Go off and get into some trouble without me?"

"You can't have it both ways," she reminded him.

He was already swinging up into the saddle and trying not to moan at the movement. Maybe the cold would be a bit of a blessing if he lost the feeling of aches and pains.

"I suppose you are going to be the voice of logic, right?" he said.

"One of us has to be."

Two of the soldiers looked away with sudden coughing fits. Merriweather grinned slightly at Mica, and he wondered if the others realized how much she enjoyed the word games they played. It was a pleasure to talk to her. Mica had never been one of those fools who thought women were lesser beings, though he did have trouble connecting with them too often -- but then he had the same problem with men, he supposed. They were no more interested in making clockwork butterflies than the women had been. Gregorian's wife had tried to find him a bride. Someday he would have to ask her just what she had thought when she presented some of those women to him. It certainly wasn't anything to do with anything approaching intelligent conversation.

As they started away, Mica looked back at Raventower itself, the old battered building still standing tall over the craggy cliffs that led down to the sea. The wind blew from north to south, and ice and snow had covered this side of the vast building. He could see one of the windows to his workshop, the shutters pulled tight and ice plastering it. The room would have been cold and drafty even with the fireplace going, he supposed. He had looked forward to a few days there, working with clockwork butterflies and maybe even talking to Merriweather about their distant wedding. Nothing more serious than that bit of fun.

Soldiers still camped in the courtyard. He wondered how long until Gregorian called the watchdogs off -- though maybe he was wise. They had beaten back the Atrians, but they had tried to kill Mica more than once. There might still be soldiers or assassins hiding in the ruins. That made going out into the storm even less appealing.

The resident soldiers were camped in tents placed near fizzling fires. If the weather got any worse, they knew enough to move into the tower for the duration, so he didn't feel too guilty about seeing them huddled in blankets and sipping from steaming cups. Half a dozen of the men already sat on horses, the animals stomping their feet in the growing snow and no one looking happy.

Mica only paused to look over Kandris; the clockwork horse moved away from the wall. The horse looked forlorn, having lost his partner and now relegated to staying inside the keep. Mica almost changed mounts, but a brush of his hand on the metal brought a chill even through the gloves.

"Sorry, but not until the weather is better," Mica said and patted the horse when he neared. Their live mounts were a little anxious but didn't try to bolt. Kandris glanced out the open gate and then gave a nod of understanding. Well, maybe he didn't want to go out into the cold weather either, now that Mica thought about it.

The soldiers seemed resigned to the ride, though. Probably, they thought about what would happen if they let Mica out on his own. What General Gregorian Raventower might do to them if something happened to his younger brother did not encourage the risk. Mica couldn't say he liked the constant feel of having people hanging over him, but he did understand. So did Merriweather. She was still tasked with keeping him alive and having a few extra eyes and swords probably seemed a blessing to her.

The gate opened wider with a slight grinding sound that made Mica wince.

"I'll need to check the clockwork mechanism," he said aloud and won a nod from Merriweather and glances from the others. Mica looked back at the building as well. "And I'll need to make certain the tower didn't take any extensive damage. I should have told Nyle and Roe to start looking for cracked walls --"

"I suspect they already have looked, you know," Merriweather replied. The gate squealed closed behind them, and the steep road to the lower ground curved downward amid drifts of snow. The horses were not sure-footed here. "They are as fond of that place as you are, my lord."

"Yes, I suppose so," he replied and held his horse to one slow step at a time. He glanced at Merriweather but said nothing --

"Yes, I am fond of the place, too," she said aloud.

He grinned. "I hope that it's stood up well. It would be a shame to lose the place now."

"Yes, it would," she agreed and glanced back over her shoulder.

Mica's older brother and sister didn't care for Raventower. Lately, he had wondered if his draw to the place had to do with being a high priest and the tower having been built over the site of an old temple. Now though -- no, he thought the draw was his own. He was a Raventower, and this was the tower that had been in their family for centuries. Honoria and Gregorian had moved on to other lives, but he had never wanted more than to be part of this unique home. It probably helped that he didn't like to socialize much, and Raventower was not a place people came to stay.

They reached the bottom of the hill with nothing more than one horse bumping another and both animals getting so annoyed that the riders had to take positions as far apart as possible.

The road curved continued to curve downward from here to the fishing village that sat at the edge of the Raventower cliffs. Those buildings had taken damage that Mica could see even in the fall of snow. Men and women were out in the weather and trying to make repairs despite the storm. He needed to do something for them. They had stood with him and helped in a dark time.

Truth be told, Mica got along better with most of them than he did with any of his peers. The other lords all thought him odd. He didn't disagree, but their complaints tended to be more about the company he kept -- like fishermen -- and not that he built clockwork creatures.

Granted, neither side knew about his link to the newly dead or the fact that some of his clockwork creatures had the souls of recently deceased humans. Mica had no intention of letting those things be known.

The storm began to die down a bit, the snow lessening as the wind only came in gusts and howled very little around the ruins. The souls of the dead? That's what some might think, but Mica watched for pretty life lights instead.

Whatever battles and deaths had taken place on this stretch of road, they had happened long enough ago that the bodies had been removed and the dead souls moved on to -- wherever they went. Mica thought he might ask Seldon one day if he got up the nerve.

He bowed his head, but not so much against the cold. He didn't want to see the destruction all around them. Shadow Walk had looked oddly untouched, but it had been a slum before the war came, and it might have been difficult to note new damage amid the old ruins. He had seen smoke from a few chimneys in there though. No one would freeze with so many destroyed buildings and pieces of wood everywhere.

The scenery grew worse beyond that already blighted area.

Buildings had fallen almost everywhere, though the main road had been cleared of debris. Mica knew this was not his fault, and yet he had been so intricately involved in everything that had happened that he couldn't help but feel a strong surge of responsibility. What if he had acted sooner? What if he had figured things out faster?

What if the assassins had killed him?

They rode along in silence, Merriweather alert for trouble while Mica considered all the things that might have gone wrong and hadn't, despite what he saw here. Kamere could have fallen to the Atrians. The entire country of Sedina would have been crushed, the people killed or enslaved. Argine, to the south, might have tried to help, but they'd have been too late. No one had expected the force of the attack that had been thrown against the city, despite the years of war they'd had with the Atrians.

Mica glanced out at the city once more, noting the sullen fires that were finally dying down in the storm, but also taking note of how much still stood, rather than everything that had fallen. He watched people working, even in this weather. Good people, here in this city. Kamere had suffered through disasters before, and it had always come back.

The Atrians had not won.

So, while he might have done better -- he might have done much worse, as well. That was something to remember on this miserable day. The signs of the war would disappear. Besides, the gods had been on their side -- literally on their side, though that was not something he wanted to think about right now. He didn't want to spend any more time working with those beings.

"I cannot imagine what the King might want of us, Merriweather," Mica finally admitted. The silence had become too filled with dire thoughts. They had gone wide of the temple district this time, the paths there still being cleared from what he could see.

"I hope it's not more trouble from the Atrians," Merriweather replied and glared out at the shadowed fallen walls and piles of debris, as though she might see one of the enemies at any moment. "I've seen no sign of new battles, though. Have any of the rest of you heard about any more trouble?"

"No, Captain Merriweather," the guard just ahead of her replied. He glanced around as though to even say such a thing might bring a fight down on them. Mica suspected they all felt that way, but at least Merriweather faced it head-on. "From what we have heard up at the tower, there's been very little going on at all. Scouting parties have found a few Atrians hiding in the city, but they seem to be just people who were left behind when the attack failed. I heard from the guard who came in last night that they've been no trouble. It's as though they lost all interest in why they even came here."

Now there was a fascinating insight, Mica thought. There had been considerable magic involved in the invasion. How much power did Atric have over his followers? Once they took Atric out of the equation -- one could not actually kill even part of a God, after all -- did he lose some special link to the warriors?

They had trapped Atric and he would not return. Mica had to believe that part because while Atric had been his enemy from the start, now he would be an enraged enemy and probably less sane. No, Mica did not want to think about Atric returning and wanting his temple back, which had once stood where Raventower now rose. He was only part of that old god, but powerful enough to be far too dangerous.

Mica could barely see a hint of the castle ahead of them, glad they were almost to their destination. Even that august building had taken some damage, though not as much as other parts of the city. They'd gotten lucky there, though Mica supposed some of the factory owners who had lost their buildings didn't feel the same way right now.

The castle, though, remained a sign of their power and a promise of their future. Maybe the others didn't realize the power of symbolism. Maybe they didn't look to the castle and understand that it meant Kamere and Sedina still stood, their pennants still flying.

Going there today didn't seem so bad after all. Maybe this was even a ride Mica had needed to make, to see the city and reconcile himself with all that had happened -- and to remember all the things that might have gone wrong and hadn't.

Yet.

What did the King want with them?

Thank you for reading this preview. If you liked the book it is available in both ebook and print formats!

About the Author:

Hello!

I am an eclectic and prolific author whose has published in a number of genres, including Young Adult Mystery, Contemporary Fantasy, Epic Fantasy, Science Fiction and numerous works on writing. While I started on the outer edges of traditional publication with sales to small press and magazines publishers, I have since moved most of my work to the Indie world, and I am madly in love with the new world of publishing and the direct contact with readers.

I live in Nebraska with my husband, my cats, and a small but entirely useless dog.

Connect with Zette:
Web Site: http://lazette.net
Facebook: http://www.facebook.com/lazette.gifford
Joyously Prolific Blog: http://zette.blogspot.com/